DEEP RIVER NIGHT

PATRICK LANE

DEEP RIVER NIGHT

McCLELLAND & STEWART

McClelland & Stewart and colophon are registered trademarks
of McClelland & Stewart

Library and Archives Canada Cataloguing in Publication

Lane, Patrick, 1939-, author
Deep river night / Patrick Lane.
Issued in print and electronic formats.
ISBN 978-0-7710-4817-3 (hardcover).—ISBN 978-0-7710-4818-0 (EPUB)
I. Title.

PS8523.A53D44 2018   C813'.54   C2017-904761-2
                                              C2017-904762-0

This is a work of fiction. Any resemblance to actual persons,
living or dead, events, or locales is entirely coincidental.

Book design by CS Richardson
Typeset in Van Dijk by M&S, Toronto
Printed and bound in the United States of America

McClelland & Stewart,
a division of Penguin Random House Canada Limited,
a Penguin Random House Company
www.penguinrandomhouse.ca

1 2 3 4 5   22 21 20 19 18

Penguin
Random House
McCLELLAND & STEWART

To the men and women who came home from war only to find the poverty, injustice, inequality, and racism they had fought so hard to end. It is to their sacrifices we owe our lives.

Midnight, we cross an old battlefield.
The moonlight shines cold on white bones.

—from "Traveling Northward" by Du Fu (712-770),
translated by Kenneth Rexroth

ONE

THE DARK CUP OF THE CAT'S EAR MOVED, the long guard hairs at the tip shivering toward the crack in the window beside her. Art finished his drink, put his glass down by the whisky bottle, and waited to see if the cat's ear would come back to rest, but it didn't. Instead she lifted her head and looked out the window, both ears pointed at whatever was outside.

Something has moved out there, Art thought, animal or man or both, and as he leaned forward in his chair he bumped the table and spilled the glass of whisky. "Damn," he said, trying to see past the cat. He took a quick drink from the bottle.

"Hey, the cabin," a man cried. "Art, you there?"

The cat leapt off the windowsill the moment Art opened the door, slipping between his legs and gone, nothing left to betray her but a few grass stems trembling where she passed into the meadow toward the aspens behind the cabin.

He looked to the river and saw Joseph Gillespie coming from the railroad grade along the path by the creek. Joseph's guitar was banging against his back, a discordant music crying. Staggering beside him was a boy hanging off his arm. Art couldn't tell if he was struggling to get away from Joseph or was just trying his best to keep going along with him. Art peered through the bright sun broken above the mountains and saw the boy's legs flutter, Joseph reaching down and sweeping him up in his arms.

Art turned and went back into the cabin, the door behind him open for Joseph carrying what had to be an accident, some injury done to the boy by himself or by some other. Either way, he was going to need help if Joseph had to carry him.

He took one more drink from the Ballantine's, screwed the cap on, and set the bottle by the leg of the table just out of sight. Dragging his grey army blanket back from the cot's thin sheet, he pulled the narrow bed out from the wall so the light from the window by the door would fall on whoever was going to lie there. As he did he heard Joseph's boots hit the porch. Art turned quick to the door and caught the soaked body of the boy as Joseph let him go, water dripping from Joseph's clothes. The man looked exhausted.

The boy and Art swept in a half-circle as if performing a step to some lost waltz, the boy's head rolling across his shoulders. "Christ," Art said looking close at him, "it's Emerson Turfoot you got here, Arnold's boy."

"He fell in the river," said Joseph, taking his guitar off his back and leaning it against the wall by the door. "Take a look by his ear there."

Art laid Emerson on the cot and pulled the blanket up over the boy's shivering body. He lifted the torn piece of what had once been Joseph's shirt wrapped around the boy's head, took a close look and, gentle, pressed the sleeve against the wound with the heel of his hand.

"What happened?"

"You know that dead fir snag that hangs out over the river just up the rail line from here?"

"Yeah," Art said, nodding as he leaned over and with his free hand pulled the first-aid kit out from under the chair by the stove. He gripped it hard to still the trembling in his hand as he settled the kit down by the cot. "Put your hand where mine is here, Joseph. Not hard. Just enough to slow the bleeding," he said, Joseph leaning in, his fingers replacing Art's by the boy's ear.

As Art got up he turned and tried not to look at the whisky bottle, its dull gleam behind the table leg. "Go on," he said to Joseph as he took a clean cotton sock from the line stretched beside the chimney, dipping it in the seething water kettle on the stove. He knelt again beside Joseph and washed the trailing blood from Emerson's throat.

"See here," Art said as he carefully took the bloody shirt sleeve away. He placed two fingers on the artery just below the cut beside the boy's ear. "Come here and feel the pulse," Art said. "Press down, but not too heavy."

Joseph went to the other side of the cot. "Okay," he said.

"The tree?" Art asked.

"The damned kid was climbing it."

"What? That rotting snag?"

"Yeah. It's the old tree the osprey hunts the river from," said Joseph. "When the kid was almost at the top, the branch he was holding on to up there must've broke. He was forty feet high when he fell into the river."

"And this?" said Art, pointing at the wound.

"Maybe the branch cut him when he landed," Joseph said. "I don't know. Water was deep where I fished him out. Couldn't have hit a rock or anything. Hell, he was floating downriver. I had to swim to get him."

Art looked close at the wound he'd exposed on the side of Emerson's face. It was deep and reached a crooked inch from just above Joseph's fingers.

"He's a strange kid, this one," said Art.

"Jesus," Joseph said. "He should be dead after a fall like that."

Art reached into the first-aid kit and took out antiseptic, tape, and a roll of bandage. He laid them out on a shirt he took from the drying line and then very gently touched Joseph's fingers. "Good. That's good," he told Joseph.

Art tried to count how many drinks he'd had before they'd come. He tried to remember, his body whispering for another sip from the bottle. Art turned and leaned down hard onto the table, pressing his hands flat against the worn wood.

"You okay?" Joseph asked.

"Yeah," said Art. "Just a little tired." He reached again into the kit and took out scissors and a razor and went back to the cot, kneeling as he clipped and shaved the skin along the cut, the razor's blade delicately slipping in and around Joseph's fingers. As he washed the last hairs away, the boy stared up at Art from his pale blue eyes, his small body tense. Art placed the palm of his hand against the boy's chest where a wild heart was beating and said quietly the one word, "Breathe."

Emerson grabbed hold of the arm pushing him down, his fingers white against Art's wrist. His frantic eyes blinked once as Art said softly, "Breathe."

And Emerson did.

Everything became very quiet and Art could hear the water roiling in the pot on the stove, the wood crackling in the firebox, and then far off the screams of a Steller's jay began somewhere down the river.

"Damned birds," Art said.

As he spoke Emerson let go Art's wrist.

"Always angry at the world," said Joseph.

Emerson stared past his wet boots at the open door and the sun on the meadow.

"When you fell out of that snag you landed in the river and cut your head," said Art. "How, I don't know. Joseph here swam out and got you before you could drown and brought you to my cabin. I'm going to stitch up the long cut you got on the side of your head and then I'm going to bandage it. You can go home after that. That sound okay with you?"

When Emerson didn't reply, Art rested the palm of his hand upon the boy's chest again. "Take deep breaths," he said. "Deep and long. And while you're doing the breathing I'm going to give you a needle in your arm that will help with the pain when I stitch that wound. When I'm done, Joseph here will let you go. You're not afraid, are you?"

Emerson just stared at him. All Art could see behind those eyes was a boy who wanted to run. Every muscle and bone in the small body wanted to be gone. Art knew Emerson Turfoot didn't like being inside any cabin, shack, or house. If the boy had his way he'd have lived in the forest in a cave or hollow tree, but Art knew his mother, Isabel, refused to put up with any such thought as that. The best she could do though was have him sleep out in the barn with the horse, the straw mattress and blanket she set there for him vacant most every night she looked to find him. She'd told Art that her son rarely spent a whole night there at the best of times, but at least she knew there was a place he could doss down that had a roof over it and an animal that loved him as much as she did. That was good enough for her.

Emerson lay quiet, his chest pinned under Art's gentle hand. He breathed, the cage of his ribs lifting and falling, the air coming deep and slow as he gave himself over to the first-aid man, Emerson's two pale eyes staring into Art's.

"You lie there and listen," Art said, taking his hand away. "Joseph here is going to tell you how you turned into an osprey when you were falling out of that snag. You didn't fall, you know. You flew right into the river. He's sure you had a big trout in your teeth when he pulled you out. You tell him," he said to Joseph. "You tell him how he turned into an osprey."

"Never saw anything like it," said Joseph as he sat down on the end of the bed, the boy's eyes locking on his as he spoke. "Never saw a young man like you turn into a bird, just like that."

As Joseph spoke Art took a syringe from a cloth bag in his kit. He tipped the needle into a small blue bottle and took up just enough morphine to knock the boy out, what remained of the drug puddled in the bottom. He capped the bottle tight and placed it back in the bag. He stared at the needle and syringe in his hand, the glisten of the morphine in its glass tube, and for a long moment felt a soft melting inside him, his dreams, his memories of the war and all else of the past he had tried to forget gone. It had been a long time since he'd taken up the needle.

He knelt by the cot and gave the boy the drug in the slender vein in the crook of his elbow, smiling as he saw the quiet shadow of morphine swallow him. The blood from the wound had slowed to almost nothing. Emerson's eyes were closed, his breathing slow and steady as Art took up the curved needle and began.

As he tied the first knot he told Joseph he could take his hand away from Emerson's temple. "Play something," he said.

Joseph picked up his guitar and stared far off as he tuned the strings. As the first notes sounded he began to sing, *I went down to the river to watch the fish swim by.* To stop himself from weeping along with Hank Williams's "Long Gone Lonesome Blues," Art whispered in Emerson's ear, "You dive deep with that osprey now, you hear?"

Emerson drifted, his eyelids fluttering as Joseph sang the song, the quiet chords carrying the boy away. Art knew the song and the singing and he remembered morphine too and as he did the temptation came again as it always did and once again he set the thought aside. The opium he smoked with Wang Po was enough, the whisky enough. He had to think about the boy. Emerson was in the presence of a gentle emptiness. Art knew that place, but knew too its other side. Whisky, morphine, opium, dreams, all the same at the end.

The needle binding the seam of Emerson's wound was something far away from the body on the bed. The boy under Art's hands was an osprey child moving feathered through the river currents in search of an elusive trout, a silver fish that was always almost in his talons and never was.

The needle moved as it always had in the war and after the war, the loops of thread gathering flesh together until what had been a crevice in Emerson's flesh became instead a gathering of tiny winged insects, each one closing Emerson's skin. Tenacious creatures, immaculate in their desire to make whole what had been broken. Art smiled as Joseph finished the song and began another. "Cool Water." Art remembered the Sons of the Pioneers singing: *He spreads the burning sand with water.* Where was he when he first heard the song? What bar, what room, what camp, mill, bunkhouse, somewhere, yes, but alone, always alone? No, not always. Not in Paris. Not with Marie.

He thought of the boy under his hands, this young, wild creature who roamed the valley and the mountains. An animal who was still learning how to be human, the restraints the world offered creating his rebellion. Art wondered what would become of such a one, and then he laughed and realized Joseph was laughing too, and though he didn't know if Joseph had the same thought as he did, he knew whatever crossed Joseph's mind was good and that the boy had found in the man and his songs his own life saved, a debt without limit.

Joseph rested the guitar when Art put the needle down, Emerson quiet beside him as Art began to dress the wound. "You think you could go up to the farm and get Arnold to come down here and get his son?"

"I can do that," Joseph said. "Won't take me all that long, I guess. It'll take a little for Arnold to get that horse of his out of the pasture and harnessed to the buckboard. I know. I've met that horse. He doesn't much like coming down to the village."

"Why's that, you think?" asked Art, knowing the answer.

"'Cause he has to haul the buckboard back up."

They both laughed.

Joseph looked down at Emerson. "Looks like he'll be resting for a bit," he said. "Mind you—keep an eye on him. I figure he's a boy could run off in his sleep let alone on morphine."

"He'll be okay," said Art. "You can leave the guitar here if you want."

"No," said Joseph. "I kind of like having it around. You never know when someone's going to need a song."

Art smiled as he watched Joseph sling his guitar across his back and head out the door. As it closed behind him, Art stood up and sat back at the table. He reached down for the bottle, raised it, and filled his glass half full. Three ounces, exactly. He'd measured the invisible line on the glass many times, his hand and eye knowing precisely when too much was the same as too little, neither of them ever enough.

—

ART LISTENED TO THE HARNESS CLINK and jingle as Arnold Turfoot and his buckboard crossed the meadow and pulled up to the cabin, the horse heaving a little before leaning down into the meadow grass to graze. Emerson was sitting on the porch, groggy, still dazed from the fall into the river and the stitching of his wound, but mostly because of the dregs of morphine running in his veins.

From the moment Joseph pulled him from the river Emerson hadn't spoken. Art had told him his father was coming to get him, but Emerson gave no sign he'd heard what Art said. Art didn't mind the boy's silence. In his rare meetings with him Emerson Turfoot had never been much for talking and Art knew better than to try and change his ways.

The Turfoots weren't a forward family. Emerson's mother was the one exception, though when she talked it was never idle chatter. Most people in the village who exchanged words with her thought Isabel spoke in riddles. Whenever anyone asked Art to try and explain what she might have said to them, the best he could do was tell them Isabel Turfoot was what he'd call spiritual. People nodded when they heard that about her. It confirmed her strangeness. She was *spiritual*, the word explaining everything they'd ever thought of her. She wasn't exactly Christian and she wasn't exactly not. What she was was someone else entirely.

Art respected Isabel. She was known up and down the river as a healer, though there were some who were a little nervous about seeking her help. She worked with old-time remedies and there were people who didn't quite trust her ways. Her healing wasn't Art's but more than once he'd gone to Isabel when he found there was nothing else he could do for someone. Isabel had helped a lot of people in her years.

One day she'd found him passed out beside the mountain trail that led to the high springs in the alpine. Why he was there he didn't know then and didn't know now. All he remembered was waking up to find Isabel beside him working threads and stems of grass into long woven chains. When he opened his eyes she said a prayer over him. He looked at her long and then not knowing what else to say he asked her what she was doing weaving grass. She told him the work gave her pleasure. She told him she was weaving chains to hold Art in this world and then she laughed. The next day he'd gone up to the farm and asked her to tell him the prayer so he could remember it. She did but he forgot it almost as soon as she told him, the whisky he'd drunk before he went up leaving him a little adrift. When he asked her whose prayer it was, she smiled and said it was given to her by an Indian from the desert country down south. "A good man," she'd said. "A lot like you"—this last leaving him bewildered.

While Emerson had been out Art told him what he remembered of the prayer. It was just a line or two, but Art repeated it anyway. *Hold on to what you are*, Art told him. *Be what you believe. Each tree in the forest stands by itself.* Art knew the boy was in a morphine dream, but he thought maybe the words might take root in some nook or cranny in Emerson's mind and be there to find if the boy needed them.

A half-hour later Arnold Turfoot had come with the horse and buckboard. Joseph hopped down from the wagon and helped Emerson off the porch and up onto the seat, Arnold lending a hand as his son settled beside him. "I'm thanking you both," Arnold said and Art nodded as if what had happened was just another occurrence in an ordinary morning. When they pulled away Art fell in behind them on the path to the village. As he walked he looked at Joseph sitting on the heel of the buckboard, his guitar in his arms. He was singing a song with wild horses in it, a song Art didn't know.

When Art got to the end of the path through the meadow he squatted in the gravel where the road ended and watched the horse haul the buckboard up the hill past the abandoned church. Joseph dropped off there, turning to wave at Art as he disappeared into the trees. Emerson sat close to his father and Art was sure it was because Arnold held him tight so his son couldn't jump off too and disappear, the trees and brush swallowing him.

The last whisky at the cabin had left him shaky and he closed a fist and leaned into the gravel with it, propping himself there as he willed the trembling to pass. He waited and watched the buckboard pass the store and the Hall until it disappeared behind the old church. Art stood up and moved into the shade of a cedar, leaning back against its trunk as he followed their journey in his head, the wheels grinding as it climbed to the high road, crossing it and climbing farther, passing the shacks where the Sikhs lived. Beyond that was the village dump and then the road veered away as it dwindled into the two-gutter track that wound its way another half mile through the forest, coming out into the meadows, fields, house, and barn that were Arnold's pride and Isabel's joy, their farm.

A strange wild creature was young Emerson Turfoot, part bird and animal, part fish, part boy. Each stitch he'd knotted in the boy's face had brought Art's war back, fragmented images of broken children standing in the mauled dirt as his tank rolled by, old women searching in the rubble for something to replace the nothing in their hands, the Calgary Highlander outside Falaise he'd tried to help breathe before a medic had taken over only to tell him the soldier was dead, Art dropping his hands, half afraid to lift them again for fear of what they might try to do next. And the old woman weeping in that doorway in Caen and, no, he didn't want to put a face to her and not to the little children piled in the ditch either, no.

But the thing with Emerson, that had been good. He had at least that, didn't he?

It had been fourteen years since he came home from France in 1946 and the war was still with him. He stayed under the cedar at the end of the path and looked up through its branches at the fire and smoke rising from the sawmill's burner into the sky above the North Thompson River. Far back in a cloud he could see the flame-throwers arching a molten fire over the Leopold Canal in Moerbrugge, the German bodies they found later when they crossed over, the smell of charred wet ashes behind the berm.

His hand shook as he picked up some loose gravel, letting the shards drift through his fingers. The cracked rocks glittered as they fell and as he heard them click against each other they became the stones in the path that led away from St. Dionysius church, its ruined tower broken against the sky.

He closed his eyes. They had fought for weeks in the battle for Caen. Then without rest they had moved on into Belgium. The struggle for Moerbrugge had left them exhausted. After three days they were pulled back to rest for a few hours, the crew sprawled in the mauled ground under what was left of an oak tree a half mile southwest of the canal. Art had stayed with the men for a while but the smell of diesel and grease, fire and smoke, and the smell of the men too, their cigarettes, their sweat, even their breathing drove him away. A rubble wall and a ruined house and store made him think there might be wine or maybe brandy in the ruins.

He'd found the German officer lying on the side of the road a few yards from the store. The body of the man lay partly buried under a skirt of gravel. The man's legs were covered in loose stones thrown up by the treads of a passing tank, perhaps their own. Part of the man's head was gone. Art could see what was left of the face so clearly, the blond hair strangely clean and flung to the side, the rest a cup of skull hanging over an emptiness that had once held a mind. The man was another ruined body and not one of theirs. Something glinted on the officer's hand and he knelt down and saw a signet ring emblazoned with an Iron Cross. He took it from the man's bruised finger.

He'd thought he would show it to the men, but when he took the ring from his pocket that night and gazed at the Iron Cross he was ashamed. At dawn he returned and found the body. He put the ring back on the soldier's finger, got down on his knees and dragged muddy rocks over the corpse with his hands, the early flies lifting around him in their croon, benisons of a false glory.

Done, he'd stood beside a breach in the rubble wall, nothing much left of the store and the house beyond but wreckage. No chance of an intact bottle of anything. Anyway, what might have been there would have been scavenged by the Germans. The garden behind what had once been a house had somehow survived the fighting, carrot and beet tops wavering. He would never forget the trembling green skirts of the lettuce bright in the sun.

He was going to pull some carrots for the men back at the tank, but as he stepped over the low wall and leaned down everything around him vanished in a fire that lifted him up from the orderly rows of vegetables, turning him into a bright star made of earth and stones, dust and silence.

The next thing he knew was Paris. He was sitting at a table outside the Café Olympique, Claude introducing him to Marie.

Between the explosion in the garden and the moment in Paris everything that had happened to him was gone. He had lost ten days, no memory of the tank crew finding him, no memory of what happened next, the medics, the field hospital, Paris, all of it remembered for him by Claude.

Art looked up and saw Bill Samuels step out of the store and get into his pickup. As the foreman turned up the hill he waved at someone from the truck's window, his hand vanishing in the dust. Art wiped at his forehead with his sleeve, the last bits of gravel slipping through his fingers. He wasn't in France. This wasn't Paris and it wasn't Moerbrugge. There was no dead officer, no Marie. Not anymore.

He took a last look down the path and got up, his hand touching the small flat bottle of whisky in his jacket pocket. He gripped it for a second and then let go of it. Down the tracks was the sawmill, the saws, the refuse chains and drive belts, and the whistles. Claude, the boss, said the great noise was the sound of money crying. To Art it was the sound of war, machines and chains, smoke and fire, the sweat and blood of men at their labour. It was Claude's mill and it was Claude's village. He hired and fired as he wished. Solitary worker or family man, most everyone's life depended on the monthly cheque from the mill. No one argued with Claude except Art and that was because he didn't care if he was fired and also because he had known Claude back in the war.

Major Claude Harper.

Art had history with him.

The sawmill whistles cut into the day, each whistle a command that cut through the noise, one whistle to start the mill and one whistle to stop it. If the whistles went to four it drew Claude from his office down to the mill and no one wanted Claude coming down so the count rarely stopped at four. The whistles almost never went to five. If the count went to five it meant someone had been injured so badly he couldn't walk off the mill floor and Art would have to go to him.

Art let go his breath when the whistle stopped at three, the foreman. Art forced his shoulders to relax. The whistles sounded all day and most of the night and each time they did he counted them down, *one*, *two*, *three*, and then the relief when they stopped, no fourth whistle for Claude, no fifth for a first-aid man, for Art to come running—no man so broken in the sawmill that he couldn't make it to the first-aid room.

And again, *one*, *two*, *three*, his body one still, terrible thing until the whistles ceased.

Wang Po would be waiting for the men to come for dinner, the day shift nearly done and the night shift crew already sitting on the benches waiting for the cook to lay out the food at ten past five. In another few minutes the single whistle would sound. Dinner tonight would be pork stew, tomorrow night steaks. The men would be looking forward to T-bones piled high on platters, cream corn, mashed potatoes, and a gravy they could drown in. Fresh bread too from the morning and apple pie for dessert.

Late tonight he'd go to the basement room under the cookhouse and spend the last hours of the week with Wang Po, the last shift's whistles as he drank, the opium he smoked with the cook adding to his vanishing. They would smoke and drink whisky as they talked or didn't talk about their lives, their wars.

Art had never fit in to the village or the mill. He was the first-aid man and he looked after the mill workers, single guys, but men with families too. Art had seen and done things in some of the rooms in the village, men and women, kids too like Emerson. Bad things happened and people could do terrible things to each other and to themselves.

The nearest hospital was in Kamloops, four hours away by truck on the one-lane dirt and gravel road that crawled along the canyons of the North Thompson River until it got past Little Fort, and even then the road could be rough. Most people didn't have the money to take the train out, let alone stay in a hotel or motel and then pay for a doctor and a hospital on top of that. The farmers and mountain people came to Art sometimes to ask for his help with an injury, an illness. He had access to penicillin and morphine, drugs Isabel Turfoot didn't have and couldn't get. Art entered people's homes in the wrong hours, saw to husbands, wives and daughters, men and boys and girls. He couldn't be a friend to any of them. He knew too much about their lives, saw their blood and tears, their frailties and vulnerabilities, their joys and sorrows.

But there was Wang Po. He was an outsider too, a Chinaman as they called him here, an alien to everyone. Men might sometimes thank him for a meal the cook made, but no one talked to him. Wang Po stayed close to the cookhouse and his room in the basement. If he did go out it was after the night shift ended at three in the morning. There was a big gravel bar by a river eddy a quarter mile below the mill. Art had seen Wang Po sitting on the pale skeleton of an old fir tree caught on shore rocks high above the river's big eddy. Art never bothered him those nights. Still, he often wondered what Wang Po thought about out there under the stars. Art often walked the night, his rambles taking him along the river, the bottle of whisky back in his cabin sitting on the table awaiting his return, the mickey in his jacket empty by the time he returned. He knew what loneliness was and knew Wang Po did too. They both had their wars, his in Europe and Wang Po's in China.

Art passed the cookhouse and the station, crossed the main line and siding tracks, and glanced for a moment at the men hurrying to load the last boxcars of the week. The morning freight would pick up the cars tomorrow and take them to Baton Rouge down in Louisiana. The freight came in an hour after the Express pulled out on its way to Edmonton. His package from Li Wei would be on the Saturday Express out of Vancouver. He had missed the Friday Express, but his liquor shipment would be in the station waiting for him, the box with its twelve bottles too heavy for Joel or him to pack back to the cabin. Bill Samuels would bring the box in his pickup. He'd carry it down to the cabin later in the day and leave it on the porch by the door. Bill said he owed Art that much ever since Art splinted the arm of Eddy, Bill's youngest. The kid had a green-stick fracture and there was no need to send him to the hospital. He'd straightened the arm and the bones healed quickly.

Art sat down in the shadow of the CNR station porch and watched the men on the train siding spear eighteen- and twenty-foot two-by-twelves into a boxcar, the long boards heavy white spears floating through the air, entering the maw of the box where other men inside directed them into piles at either end of the car. He couldn't see them but he knew how dangerous the work was. The lumber came hard and fast and the men in the boxcars had to be careful. He'd had to put a man in a freight train caboose and send him out to the hospital last winter. The man had been struck in the back of the head by a two-by-ten. The man never returned to the mill. Billy something, Foster, Forester, his name the same as all the men who passed through the mill, someone forgotten the day they headed south or north. No one ever came back once they were gone.

The boxcar was close to being full. The men on the platform moved together in the synchronized repetitions of hard labour. The dance at the Hall was tomorrow night. Everyone who could walk or crawl would be there.

Saturday night.

He didn't always go to the dance, but if there was trouble later on, a fight, a woman hurt, someone injured, they'd come to his cabin and get him to come and help. There were a lot of men working at the mill. Some had wives and families in cabins or shacks, but most were single and lived in the bunkhouses. And there were the people from the mountain, women and children, sons and daughters too who were looking for a way off the farm or ranch so they could leave and go somewhere where they could pretend they were in a place where real life happened, Edmonton, maybe, or even Vancouver.

The hill people kept mostly to themselves, but come a Saturday night dance they'd be all dressed up, shiny shoes, polished boots, worn high heels, a pair almost new, a homemade dress or one they'd worn ten times or more, a starched shirt ironed on a kitchen table, a pretty necklace, whatever it took to make the night special. The girls who went there danced for their lives, men standing outside the Hall drinking on the deck, behind the Hall in the trees, or standing along the wall inside as they waited for a chance to cut in on someone, anyone, just to hold a woman in their arms. Their wildest dream was to take a woman back to their truck or into the darkness of the trees while "Dream Lover" or "Stagger Lee" played back in the Hall, any song so long as they weren't alone on their bunk at three in the morning holding themselves in their hands as they stared at a shadow on the wall.

And there was the new girl, Alice, at the store. The Rotmensens had brought her in to work for them, nearly a month ago now. They'd paid fifty dollars for her at the residential school in Kamloops. She was theirs till she was sixteen. Piet and Imma kept her locked up at night in the shanty hanging off the back of the store for fear she'd run off with someone. People shook their heads when they saw her pulling that wooden wagon down to the station to pick up the food shipment from Woodward's. Sometimes she'd have to make four or five trips. When she was working at the lunch counter men would come by and get a coffee or sandwich just to look at her.

A lot of the women in the village were upset by her being locked up at night, but what had really got them talking was the Rotmensens buying a girl and an Indian girl as well, no matter them saying they were giving her a chance to work. Molly Samuels was especially upset and Art had heard her say so more than once to Imma. Molly hated that anyone could just buy a girl and she told her so, but Imma said she and Piet were giving her a chance to have a life and how was it Molly's business anyway. Who did she think she was? Just because her husband was the foreman at the sawmill didn't make her any more special than anyone else. Bill had told her she should let it go, but Molly wasn't the kind of woman to do that. Art heard she'd asked Bill to talk to Claude and he did, but Claude wanted nothing to do with it. He said the girl was lucky they'd rescued her from the residential school given the kind of stuff that went on there with the Brothers itching to get their hands on a pretty girl.

Art said he'd help if he could, but he didn't know how. Molly told Art the village wasn't some place down south in the States. Alice wasn't a Negro from a century ago. She said Alice was the same as anyone except maybe she was an Indian. And who gave the Rotmensens the right to lock her up just because of that?

What was Art to say to Molly or anyone? Like most things he was asked to confront, it made him feel useless.

Claude was the one watching over Alice while the Rotmensens were away this weekend. There was talk Claude was going to let her go to the dance. The Rotmensens had never done that. One thing Art knew, if she was allowed to go to the dance tomorrow night there'd most likely be trouble.

What young Joel would do about Myrna and Alice if they both showed up was anyone's guess. The kid was besotted by both of them. He spent half his weekend hours up at the Turfoot farm with Myrna and half his nights standing on a cedar round peeping through the lean-to window at Alice sleeping.

Joel.

The kid Art had saved from freezing to death in a gondola car the winter past during a blizzard. The shift at the mill was ending and after Joel had finished sweeping up he'd hotfoot it up to the store so he could sit with his bottle of Coke and moon over Alice as she worked behind the counter. It was all too painful to think about.

Art tried to remember when he'd been that crazy over a girl. The only one he could remember when he was that young was Margie Sandovitch. There was a night long ago when he'd dared to touch her breast after their kissing and she started to cry. She'd looked so frightened, her hands covering her face. He had fled from the alley behind her house thinking it was his fault, that he'd hurt her somehow. It was only months later he found out her father had been raping her most nights since she was a little girl. Margie and her little sister Joyce. Some of the men around Pender and Keefer found out about it from one of the wives, the mother's face cut and bruised from being hit too often, Joyce hidden away sick too long, too many times. One night a few of the men took Margie's father into an alley off Water Street and beat him blind and broken with boots and two-by-twos. He didn't need a white cane after that. There was no need. He never walked again, the family gone when he got out of St. Paul's Hospital.

Art slipped the mickey out of his pocket and took a quiet

drink. He looked at the tracks running north and south, stepped away from the station, and headed back toward the village. He passed the cookhouse and the bunkhouse where Joel lived, the one he'd taken him to after Claude had Bill Samuels haul him out of the gondola car last winter. Art had worried at first about the kid bunking with the older men, but Joseph told Art he'd keep an eye on the boy. There were men like Ernie Reiner who would bully the kid if they could. He knew Joseph wouldn't stand for that. Most of the other men wouldn't either. Still, Joel had to learn to look after himself.

Just up the road from the store he could see the single clapboard schoolhouse and beside it what remained of the old church on the corner, both of them empty. The schoolhouse wasn't much bigger than half a boxcar. It had been abandoned for a couple of years now because there weren't enough children to allow for a government-paid teacher. They needed twenty kids and the village and hills could only come up with eighteen. And there was Claude's house just below the store, the Rotmensens' across the road from his. The rest of the village was what it'd been when Art came up from Vancouver, a few small houses, the bunkhouses, rundown shacks, trailers, and cabins.

Piet and Imma's house had a covered front porch with a couch on it. Claude's house was larger than theirs. The last mill boss had a family, according to Claude. The old boss had tried to fix the house up before Claude came up from Kamloops, but the job was done badly, the paint he brushed on peeling, the windows swollen shut. He'd told Art enough times how his job was to run the mill into the ground, the last good timber dwindling in the cut blocks. The bribe money the mill had paid to the Forest Service guys had dried up along with the fir and hemlock in the valley bottoms. In the end none of it would matter. In a few more years the bosses down at the coast would have taken everything of value from the river valley. After that they'd likely torch the mill in hopes of getting what insurance they had on equipment, the building itself worthless.

This was where he lived, this half-assed village, this almost-town where he was the first-aid man for a sawmill on its last legs. He scuffed his heels in the cinders and gravel under his boots.

The mill whistle sounded to end the shift. The saws stopped their screams. There was only the clanking of the chains as they hauled refuse up the flume into the burner. Art didn't think he'd go to dinner. He couldn't eat, his belly grinding on glass. He put his hands together and made one fist. The sawmill chains kept banging, louder now the mill was quiet, Joel and the rest of the cleanup crew loading chips and bark to be carried up to the burner's gaping mouth. Caen, Moerbrugge, the Scheldt. The only thing that never stopped was the great fire, the smoke boiling from the beehive cone drifting south into the canyon along the river, a grey swath eating into the forest along the river's hard banks.

TWO

REINER WAS ALWAYS AT THE CAFÉ before Joel got there, no matter Joel's struggle to get the last cleanup under the trim saws done faster. Joel would arrive draped in a veil of sawdust stuck to the oil on his clothes, his hands and face. Dust stubble stuttered on his cheeks, a slick festoon in his hair, his boots streaked with grease and oil from slogging through and around and under machines, the trim saws, the edger, the gang and head saws, the belts and conveyors, and the floor that needed endless sweeping, shovelling, and scraping, the foreman keeping a close eye on him, making sure he did his job right even as he knew all Joel wanted was to be get gone.

Joel straightened his stetson and brushed at his canvas pants and wool shirt. The door slammed behind him as he went past the till where Imma Rotmensen sat on her padded chair, her heavy blond head angled down to the side as she jotted the sums paid against what was owed by Oroville Cranmer, his whip-thin wife, Gladys, beside him counting out her four dollars onto the counter and Imma picking up the two bills and pushing at the coins with her stubby forefinger, counting herself the silver and coppers carefully, dragging the metal across the scarred wood into the tacked-on kitchen drawer she called her till. Imma told the two of them then exactly how much they still owed from the spring when the mill was shut down for breakup, the bush roads impassable because of the snowmelt, and their pogey ran out, welfare nowhere near enough to feed their brood.

Joel both saw and didn't see them, heard and didn't hear as he sidled past and down the aisle where the canned goods were stacked, tomatoes, corn, green beans and pork and beans, peas, canned peaches and pears, scabbed labels scratched and stained, the bins where the weevil-soured flour and sugar, the mottled rice and cereals were kept below the flats of withered week-old vegetables, carrots with hair roots flaring and potatoes gone soft, stained with black eruptions, pale turnips, onions and cabbages gone to brown and grey reek. He passed all of such sundry and went on down the aisle to the counter at the back where he took off his hat and sat down on the stool he always took.

He looked around but Alice wasn't there. He thought he could hear someone rummaging in the storeroom and thought she might be in the back getting something. He glanced at Ernie Reiner sitting at the end of the counter and looked away when he heard Molly Samuels talking to Natalka Danko. Natalka was a woman like the ones he'd known back on the Arrow Lakes, sometimes poor, sometimes not, but mostly angry, mostly miserable. Molly was different. She had been kind to him ever since the night last winter when Art Kenning rescued him from the gondola car in the blizzard. Art had taken him to the cookhouse where Wang Po fed him and then he took him to

Molly's house. It was a freezing cold winter night and Joel had never forgotten her kindness. She gave him a hot cup of tea and asked him where he'd come from and what his life had been before he jumped the gondola in Edmonton, the blizzard swirling all the way through the Rockies and down the North Thompson River.

Molly had checked his teeth and feet and asked him if he'd kept himself clean. Even half frozen, he knew what she meant and told her he did. Joel had trusted her that night in a way he'd never trusted anyone before. He wondered sometimes if it was just because he was so weak right then, but he knew it wasn't only that. Molly was someone who just took charge of things. She was what his own mother would have called firm. There wasn't anyone in the village who didn't respect her and her husband Bill too, the foreman. When there was trouble people turned to them for help. When Art took him to the bunkhouse after Molly was finished Art told Joel he'd be okay. He said too if Joel was ever in trouble and he wasn't around then Molly and Bill Samuels were two people he could count on. Joseph too.

Joel looked over and said hi to Molly. She smiled at him and then turned to Natalka who was going through bolts of cloth, unrolling each one a little ways and holding it up to see the patterns. As Joel watched, Molly pointed out one she thought Natalka's daughter would like. She told her to buy it, but Natalka said it was too expensive, saying her daughter didn't need fancy.

"But I know Kateryna wants something nice to go to the dance with," said Molly.

"She can wear ordinary," said Natalka. "It's not like it's any different than this here cloth." She held up a plain white cotton. It looked to Joel like it had sat on the shelf for years, a cloth like what dish towels were made from.

"Kateryna shouldn't get any ideas about who she is or where she's going to end up," said Natalka.

"She's a good girl," Molly said. "Why don't you spoil her a little bit this one time."

"The time for spoiling is when a man can give her the money to buy her own. When Kateryna's under my roof she can do with less. Besides it's me has to keep an eye on her when she's cutting out the pattern tonight, me who's got to keep a lookout when she's sewing it up all the way into tomorrow for the dance. Plain is easy to work with. Why buy her good cloth just to ruin it."

"She'll be so disappointed," said Molly.

"She might as well get used to disappointment when she's young," said Natalka. "It's a woman's lot, no matter who."

"It doesn't have to be that way," said Molly. She reached for a roll of pale blue ribbon on a shelf and took it down. "Why don't you let me buy two yards of this ribbon here for her. You could get Kateryna to sew it into the bodice. It would make it look so nice."

"So you say. You'll buy it for her?"

"Yes," said Molly. "I'd like to do it. A little gift."

"Blue ribbon, yes," said Natalka. "Not too much," she added, tucking the roll of white cotton under her arm. "I don't need her getting big ideas."

As they turned to go, Molly lifted a hand. "Hey," she said. "You all right, Joel?"

"Yup," said Joel, not turning now, his eyes on Alice as she passed in front of him with a bucket of ice. Joel was going to say how he'd have helped her get it, but she was pouring it into the cooler by then. Joel sat there wiping the bits of sawdust off the counter that fell from his hair, waiting for Alice to take a bottle of Coke out of the cooler and bring it down to him. It's what he always got.

Alice went over to Reiner's end of the counter, setting down in front of him a curled baloney sandwich on a chipped saucer. Reiner picked up the soft pickle and wobbled it at her, a grin on his face like a wrong blossom. His Browning .308 was leaning against the counter beside him.

Joel watched Alice's back as she went along the counter, heard the jangled wet sound of dead ice dragging, a bottle opening with a sudden whimper of air, and then he dropped his eyes again to see only her small hand as she put the Coke down in front of him. No glass, no straw. He watched her slide his quarter across the scarred wood, her hand taking the coin between her fingers and then stopping a moment and looking at his bent head and hat before going to the cardboard cash box and making change, giving him a nickel and dime back. He dropped his head lower as she placed the coins into his palm, not wanting to know what it was she might be seeing in him.

He stared instead at the cotton string cinched at her middle to hold her stained white apron, fold creased upon fold to fit her narrow waist. He watched her back as she went down the counter. Thin beads of water ran down the sides of his bottle and pooled on the pine boards. He wanted to say her name out loud, Alice, but couldn't think of a reason. He looked at his clutched hands and wondered how anyone could be as wretched as he was. He sneaked a look at her face and saw a smile that was almost there, her lips moving, saying nothing he could hear, the blood sloshing loud in his ears, his head drowning.

It was the same each afternoon at the end of his shift at the mill, his quarter, his change, her hand with the bottle of Coca-Cola she lifted from the wheezing cooler and him afraid to look directly into her face. Whenever she seemed like she might start talking to him he'd turn away or stare down into his hands, anything not to look at her when she was looking at him. One thing was for sure, she wasn't afraid of him. He'd seen her be different with other men, more careful. He'd watched her serve the mill guys, saw her eyes go thin as she looked at some of them warily. Ernie Reiner was the worst.

Joel hated it when he saw Reiner whisper things to her. Joel would see the nervous look on her face as he beckoned her close and her having to bend forward to hear him. It was then she seemed to Joel to be confused, Reiner's lips sliding across whatever it was he was saying, Alice leaning against the counter across from him, hands flat on the scarred pine, then turning away and wiping a stray hair from her dark cheek, jewels of sweat on her forehead.

Joel hunched deeper over his Coke and stared into the puddle on the counter. The grin on Reiner's face made Joel bite at his lip until it bled. He turned at the sound of boots clacking on the worn linoleum and saw Cliff Waters leaning against the shelf of canned goods.

"Ain't she something else," Reiner said, just loud enough for Joel to hear and Cliff too.

"Leave off talking like that about her, Ernie," Cliff said.

Joel had heard Cliff straighten Reiner out a few times, but he didn't know what was going to happen this time. Cliff teased Alice too, but he wasn't mean like Ernie. Cliff's teasing was liking her, not hurting her.

"Hey Alice," Ernie said with a grin, ignoring Cliff. "You oughta come to the dance tomorrow night. I could show you a good time."

"I don't know how to dance," she said softly, turning her head a little and looking at Cliff, not Ernie.

Joel marvelled at the quietness of her. She seemed to be speaking from far away, a small voice sent out from the lighted end of a tunnel. For a moment he imagined her speaking like that to him, maybe saying she liked him.

"Hey," Ernie said. "Don't know how or don't want to?"

Joel's head sank a little more, his hat blocking his eyes of everything but his hand and the Coke bottle.

"I can show you some steps if you don't know how," said Ernie, his fingers tippity-tapping his spoon, his coffee cup jiggling in its cracked saucer.

"I can't go," she replied. She walked along the counter past Joel to where Cliff was standing. "They won't let me," she said to Cliff. He nodded, her smile in return a whisper. "You know that," she said.

"Who? Piet and Imma?" called Ernie, his coffee cup still, his spoon gone quiet. "There's ways around them."

"She's not talking to you," said Cliff. He didn't look at Ernie. "She's talking to me."

"I wouldn't let her go anywhere if it was me in charge."

"Imma and Piet are going away tomorrow," said Cliff, ignoring Ernie again. "Down to Kamloops." As he spoke he moved around the end of the shelf to the counter and leaned across the counter toward Alice.

She didn't speak and Cliff smiled at her. "Who says you can't dance?" Cliff said softly.

Joel cut his eyes down the counter to her and tried to hear what she said back to him, but Alice's face was turned away, her words even more of a whisper.

". . . and you know they lock my door," she said at the end of what she was saying, Joel catching at the last words.

There was a silence along the counter.

"There's no such thing as a locked door that a man can't open," Ernie said. He got up, cradling his rifle under his arm.

Cliff leaned away from Alice and turned to Ernie standing by his stool. "What the hell you doing with a rifle in here?" he asked.

"Nothing you should worry yourself about," said Ernie, shaking the rifle into the crook of his elbow. He slipped his finger into his watch pocket and slid out a dime, placing it on the counter by his coffee cup. "There's supposed to be a big bear coming through here nights, Cliff," he said. "Thought I'd go down and hunt a bit along the river. Might be that bear holed up there for the day. Want to come along?"

"Bears go high to sleep," Cliff said. "And that rifle of yours should be in the rack in your truck. Not here in the café."

"Yeah, well, what I carry and where I take it is none of your business."

"It's my business if I make it mine," said Cliff.

"Yeah, yeah," said Reiner.

"Well, you're done here today, don't you think?" Cliff said, stepping back and making elaborate room for Reiner to pass by.

Reiner took a long look at Alice but she was at the sink again, her back to him, her hands deep in soapy water.

"I'll be back for coffee later," Ernie said to her, the rifle snug under his arm. As he went by Joel, Reiner flipped the back of Joel's hat, the brim falling hard onto Joel's nose. "How's it going, kid," he said over his shoulder.

Joel turned, Coke spilling over his fingers, but before he could think of what to say Reiner was past Cliff and walking toward the front door, muttering something about Alice that Joel couldn't hear.

"Leave him alone," Cliff said to Ernie's back. "I mean it."

Joel listened to Reiner's boot clumping down the aisle to the front of the store, the door slamming. He didn't move as Cliff leaned over the counter and reached out to touch Alice's shoulder. She jumped but, seeing it was Cliff, bent her head away, looking up at him sideways from her dark eyes.

Joel stared down into his Coke, wishing it was him talking to Alice, saying things like what Cliff was saying and her listening to him, saying things back.

"You never mind Ernie," Cliff said to her as he turned away from the counter and followed Reiner's footsteps down the narrow aisle between the shelves with their tired food and out of the store, the door banging behind him.

Joel waited a moment before pushing his hat back up. He hoped she hadn't seen what Reiner had done to him, but he knew she had. She was down by the cooler now squatting as she drained grey water from the spigot into a bucket. He wanted to say something but he didn't know what, so he said, "It's sure hot in here, isn't it?"

"Yes," she replied, not looking up from the rag she was pushing to sop up spilled water.

It was quiet as she dried the scuffed board floor. When she was done she wrung the cloth out over the sink and said over her shoulder, "You want another Coke?"

Time got still then, everything in the world moving except for what was in Joel's head.

He waited while she set the new bottle down in front of him and took the empty one away.

We're alone together, is what Joel thought. Everyone else is down at the cookhouse eating dinner.

Alice went down to the end of the counter and began to fill the salt shakers, her mouth open a bit and breathing as she concentrated on the pouring. As she worked Joel stared at her lips and nose and chin, the small earlobe above the slender muscle by her cheekbone, the way her neck vanished into her blouse leaving the hollow at her throat open. He wanted to taste the dampness he saw glistening there. He could see her arched collarbones, could feel his hand reaching out to touch them, feel her skin. Her hair was bound with a red band tight around the gathering, the long tail of it falling down her back, alive, and him wanting to cut the string with his knife to see the black hair flare into sudden feathers around her face. It's what he thought she was sometimes, a captured bird, that hair of hers tied back, and him wanting to undo it and let it fall through his fingers like loosened wings.

As he watched her he thought of Myrna up on the mountain and what they did together in the high pasture of her father's farm. He liked Myrna and when he was with her he almost never thought of Alice. They were both so different. With Myrna he could do and say most everything he wanted, but with Alice he was completely tongue-tied and he didn't know why.

But he didn't want to think about Myrna. What he wanted was to sit somewhere with Alice down by the river. They would talk and that'd be all, not like what he did with Myrna. Alice could tell him what it'd been like down at the residential school in Kamloops and he could tell her about where he came from. He could tell her about the lakes and the long nights of winter when the northern lights danced over the Monashee Mountains. He could tell her about Alberta and the prairie, what the Rockies looked like when the morning sun lit up the high peaks, and while he was talking maybe she'd let him hold her hand.

And he was going to say something to her, but right then she started back down the counter toward him and he didn't know what to do with his hands. He tried to pick up the Coke bottle and pretend to drink, but his hand trembled in the same way his father's did each time the old man came back in the old Ford pickup truck from the bar at the hotel in Nakusp. It trembled like Art Kenning's did in the morning when he reached for his whisky, the dregs in his glass or the inch or two he always left in the bottle by his bunk. He hoped Art was all right.

Joel would go down to Art's cabin in the early morning on Saturdays and Sundays, other times too, and see if he was okay. If Art was awake and not too drunk or wrecked Joel would sit with him. Mostly they'd be quiet, but sometimes Art would go on about the old days when he was in the war. Joel felt safe with Art. Most of the stories were ones he'd heard before, but he liked hearing Art talk. Sometimes he wondered if Art even knew he was there. Joel wondered if he'd ever go to a war. There'd been the Korean one but he'd missed that.

Some early weekend mornings he'd go and Art wouldn't be there, so Joel would go to the cookhouse to see if he was still there smoking opium with Wang Po in the room below. Wang Po looked out for Art too, but in a different way than Joel. When he and Art were on the pipe they were lost in their worlds. A couple of times Joel had helped Art back to his cabin and stayed with him until he drifted off. It was Art who'd saved him from the train last winter. Joel owed him everything.

Wang Po had explained a lot to him as well. Joel liked to sit in the kitchen, just the cook and him. Wang Po knew a lot of things. He told Joel that Art had a sickness. "Many soldiers had that same sickness in China too," he said once when Joel asked about Art and the war. "Terrible things happen in wars and there are some men who can't let them go. Women too, they suffer the same." Joel asked him why he didn't and Wang Po said he'd learned to forget them. He told Joel he was a Buddhist and because of that he was able to let things like the past go. "I saw bad things happen and I did bad things, some good things too, but they are far away now in the place I call the young man's war. But it was a war," he said, "I never forget that. In wars people do things you can't imagine. In your

English you say you forgive your own life back then. I am that," he said. "I am a man who forgives."

Wang Po had gone back to cutting steaks from the side of beef, his saw cutting through the bone of the spine. When he finished he put down his saw and knife. "No one saves us but ourselves, Joel. Buddha told us the path each of us walk is our own." Joel looked at him and Wang Po said, "Art is between two things: not going all the way and not starting. He has stayed between sword and shield. The war left him in the empty place called grief. It is what he has now."

Joel didn't always understand what Wang Po told him, especially when he spoke in poems, but he liked to get lost in Wang Po's spare stories of China, how he escaped, and how he came to Canada. Mostly he loved the quietness around him. There was a silence in Art too, but it wasn't quiet. Inside Art there was a craziness, many worlds fighting each other, battles without an end.

Joel loosened his grip on the Coke bottle and the trembling stopped. It was Alice who did it to him, not Art and not Wang Po, not whisky, not opium. She'd asked him if he wanted a second Coke and he'd nodded. "Sure," he said, and she gave him the Coke and that was all. When he didn't say anything else she took his dime and went back to the counter where she began to lay out slices of grey baloney, a chunk of margarine, some watery mayonnaise, and curled slices of white bread.

Watching her put the food down on the counter by the sinks he remembered he had to go to the cookhouse to eat. Wang Po would have laid out the stew and he liked stew and if he didn't go soon the other men would be grabbing for seconds and there wouldn't be any left for him but gristle and cold spuds. But he wanted to say something more to her after saying it'd sure been hot today. The coldness of the glass entered his

fist, water beads squeezing wet between his fingers. He wanted
to say at least something like, hey, hi, how are you doing, not
knowing how to say those words in that way or any word to
her, say: thanks, thank you, for sure, okay, or words like, you're
real pretty, and what fear he had to say such a word, to say,
pretty, to say, beautiful, you, your hands, your skin, stunned,
to say such a word as strange to him as lovely, to say the word
love knowing what he had inside him was and wasn't love, for
how could he have what he did not know, a word he had only
read, had never heard once in the home he came out of, his
chest tight, his shoulders, belly, hips, and his legs, his legs
jumping so that he had to let go of the Coke bottle, slide his
hands under the counter and grip his knees, his cock suddenly
hard, his belt cinched tight, his body gone crazy again, and
then bowing his head, his face hidden by his stetson, looking,
he knew, like some cornered animal, a badger gone mad, a fox
frothing, a tick-thin bear, a rat, a rabbit screaming, and all and
none, and wanting to say instead of nothing, hey, it's a nice,
good, pretty good, day, night, to her from under the shadow of
his hat, and her turning from a sandwich saying at last into his
frantic silence:

"You want anything else?"

THREE

ART LOOKED AT THE KID UNLOADING at the woodpile. Joel had come over from the cookhouse and begun working beside him in the cool evening air. Art hadn't asked him to help. Joel just showed up like he always did when there was work to be done. Art set his axe down, loaded six split chunks on his arm, and carried them to the lean-to behind his cabin where he stacked them in new piles across from the four rows of dry wood left from last winter. He was drenched in wet salt sweat, his pants clinging to his thighs. He gripped the edge of the pile to stop his arm from shaking. As he did, Joel came up beside him, his arms full of split fir. Art let go the shed wall and lifted the chunks from the kid's arms stacking them there with the others.

They went back nine more times before Art sat down hard on the chopping block and said, "Enough."

When Joel looked at him, Art said, "Enough for now."

"There's still lots here," said Joel.

Art held up his hand. "Enough," he said. "It'll be dark soon."

"You told me you were going to finish the wood today."

"When did I tell you that?"

"Yesterday," Joel said.

"I don't remember you being around here yesterday."

"It's okay," Joel said. "Never mind. Just let me help you finish."

"No," Art said as he reached behind a broken stud in the shed wall and took down a half-full mickey of whisky and took a drink. The slide of the liquor down into his belly eased him. He shook his head to clear away the wraiths that shivered behind his eyes. Joel stood there waiting among the last of the scattered wood. The kid was always around.

"You ever think about what you're going to do?" he asked as he put the bottle back, what was left of the whisky swirling behind the pitch-stained glass.

Joel shuffled his feet, suddenly feeling awkward. "Tonight?"

"No, not tonight or tomorrow. I mean you're getting deeper into the life around here. You've got Myrna Turfoot on that hill farm up the mountain. And by the way if I was Arnold Turfoot I'd have your hide nailed to my barn door. Don't think I don't know what you're doing up there with her."

"What do you know about it, anyway?"

"What? You think nobody knows about you and Myrna?"

When Joel just stood there, Art said, "It's hard to keep a secret in a little place like this."

"Yeah, well," said Joel, hesitant and awkward.

"And there's that Indian girl at the store too," Art went on. "If you're not up the mountain you're mooning around her at the café or standing on that cedar block back of the lean-to where she sleeps. It's a wonder she doesn't know you're peering at her half the night. A dead-end mill town like this is no place for a young guy like you to make a life."

"But you're here. Why are you staying if it's so bad?"

"Jesus," said Art. "It's different for me. You know, sometimes I wish I never asked Claude to have you hauled out've that frozen gondola car last winter. You never mind me. I've had a life. You're just beginning yours."

"I don't know," said Joel, fiddling with his hat. "I like it here."

"I know what you're thinking. You've got Myrna in the rocks and Alice in your head."

"Yeah," Joel said. "Well . . ."

"I know, I know," said Art as Joel walked back to the chopping block and began piling another armful of wood to carry to the shed.

Art crossed his arms on his chest and held himself tight as Marie slipped in and out of the shadows in his mind.

Their tanks had moved on to Holland. Claude had told him the army had left Moerbrugge behind. It was the deepwater port of Antwerp the Allies needed and that meant taking back the fortress of Walcheren at the end of the Scheldt peninsula. Moerbrugge was being left for another day. Claude told him he was being sent back to his unit. Back to the war.

He wished he could remember more of what had happened to him the day he was blown up, but all he could remember was the dead officer and the ring, the empty cup the soldier's skull made. Yes, and the fieldstone wall, the garden. He had tried to reach for a carrot. How crazy was that? A carrot and a war?

It was Claude who had sent him to Paris to recover. It was Claude who introduced him to Marie.

It was the night before Art was going back to his unit. His shoulder had healed. There was nothing left of the shrapnel wound but an itch. The concussion was never talked about. He had always wondered if Claude arranged that too. And he could put his arm over his head and clench his fist. That's all the doctors needed or wanted to know.

He had sat on the edge of her narrow bed with a drink in his hand. Marie had looked up at him from the rumpled sheets. On the night table by the bed were the syringe and her little bottle of morphine she'd brought back from Marseille. How she guarded it. He could see it so clearly, the black leather thong coiled like a snake under her wrist, her pack of Gitanes with the gypsy dancer dressed in blue, and her Johnnie Walker whisky. Always the whisky, her glass half full, half empty, his own the same, another bottle of whisky waiting for him, for them, the one on the table by the door.

She smiled up at him with the cunning innocence morphine gave her as he told her he would come back. She was so beautiful.

"Jesus," he said, rocking back and forth in front of the piled wood. "I went back to Paris. I came back to her."

"What's wrong?" Joel said. "Is it that Marie from the war?"

"Never mind," Art said as he tried to still the invisible shakes inside his body. "It's nothing," he said. "Listen to me. The package from Vancouver is coming in on the Express in the morning. You'll remember to pick it up, right?"

"Yup," said Joel. "The same as always."

"That's right," Art said. "Now go away. You've got the night ahead of you."

"You sure you're okay?" Joel said. "There's only a bit more wood here to stack."

"It'll be there tomorrow. Now, go, go. And Joel?"

Joel turned around.

"Steer clear of that Indian girl. She belongs to Piet. You go up the mountain to Myrna if you want to get laid. She's the one girl around here who is guaranteed to give you the kind of trouble you can spend a life with. Stay away from what's not yours to have."

———

ART WATCHED JOEL CUT ALONG the gravel road and disappear in the shade of the brush line that separated the railway and the river from the village. Joel would pick up the package from Li Wei. The kid wouldn't forget.

He took the mickey from behind the stud, lifted it to his mouth, and drained it, shaking the bottle gently to get the last drops to fall on his tongue. He dimly remembered breaking a bottle so he could lick the broken glass for the whispered sheen of lost whisky. Where was that, Caen, or was that Utrecht? Somewhere in the war. In the distance smoke poured from the beehive burner at the sawmill. The last shift of the week. Six o'clock through to three-thirty tomorrow morning. He'd maybe go to the mill in an hour or so, but not yet. If he was needed they'd let him know. He'd hear the whistles. And Claude didn't care if he was at the sawmill or not so long as he was close enough if there was an accident. At his cabin or in the village, so long as he was close by. The whistles were his tether. Art listened. Behind the sawmill's cries there was the deep sound of the river, a tree fallen in and sweeping against the bank, a hushed noise above the sullen heave of the heavy waters. Cobwebs came down over his eyes.

The two of them were sitting in the afternoon at a table in front of the Café Olympique. Claude had just introduced them. After buying them a glass of wine Claude left with the blond girl who had come with him. She was very drunk. The last thing Claude said to Art was that he had a couple of weeks. "Don't waste them," Claude said as he stood up, his chair rocking back. He was smiling as he pulled the girl to her feet.

And then it was twilight, a break in the cold rain, and they were walking together, he and Marie, along the Seine by Notre-Dame, the river whispering against the stones, and then another glass of wine back at the café, a bottle of whisky in his pack, the climb up the back steps to her room. He'd thought she was just another pretty *putain*, but she wasn't, was she? She'd brought him to her room because she said she liked him. He was an injured soldier with extra leave, money, chocolate, cigarettes, and whisky. Sometimes it was all that was needed to get a girl to follow you or you her.

What he remembered when he stepped into the room was her falling back on the narrow bed by the wall and scissoring her legs in the air. She asked him if he liked her legs and he told her he did, yes. *Oui*, he said, awkward, and she laughed at his wretched accent and pointed at the bottle of whisky he had taken from his pack. He grinned and filled glasses to their blue rims. She smiled a pretty smile and asked him if he had any silk stockings in his pack. *Bas de soie?* When he held up his empty hands she laughed and laughed.

And then, standing there, he had suddenly forgotten her name, the one she had told him at the table outside the Olympique when Claude introduced them. His mind after the concussion opened and closed. It lost things, faces, names, the days and weeks of his life. He stood there by the bed, helpless, and asked what her name was and she turned her head to the pillow and looked sideways up at him as if she wasn't quite sure who he was or what he was doing there.

"I am Marie," she said.

Marie.

The river and a tree brushing against the bank, the drift booms on the North Thompson River riding a fallen tree out into the main stream, the roots and trunk and branches rolling over and gone to the rapids miles downstream. He could hear them, the sound diminishing as it drifted away. The Seine, the ripples brushing against the stones just past Notre-Dame. Marie leaning over, pointing at a bouquet of flowers someone must have thrown into the river. *Quelle tristesse.*

How sad, she had said.

Marie.

She was all around him and he wanted her gone. He went over to the chopping block where the tumbled pile of wood waited and began again.

His heavy axe cleaved the cool evening air, the fir breaking under the iron fall of his thick, splitting blade. The green wood sucked apart, the three-foot rounds cleft in two, the chunks dropping to the dirt on either side of the chopping block. He rested the axe with its blunt head against his leg, leaned down and picked up a half round, setting it on the block. He stood there trembling, his shirt hanging wet. He stared through the salt in his eyes and found the fracture line in the wood where there were no knots to bind his blade. His axe swept up into the sky and down, the edge of blunted iron finding the mark he had chosen, the wood breaking perfectly in two. Wiping the sweat away he repeated the blows, the rounds behind him disappearing, the quarters breaking down into eighths. They piled around his legs until he could hardly move to lift a round to the block. When he was done he began stacking what he'd split, trying not to think of the whisky in the cabin, the bottle of Ballantine's sitting on the table just inside the door. He could use a drink, just one, a couple of fingers to calm the shaking and stop the sweats.

But no, not yet.

The pure mindlessness of the work was what he'd needed. He'd wanted his body to go through its steady paces, no thought intruding, no memory roused in the labyrinth of his brain. When he was breaking the fir rounds it was the work of muscle, blood, and bone.

Splitting firewood for the winter to come was work he loved no matter winter was months away. It was the same work as what he'd done off and on his whole life. Except for the war years and he shook his head to drive the thought of them away. He didn't want to drive a forklift, truck, or Cat anymore. He didn't want to work on the mill floor feeding an edger or working the trim saws and gang saws. He hated machines after the war. He hated what they could do.

Yet he hadn't always. He'd loved working in the mills along the coast and up north before the war. He'd loaded boxcars, pulled lumber off green chains, stacked rough-cut boards as they came down from the trim saws until the piles were backed up three deep and five feet high. He'd driven forklifts and hauled the stacked lumber away to drying fields beside oceans and rivers. He'd dug ditches and driven water trucks to spray the dusty roads. He'd driven logging trucks. But he didn't do that kind of work anymore. He was the first-aid man at the mill now.

One of the best jobs he ever had was when he went north for the first time. He was young, sixteen or seventeen, and working behind a D8 tractor and an arch in the bush up on Highway 16 east of the Hazeltons. He'd set chokers on logs, the heavy treads of the Cat working to drag the timber out of the quagmire that was a late spring logging show in the north interior. The Cat hauled them down to the sorting ground where forklifts loaded them onto the trucks to be taken to the mills and the saws in

Smithers. He loved dragging the heavy cable with its four chokers through the tumble of limbs and stumps, his muscles screaming, his body filthy with mud and needles, blackflies, deer flies, blowflies and mosquitoes coursing over his body as they searched for a bare patch of skin they could settle on and drink the blood that would feed the eggs that grew inside them. He loved getting down on his hands and knees and scrabbling in the muck, digging under a trunk of hemlock so he could get the choker cable around it, the satisfaction he got as the Cat winch dragged away the logs he'd choked, the forest shuddering around him, deer and moose breaking for the estuaries, the bears watching them carefully, birds screaming above fallen nests, squirrels, weasels, porcupines, and marten looking for something, anything to run to or climb up to get away from the destruction, nothing left in the cut block but limbs and stumps, bewildered animals, forgotten birds.

Setting chokers had been mindless work, his body alone, complete in itself. No one to talk to, no one to interfere, him and the Cat operator two separate creatures, one in deep, hard labour, the other driving a machine as he breathed diesel smoke, the blade of the D8 pushing down anything it could just for the pleasure of seeing it fall. He tried it once over in the Kootenays the year after he came home from France, but he quit the job the second day, the roar of the engine and the clanking of the treads reminding him too much of the war. The Caterpillar tractor he worked behind was the same as a tank, the difference being the Cat was a machine without a turret and a gun and a belly full of men intent on killing other men.

Asking Joel what he was going to do with his life had brought back the Depression years, his father's drinking, the afternoon he found his mother unconscious, bleeding on the kitchen floor, his drunken father being taken away by the police. Art remembered how he'd tried to scrub clean the floor so his mother wouldn't see her blood when she came home, and then her never waking up, her never coming back from St. Paul's, her body in the basement morgue and him standing there by a man in black pants and white coat and saying to him, "Yes, this's Missus Kenning, my mother, her name is Elizabeth Mary Kenning. Yes."

The early years in the thirties, his gang on Gore and Pender, the stealing and the fighting, the drugs and liquor, all of it, his being thrown out of their basement rooms by his uncle a week after his mother died, his father in jail on charges he would later beat only to find his own death two years later in an alley behind the Marble Arch Hotel. Art was fifteen when he first worked the camps up the coast, then the mills on Vancouver Island, Tahsis in the rain, and Honeymoon Bay, the booms on Lake Cowichan crowded with logs, men walking them like pond spiders as their pike poles sorted the fir from the hemlock, the spruce from the cedar. It was in a float camp up Seymour Inlet where he first tried heroin, though he'd sworn he'd never touch the needle after seeing the junkies in the East End, the whores and pimps, the sailors and hustlers.

He'd never forgotten a Bible puncher saying Art's people were *the wretched of this earth*. The preacher cried it out on the corner of Main and Hastings week after week the summer of '37, people passing him by, women laughing, a kid throwing brick shards at the man, the derisive shouts, the cries, the laughter, and the tears. Art had been just a kid, but when he heard the preacher speak of the wretched he knew who he was talking about. It was his mother and father, his friends and enemies, the Eastside and all who lived, lied, loved, and died there, all and everyone who struggled to survive in the houses, shacks, and walk-ups, the basement rooms, the hovels and hotels, the shooting galleries, the tunnels under Pender Street and Main, the whores on their knees, the cops with their truncheons walking the back streets and alleys as they beat the helpless and the homeless into a deeper submission.

Art's mind was floating now, his body slow as soft air, too many things to remember, too much to forget. There was a shivering absence in him. He didn't want the image of his mother in his mind, the startled halo of blood around her head. He reached down and picked up an armful of wood, four pieces, six, and another until his arm seized up, his muscles straining, and staggering to the pile and slowly, carefully laying them down one at a time to prolong the ache, to make the burning in his arm last, to turn what his mind remembered into nothing but what hurt, the pain eating up the past, *the wretched of this earth*.

But the memories wouldn't go away. When he came back from the war East End Vancouver had changed. It was 1946. He was twenty-six years old and the people he'd hung around with before the war were mostly gone. A few old guys were still around, but the girls he'd known were married with kids or without, nuns or nurses, or working in the city. The guys he'd hung around with were in jail, moved away, or dead. He had his poke from leaving the army. He holed up with it in a nowhere room on Water Street and a little later in a basement off Trounce Alley. The bars were what kept him alive. When he ran out of money he could always lose himself in some float camp or another, some bunkhouse, shack, or cabin, any shack, any cabin, the one he lived in now in this wretched river valley, this North Thompson River mill town. His hand settled a crooked chunk of wood on top of the pile, his other hand clenched into a fist.

The mill chains clanked and the treads of his tank ground through the mud of Holland. He wasn't on the push into Holland. There was no farm, no mother, no girl called Godelieve, no pig, no fire, no Tommy. And Paris was a dream too. There were no tanks anymore, no Marie. He was the first-aid man in a sawmill up the North Thompson River. He could feel the split wood under his hand. The film of sap sucked at his fingers. But the sounds of the chains in the mill banging were the treads of their Sherman Firefly on the road to Antwerp, the far-off rapids in the river the waves eating the beaches along the North Sea.

He staggered into the shed and bent over beside the last row he'd stacked. Lifting his calloused hands to his face he pushed the heels against his eyes, dragging the worn skin of his palms against his eyelids, the wet salt from his sweat stinging his sight, and then rubbing even harder as if by doing so he could rid himself of what he heard. And he scoured his face and struck his head with his fist and as he did the sounds fled back into the cul-de-sac where they kept themselves alive waiting to torment him.

He dropped his hands hoping what he saw next would not be the flooded fields of Holland, and they weren't. It was the grass and shrubs beyond his cabin, the CNR railway and the river beyond, the huge murmur of its brown heave and the mountains rearing up in waves of dense green on the eastern shore. That other world was gone. He took a single step and stopped. Standing in the shadows at the edge of the field where the path turned from the dirt road and wove its way down to his cabin was the figure of a tall, thin man.

Art knew who it was.

"I'm the first-aid man," Art said to the mountains, the cat suddenly between his legs, passing through him and around him and gone. He closed his eyes. "That's all I am. There's nothing I can do for Jaswant Singh Gill."

Jaswant's standing alone there was a reprimand to Art's futilities. Art knew that and because he did he couldn't refuse him. The man would stay where he was at the end of the road, at the head of the path, right into the night out of some misguided politeness, some formality he'd learned back in India and which he practised at the mill and in the village, speaking only when spoken to, moving aside from men who were not Sikhs, white men whose surly, good-natured casual ways defined who they were, white men whose fear and hatred of anyone different ran deep in their blood.

Art went to the pile, picked up the splitting axe, and drove it into the wood, the block shuddering. Leaving the axe buried there he walked over to the cabin and beckoned with his arm for Jaswant to come down. Art didn't want him to. But he knew if he didn't call out or make a motion Jaswant wouldn't move from where he stood. As it was, he could have already been there for an hour.

He knew why Jaswant was there. It was the sick baby. The mother must still be up there in that shack Jaswant had found for them. Art had been sure she'd go south following after the man who had left her there, the man who'd promised he'd come back. And maybe he had come back and got her and the little one, but even as Art thought that he knew the man hadn't returned. Art knew that men who leave women and sick babies on the side of a road never come back. There are no eyes in the backs of their heads. All men like that have in them is where they are going and it's always alone.

It's why Jaswant was standing out there right now.

They'd been two down-on-their-luck drifters with a sick newborn. They'd been dropped off on the high road by a trucker they'd caught a ride with up in Tête Jaune Cache. Why the trucker dropped them off instead of taking them the whole way south was anyone's guess. From what Jaswant had told him a week ago the family had intended to head west to Prince George along the Fraser, but they got confused and took the truck heading south down the wrong river. It was Jaswant who found them and took them to the deserted shack. And then the man leaving, saying he'd be back. When? As soon as what? As soon as he got some money together? As soon as he found some help?

Jaswant and his wife had been helping the woman as best they could, but the baby was sick, the woman helpless. When Art first saw it the baby wasn't much more than a weightless bag of tiny bones wrapped up in a wool shawl, the skin of its head pulled tight around its skull and two huge blue eyes that stared out at a world the tiny body had entered however briefly, the life in it raging with a sickness Art did not understand, an illness he knew he could not cure no matter his first aid, no matter his wanting to. He told them the baby needed to see a doctor, that there was nothing he could do. He told them they had to make their way south to Kamloops. And he'd thought that's what the woman had done. After her man left Art had been sure she would follow hard on his heels, the baby in her arms. But he knew Jaswant standing there meant she hadn't.

Art stepped up on the narrow porch, stilled his trembling hands, and waved to the waiting man. He stood by the door as Jaswant came along the path. Art's body cried out for a drink from the bottle that was on the table inside. He knew he couldn't help that baby. Art's was a first aid, not a last.

The Sikh's feet were too narrow in boots too large for him. Art could see his feet slipping inside them. His turban was a faded yellow, subdued, its paleness a failing sun. Jaswant did not look down as he walked over the uneven ground. It was like his feet in those loose boots knew the ground before they stepped on it. He had come from a place in northern India. Somewhere in the mountains. Jaswant walked on the ground like he knew what the earth was, uneven, stone strewn, yet forgiving. Art knew the place he'd come from was the Kashmir, but why he knew he didn't remember. It must have been Wang Po told him. The cook knew about everyone who worked in the mill, everyone in the village, everyone on the hill farms. He knew because no one paid attention to him beyond eating the food he served. He knew because he listened.

Jaswant had to know there was nothing Art could do for that baby. And there was no penicillin in Art's stash, no sulpha. He'd left it all out on a shelf by the door four or five days ago and the cat had knocked it to the floor into a spilled drink when she was trying to catch a hawk moth. He didn't think the drugs would have helped anyway. But maybe they might have. Maybe they still could.

The new supply would come tomorrow when the package came up from Vancouver on the Express with the morphine for his kit and the opium for Wang Po and a little for himself. There would be medicine in the package if Li Wei had found medicine to send. He might not have. And even if Art risked giving the baby some penicillin he knew it could easily kill rather than cure, the baby so impossibly small.

"Yes," Art said, as much to himself as to the man approaching.

Jaswant stopped, his boots a foot below the porch deck, his head even with Art's. There was a silence and Art waited, hoping for what was not going to be said and knowing it would be. They waited and finally Art broke and said, "Is it the baby?"

"It is the baby, sir," said Jaswant.

"It is no better?" replied Art, the word *sir* dumbfounding him as it always did when he talked to the man, Jaswant thinking because Art was the first-aid man he was the same as a doctor. And Art's own reply, his words slipping into the odd clipped formality Jaswant used when he spoke in an English that was Art's language and was not quite.

"She is no better," Jaswant said. "The woman has milk, but the baby throws it up. That baby is feeble now and I think she will die."

"A girl?"

"The baby," said Jaswant. "A girl, yes."

He hadn't known it was a girl. When he'd seen it last it was only a tiny face and two fists wrapped in a yellow shawl Jaswant's wife had given to the mother. Art didn't want it to be a girl, a daughter. And he didn't want it to have a name. He wanted it to be just a baby. A daughter was too real. If it was a daughter she would have a name and if she had a name he would have to try to do something, anything.

"Her name is Beate."

"The mother?"

"The baby, sir," said Jaswant. "The mother's name is Gerda. Gerda Dunkle."

"And the father? Is he back?"

"No."

It was quiet as they waited for one or the other to say something more. There was a soft thump at the edge of the porch and both of them turned and stared at the cat with a mouse in her jaws. The cat stopped for a moment and then walked across the worn boards and wound her liquid body in and around Art's boots. As it did Art reached behind him and opened the door, the cat making one more pass by a boot and from there into the cabin. Art pulled the door behind it, the single thought in his head a bottle of whisky glinting.

"It is the cat," Art said, asking himself why he was speaking like this. Jaswant knew the cat was a cat. He didn't have to be told.

Art waited again in the vain hope he would leave and then Jaswant said, "What can you do?"

Art stood there stunned. For a moment he found the question impossible. What had he ever been able to do?

Art stepped out onto the grass and said, "I don't know. Something. Nothing. The woman shouldn't be here. She should be in Kamloops."

He waited, but Jaswant said nothing in return.

"Maybe tomorrow," Art said. "If the medicine package comes on the Express. But only if the package comes and only if there is medicine in it," adding this last even as he knew the package was coming on the Express, but needing a way out. He didn't want to have to make good on a promise he knew would change nothing and probably make everything worse. It was the hope a promise gave that worried him, the offering an obligation.

Jaswant nodded, his gesture in deference to Art and his decision. He waited a moment and when Art didn't reply, Jaswant said, "Thank you, sir."

Walking away his body seemed a slender stem of grass moving in a breeze come off the river, Jaswant Singh Gill, tall and thin in his worn work clothes and yellow turban on the path back to the dead end of the road, the tall grasses swirling as he passed into the pale beginning of night.

He didn't turn again.

Art had known he wouldn't. To turn would have been for him an even greater intrusion and Jaswant would not want that.

He thought of the baby dying. What would the woman do if it died? If *she* died, the baby, the girl, and he tried not to name her and did, saying out loud the word, *Beate*. There was the church up past the store. It was still standing. It was just another unused space in the village, an empty box of boards and shingles in a square of dirt and weeds. Emil Kosky's baby was buried in the cemetery out back. It was the only new grave in a long while. Last year. The child just died, Art didn't know why. Lydia Kosky had gone over to the apple-crate crib one morning and picked her dead baby up. People said her screams were still alive in the forest around their cabin. No one had lived in it since they left.

The humps and sinks in the graveyard were mostly mountain people who'd been buried over the years, old graves whose wooden crosses had weathered away or lay broken from the heavy snows. You couldn't read the names on most of them. The perimeter was marked by a few rotten posts, rusted barbwire strung twisted through the grass and stunted trees. It was outside the fence he'd found the graves of babies in limbo, the unbaptized ones the Catholics wouldn't bury in holy ground. Tiny crosses made from twisted welding rods, one was made of black rocks arranged in the grass and ever since first he'd seen the cross he'd wondered who in the village kept restoring it, the rocks so easily disturbed by animal or man. There was another old place of worship down the river a ways. People called it the Someday Church but as far as he knew they didn't bury anyone there.

He waited until the Sikh disappeared into the dark of the brush line below the village and then he went into his cabin. The cat was sitting on the windowsill finishing off the mouse she had caught in the field. The tiny bones crunching in her jaws were a distant clicking, an insect sound, the kind of tolling sticks might make in a land without bells.

"Hey, cat," Art said as he sat in his chair, the bottle of whisky beside him on the corner of the table, his empty glass beside it.

The cat ignored him.

He'd been chopping wood for hours and he had not had a drink all that time. No, he'd had one when Joel was there. No, and then one after. Two drinks.

The cat moaned, the sharp bones in her belly turning.

Art heard himself in her groan. There were nights in Paris, later, when Marie locked him in his room for fear he'd hurt someone or hurt himself, the muttered shouts, the guttural moans, the mangled monologues, the fear and the anger. She told him she was sure hearing him he was going to kill someone, or kill himself.

The bottle of Ballantine's gave off a glow, alive behind the glass. He stared at the swirls the whisky made, golden shimmers that withered as he watched. He picked the bottle up, the square glass familiar under his fingers. There was the night. There was at least that.

FOUR

WANG PO SAT AT THE SMALL TABLE in his room below the cookhouse and turned the ink-stick in the water drops on the stone. The sound made him think of a wet mouse crying and he smiled as he thought of the mouse he saved as he floated across the Qinhuai River, light from the fires glittering in its wet fur. It was the only time he looked back, his old Nanjing burning behind him.

His hand moved in its circles, the ink-stick giving up its carbon, the ink darkening. The first stick he'd made was from raw carbon he'd scraped from charred fir slabs left in the saw-mill's beehive burner during spring breakup three years before. It was the third month after he began cooking for the mill. He had decided he would draw again the day he arranged for his bride in Shanghai, the first money sent, the arrangements with her family completed. It would be the first time he would finish a drawing since he left Nanjing all those years ago.

The day he escaped he had hidden among stones behind a deserted temple on Stone Mountain. Lying there in the curl of the sleeping dragon he had looked at his trembling hands and known then that the war was taking his brushes away. He had tried only once to take up a brush during the first year he was in Vancouver, and it had hurt him that he drew so poorly. He'd placed the simple brushes and inks back in their box and gave them to a boy he found drawing in a park down the block from Li Wei's little house on Gore Avenue. The picture he had tried to make was of the ferns along the Qinhuai River back home, a grey moth sleeping on a drooping blade. It was an image that had stayed in his mind from the old days when he was just a boy, but when he tried to make the first fine line the brush wobbled, his hand shaking.

The war had been with him then, the years he'd survived in occupied Shanghai, the terror the Japanese brought with them, the casual killings along the docks, the women young and old hiding in attics and basements, the fear so much a part of life it became you. He had worked as a labourer loading freighters until the Liberation in 1949. Then the Communists began the executions in the Canidrome stadium, tens of thousands of Chinese slaughtered by Mao Zedong. A few months later he stowed away on a small fishing boat and made it down the coast to Hong Kong and then to Vancouver as a refugee.

A month after he arrived in Canada he had been walking late one night on East Pender Street and Li Wei came out of the Dart Coon Club and stopped him, asking who he was. He took Wang Po to the Pearl, a small restaurant nearby, and bought him tea and a meal. They talked and he learned Li Wei was also from Nanjing though he had come to Canada earlier, in 1935. They had many stories to share and so became friends. Li Wei found him a job cooking in a little backstreet restaurant in the

alley behind Pender Street just off Main. Li Wei's opium par-
lour was in the rooms above and there were times Wang Po
climbed the stairs to forget the war. He would rest on a thin
mattress and chase the dragon with his new friend.

Wang Po left the pain of Nanjing behind with the help of Li
Wei. You have to leave the past behind, Li Wei said that night
in the Pearl when Wang Po told him how he managed to escape
the Japanese. Telling Li Wei the story had brought those days
back and he had lamented the loss of his mother and father,
their murder by the Japanese. Wang Po told Li Wei he had hidden in the narrow space above the attic in a stranger's house.
The soldiers had searched the house but didn't find him.

Wang Po had thought he had escaped the past, but he had
just buried it deep inside him. It was from Li Wei he learned
that the path he walked was his alone, that no one could save
him but himself. Wang Po worked and saved his money so that
he could have a family to honour his parents who had lost
their lives.

Li Wei listened to Wang Po's stories of his life before the
invasion and many times he encouraged him to draw. But Wang
Po didn't work with the brushes again. Just thinking of his
hand moving ink on paper caused him pain. He could watch
others create beautiful pictures and calligraphy. He loved to
look at an artist's hands, the lines forming behind the brush,
fine paper coming alive with a single blossom on a gnarled
branch, the wing of a swallow, a mountain in the mist.

Two weeks after he arrived at the mill he received a photograph, his second, of the woman he would marry. Her name
was Chunhua, *spring flower*. She lived in Shanghai. It was Li
Wei who had introduced her family to him. They were not
from wealth, but they were honest people who desired a better
life for their daughter than the one she would have in China.

The negotiations had gone on for months with a cousin of Li Wei's conducting Wang Po's humble offer. Three months before he took the job at the mill he had sent her the ring that bound their engagement. What he needed after that was enough money to pay the full dowry to her family, but also to bring her to Canada. It was Li Wei who had heard about the job at the sawmill. It paid double what Wang Po made cooking at the restaurant in Vancouver.

He loved the image her family had sent him. The picture showed her sitting under a blossoming plum tree, her hands resting on her lap. The ring he had sent was on her finger. It was her modesty that made him want to draw again, but he had no ink and no brushes.

A month after he received the photograph the mill shut down for spring breakup, the bush roads impassable from the snow-melt. There was only a skeleton crew working and in the new isolation he found the peace he had been seeking for so many years. It came to him one day when he saw an orb-weaver spider building her web outside the cookhouse window. He watched for hours as she created something that he'd learned the Shuswap people of the valley called a dream catcher. When the web was complete he saw the spider settle herself in the centre. The sun caught at her tawny skin and she shone like a gold pendant. At that moment of completion they became drawn together in a perfect moment, the spider and the cook from Nanjing.

The spider and the man, two creatures whose work was to create something so beautiful they could hang their lives from what they had made. It was on that day he got up from where he was sitting by the river and began the search for what he needed to make his ink. He spent days combing through the cold ash along the outside edge of the burner for wood that hadn't completely burned, the cedar slabs that had charred slowly beyond the flames. The best pieces were crinkled like the scales of Chi, the hornless dragons that were the snakes of his childhood.

He liked the fine char he made from the fir coals, but his best ink was made from a delicate soot he scraped from the chimney of an abandoned cabin a few miles up the river. The soot was thick with oil from poorly burned wood. The moisture in the charcoal was important. Travelling south along the river he gathered wet and dry pitch from pine trees near Little Fort and Kamloops, boiling the soft and hard clumps in water to loosen their oils. He made glue from the hooves of wild horses shot by a rancher up the Barrière River. He traded for the hooves, giving the man in exchange a quick pencil drawing he made of the ponderosa pine in front of their house. The rancher's wife told him she'd never seen the like of it and nailed it to the wall in their living room next to the head of an eight-point mule deer. The ink Wang Po made was almost as good as the ones he had used in China all those years ago. Whenever he mixed the ink he always thought of how his drawings were made from horses in flight in the fields of heaven.

Later Art Kenning would come to visit and after he arrived Joel sometimes followed. He remembered when Art had brought the boy to the cookhouse after they took him off the gondola car. Wang Po had placed a hot bowl of soup in front of him and Joel had held on to the bowl so long with his red hands that Wang Po had to heat it again before the boy drank it. Joel kept asking about an old man who had to be saved. Art told Wang Po the story when he came back after taking Joel to see Molly Samuels and then putting him to sleep in the bunkhouse, how Joel had stood in the snow beside the train tracks and begged them to save the man who had saved his life. That night Wang Po had dreamed of that old man in the gondola car as he crawled back into the storm. He imagined that aging face resting on the frozen iron railing as the train dragged him through the canyons to his death. Many times he had wondered if there was a way to draw such a face. The thought of it made him think of the faces of Shanghai, the old ones in the alleys, the slowly dying, bodies wasted away, bones with skin stretched over them thin as rice paper, their eyes huge as dark moons.

The stick in his hand turned slowly, the black pool shining. The ink was ready.

He sat quietly and rested himself. He did not want to stay in the Old World. Shanghai had become another Nanjing, people dying everywhere as the Communist cadres roamed the city looking for those they called collaborators. It was no different under Jiang Zhongzheng, the purges, the massacres. The wars in China never seemed to end. Now he lived and worked in a place the village people called the Interior. It was a strange word to use for where you lived. Here they called their land an inside-place. And perhaps that was what this land was, something hidden and not to be seen. He would never fit into the village or the mill and he did not try. He would go back to Vancouver in two more years. He would live in the place these people called Chinatown. Chunhua would be with him. They would have children, they would have a life.

Old China moved through him, wisps, thin steam from a seething pot on the stove. He had let go of the old years the same way the river let go of the mist that rose from winter waters only to vanish in the air. He sat at his small table, the ink and brushes ready. The wet-on-wet drawing he wanted to finish was of a branch on a deodar cedar tree that had grown on the bank of the Qinhuai River a few blocks from his father's home. He had watched the tree burn through the bamboo slats where he was hiding. But one image of the tree had been preserved from childhood. He could see the branch so clearly, the cone, the needles, the flakes of bark at the interstices of branchlets, a black ant that crawled across the face of the cone. He had called it up from memory many times over the years and now he would give it life again. This new work of his was a close-up, not a far-off scene. He had made many drawings of the things that lived in him, the present one to be done in the style of Ni Zan. The Yuan dynasty painter's works had a spare simplicity he had tried to find in his own pieces.

What he wanted to capture was the sound of early evening, the faint click and scrape of the deodar's needles when the wind rose along the river just before dark. He wanted to be able to hear the drawing when he was done. He could see the fine lines he'd make when he used the point of the wolf hair to draw the needles. The brush rested on the brass butterfly Li Wei had given him when Wang Po slept in the basement room he had offered him. Gore Avenue, the little house where he lived the year he arrived in Vancouver.

The spring breakup the year after he made the ink and brushes he went down to Vancouver and stayed with his old friend. One of the first things he did was to buy paper to take back north. He brought Li Wei drawings he had made on lesser paper, modest gifts given to repay the kindness his friend had shown him since that day when they'd met on East Pender and Li Wei had bought him tea. Wang Po was happy that Li Wei could help Art get the medicines he needed to do his work, happy too that he sent the opium.

He knew close studies of deodars were rarely drawn, the needles too short to display the flare other pines had. The deodar's was a minimal spray from a single twig. It was not the

Mount Hua pine with its long needles. He prepared the paper with a light ink wash and while it was still wet picked up a brush, dipped it in the fresh ink and without thinking drew three needles and beside them a pine cone. Four times he did this, the last needles more heavily inked, the lines sharp and clear above the ones below, the branch fading deep into the picture. Three small moves with the tip of the wolf-hair brush gave him the ant on the side of the cone.

It would do.

Satisfied, he cleaned his brushes and his ink stone. He held up the paper and looked carefully at what he'd done. It was not the work of Ni Zan. It was the work of Wang Po and he was content. He looked up from the inkstand at the wall and the drawing of Chunhua waiting in Shanghai. Soon he would send for her. Two years more and he would have enough to finish paying the bride price. The customs would not be the same as in China. He was also saving to send gift money to the bride's family. The matchmaker lived in Vancouver and she was very careful that traditions be followed as best Wang Po could. When Chunhua arrived Li Wei's wife would look after her until the ceremony could take place. Two years more. He would be patient.

He looked around his small room. Nothing much had changed in the years since he first arrived in Canada. He was still living in a basement. But Li Wei had helped him buy rooms in a small place close to where he lived. Wang Po had rented the rooms out to a family. When Chunhua came and they were married it would be where they lived.

He was far from Vancouver now, far from China. He was the Chinese cook and many of the men didn't know his name. They called him Hey You or Cookie or the Chinaman. He was much alone, but he had been that way ever since the war. Living in the Interior in the mountains was to be separate from everyone until the night Art Kenning came to the cookhouse with a bottle of whisky and offered him a drink. When Wang Po asked him why he had come Art told him he had been out walking in the night and saw a light in the narrow window of the cookhouse. Art had looked down into the basement room and saw Wang Po making a picture with a brush. He thought a man who could do that might like a drink, he said. Wang Po hesitated a moment and then invited Art into his room. They shared the whisky, just as later they shared Wang Po's opium. They spoke carefully of their lives. There were silences, but both were comfortable with them. That was the night they discovered they both had a war, his in China and Art's in Europe. Over the following months Wang Po understood more and more how Art could not let go of his war. Art could not forgive himself what he'd seen and done. The war was trapped inside him and he wouldn't let it go.

Wang Po placed the wolf-hair brush back on the butterfly's back. He looked again at the picture. The pine needles were very fine, he thought. The drawing one of his best. The brush's tip was perfect for the finest of lines, the swelling of the barrel right for holding the precise amount of ink. The brush would last him a long time as long as he cared for it. Wolf hair was hard to come by. The wolves had been driven into the backcountry by the farmers and ranchers. Their prey were caribou, the wolves following their yearly journey north to south and back again. They wintered up the Clearwater River, eating the hanging moss off the trees. The brush he used came from hair he found caught in the barbs of an old wire fence near White Horse Bluff. He was lucky to get the long hairs with the black tips. He gave thanks to the wolf for leaving such a gift for him.

FIVE

THE SAWMILL SPRAWLED BESIDE THE CNR railway that ran north to Jasper, south to Kamloops. A pockmarked gravel road crawled out of the mill yard. It crossed the railway siding and the mainline tracks, reaching past the three-room CNR station, circling round the cookhouse at the first bend of the road by the swamp where the three bunkhouses lay side by side. The long, low buildings squatted at the edge of a bog, the line of six windows under the eaves propped open with cedar kindling sticks in the faint hope of a breeze to move the fetid air. The screens that tried to cover them were rusted, cut, and torn, prickled edges bound back together with threaded haywire and woven butcher string. The gaps and holes let in the flies and the mosquitoes in seething streams. In the lines of bunks along the walls the sleeping men turned their bodies over and over as insects settled to feed on their bare arms, their chests and shoulders.

The men's faces stared blind into the dark, a rare hand rising vaguely into the night, brushing at the whining air as if to drive the sound of darkness away.

Joel lay awake on a thin mattress at the bottom end of the last bunkhouse. His bed was the one closest to the bog. The musk from the still waters eased across the floor, a thin mist creeping. The welded iron bed he'd been given a year ago had been pushed three feet from the corner by the back door and there it had stayed. There was no window above his bed, only an apple box nailed to the wall with his weekly towel draped across it. The box held the little he called his own, a safety razor with the rusting blade he used for two weeks, a bar of soap in a cracked saucer with bits of sawdust and grit embedded in its scored surface, and a plastic comb with the tail sharpened to a point. Under his bed was a small cardboard box where what clothes he'd scavenged were stuffed, two shirts, one with its tail torn off, the other missing buttons, his other pair of work pants, some assorted socks of different kinds, and the blue wool coat Art gave to him that winter night he'd been dragged off the train.

The twelve men he shared the bunkhouse with lay stretched out beyond him in a row of army bunks, their bodies barely covered, damp sheets coiled around their shanks. They had long ago fallen into restless sleep, their snores and grunts breaking below the nag of the mosquitoes. Joel lay naked, his yellowed sheet drawn across his legs, his pants and shirt slumped on the floor by his boots. He refused to let his hands wander his body, keeping them clenched into fists at his sides. His hard cock stood stiff from the wisps of blond hairs matted with sweat in the crutch of his legs. On his belly lay a slug trail of semen. His penis obeyed only itself. A drool of spunk shone in an oval pearl at the end of it.

He lay there deep in an empty place as he tried to take his mind off Alice sleeping in the lean-to behind Rotmensens' store. Myrna too, up at the farm, her blond muff glistening. He opened his eyes and stared at the smoke-streaked boards above him, seeing in the twists of blackened wood the outlines of the land he had left behind, the bush along the creek behind his father's barn where deer and cattle slept through the heat of the day. The Arrow Lakes glinted in the distance, a stretched pool of beaten iron. The wraiths of his two sisters drifted toward him across the waters and then the three of them were sitting silent at the table as they waited for their father to rise from his bed, the Bible clutched in his hand, prayers stumbling from his mouth: *There shall the great Owl make her nest, and lay, and hatch, and gather under her shadow: there shall the vultures also be gathered, every one with her mate.* His mother hovered at the stove, the morning mush seething, the coffee clearing with the eggshells she'd saved for its steep. Joel remembered those coffee-stained shells. They lay cupped like brown nests in the bottom of the iron pot.

"Holy, holy, holy, Lord God Almighty."

His father loomed behind Joel's eyes as a bat careened past their kitchen window, a pale moth in its delicate jaws. Demented weather poured over the mountain crest to the west, a boil of cloud across the rimrock below the stars, his mother warning against the bad luck of a single bat at dawn.

Joel blinked, the clapboard bunkhouse ceiling still there, grains of sawdust, ash, and insect corpses swaying in the drooped nets of old webs. Joel kicked at the yellowed sheet, swung his legs off the mattress, and sat on the edge of the narrow bunk, wiping at his arms and chest. He didn't want to think of his mother or his sisters. His father had told him God wanted Joel to stay on the land. The old man had knelt by the back door and, staring across his mown fields to the mountains, begged the moon and the stars and the god who lived among them to keep his son in the valley.

His mother whispered daily to Joel of the neighbour's daughter, Elsie Crapsey, the cripple-back one his father had chosen for him, a girl his mother called saintly, the one who would come with a virgin womb, a spit-thumbed Bible, a three-room shack, an outhouse, a tumbled barn, and eighty acres of woodland and fields north of his father's land along the lake. But Joel wanted none of a girl with the Good Book between her legs. He wanted none of the farm she held out to him on a page from Revelation, the land title writ there in moans and lamentations: *Thrust in thy sharp sickle, and gather the clusters of the vine of the earth; for her grapes are fully ripe.* Joel's mother admonishing him to gather up the land his father coveted, all of it to be his someday, his sisters getting nothing but a husband elsewhere.

A barred owl cried down by the river, the creature's barks and hoots a comfort in the night. Moonlight stretched out from the bunk next to him, dust devils shivering. Joel gazed into the faint oblong of light on the floor. It seemed a shining trap door and for a moment he imagined stepping into it and following that light down into the earth. Ever since he was small he'd dreamed of finding some hidden treasure. When he was little he'd sit behind his father on the grey stallion as they rode down the shore to the post office in Nakusp. Why his father took him there he didn't know. The only other times he was allowed close to town was to go to the church on the flats each Sunday. What schooling he had when he was small was from his mother's teaching, her books the same ones she'd learned from when she was a girl down in Idaho.

The mornings he rode to town with his father he was told to wait outside the post office and watch the horse didn't spook at some logging truck passing by. While he was outside one day he'd looked down through the cracks in the boardwalk and caught the glint of a silver dollar in the dirt. When he crawled out from under the boards with the shining dollar clutched in his fist his father stepped from the post office door, leaned down, and took the coin from him, flipping it into the sun, the King George face grim as he fell into his hand. He told Joel that the Lord giveth, and hoisted him onto the horse for the long ride home, Joel mumbling, *and the Lord taketh away*. He remembered it had been the new 1949 dollar, the Newfoundland one with the ship on the tail side. There were nights Joel dreamed of that wooden sidewalk in Nakusp and the dollar he'd held for a few moments, the silver ship floating on his palm, its sails unfurled, going somewhere across an ocean to another land. He wanted a life, but he was a little afraid of what he might find out there. He knew one thing: whatever it was he needed to find it wasn't on Arrow Lakes.

Joel had never seen an ocean, his only journey the one he'd taken when he finally left home, a little bewildered, a little afraid. There were the rides he begged and bummed through the mountains and the plains, and the train he'd jumped last winter, the freight that brought him down from Edmonton through Jasper into the narrow valley canyons of the North Thompson River. He remembered the cold of that January journey in the open gondola car and the old man who shared his rolled newspapers, crumpling them and stuffing the papers into Joel's pants and coat. The man had helped cover him with snow, telling him it was warmer than the winds that worked like withering fists inside the car. Joel ended up in a front corner in the lee of the wind and staring into the chimera of dark thunderheads. The two of them huddled against the iron, Joel in the old man's lap with his back to him, thin arms around him holding tight. The other men in the open car curled up like fallen ghosts in their blankets and broken cardboard boxes. The old man behind him wouldn't let him sleep. He told Joel sleep would find him dead come Kamloops Junction far to the south.

It was Claude Harper, the big boss at the mill, who ordered Bill Samuels to bring him down. But it was Art Kenning who asked Claude to do it. The first-aid man had taken a long look at Joel, his words to Claude lost on the wind, Joel leaning out from the roofless car into the wind and blowing snow as he tried to hear them. When Claude raised his arm everyone stopped and waited to see what he wanted.

"The kid," Claude said, pointing with his gloved fist. "Haul him down from there."

Art had saved him, not Claude. Joel knew that even though Art always said he had nothing to do with it. Joel had been standing with the freezing men leaning over the iron lip of the gondola, the car a rectangular boat with no mast and them like lost sailors in a storm. The snow was falling heavy and thick around them. It was the hammer blows on the side of the car that had woken them from their numb sleep, Bill Samuels wielding his sledge, the *boom boom boom* of iron blundering in their heads as they rose from the snow and ice to see whose god was knocking at the wrong door.

Joel was half-dead when Samuels climbed the ladder at the end of the car and hauled him over the iron, his feet near frozen, his hands so cold he couldn't bend his fingers, couldn't feel his face. His old stetson was bent and crushed like cheap plywood and stuffed tight under his arm.

"Please," Joel managed to whisper. "Can you help save the old man too?"

But none of them heard him, his words half-frozen on his lips.

"Look at him, for Christ's sake," said Bill. "The kid managed to save his hat."

"There might be something in him after all," said Art.

Claude was already walking down the line of gondolas toward the boxcars. "Not bloody likely," he said, the wind pulling him away. He shouted then: "Grab your sledge, Bill. I'm not paying you to stand around."

Art Kenning was the one who had spoken to Claude and it was Art who started to lead Joel to the cookhouse along with two other men Samuels found in a boxcar farther down the line. But before Art could take him away Joel had begged Samuels to help the old man who'd taught him how newspapers and snow could keep him alive. Samuels had waited a moment for a nod from Claude, but he never got one.

The old man's grey hair hung in frozen strands from the ledge of the iron parapet. He stared down a moment at Joel then fell away, his hands and face disappearing into the cold of the gondola, the sound of his lament a silence held in the flailing arms of the wind. Joel was the only one taken from the gondola, Bill backing off the others when they tried to climb out, Claude refusing them a place on the siding.

The muffled lights of the cookhouse had been a mirage that promised food and somewhere warm enough to eat it. In the kitchen that night Joel had sat in a chair right next to the stove, the fire warming him up enough to eat the food the Chinese cook placed on his lap, a bowl of hot soup full of vegetables, fried bread, and sausage. His feet and hands burned with pain as the frost went out of them.

Art had taken him then to Molly Samuels' little house where she looked him over for what he didn't know, asking him if he kept himself clean, giving him salve for his frostbitten hands. After her it was the bunkhouse, Art leading him to the bottom end past the beds where men lay on their bunks, some sleeping and others rolling awake and watching.

Ernie Reiner had woken as they came past his bunk. "Who you got there?" he asked. The question wasn't a pleasant one. "This ain't a place for boys, you know."

"Shut up, Ernie," Art said. "You don't like it, take it up with Claude."

Ernie said nothing to that, but he grinned and pointed one thick finger at Joel as if to tell Joel he was watching him.

Art said nothing as he gave Joel the iron bunk in the corner by the back door. When Joel lay down, Art covered him with a couple of grey army blankets.

At dawn that next morning Art came by and dropped off a pair of worn boots and some dry clothes. He waited for Joel to dress and then took him down the road to sign on to the crew. Art didn't say much at first, just told him not to argue with Claude, not to explain. "You're lucky to be alive," he said.

"What about the other guys?" Joel said. "That old man really helped me. He stuffed newspapers inside my clothes, he kept me warm."

"Everybody takes their chances in this life," said Art. "He took his for you. Anyway, maybe he made it. He looked like a tough bugger."

"He was old," said Joel. "And what about the others?"

"Just count your lucky stars you're here and breathing."

"But—" said Joel, Art interrupting him.

"Never mind all that," he said. "You're going to see Claude. Just do as he says. He's going to put you on the crew. That's you having good luck twice. Keep that up you're gonna run outta luck before you're grown." He laughed and said, "Just shut your mouth and start listening. It'll take you a long way in this life."

Saying that, he'd reached into his coat pocket and took out a short bottle of what looked to Joel like rum or maybe whisky, unscrewed the lid, and took a long draw on it before holding it out to Joel. When Joel shook his head Art smiled and said, "It's a cold night. Just about as cold as yesterday and about to be as cold again tomorrow." He looked long at Joel then took him by the shoulder of the blue wool coat he had found for him somewhere. "Hell," he said, his voice gruff, "I'm not sure yet Claude should've pulled you out of that gondola."

"But it was you who told him to," said Joel.

"You never mind that," said Art and told Joel to follow along, taking him to the mill. When they got there he shoved him into Claude's office.

Joel stood just inside the room, not knowing what he was supposed to do.

Claude didn't look up from what he was writing.

"I'm Joel," he said into the silence. "I'm the one you . . ." but he never got another word out.

Claude held up his hand, his head bent, his eyes still on what he'd been looking at. "I know where I got you," he said. "What's the rest of your name?"

"Crozier."

"You French or what?"

"No. English, I guess."

"Sounds French to me. I never met a Frenchie yet who was worth a bent nickel."

After he wrote Joel's name in his ledger, Claude told him he'd be working cleanup on the day shift. "And don't fuck up like those two out there are trying hard to do." Claude pointed out the grease-streaked window at the other two men he'd got off the train. They were at the other end of the yard. The men were walking a narrow path around the log pond that was fed by the river. They shivered at the ends of their pike poles as they pushed logs through skim ice toward the iron dogs that would lift them on winding chains into the mill and the waiting saws.

"It's likely I'll regret the day I ever saw you hanging frozen from that gondola, kid," Claude said. "You're like a small fish snagged by a man who isn't paying attention to the job at hand. Just remember, it's easier to throw you back in than keep you. Don't ever forget it."

"No sir, I won't," Joel said as he backed out. "I mean I won't forget it," but Claude was looking at the paper in front of him, not at Joel.

"Shut the door after you," Claude said.

The storm had held on through that night and knowing how frail the old man had been, Joel knew he'd never have made it to Kamloops alive. One of the men in the cookhouse said the railroad police threw any dead bodies they found into the river. They said the bodies always showed up drifting in Kamloops Lake. A guy who'd worked at the Savona sawmill said two floaters had come ashore when he was there. He laughed when he told the story. Those people in the railroad cars are just like us, Art had said, but the guy just laughed again. Joel didn't say anything else. He remembered Art telling him to keep his mouth shut, so he did. Still, he thought, the same kind of poor people wandered the road that passed through Nakusp on their way to the Okanagan looking for work in the orchards there. He'd met a lot more of them along the Alberta roads before he got to Edmonton. The old man in the boxcar was the same as all of them, and the other two men in the gondola too. Joel never knew their names. Poor people who lived everywhere and nowhere.

Poverty eats the heart. His father told him that often enough as he tried to warn Joel away from leaving the farm.

"You go out into the world and sure as hell you'll get trapped by the life of drifters," his father had said. "Just remember, people without a house and home spend their days burying hope in alleys and under bridges in the cities. You can always eke out a living on a bit of land. And there's eighty acres waiting for you right here and a woman too. Remember, women are all the same in the dark. Pretty or ugly, crippled or straight, they're all the same." When Joel said nothing to that, his father went on, saying, "A man needs satisfying and sometimes a wife's not enough. You'll learn that too someday. That land Elsie Crapsey's father is offering is what you should be thinking of and not her crooked back."

Joel wasn't sure anymore that he wanted the wandering life his father had warned him against. The months he'd spent drifting through the mountains and the plains had left him feeling lost and lonely. And he liked working at the mill. There was Art and Joseph and Molly and he liked Wang Po, the cook, too. And especially Myrna up on the hill farm. And Alice too, even though he knew deep down she wasn't ever going to be for him. Still, he knew his dreams were worth more than not having her at all. It was just whenever he saw her he lost his head.

He had saved most every penny from his dollar-twenty-an-hour paycheques. There were a hundred and ninety-seven dollars and forty-seven cents hidden in a green Export tobacco can buried under a boulder out in the bog. He hid it there for fear someone might steal it. The only person he could see doing that was Ernie, and that was enough for Joel to hide it. The money was a fortune to him who'd never known much more than nickels and dimes in his life. He'd grown up a lot since his father had tried to burn God into his head. Joel had sent the flimsy pages of the Bible flying away like crows the day he walked away from Nakusp into the dark folds of the Selkirk Range.

He wasn't a kid anymore, no matter Ernie Reiner telling everyone he was. He had a real job, just like all the other men at the mill.

He looked along the row of beds to see if anyone was awake. No one moved. He slipped from the cot, grabbing his shirt hanging off the nail on the wall, and pulled on the socks and pants that were piled on the floor. He cinched his belt, picked up his boots and hat, and stepped out onto the weathered porch. Drawing the boots over his feet, he bound the laces tight around his ankles.

Joel sat on the round of fir on the back porch of the bunkhouse and looked up at the narrow band of stars between the mountains, the moon rising low in the east. The dark clouds that had poured over the mountain's rim earlier had flown into the Selkirk Range and were gone past the Rockies to the prairie where he'd wandered only months before. He lifted his head to Orion tilted in the southern sky and drew some cool air into his chest. Alice would be sleeping in her lean-to back of the store. He could almost smell her. He thought of what it would be like to put his face into the bend of her neck and breathe her in. He sniffed at the fusty air lifting off the bog, his cock rising hard as he breathed the thickness of the swamp. He bent his cock back down, gripping it between his legs, the pain dwindling, his cock going slowly limp.

He clenched his fists to stop himself from thinking of Alice that way. Even just to talk to her would be enough. Even just to hold her hand. But he couldn't stop his body wanting her.

Behind him in the bunkhouse the men slept on. The second bunk from the front was Cliff's and the third bunk was Ernie Reiner's. He was lying on his back snoring. Through the wheezes and sighs of the sleeping men Joel could hear the wet in Reiner's throat and mouth, a choking as if the man was trying to swallow something thick that would not go down no matter his sucking on the clutch of phlegm stuck there.

It was Ernie who ragged Joel from his seat in the cage above the trim saws. Joel would be under the sloped saw bank late in the lunch break cleaning up fallen trim ends, sweeping up sawdust, and gathering into his wheelbarrow the scraps of bark and broken wood fallen from the trim saw chains. Ernie would sometimes come back early when Joel was working the lunch downtime. Joel never knew for sure when he'd show up. For a big man Reiner could be quiet as a thin cat on narrow paws. He'd wait until Joel was in a spot where the chain bank was low and then Ernie would pull a lever and send a saw down, the sting of the teeth biting the air just above Joel's head. He'd sit and watch Joel work, Reiner's hands playing with the saw levers, touching one and then another, laughing as Joel moved hunch-backed across the floor to fill the barrow, his body flinching each time a blade cried in the air above him. He always laughed at Joel jumping away. Every few days it would be the same. Ernie would be up there with his hard face and that black hair of his sticking out like a wrecked wire brush from under his hard hat.

Joel thought of the .308 Browning hung on padded spikes above Reiner's head as he slept. On a shelf above the rifle were the bear skulls he'd boiled clean, long yellow teeth jutting from heavy jaws. Beside them were three-and-a-half boxes of shells stacked in a neat pile. The skulls were from bears Ernie had shot up the river on the alder flats, two of them just that spring, the bears feeding on roots, young grass, and Columbia lily bulbs. They were easy prey in the meadows.

Ernie was a solitary hunter except for a few times he'd hunted with Jim McAllister, the new sawyer at the mill. Joel had seen the two of them take off in McAllister's black pickup a couple of times with their rifles. Jim had shot a moose earlier

in the summer on one of their hunts, but no one on the mill
crew said anything about it being out of season except to wonder why they left most of the kill behind. Jim and Ernie had
packed the hindquarters back to the road across their shoulders and left the rest. That was good meat they left out there
in the bush, Joseph told Joel. He said people up on the hill
farms could've used that meat instead of just leaving it for
bears. But Jim McAllister was the top sawyer. No one was
going to say anything about what he did or didn't do.

Not much was known about McAllister or his wife, Irene.
When he wasn't sitting in the saw box Jim stayed close to
home in his trailer. The first week he arrived he'd backed the
trailer up into a hundred-foot track he cut into the bush at
the edge of the village. You couldn't see the trailer from the
sawmill road. He told people his wife liked to be left alone too.
He told people not to bother her and no one did except for
Molly Samuels. Joel knew she'd been around to their trailer a
couple of times to welcome Irene and partly too, she said, to
find out a little about her, people saw her so rarely. Joel heard
Molly say that Jim's wife was a strange little thing half afraid
of her own shadow. She told Art she'd asked Irene to come
down to her place and have a coffee with some of the other
women but Irene McAllister told her she liked being left alone.
Molly thought that was kind of strange. Joel remembered
exactly what Molly had said after that. "Alone? What woman
doesn't want her own kind with her? Women don't want to be
alone, not all the time."

Art had said nothing to that, only nodded like he mostly
did when Molly got excited talking. Joel saw Irene at the store
a few times when he was there but she never stayed long and
spoke nothing to no one except for a nervous nod sometimes
if she was cornered. She stayed her days and nights quiet, with

Jim or without him there. The sawyer kept her close is what Joel knew. Some men were like that with their women.

Ernie Reiner looked up to McAllister. The sawyer was the head of the line in the mill. Jim McAllister was the top sawyer and Claude made sure he got the finest fir and hemlock because Jim could get the best from a log. The sawyer on the other shift, Charlie Sangster, was good too, but not in the league of McAllister. After them came the gang sawyer, the edgerman, the trim sawyers, and then the rest of the men on down depending on whether they operated a machine or were straight bull labour like the green chain or the cleanup crew. The logs came up from the pond riding the chains and were rolled onto the head saw carriage, Jim setting the dogs to hold the logs fast to the carriage and then driving the log through the saws. The mill's production depended on Jim and Charlie. They controlled what came out the end of the mill. If either one slowed down the mill slowed down and if that happened there'd be no bonus at the end of the month for the men.

Ernie said what pleasure McAllister took from the one bear he shot was in the kill and nothing more. That Reiner pulled the claws and took the bear's head to boil out the skull had meant nothing to Jim. Joel had heard Ernie telling Joseph that Jim was a cold hunter. Ernie seemed impressed by that. He said once the bear was down Jim didn't even walk over to look at what he'd shot. To him the bear he'd killed was just something for crows and ravens to argue about, wolverines and wolves to fight over, a carcass, nothing more.

When he heard Ernie say that, Joel looked at Jim McAllister differently than he had before. He asked Joseph one time what kind of man wouldn't even bother to look at what he'd shot. Joseph told him he'd seen men in the war who were like that. They could walk past a pile of corpses and not even notice they were there. He said there was something missing inside men like that, why he didn't know. "Just stay away from him and from Ernie too," is what Joseph said and Joel did, though with Ernie it was harder seeing as how they shared the same bunkhouse.

One night when Ernie was working Joel had taken one of Ernie's bear skulls down from the shelf and a funnel spider crawled from one of the eye sockets. Joel stared into the cavity at the web where the bear's brain used to be. Some nights he dreamed of being pulled into such a tunnel, a white weave filling his lungs. The nightmare always woke him, Joel lifting from his pillow as he tried to get air into his chest.

Three black bear skulls and now Reiner going on about the grizzly he was going to shoot one day. He'd sit on his bunk and clean his rifle over and over, loading and unloading it, the brass shells falling onto his blanket, the jackets of the bullets gleaming. Each time Joel heard him go on about killing a grizzly Joel imagined one of the great bears biting down on Reiner's head, the man's face peeling off, the huge teeth of the grizzly piercing his skull.

Art Kenning had told Joel he shouldn't pay Reiner any mind, just like Joseph had. Art said Reiner was a drifter, the same as a lot of the men in the bunkhouse. Joel asked him if Joseph Gillespie was a drifter. Art said Joseph was just older and a different kind of man than Reiner and the rest of them. He said Joseph had fought the last few months of the war in Germany. "War makes men different from the ones who weren't over there," said Art. When Joel asked him what the difference was, Art just said, "Joseph's a good man."

Most of the single men at the mill were footloose, half-grown boys is what Art told him. In the early fall they followed the grain harvest on the prairie and later on picked fruit in the orchards along the mountain valleys. Some seasons they worked a winter at a mill or mine for a few months before moving on in the spring and other times they put in a month on the fish boats out of Prince Rupert. Like all their kind, Art said, in the end their wandering would take them to Edmonton or Calgary or Winnipeg, but winters they'd hole up down in Vancouver. They'd mostly end up in the East End, Chinatown, Japtown, Main and Hastings, the cheap hotels and dives along Cordova and Water Street, Powell and Pender. Joel knew it was trouble they looked for down in the city, just as it was trouble they were looking for at the store in the afternoon or at the Saturday night dances at the hall or at the beer parlours in Blue River and Clearwater. He didn't need Art to tell him that. Reiner called their going to the bar "hunting poontang." The first time Reiner said that word, Joel didn't understand. Everyone at the cookhouse laughed when he asked what a poontang was.

Joel knew who Reiner was from the first day. Art told him the trim saw man's bullying came from the fear he was weak, that when it came time to be brave he'd somehow fail and people would know him for what he was.

The bunkhouse was off limits to Reiner's petty cruelties now. When Joel first arrived there, though, Reiner casually preyed on him there as much as he did at the mill. One day Joel got up and his boots were gone. Ernie laughed when he saw him looking for them in the bunkhouse. He told Joel he'd be better off looking out in the swamp. It took hours for Joel to find where Ernie had thrown them. Another night his sheets were soaked with swamp water and weeds.

Ernie played his small miseries on Joel for as long as he thought he could get away with them. Joel didn't like it but he knew he couldn't tell anyone. He knew complaining was something you didn't do. He knew Ernie was his problem and no one else's. But one night Joseph saw Ernie trip Joel when he was passing. Joseph came down the line and told Ernie to stop. "Leave the kid alone," he said. Reiner had blustered, but Joseph looked hard at him and Ernie backed off. That was the end of most of Ernie's ragging him.

Joseph Gillespie played guitar most nights out on the front deck of the bunkhouse after his shift was over and he was done with dinner. Sometimes too he'd sing. Old songs mostly, ones that made you feel lonely, tunes that were sweet and sad. "Wandering Boy" by the Carter Family, and another one Joel liked called "Way Down Home." When he sang men got quiet. It was like his singing drove the fear out of them, the hate. Come a restless night, an argument or fight, it was often Joseph who brought everyone back into what a bunkhouse had to have to survive the weeks and months of men living together in a narrow space. Joseph Gillespie had a strength in him that even Reiner feared and respected.

Still, Joel did his best to stay out of the trim saw man's way. In his free time Joel would go off alone up the mountain or range the trails through the swamp and along the river. He knew a hundred secret places, caves and hollow trees, the deep root pits trees left behind when they fell into the river. Art had said once Joel would never be a drifter, but he sure as hell was a wanderer. When Joel asked him what he meant by that, Art just laughed.

On Saturdays he'd climb to the ridges above the treeline, stopping at Arnold Turfoot's hill farm in hopes of seeing Myrna. He'd always hang a red kerchief on a fence post to let her know he was there. Most times when he did she came running.

She wasn't quiet and shy like Alice. He could talk to Myrna, tell her his secrets, his dreams too. Alice left him unable to talk and he didn't know why.

But his need for Myrna always overcame him by the end of the week. He dreamed about Myrna too, but his dreams about her didn't drive him crazy. Myrna was real.

One thing Joel knew was Alice might be going to the dance tomorrow night and if it was true and Piet and Imma were going away and she somehow got to go then there might be a chance for him to maybe get close to her in some way, to dance with her and . . . and he didn't know how to dance that well to the fast songs. He was better at the slow songs like Elvis's "Love Me Tender," and she'd said in the café she didn't know how to dance, and he thought that maybe if he could dance the Elvis with her he might have a chance to teach her a little about slow dancing. But maybe he'd just be making a fool of himself trying to be with her at all.

She wasn't Myrna, she was someone else entirely.

And then he couldn't think any more about what it might mean to be alone together, on the dance floor or maybe somewhere else, maybe under the trees behind the hall, or maybe just walking together, him finally talking to her in the night.

"Oh, damn," he said, Myrna coming slow into his mind, her laughing as she wrapped her arms around his back.

Joel listened to the barred owl cry its hoodoo song down by the river. The owl always perched there on a dead cedar branch that hung out over the log pond. The owl had been hunting rats and mice in the grass tangle along the riverbank. He'd heard its cry for the past two weeks. He touched his cheek and felt the roughness there. There were times listening he thought he was as much feathers as skin.

As the owl's cry faded away he thought of the path through the bush that started across the mill road. At the end of it were the store and the lean-to where Alice slept. He'd go to see her as he always did.

There were the mountains and the river and the shadows.

He knew the night and the sickle moon.

As he passed along the side of the bunkhouse he stopped at a window and listened for a moment to the glut of Reiner choking on the dark.

SIX

THE SKY HAD BEEN GREY AND THE SEA TOO, grey, and the dust from the dunes thin whispers sliding over iron. The light was almost gone from Holland, the light wind steady out of the north. There was a dead bird on the tank's front apron, the feathers drab, freckled streaks of brown on a paler brown. A skylark, a little bird he'd seen and heard when they were stationed in Kent waiting for the invasion that never seemed to come until it did, ferocious and terrible. He remembered thinking he'd read a poem about such a bird in a book some soldier left at an aid station. The end of the poem was about madness, and there were old-fashioned words at the beginning he hadn't forgotten, *Hail to thee blithe spirit, bird thou never wert.*

He'd never forgotten those strange words, *wert* and *blithe.* And then a bird fell from the sky, a small, brown, feathered thing plummeting down. It landed soft on the front of the tank, its wing catching on a seam of sharp weld and holding there. The feathers fluttered in the wind, the sea rough, the surf booming just over the crest of weed-choked sand. The birds he'd seen in Sussex had nested in the fields where they'd been bivouacked back in England. Maybe the skylark got tired of listening to the guns. Maybe that's why it fell.

They'd been a little east of Diksmuide in Belgium when he caught up with his unit after the medical leave Claude had given him in Paris. Their tanks were helping clear up the pockets of German soldiers left behind to defend the coastal approaches to the port of Antwerp. His group was pushing now to the Scheldt peninsula to catch up to the advance on the fortress of Walcheren island. He looked at the crooked line of weld where the bird had been caught and he remembered Marie reading his palm in her room above the café. He still couldn't remember the explosion in Moerbrugge, the concussion having hurt something deep inside his head, that day and other days too, gone.

She'd showed him the line in his hand, scrolling her fingernail down the scrawled groove as she pointed out the break. *Pauvre garçon*, she said, poor boy, and she laughed. She said his lifeline was broken. He sat there staring into his cupped hand thinking obscurely of what it meant to have a broken life and not caring. Reading palms was just a game Marie played. It's what lovers did. They played.

But he'd seen people whose lives were torn apart. He'd seen them break into so many pieces you didn't know it was a man anymore, or a woman.

Tommy hadn't joined their unit yet, but he was only days away. The Scheldt and Walcheren were only a day or two away.

The treads of their tank tracked on scattered stones, grinding them to powder. Alvin down in the tank's belly had jerked them to the right to get around an overturned truck and a crosswind caught at the bird, breaking it free from the iron. The brown feathers lifted and for a moment Art had thought the bird might take flight and give itself to the wind. Then Alvin pulled the tank back onto the narrow way and the bird slid across the apron and fell under the grinding treads. It was a grey day when they pushed along the lone and level sands, his tears drying in the wind coming in off the sea.

It was quiet in the cabin. Art closed his eyes and saw again the long falling of the bird and he was crying just as he had cried back then, and he didn't know why. A glint of yellow flame in the lamp chimney flickered on the wall, the far-off glow of a burning village. Strands of sunlight came through the dark slit between the worn Five Roses flour sacks hanging over the window. The whisky helped. He wrapped his arms around his knees, pulling them to his chest, his arms heavy. The *clank clank clank* of the great chain at the mill went on. Each night after the night shift crew went to their beds, the refuse chain kept banging. It was the last sound of night, iron on iron, dragging chips and sawdust, trim ends and slabs the cleanup men threw into the flume that went to the gaping hole in the top of the beehive burner at the mill. He could smell the acrid smoke on the wind from the south.

Art's belly cramped again and he dry-heaved into his lap, a string of spittle hanging from his lip. He took a long drink from the bottle and gazed at the newspaper walls of his cabin. The pages had been glued flat to the logs to keep out the cold drafts of winter. There were many hundreds of nights Art had lain on this cot, the lamp turned low, the chimney grimed with soot. It was in the dimness Art imagined the old prospector who'd built the cabin lifting a fragile sheet of damp newspaper up to the wall and sticking it there with glue made from melted moose hooves. The walls revealed the sixteen years of the man's solitude. The earliest paper Art could find was a fragment stuck under the lintel above the door. The date in the corner of the fragile shard was August 7, 1898. The last was October 4, 1914, two months after war was declared. It had been pasted neatly beside the cot where a man could lie and read it over and over. It would be the first thing a man would see when he opened his eyes.

Art liked to believe whoever built the cabin had come to the far west by sailing out of Liverpool on a steamer. Someone who had left England in the last century, the wind carrying him around the horn of South America through the Drake Passage and then on to Vancouver Island. The gold rush had run out in the Yukon, and the man went up the Fraser and then east and north along the Thompson rivers. He stopped when he got to Little Hell's Gate and, turning south, began his search for gold in the narrow valley where little or no gold was. The North Thompson and the Clearwater were pyrites country, dead volcanoes dreaming of older days.

Art sipped at his whisky as he imagined the old man moving in the shadows of his room. He closed his eyes and saw the old prospector pick up a fragile sheet, the last one he glued upon the wall. He wondered how many hours the man had spent lying on the cedar boughs of his poplar-pole bunk staring at the words about his war.

Before the old remittance man, Sinjun, died he would sit and drink with Art and tell him stories about those early years. Art had asked him about his strange name and Sinjun had laughed and said his name was St. John. "It's how we say it," he told Art as they shared a drink. Sinjun had remembered the man who'd lived in Art's cabin leaving on the train an October night back in 1914. "I called him Smith," Sinjun said. "He never offered me no other name. He was a prospector who received money from home. He was a fearful drinker," Sinjun had said before pouring another couple of ounces of Art's whisky into his glass.

Both those old-timers had been looking for gold back then. They wanted to find the colour that had run out up in the Yukon. Sinjun said Smith had worked every creek from Tête Jaune Cache to Little Fort but all he ever panned were mica flakes and Gobi dust, pyrites and the wrong quartz. But he kept trying, Sinjun said. Prospecting was a curse, the searching for gold almost more important than the finding it. "We love to lose," he told Art. "Losing is what we want. We wrap it around ourselves and call it loneliness."

There were times Art thought long of those two solitaries at their steady work, a bottle of homemade hooch between their legs at night and gold dust in their heads. Smith's bones were most likely lying in a grave in France and the other, old Sinjun, was buried in back of the village church. Before he passed on he'd taken Art to the graveyard and shown him where he wanted to be laid. Don't say any words, he told Art. I never talked to anyone from the summer of 1920 to the spring of 1925, he added. There are far too few good words in this world to waste even one on me.

It was Art who found him dead, empty bottles of lemon extract littered by his mattress. There were only a few days left in the month and Sinjun had gone through his monthly remittance by the third week. He drank extract after that, every month the same. His skin was stained yellow, scratch marks on his arms and withered chest where he'd scraped at the lemon sweat come out of him in hopes there would be alcohol left in the stain. Art buried him under the young cedar Sinjun had chosen, the old prospector having told Art he thought cedars were like women with long skirts and he wanted to rest under one. Art missed the tales of the old days on the rivers, the Yukon and Nass, the Fraser, Skeena, and the Thompsons, the stories of Sinjun's years in Africa, the Boer War. He said Africa was hell for soldiers. It seemed like the wars ate everyone in the end.

Art's bottle perched like a carrion crow on the corner of the dead stove. There were still two or three inches of whisky left. Art was amazed he hadn't finished them.

A white moth flew out from behind the Five Roses curtain and crashed against the kerosene lamp, swirled up, caught in the dark heat of the chimney, its wings withering to ash. Art watched it fall as the boulders deep in the river bottom rolled on bedrock, their low thunder a dark drum. The guns of Walcheren was the song the river sang.

"Where am I?" he said, his head hurting.

He spoke quietly into the night, the cat answering him with a guttural moan. The animal was under the bed. He could hear the thin bones of some small creature breaking.

Art rubbed his knuckles into his eyes and the darkness there exploded, a Fenian fire behind his eyes, a phosphorous bomb in his brain. He pushed his knuckles deeper, grinding there as if he could destroy what he saw. Lightning balls burst and turned into incandescent bats, their shining wings fluttering as they receded into the dark. Art lifted his glass and emptied it. He poured another and took a swallow. As he drank, the guns of Walcheren became the river again and he saw Claude Harper as he had first seen him.

Claude was in an alley behind Pender Street with a young girl. She was struggling to get away and Claude was laughing as he pressed her against a wet brick wall, his forearm across her chest. A garbage can spilled down the block, some street woman looking for her dinner behind the Pearl Restaurant. It was Chinatown. It was 1935. Art had yelled at Claude to let her go and Claude, surprised anyone was there, turned to see who was trying to stop his fun. As he did the girl twisted out from under his arm and ran past Art out of the alley, her bare feet slapping puddles, her scuffed high heels hanging from clenched fingers. *You fucker*, she cried. *You dirty fucker!*

And that was where it began. He never really understood why Claude took a shine to him. Art was fifteen years old and Claude was ten years older. They were different in other ways too. Art was a homeless East End kid and Claude with family money and a fancy apartment in West Vancouver. They argued, Claude taunting him, a little angry, a little amused, and then he took a flask of whisky from his hip pocket and offered Art a drink. They stood in the alley and finished the flask. Then Art took Claude to his first opium room. After they smoked, Art took him down a side tunnel under Pender Street. It was where Art had lived the past five months. The stone wall up against his mattress was always warm from a sewer pipe that ran behind the rip-rap wall.

They were to each other a strange kind of friend. Claude had whisky and money on him all the time while Art struggled daily for the dollars he needed to keep alive. He showed Claude around, introduced him to some of the guys in the Alma Dukes and Riley Park gangs, the pimps and whores in the late night Blue Danube, the after-hours at the Mocambo, the Silver Fox dressed to the nines with his ladies on show, Dainty Thelma too who came with her girls and her man, Fat Alfred, who was known to have maimed a dozen johns for his private pleasure. It was always two or three in the morning, the street trade done for the night. And there was the opium. Art could always get Claude opium. Then the war came along and Claude stopped using the drug. He drank, but then who didn't back then.

The Depression ate up everyone's lives. Claude came and went. Art got occasional work on the boats and camps up the coast. When those jobs dried up he scrambled in the street selling heroin, stealing, doing whatever he could to make ends meet. Claude was slumming when he came down to the Eastside. Art knew Claude could always escape back to the safety of West Vancouver when it pleased him. Claude had money. He didn't have to work.

After the shell landed near him at Moerbrugge Claude sent him to Paris, Art's brain concussed, shrapnel in his shoulder. They were going to send him to England and then home, but Art had asked Claude not to let them send him away. Claude told him after about his begging. "Christ," he'd said, "you got the perfect wound and there you were asking me to keep you in the war."

Claude said he liked having Art around. He told Art once that he was his bad luck charm.

And then Paris again just after the Liberation, the Germans gone from the city. One night he and Marie had made a slow love, tender, and after sat at the window looking out at the people passing by, the lights, the laughter, the sound of Paris newly free. They sat side by side and watched as a truck came careening down the street and crashed into a car turning into the corner. There was the huge cry of wrenched metal, a sudden silence, and then the blaring of a horn that would not stop. Art pushed Marie from under his arm and as he made a move to get up from the edge of the bed and go down to the street to see if he could help he saw a flame lick out from under the back of the small car, a woman's scream, and then the gas tank blew.

Art heard the explosion, he didn't see it. His eyes were closed and he was back in Moerbrugge and the shell was bursting behind him. Something punched him hard in the shoulder and he was thrown into the air, gravel and dirt spraying around him in a fan, smoke and dust and nothing.

The explosion in the street outside her room brought back the scattered stones of Moerbrugge and it was only then that he remembered lying by the rubble wall, the garden he had stepped into gone. He remembered staggering into the night and one of the men finding him, he didn't remember who. The medics got him then and he was taken to the field hospital, Claude intervening two days later when they were going to send him to England, Claude taking him to Paris, the hospital, and then Marie.

Even now, fifteen years later, his brain would break and he wouldn't be able to find anything to hold on to. There were places beyond the curtain, but he couldn't find a way through. People talked and shouted there. They lived and died and he didn't know how to save them. Fragments, nothing more. And still the nightmares, someone shouting, his own cries to someone, no one.

He'd loved Notre-Dame, loved to lean back against the ancient walls while they talked. They had begun to learn the rudiments of each other's language, enough to laugh at their mistakes, enough to be sure of the silences that lay between them.

He remembered their first time together and the milk from her breasts. He hadn't known there was a baby until she lay naked beside him. Her milk leaked and when he pressed her breast gently the milk sprayed out in tiny fountains.

Confused, afraid he was hurting her, he said, "Is it okay?"

And she said *oui*, her eyes looking up at him as if he were a man far off, someone she had found for a moment only, no more. She told him he was the stranger in her life. You I cannot know, she told him.

Her milk was a last blue, the colour of the winter sky in the north just before the night has arrived, the colour darkness dreams before it can become a colour. After they made love he had licked the milk from her belly, the sweetness pooled in her navel, and they talked. He had no French beyond a few words. Her English was better, but not much.

"A baby?" he asked, pointing to her belly. "Where is he?"

"A girl, no boy."

"Where is the baby?"

"Not here," she said, rolling away from him.

And her milk began to dry up and Claude sent him back to his unit in Belgium, the battle for the Scheldt begun.

She would be sixteen years old now, that baby of Marie's. Two years older than the Indian girl in the store, Alice. Marie's baby would be a beautiful young French girl laughing in a café on the Left Bank, a café like the one her mother knew. The Café Olympique, perhaps. Or not. Maybe the baby was dead when they lay there together back in Paris. Why didn't she have a name, that baby?

He didn't want her to be dead. A few days after that first time Marie had told him the baby was with friends in Lyon. Days later she said the baby was with her family in Marseilles. If the baby was alive why wasn't it with her? If the baby was dead then why was it dead? What happened?

And Marie?

She told him not to love her. She said love in a war is only an hour. *Rien de plus.*

But that wasn't nothing, was it?

When he left to go back to the fighting she told him he would forget her. But he wasn't good at forgetting. He told her he would come back to Paris, to her. The war will end, he told her.

Some nights he wished he could put it all together. He wished the past would stay in the past so he could forget it. But it wouldn't go away. It lived inside him, the war, Marie.

Who was he to feel sorry for himself? He'd made his life. Who was Marie? Who had she ever been? And for a fragile moment she was there in his cabin standing by the stove warming her hands over the fire, her dark hair hanging loose against a white shift, and then she was a wisp, a thread of smoke in a dingy room above a sad café.

He opened a new bottle, whisky splashing, waves and tremors swirling as he filled the glass with its three ounces. He screwed the cap down on the bottle, setting it gentle on the table, the whisky trembling into stillness. He was about to reach for the bottle again when the cat leapt from under the bed and up onto the windowsill. She turned her body sideways to the night, her ears erect, the hair on her neck stiffened, and a *hack* and another *hack* from her throat as if trying to dislodge something, a bone gone down wrong, a smell she wanted gone, or a need to have her lungs clear for whatever was outside. She settled on her paws and softly hissed.

Then Art heard a noise far off.

Outside was something close and closing. Whatever it was it hadn't lost its way in the dark. There was only the faint sound of grass brushing against a body, boots on the path.

Art didn't think. He got up in a single motion, his legs obeying muscles that had long ago learned how to move by themselves, took two long steps to the door, reached around a padded coat for his Winchester, and then stopped himself. He stepped back and waited, wondering at his reaching for his rifle. There was nothing strange about someone needing him in the night.

A boot came down soft on the porch and then another boot, quieter, and then nothing.

A man, then, Art thought.

"Hello, the door," Art said, and when there was no answer, asked, "Who's there?"

He watched the handle turn and the door push slowly open. Jim McAllister stood just beyond the doorway on the porch. The darkness was behind the sawyer, the light from the kerosene lamp on the table, faint glimmers feeding on his face.

"Jim?"

"It's my woman," the sawyer said, his voice quiet.

"Your woman?"

"You come," said Jim. He spoke as if from a place far off only he knew was there.

SEVEN

JOEL'S SWEATY HAND LIFTED from the butt end of a log beside the path, a chip of bark falling away. The shard slipped through the air and came to rest in the dust beside the sill. He stood quiet as he watched a rat poke its head out of its burrow and touch the fallen flake. It sniffed at the bitterness of what he had touched and he imagined the alien smell of sweat and salt melting in the rat's delicate nose. Joel took a step. He could see the pale cups of the rat's ears catch at his footfall, his slightest breathing, the frayed cuff of his shirt catching at a leaf, a shard of stone flittering away, a choke-cherry branch whimpering as he bent it back upon itself. The dry limb of a cedar shifted as he moved again along the trail, brittle red needles sweeping the air behind him.

He had watched the small creatures many times, just as he watched birds and bears. He closed his eyes and imagined the rat rubbing its face with praying paws before retreating to its burrow, the small hieroglyphs left by its clawed feet faint in the dusty earth. He knew the rat would sit in its dark mouth of dirt and suck at its teeth as it listened to the worn threads of his pants brush against the chokecherry, his boot heel click against a rock as he moved away.

The dark caught at Joel as he passed along the trail. His muscles hadn't yet caught up to his bones. Scrawny, his lean legs stuck out from his stagged-off canvas pants, his narrow feet bound in boots too wide and too short for him. He'd pulled the laces tight and wound the rawhide strips around the boot tops, lapping the eye holes, binding the stiff leather to his skinny ankles.

He thought again of the morning he got the boots, Art Kenning standing at the bunkhouse door holding them crooked in his two fingers. Art had dropped them on the bunk and told him to get dressed and come down to the cookhouse. As Art left, Joel asked him where the cookhouse was. Art told him he'd been there last night, but Joel said he didn't remember, it was so cold, there was so much snow. Art just said Joel would find it if he was hungry enough. Joel had slept past breakfast, his muscles still aching, frost burns on the backs of his hands, his face chapped and brittle. Even his hair hurt. Pain, yes, but not enough to go hungry. The thought of food drove it away.

He remembered that morning, his walk around the bunkhouse, half the men gone on shift at the mill, the rest sleeping or staring vacantly into the shadows. He'd walked between the rows of bunks, each one defined by the man who slept there, cots left rumpled, blankets askew, and others with sheets and blankets pulled tight to keep the winter chill out. He didn't know then that the men who had made their beds were veterans from the war, the messed beds left by younger men. On the wall above the cots men had nailed shelves to hold what they had, soap, razors, knives and such, nails to hang their coats and jackets from. Some had photographs of family, people left behind or people a man might be going back to, a woman, kids, someone waiting for the man's return. Joel had looked at the faces of happy strangers as he wondered if he'd ever have a family. Maybe someday. There were books too, ratty magazines with girls on the covers, quiet things, a postcard from somewhere, thin letters bound with string. Each man had made the space he was allowed into a room without walls, a kind of home, its space clear and defined, an invisible line marking off where one imagined room stopped and another started.

There was one bunk in the row that had stopped him dead. A shiver had run up Joel's arms when he saw a bear skull on a shelf. A man who would kill a bear for his skull alone was the worst kind of man to Joel. He believed men who hunted for trophies had an illness in them. His father had always told him such men were weak. They needed to kill to prove their manhood. When Joel was fourteen he had sat in a meadow high above the Arrow Lakes and watched a grizzly bear sow feed her two cubs. She was no more than thirty feet away. When he saw her he fell to his knees and leaned back on his haunches. The cubs were yearlings, spring bears, and one to each great breast. She knew he was there and did not mind him. He stayed long after she left, the cubs playing, their squeals and mock growls a joyful noise as they stumbled and bumbled into the bush after her. Whoever slept in the bunk with the bear skull Joel knew he wouldn't like.

After Art had dropped off the boots and left Joel had gone out, sat on the back stoop, and taken the boots off. He took out the hunting knife he'd arrived in the village with and carved his toenails back. The blade's homemade scabbard was from the hide of a mountain caribou he'd shot the year before he left the farm. His mother had canned the meat, a farmer down the road tanning the hide. When he put the boots back on his toes still cramped against the hard, steel-cupped leather, but having cut the nails close he knew the toe-ends would callous up.

The boots didn't bother him much anymore. The dull pain he felt in his cramped feet was part of who he was now, a sawmill worker, a man. His canvas pants were held up by a worn belt slipped through the three surviving loops, new notches punched by a nail, the drooped leather tongue hanging twisted at his waist like a dried-out roadkill snake. The denim shirt on his back was worn, its cotton threads cross-hatched white on stone-bruised blue. Like the boots, the shirt was too small for him, the frayed cuffs high up his wrists, three buttons at the breast left, the rest gone, his scarecrow arms sticking out, cords of spare muscle taut. The sunburned skin on his hands stretched tight over castanet bones. Around his throat was a soiled red bandana tied in a reef knot, a frayed V jutting out from under the yellow hair that hung scissor-cut upon his pipe-stem neck.

The grey stetson was pulled down on his head. Day or night, he always wore it. On the tip of the crown was a worried hole rubbed there by the fingers of the man who had the hat before him and worn even thinner by Joel's fiddling with it. Stuck into the woven leather band were three red-tail hawk feathers he had found outside the chicken coops by the sawmill cookhouse. Wang Po had shot the hawk that spring with his antique Cooey .22, nailing the hawk's body by the wings to the cedar wall as a warning to all who hunted the chicken yard to keep away. The stetson was an old one, a hat that had survived other heads, other hands. Joel had found it perched on a fence post alongside a road by a stump farm five miles west of the ferry landing on the west side of the Arrow Lakes. Joel figured the man who had forgotten the hat had grown tired of setting posts and stringing barbwire in a land whose shadowed forests ate at his brain, someone who had put down his rock-stubbed shovel and walked away from the solitary work, his bare head burning as he trudged the road west into the Monashee Mountains where the sun set every day.

He stopped and hunkered down by the butt of a fallen tree, the dried roots a tangled frieze between him and the stars blinkering through the trees. He stood there and remembered the day he'd walked north to Revelstoke and then the days trying to hitch a ride south into the Kootenay country, the Selkirk Mountains huge around him. He'd caught rides with two short-haul logging trucks. The road had been barren but for the occasional bear and moose, the rare cabin with no one at home for years. He'd walked most of the last ten miles to Lardeau then caught a ride down the lake to Nelson in the back of a rusted pickup. When he got to Salmo he'd turned east and found his way along the twists and turns of gravel through the Cascade Mountains to the Rockies and the Crow's Nest Pass beyond. From there it was rolling country through the foothills to the high plains, Pincher Creek, Lethbridge, Medicine Hat.

He'd spent the next weeks wandering through small towns and ranches and farms as he drifted north, ending up in Edmonton. He arrived in the city in the first of winter, a snowstorm riding out of the mountains in mid-September. Desperate, broke and hungry, he got a job working for bed and board in the Canada Café on Whyte Avenue to keep himself from freezing. He became the café's dogsbody, cleaning garbage cans, sweeping floors, and washing dishes in exchange for a closet in the basement, a worn blanket, and three strange meals a day. The first night there he sneaked into the kitchen and soaked the hat brim of his stetson in sugar water, dry-curling it into the shape of the cowboy hats he'd seen in the movies. He formed the crown with an oblong stone he took from the bank of the North Saskatchewan River, the stone the shape of his narrow skull. Now streaks of embedded grease ran around the band, the soak of salt leached there. The stain looked like the horizon line of hoodoo rimrock, his daily sweat in the sawmill and the yard bleeding up toward the crown, turning the salt lines black in the sun, only to find them dried-out white come morning.

The brim of the hat lay creased just above his eyebrows. It made of his face a deeper shadow than the night. Anyone seeing him on the path would have thought it was the heat in the bunkhouse that had driven him outside. That or the shard of a smoke-stained moon, a comet's flare careening among the dim stars, some ill light that had brought him from his bed to brood along the paths that led among the cabins and trailers, the weathered shacks that squatted like belled knots of choker cable along the rutted road that cut the village in half.

The barred owl called again and he rose up to its cry, moving through the cedar fans, their thin whispers a song left wilting in the still air.

He stopped on the other side of the double-plank bridge, squatted by a clear pool, and lifted a handful of water to his mouth. The creek came down from the spring on the mountain, but it had been thinned to a trickle by the summer heat. There was one pool he liked to climb to, the glacial water rising clear from a cleft high in the alpine, a place where he could sit and see as far as the next world, mountains folding into mountains, blue following blue until they were nothing but light. He'd climbed mountains all his life. They were there was all, not obstructions, but like questions, asking.

He licked the water in his palm and remembered when he first asked Art if there was a path leading up into the high country. The first-aid man had told him he had to pass through

Arnold Turfoot's last field to get to the trail by Lost Line Creek. Turfoot's was the last stump farm at the end of the dirt track Joel had followed from above the village. The farm was two hayfields and a fenced meadow where a horse and cow kept vigil to the sun's rising and falling. Seven shit-splattered sheep lay in the crescent shade along the fenceline where scrub cedars swayed. Joel had walked quiet in the cover of the margin trees, not wanting to disturb the animals. If they scared then Turfoot would know someone or something was prowling the land, a bear or cougar, or a man. Joel hadn't asked permission to cut through the fields, but Art had told him the mountain trail began just above them. He'd crossed behind a pile of stones beyond the barn and skirted the upper side of the last field by the trees. At the sound of rock scraping on rock he had looked back the way he'd come. In the middle of the field was Arnold Turfoot's daughter.

She saw him look at her but she didn't run like he thought she would. He turned away from her steady gaze and kept on going. When he got to the corner of the field where he thought the trail began he saw her slip behind a hollow tree not twenty feet away. She moved quiet for a girl. He wondered at her being there so close and sat down on a deadfall stump, waiting until she stepped out. He could tell she wasn't hiding from him. It seemed she had more fierce in her than fear.

Months ago and now he was squatted by the creek staring into his open hand, Myrna on his mind, the water from Lost Line Creek drying in his calluses.

She'd stepped out and he'd watched her walk toward him through the stubble grass. She had a grin on her round face, a kind of happiness in her, a stunned joy.

He waited and as he did he remembered her look that time at the station when first he'd seen her sitting there on the back of her father's wagon. She'd looked right into him and he knew even then there'd be a time.

And she did come to him that day on the mountain, the ragged edge of her dress riding up her pink legs, her hands lifting the frayed hem past her knees. He felt an ache deep down and told himself not to think about her, knowing even as he pretended not to that whatever might happen was going to be her fault for following him, her fault for lifting her skirts, for wanting anything as bad as he was. Joel had imagined being with a girl so many times before and had wondered what it would be like. He had watched animals, cattle and horses, cats, dogs, and chickens, but they were animals, not people. He'd seen his father with a neighbour woman in a field, had seen Oroville Cranmer ride his wife in their narrow bed, their outcries and thrashing. Myrna Turfoot was going to make what he did different than he thought his first time would be, but it was because she was different that he thought he could do it at all.

She was a stranger girl than any he'd known. She had a kind of happiness at everything he did with her, what she did with him, at everything they did together. A butterfly was something perfect to her, a lamb, a jay, a chickadee. She would go crazy looking at a flowered grass stem in the field. She'd tell him to look and he would, but he didn't always see what she saw. To her it was the most perfect stem of grass that ever was. There were times too looking at a fir cone or a warbler's lost feather that she'd be taken somewhere else. It was a place he couldn't get to, try as he might to find it in himself. And she carried a special kind of pebble with her, a shining black stone shot with crystals. She sometimes rubbed it when she was quiet or when she was alone. He'd asked to see it once but she tucked it away in the pocket of her dress. She said her mother had given it to her when first she came to bleed. Her mother called it a waiting stone. She'd kept it for her until the day she became a woman. He'd seen Myrna singing words over it, words he couldn't make out, whispered as they were, but the singing of them made him feel at peace with himself, with her.

That time they did it was Myrna's first time too. He knew it was supposed to hurt a girl. It hurt animals. He'd seen it enough times, heard the scream of a cat, a queen turning on a tom and striking him after he pulled out, chickens screaming, horses, cattle. But it was strange how Myrna's shouts and crying didn't sound like pain. They were different than what hurting was. Just as her smiling when he fell on her white breasts after he was done.

He remembered how Myrna touched herself down there and brought up her fingers touched with blood.

"This is me," she'd said in wonder, her tears like wet pearls on her round cheeks.

Arnold Turfoot's daughter, Myrna, holding him tight in her pale and heavy arms. As she did most every Saturday, waiting for him in the high pasture. With her he could be who he was and not the tongue-tied boy who sat mooning in the café over Alice. Still it was Alice he dreamed about.

Joel reached down into the pool again and cupped his hands, splashing water into his face. The cold startled his skin, his eyes drawn to the slender rivulets filling the little pool. For a moment he felt like Myrna must feel when she looked at things, each small pebble perfect and alive.

He was torn by knowing Myrna, this girl with her odd beauty. When he was alone on the mountain or in his bed he wondered at what he felt for her, just as he wondered at his happiness each time he walked away from the farm. Why was he happy when he was with her when hours later he wanted to be with Alice too? The day he saw Alice getting down off the train at the station, she'd stood at the open door of the passenger car, the porter below with his hand out and his stool there for her to step down on. Imma Rotmensen was standing behind the porter urging Alice to hurry. She didn't look frightened at where she was. What fear was there had taken place a long time ago. She looked as if the journey through her life was something she'd had to endure. Whatever wound she carried was hers alone and because it was Joel knew he'd do anything for her.

That was when Alice and Myrna became confusions in his life.

He knew from the day he first saw Alice everything would be different. He knew it like he knew trout dance and mice sing. Seeing her was like seeing light when first it spilled into the valley.

When she came to the village, he thought he wouldn't want to be near Myrna anymore. Yet he'd climbed up to the hill farm a week after Alice arrived at the station. He lied to himself about why. He told himself it wasn't Myrna, it was the clear spring pool high on the mountain he was going to. He told himself over and over he didn't want Myrna to be there. He wanted to be clear of her, promising himself each night he wouldn't go back up the mountain, but the need to lie between Myrna's legs and feel her soft breasts had driven him again to the Turfoot fields. And once there they did what they'd always done.

He had a feeling there was something about Myrna that drew him to her besides their bodies. Part of it was her laughter, the crazy kind of joy she had. She loved things he didn't know you could love. It could be a yellow lichen on a rock, a jay's scream, a single chocolate lily nodding on the scree. He was undone by her touching the soft belly of a frog. No matter what he told her she found some kind of happiness in it. When he spoke of his father she told him how lucky he was to have been so hurt, because it made him the happier for being away from him. She made him feel blessed. He'd never thought his life could be that.

Whenever he'd get to the end of the upper field he'd take the red bandana from around his throat and tie it to a broken stub in a cedar tree so she'd know he was waiting for her in the clearing behind the rocks. Once he had it knotted he'd turn around and there she'd be. She would walk the edge of the field toward him, this strange, imponderable girl, unstoppable in what he knew was her want and his own need for her, his rut and hers under the sun, her wild talk after when she said she loved him.

Loved him?

He realized she must wait for him and the red bandana the whole morning, so soon would she be there. He'd never know how deep the shadows were that she hid in when she was waiting for him, only that she'd appear from out the cedars, a girl of flesh and blood, walking the pasture toward him. Each time she saw him turn to her from the rocks, she lifted her dress, her heavy legs mottled against the meadow stubble. She wore nothing underneath, the blond hair at her groin a sudden light flaring against her pale skin.

Her nakedness stunned him each time he looked at her. Myrna wasn't Alice. Each time he looked at Alice at the back of the store she was broken into rectangles by the pig-wire nailed across what could be called a window and wasn't, there being no glass. The Alice he saw lying under her covers, the blanket pulled down off her shoulders, the scroll of her ear, her slender hand, each small, discrete part of her broken by the wire that separated her from him in the prison room where she lived out her nights. He had wondered what would happen if there was ever a fire and he imagined coming to her rescue, tearing the pig-wire down, ripping at the poorly-nailed boards with the axe he somehow had with him, or running into the burning store and tearing the padlock off, each possible rescue a moment where he would save her from harm.

Alice's was an imagined body whose shape was all he had, shrouded as it was by covers. He was allowed glimpses only; the night he saw the back of her neck and her bare shoulder, the curve of her skin as it fled into her long black hair and the single mole riding on the top of her shoulder blade, a small living thing that was a part of her and he had imagined touching it and then, overcome, had fallen backward off the cedar block and landed on his back in the gravel.

What he knew of Myrna was that each time he lay with her up at the farm she overcame him entirely. The second time he had gone back expecting her to be there, but expecting her not to be there too, for why would she after what they had done? But he had climbed the field anyway, drawn to her, his body crying out the same as hers must have been, and when he turned she was there.

Look what I got! she had cried.

He knelt beside Lost Line Creek, the pool trembling and those four words coming back to him: *Look what I got.* He'd been angry at himself for being there, angry at her for saying aloud what he had thought of the long days and nights since that past Sunday. He had pretended he couldn't see her no matter his wanting to fall like any animal upon her.

"I'm down here," she'd cried, her voice high and wild.

When he made no move to show he'd seen her, she pleaded: "Look at me."

And then at his refusal to shade his eyes and look at her, she said, plaintive: "Please."

There was such want in her saying that word.

He had stared past her at the trail she had taken across the meadow, the track where her bare footprints had disturbed the dew in the mountain shadows of the grass.

And then he looked at her.

There was such an odd and terrible smile on her face, a smile he'd never seen before on her or anyone, the soiled hem of her dress held high in her clenched fists, and saying through her tiny, stuttered teeth: "Look at me!"

And he looked again.

He told her at the last to hurry, his shirt undone, and him sitting on a patch of dust between two boulders, pulling at his boots to get them off his feet. As he did she had said *Joel* over and over as if she'd spent the day with his name in her mouth just as she had the first time. How she'd known his name even then, he didn't know. He'd never told her.

And when they were done that day he'd left her in the cleft of rocks. He'd pulled on his clothes and boots and gathered himself for the trail, catching Lost Line Creek just above the farm, and then he had climbed three thousand feet more. At the alpine spring he gazed down at the house and barn far below. He imagined for a moment he could see Myrna white and still in the field, but whatever it was he thought he saw moved and he wasn't sure if what he was seeing was her at all. He watched until whatever it was disappeared into the trees, a sheep maybe gone astray from the others and not a girl he'd lain with in the swale between the rocks.

Joel, Joel, she'd howled as he'd left without a word.

He'd never asked her to be there.

None of it was his fault.

Still.

Now there was the dance tomorrow night. Myrna had told him her father was taking her there. It was going to be the first time ever she'd gone when she could dance most of the dances knowing how. She said her father had been teaching her box steps and walk steps and other kinds too.

Waltz and *polka* fell from her lips like magical words.

He did want Myrna to be there, wanted to dance with her, and it didn't matter if Alice saw them dancing because he'd be dancing with Alice too if she'd let him. And Myrna wouldn't tell anyone about what they'd done or did. Not her. Not Myrna.

The creek and the bridge were behind him now. He'd moved on into the night. As he walked he caught glimpses of the moon's hook as it kept trying to catch at the rimrock above the cliffs on the other side of the river, its vagrant light lingering among the stunted trees along the alpine.

A rustle in the brush ahead stopped him, a thick stench creeping.

And then a quickening, a heat flare, a stink, all of it a thickness moving.

The night was then an absence, a breath untaken.

He stood motionless as something coarse brushed against a rock. A stillness and the scrape of sound, the smell of bear and it knowing he was there.

The sound flowed, an open mouth, a *ffhhhhh* stretched out, wet air moving over hot stone steaming.

It was a bear and it had to be a big one come along the cliffs above the canyon, or from the south pacing the creeks below Mad River, or down from the mountain runnels to the dump. One who had come into the village to forage at the burning barrels behind the cabins and shacks, the covered barrels down at the cookhouse. Or not hungry, but walking the path for something other than garbage, walking like this was its place, its land, its right to be anywhere. The trail belonged to the bear, and any beast—bear, wolf, cougar, or man—must step aside. He'd seen what a bear could do. The torn-up body of a faller down on the lakes, a man who thought the forest his to reap, and the bear with its right-of-way, perhaps guarding a nearby kill, a cub to protect, something, or nothing, just a man in its way. A bear could smell death in a man.

The bear heard him breathe. It matched him breath for breath.

And in the long quiet he waited, knowing if he tried to run the bear would be on him in seconds. He stood in the stillness and then he heard the bear tear at a rotting stump, a root, a stone.

Hhhuuuunmfff.

Deep in the gutter of the bear's throat, that sound, and he listened as it began to move up the trail. He could feel the steps of the animal as paw after paw placed itself heavy on the earth. He felt the bear's bulk in his bones, the way it shouldered its way through the bush a few yards ahead of him, leaving behind it a cloy caught on the air, the thick of a boar's musk.

He wiped at the smell in his nose, his wrist across his face. The animal had left itself on the night, not just its rankness, but a gravity that inhabited what it was and where it had been.

Joel waited long, his heart slow, his breathing quiet. The bear had let go of whatever had brought it along the path and it had let go of him. The bear was deep in the night, but Joel walked more carefully now, each small step he took aware, each bend in the trail a moment to breathe, to smell and listen. Twenty feet along the path a fir stump lay in pieces, pulled apart, fragments of wood lying everywhere as if it had exploded. Dry kernels of bark turned to dust under his boots.

Three bends, a big root in the trail, and the next cabin appeared, the one under the triple aspens. A stove-in bucket was tilted by the door, dandelions growing through the rust holes. Joel knew Oroville was behind those chinked logs sleeping with his skinny wife, their gunny-sack shades pulled tight and bound down with baler twine. He figured they'd heard his footfalls by their window some night back in the spring. They'd stayed hidden after that, but he didn't need to sneak looks into other people's lives so much anymore. Not now there was her. And then he wondered which her he meant, Alice or Myrna. He wanted both or none or one, but which one?

The burning barrel beside Oroville's cabin was tipped over on its side, half-burnt pork-chop bones, remnant potato skins, tin cans and damp ash spilled across the trail. The big bears mostly stayed away from the village, though Jaswant, the Sikh on the green chain, had told him a week ago he'd seen bear sign marked in the mud by the road leading to the dump. He told Joel the claws alone were two inches long, the paw prints huge, too large for even the biggest black.

Joel ran his hand over the scuffed fir needles. There were claw marks on the barrel, and in the damp earth beside the overturned barrel was a smudged print. Five long claws in a straight row and not rounded on the paw like a black bear's.

He'd smelled the bear just minutes ago.

Grizzly. A real bear, not a spirit.

But why come here?

The great bears got more than enough to eat feeding upon berries in the meadows, salmon on the creek bars, a moose calf. Little Hell's Gate was many miles north of the village, a sixteen-foot-wide dogleg canyon even the spring salmon couldn't force themselves through, the river pouring from the twisted gut in a wrench, a gasp of water. He'd seen eighty-pound springs spawning on Cougar Creek across the river from Aspen Flats just north of the village, the bears throwing the huge fish like silver leaves from the shallow waters, then tearing off the tops of their heads for the fat in the brains, ripping open the bellies for eggs, and leaving the mangled bodies for ravens, crows, and gulls.

The signs by the burning barrel were rough, but Joel knew bear sign and knew the paw print was a grizzly's. He'd hoped it was just some errant, aging black boar or sow, some oversized yearling come to feed upon what Oroville's wife, Gladys, had thrown away. Gladys left her waste sometimes unburnt and for that he'd thought a bear might come. But not this grizzly. It had a reason to be here. A grizzly wasn't a garbage bear. Joel stepped over the charred waste and ducked his head under a limp fir bough. He passed among random stones, an old log with stubs that had to be stepped over careful, and then he was looking down through gravel and brush tangle at the faint glow of a light at the back of the sawyer's forty-foot trailer. Jim McAllister's place.

There was a thick chokecherry bush a little ways down the slope and Joel picked his way down to it. Pushing aside a branch he looked along the side of McAllister's trailer where a light was coming from an open door farther down. It shone dimly into the shack attached to the side of the trailer. Jim had built it the week after he moved in. Joel had seen it go up on his night walks along the forest path, the stacked cement blocks and crossed railway ties the trailer rested upon, then the framing of the shack beside it. Trailer people called the additions joy-shacks—why, Joel didn't know. There didn't seem any joy to the clutter people stored in them. He looked through the joy-shack door at the shadowy boxes and cartons in Jim's extra room. There were a couple of chainsaws, a workbench with a metal box, tools lying out as if Jim had been fixing something, cardboard boxes stacked in the back, and anything and everything else that wouldn't fit inside the trailer. There was a washing machine, a half-size box freezer, and a tube vacuum cleaner, things there wouldn't be a use for in the village. Like most everyone McAllister had no electricity. The only places that had power were the Rotmensens' store and home, the Community Hall, the cookhouse, and the Company house where Claude lived. The mill's diesel generators lighted those buildings alone, the workers, farmers, and hill folk getting by as they always had with coal oil, kerosene lamps, candles, and flashlights.

Joel stayed hidden behind the bush and looked up at the muted glow coming through a window above him at the rear of the trailer. Joel knew trailers from back in Nakusp when he'd roamed the night streets. The light was where the bedroom had to be. The narrow window was open, a thin curtain pulled to the side. Joel lifted his hands from between his shanks and settled deeper on his haunches just as Jim's voice came through the window.

"This goddam woman," McAllister said, each word as if bitten off, each sound he made a severed absence as if he was speaking only to himself and to no other.

Joel waited through the following quiet and then heard a woman cry back, her voice wrenched, a choker cable stretched across the dark. "No, not damned. Not that."

And then, strange and sudden and out of place, Joel heard Art Kenning speak. "Don't curse her, Jim," he said.

"I'll say what I want to say," the sawyer replied, his voice thin and hard. "Irene's my woman, not yours."

"What's wrong with you?" Art asked. "She's hurt."

Joel could hear the whisky as Art spoke, a soft slur Joel knew was liquor talking.

He listened as Art told McAllister to let him do what he'd been brought there to do.

McAllister said again it was his woman to speak to and do with as he pleased and Art asked him to get out of the bedroom.

There was a long silence. And then Art said, "Why'd you cut her?"

"Who are you to ask me anything?" Jim said, his voice bent iron straining. "I got you here to fix her, nothing more."

It was quiet again and into that emptiness McAllister spoke one word, but not to Art, and not to Irene, his wife, the one who was making with her mouth a sound like wet leaves turned by a boot. No, not to them, but to someone else entirely, who Joel didn't know. "Women," said Jim. He spoke as if the world was made entirely of them and therefore entirely damned.

Not damned, Joel thought, not her or anyone.

"Get out," Art said. "Let me do this."

Joel leaned forward, his hat low, one hand stretched out, the muscles in his legs tight, his other hand flat on a boulder, dry lichen bristling in his palm. The other gripped the choke-cherry branch, a few last berries falling, rattling dry and bitter on the leaves at his feet. He heard then what had to be the bedroom door sliding closed, carefully, not slammed, and then Jim's horseshoed steel boot heels clicking slow and steady down the trailer toward the front where a second kerosene lamp burned, its glow shining out into the joy-shack. Joel crept farther down the slope until he could lean against the scarred siding below the window at the back, blue aluminum paint dust sifting down on his shoulder, his feet set to run.

Two small aspen saplings gave him cover as lamplight flowed like burnt water over his head. A grey moth fluttered past his brow, the moth's wings beating against the limp curtain, flaring as it tried to reach the light inside the room. Then he heard Irene McAllister cry out, her voice soft as a child's in a strange dream.

Art Kenning was whispering things to her. They weren't words. They were sounds, the kind someone would make to a fevered child, croonings mostly, like what women sing to something that's been wronged, animal, bird, or child.

Joel thought about what Art was doing in there with Irene McAllister, wanting to hear more and not wanting to know, Art's hands on her, and then, a little crazed, bewildered by thinking what he was, he climbed up the slope to the trail. He looked back only once, the light from the two lamps still shining, the one from the bedroom where Irene and Art were and the other from the front where Jim was, doing what, Joel could not imagine.

Standing a little straighter now that he was hidden from the trailer and the road, he walked on past a pile of scrap lumber, tar streaks on the boards, and on from there to a tumbled woodpile, the split fir and hemlock riddled with worms and black rot. He stopped beside a burning barrel, this one upright, balanced on three flat stones, the white ash in the bottom of the scorched oil drum shivering from air that bled through the torch-cut holes in the iron.

McAllister's trailer was best left alone.

He'd heard what Jim had said: *That goddam woman.*

No, what the sawyer had said was *this*, not *that*. *This goddam woman* is what McAllister said. It was as if he was trying to make sure of who she was, his woman and no other's.

And Art had ordered the sawyer to *get out* in Jim's own trailer.

Joel wondered how bad she was for Art to say that. He'd seen Art sew a logger's thumb back on one time last winter. The man had come out of the bush with it hanging from behind the knuckle, tied off at the stump with twine to stop the bleeding. The thumb didn't take after Art put it back on, but it'd been something to watch Art fit the bones together and then sew it on, the stitches at the end looking like a fringed necklace around the logger's thumb. He remembered the paleness of the bone. It was the first time he'd seen a living bone. Art had told the guy it wouldn't work, but the logger insisted he try. Art said the thumb was pretty well dead by the time it got to him, but he sewed it back on anyway, the man thanking him for the time he took to do it. Art took the thumb back off a week later because of the smell and sent him down to Kamloops, telling him he'd likely die if he didn't get it seen to. The man never blamed Art for his own insisting on the trying. He went down on a train that night. He never came upriver again.

As Joel tried to imagine the shadows of Irene McAllister's body and wondered what part of her Art was sewing up, he stumbled on a root just past a deserted cabin, sucking in one breath and then another as he pushed down on his crotch, Alice alive in his head. It was like sometimes women were under his hands, the ones he'd sometimes see in the dark, and in the light too, the ones who walked moving like they did and do down the road, the wives sometimes and the daughters too like Myrna. Myrna Turfoot in their hiding place above the trees behind the rocks.

"Myrna."

And then in a whisper, "Myrna," again, thinking of her laughter, the joy she took in things, in him, her pleasure. He wanted her and didn't want her. He wanted Alice too mostly because he couldn't have her. But knowing the *didn't* and the *did* was never going to change the way he felt about the two of them.

He thought of the men sitting around the bunkhouse at night telling stories. If they talked about women it was about ones who lived everywhere else but the valley, the village where they worked. Some of the men would start drinking heavy and then they'd go on about what they'd done to a girl down in Little Fort or up in Blue River or Jasper. I did this or I did that. *Bitches* and *whores* is what they called them. *Cunts* is what they'd say.

One thing Joel knew, the men seemed to hate the women they talked about, the ones they said they'd been with. Some of the men when they got really drunk would talk about beating a girl up. Reiner was full of stories like that. He bragged about the times he'd had to bring a woman into line. It was because one had either mouthed off to him or come on to another guy. Or else he said it was because she'd wanted to get hurt, that she was looking for it from the start. It was almost as if Ernie was afraid of women.

There were some, Art and Joseph and a few others, who wouldn't put up with Ernie going on about what he'd done to some girl or another. Joel thought maybe it was why Reiner hung around Jim McAllister. McAllister never said much one way or the other, but Joel had seen the two of them take off for Blue River on nights when there wasn't a dance going on in the village. Reiner was always drunk when he got back, but if Jim was he didn't show it. The times Joel saw them return McAllister never staggered or fell like Reiner did. Art always said they were a strange pair, Jim dead quiet and Ernie a loudmouth.

The thing was, men never said they missed the women they talked about, wives, girlfriends, daughters. But there were times when Joel would see a man sitting alone, down by the river or up on the high road watching the trucks heading toward the cities, dust riding in rooster tails behind them. The guy would be sitting on a rock or a stump and there'd be a look on his face so lost it made Joel turn away. He knew what that look meant now there was Myrna and Alice. It wasn't just loneliness the man had been feeling. There was something else in his heart, a need, a kind of wanting, and though Joel couldn't name what it was, he knew it lived somewhere deep inside him too.

Something bad had happened back at the trailer to have the first-aid man there, him having to sew up Jim's wife, and Art talking to McAllister like he did.

Only the boss could do that and even then Claude was careful around him.

But Art Kenning did.

Joel took a step and stopped, resting his back against a dried-out cedar trunk.

Thick air pooled on the stones at his feet.

A frog sounded in the tired mud back at the creek.

Creaak . . . crik . . . creaak.

And a rat in the fir needles rustling.

Was the owl still down by the river, the bear on the trail to the dump?

Ernie Reiner sucking on air.

There was the lean-to behind the store with its pig-wire window.

Where he was going.

Where Rotmensen kept Alice.

This goddam woman. This goddam woman.

McAllister's Irene.

What McAllister could do, anything he wanted to do, to her.

Scared of the pictures in his head, Joel took a deep breath and bent over, his hat falling off, his hands between his thighs. He felt himself get hard again, the blood in his groin stirring, his cock quick against his palm. He squeezed down, gripping himself, wishing his body gone. He was afraid Alice would be able to smell him when he got to the lean-to and stood on the round of cedar looking down upon Alice sleeping. Standing straight, he leaned his head and shoulders back so the stars were cold on his eyes. He pushed his hand down the front of his pants, pulling his cock up so it rested hard against his belly. Dragging his low-slung belt down, he pulled it tight, binding himself, the leather like a hard lace cutting him. He thought of where he was going, the lean-to, the window, and he struck low at his belly where it was, struck at himself with his closed fist. He punched at himself again, but it wouldn't go away.

It just got harder.

He pulled his hat down onto his skull. Shoulders hunched, fingernails gripping his palms, he passed behind a clutch of young alders, their leaves shaking. The shadows ate him, nothing to mark his passing but the dragged scuffs in the dust his boots left walking.

EIGHT

ART KENNING HAD COME DOWN from McAllister's trailer to Lost Line Creek where it ran just beyond the path that led to his cabin. He knelt in the moss and placed his hands deep in the pool he had made when first he moved up the river. He'd carried stones there so the water would stay clear. Ever since, he'd got his drinking and cooking water in the end where he'd dug it deep. Below the pool the creek re-formed and ran another fifty feet before disappearing into an iron culvert and from its far mouth beyond the railway grade fell at last into the North Thompson River.

The cold wreathed his wrists under the moon, blood lines in the water shivering like stretched green copper left too long in the rain. Irene's blood was like that, metal vines writhing in water come down from the high springs and alpine snows. He knelt there in the moss and wrung his fingers together, his palms scouring the backs of his hands. Bits of brittle blood sheared away, fragile flakes of Irene McAllister floating from among the golden hairs on his wrists.

Deep under the waters beyond him great boulders rolled on the river bottom, their thunder the guns of the Scheldt, the guns of Walcheren. He clenched his fists, the ghosts of Holland dancing wisps in the cul-de-sacs of his mind. The whispers were always there.

He sat back by the pool and thought of his squatting in front of McAllister's wife as she sat on the edge of her bed. She'd looked more child than woman, she was so small. If she'd stood she wouldn't have reached five feet. It's going to be okay, he'd said to her when he got there. She didn't speak except for those few words to him after McAllister cursed her: "No, not damned," she'd said, and Art then telling her it was going to be all right.

As Art spoke she had tilted her head back, her necklace with its Alaska black diamonds rising on her white throat. The bits of cheap glass glinted in the light from the lamp. Her small mouth gaped. He thought, looking at her, of a wolf he'd seen once in a winter meadow howl at a severed moon. The cry before him was the same, the moan diminishing to a gasp of spittle-choked air.

And then there was a sudden noise, something breaking in the front of the trailer, and her eyes startled, stared out, and, "Don't let Jim back in," she said, and whispered, "Please."

He'd watched her eyes look from him to the ceiling above and followed them with his own to a water stain, a dark blotch spreading there. He imagined her lying on her back in their bed and staring at it as it slowly grew, misshapen, alive. He'd tried not to look at her bare thighs and the deep cuts in her flesh. She had pulled the skirt of her cotton dress up in a tangled roll at the bottom of her belly, holding it there in her fists, the blood from below gathering there. The folds above her groin were blotted too with blood. Her bare arms and her legs below the wounds were splotched with bruises, some a pale yellow healing and others still purpled. He'd seen such bruises before and knew she hadn't got them by bumping into things. Her dress was stitched high at the neck, tiny scarlet crosses embedded there as if to match the stains below. On her one foot was a red high heel, the colour of her wounds. The other foot was naked. It looked lost against the brown linoleum on the floor as if it had somehow been a foot someone had forgotten, someone who had put it gently down and then gone away without a thought.

"Was it Jim did this?"

He'd asked and she'd answered him by letting go of the blood rolls at her waist and putting her wet hands over her eyes as if to protect herself from the walls and the black smut that grew in the damp corners, saying, "No."

Before she could cry out again he, gentle, said, "Okay, it's okay."

And she was quiet.

Her hands were still over her eyes as he took the slip and blood-soaked dress and rolled them tighter, tucking them higher across her waist. He tried not to look at the swell of her mound, the dark hairs like fragile fronds pasted to her flesh at the edge of her panties.

She lowered her hands then, the blood prints of her fingers and palms on her face. When he was done with lifting the folds she placed her hands again upon the rolled dress, gripping it tight, holding it there, the knuckles of her hands wet.

Slow and careful, tender, he touched her skin.

A tremor crept from her thighs to her belly. Her hands lifted and she cupped her face again. When he tried to move them away, she said one word, a small no.

Silent then and utterly so, she was, and he left her to be such, alone and blind, and him, to her, someone far off as if not there at all, his hands on her imagined things and, belonging to no one, nothing more.

He went out to the kitchen, the living room a larger space past the small sink, stove, and counter. He filled a pot with warm water as the sawyer stared out the front window at the darkness over the river. McAllister turned and started to speak, but Art raised his open hand and Jim was silent.

Art walked down the narrow hall back to the bedroom feeling Jim's stare on his back. He took one of the clean cloths he found in the bathroom cupboard and washed her wounds, cleansing them with antiseptic. The tourniquet he had tied on the leg with the deepest cut had stilled the worst bleeding. He knelt in front of her and took a curved needle from his kit, drawing the point over the narrow Washita stone he kept there. The sound the needle left behind was a faint *whish whish whish* as if there was somehow hope in the tiny steel blade. The needle had to be perfect to enter her skin without mar. When it was ready he laid it down on the clean dressings beside the syringe. The pool at the bottom of the bottle was all that was left of the morphine after looking after Emerson Turfoot that morning. Art's stitching the boy's face seemed a long time ago. It was strange that he was doing the same again.

Irene McAllister sat very still but for her breathing as she waited for him to begin what he was going to do.

Here, he was here, he thought, as he prepared the syringe.

He leaned over Irene then and tied off her arm, a vein rising in the crook of her elbow. The needle slid in, the morphine entering her as he untied the strap on her arm. In a moment her eyelids began to flutter, but she held fast to the roll of cotton in her fists. She didn't let go.

The kerosene lamp on the half-moon table beside the bed was the only light in the room. Beside the lamp was a china figurine of an antebellum Negro girl in a long white dress. The little creature was trying and failing to look both innocent and coy. She held a frilled lace umbrella with pink china flowers embedded in the porcelain. The bulb she was supposed to hold was missing, the receptacle empty, the lampshade balanced precariously there as if to give the illusion of another kind of light, there being no electricity.

Art shook his head at the craziness of it all, McAllister, the woman's wounds, the long night that wasn't over. He knelt now in the moss by the river, thinking of the Negro lamp and how odd it was for Irene to have kept such an object with nothing to bring it to life. Who knew but that the lamp was a gift given her by some older woman, a spinster aunt maybe, or a widowed mother, someone foolish enough not to understand its uselessness, the irony of such a gift brought to a narrow northern valley far from the world of porcelain and pretty hats. Or Irene had bought it herself when she was younger. It was the kind of sentimental thing women from the backcountry loved. Perhaps some odd hope had come to her by having it, but hope for what?

What hope was hers?

For a moment Art imagined her standing at the foot of the bed when Jim was working night shift at the mill. He could see her turning the lamp switch on and off, on and off, and no light ever there in the darkness.

He held up his arm. A thin line of her blood had run along the side of his wrist and soaked into his shirt cuff, the stain looking to him like the mushroom his mother called Scarlet Devil's Tooth, the blood having grown there like the mushroom, blots of blood on flesh.

Back in the trailer he'd willed his hands not to shake, the right hand because it had to thread the needle, and the left to hold everything steady. The lamp glimmer had been dim and Art could barely see the hole in the needle.

Was hope what she'd allowed herself?

He didn't think so. That kind of thinking could kill a woman. Or a man.

The boulders rolled in the river below the tracks, the thunder of far-off guns. Tommy laughing as he brought the girl in from the dark where she'd been hiding.

Irene had sat utterly still. She had let go the rolled dress, her hands curled over, resting like supplicant cups on the bunched cotton at her belly, waiting.

The morphine he'd given her had done its job and he knew she drifted soft inside her mind. Most nights he chased dreams too, but his were confused these past months, his nightmares limbo.

"Let the morphine do its work," he'd said to Irene, and then almost pleading: "Why did Jim cut you?"

She looked at him out of her blue eyes, wide open at his question, staring. He saw her then clearly for the first time and wondered to himself how he could have been mistaken.

Not Jim then.

Her.

She was the cutter.

He understood then the ladders of pale scars that crissed and crossed her arms. She whimpered and then she stopped, her mouth as if closed forever.

"Just breathe," he'd said in wonder.

Softly, he'd spoken softly, and bending, he helped her get unstuck. He shifted her hips away and leaned her back upon the quilt. He lifted and turned her, straightening her legs and slipping off her high heel shoe. He placed it on the floor under the bed with the other.

Blood welled a bit in the deepest cut she'd made with the knife, her hand by then sure.

He knew she'd had no care for what he tried to say: "Easy, careful, it's all right, I have you . . ." What? Have her, how, and how, lying in her blood, was she anywhere near all right?

Irene McAllister had stared up at the ceiling, seeing, he thought, the same thing he did back in his cabin when he read the ceiling and the walls, the damp rot above her formed into odd and terrible shapes in the cheap plywood veneer above her. She was buried in visions of what to her must be ruined cave paintings made in some far-off time, but what those visions were he did not know. Women's dreams were a mystery to him and perhaps to all men. He couldn't imagine their hallucinations, living as they did in their moons of blood. He didn't understand his own.

Irene must have looked at that ceiling a thousand times in her months alone. He knew. He'd laid himself down on beds in rooms with stained walls and ceilings and watched terrible creatures come out of the cracks with screams in their teeth, monsters living between the boards in the ceiling at his cabin.

The water purled across the rocks in the creek below the pool. He took another drink from the bottle. It was close to empty now. He had to stop thinking of Irene McAllister and the man who had driven her to such a place as was hers. He placed in his mind the hand-split cedar boards of his own cabin walls and the newspapers that had been glued there to keep out the drafts in winter, cracked now and torn by years of worms and wasps and beetles.

The river beyond the railway grade moved past, always

different, always the same. Art clenched his hands and opened them, his fingers steady again.

He thought of how he'd gripped them over and over back there in that room in McAllister's trailer, squeezing his fists tight and letting them go slowly. When his hands had quieted he'd lifted the needle to his better eye, the left one, and slipped the silk through the tiny slot, the thread moving with his breath as he drew it down, a single strand of web hanging as if left behind by a spider in the night, as delicate, as strong as that. Then he'd loosened the tourniquet just above her wounds. The peroxide had foamed pink in the cuts and dribbled down her thigh. Blood had bloated in the longest one, a thickness swelling in the crevice. He tightened the tourniquet again until the bulb of blood stopped growing. Blood thick as rubber had welled into the other cuts too and he wiped them gently with antiseptic on the clean cotton he'd found in the bathroom cupboard.

He'd told her there was more stitching to do, but she'd neither moved nor minded as he pushed the needle through her skin, the flesh resisting slightly as the needle sank like a delicate silver fish and rose from her body as if from shivering water. Art tied a knot in the first suture and moved steadily on, sewing the gaped lips of each wound, pulling her together. He tried to remember where he learned the double loop of the square knot. Somewhere.

When Art finished he'd bound her thigh tight with pressure bandages. No one had taught him how to do what he had done. What he knew of injury and the care of others he'd learned by watching the medics in the war, his own regiment's medic shot dead outside Tournai. Tournai? Somewhere in Belgium, nowhere, the goddamned war. After they took the medic's body away they came to him for aid. He didn't know why.

Wiping his fingers on the sheet, he'd wished her scars to be as thin as stretch marks, something a man if he saw them when she was naked or wearing a bathing suit might forgive her for, thinking childbirth the cause of her suffering.

He'd collapsed his fingers into loose fists again as he looked at her wounds. He figured she'd made a whispered cut along her left thigh first and then another, slightly deeper, the last the heavy bleeder he'd just finished stitching. The two cuts in her right leg were shallower, skin deep, the slices crooked as if she'd almost forgotten what she was doing and had to start over. She had to have been in shock by then, the muscles in her arm heavy, her fingers without feeling as they dragged the knife awkwardly.

He closed his eyes and imagined her as she must have been before he saw her sitting in her blood, still trying. It was as if she'd been patient when she made the first cut, placing McAllister's hunting knife sharp against her white skin and drawing the blade across in the same way she might have tested a ripe tomato, the blood rising behind the steel, a red furrow forming, the blood lines sudden, draping down the sides of her thigh in slender rivulets and drying in a pool beneath her hips. She had to have worried the bigger cuts with the knife or with a finger to keep the blood flowing. She had cut into veins, the big artery in her leg too deep for her to get to. Or maybe she hadn't wanted to. Someone so close to her own blood must have known the artery crossed the groin in a place so shallow she could have cut it open without trying and bled to death in five minutes.

She didn't want that.

Art could see her sitting there waiting to see what the inside of her leg looked like when they were opened, and then going on, cut after cut, each one a little deeper than the one before. After the first three she must have stopped and waited, he thought, to see if they were enough.

They weren't.

So she tried again on the other leg, the knife wavering, the weight of her hand and the knife doing what they could alone, her body not helping the blade to go deeper.

Where was he?

The pool shimmered under what was left of the moon, the water he'd washed his hands in clear again, her blood gone on to the big river. Fish were lifting from the deep pools and eddies to sip at the wisps of her lost body, his hands having washed what of her he had taken away. At the thought of the great fish rising to her smell, he rocked back on his heels and fell against a huge granite rock rolled off the risen grade by the railway years ago.

He stretched himself there, his hands pressed into the moss.

A clutch of daisies nodded by his shoulder, the petals worn by the wind the trains dragged passing.

Irene McAllister had made of herself a long thinking. He knew what it was to live in the holes you found inside your head. A woman too could burrow there. Live too long in the tunnels and trenches and your body becomes a stranger, your skin and bones things you look at from far off. You hang in obscure caves and crannies. You're the dream you don't remember, but you know you're down there if only you can find yourself. You're a fish in the river, a trout with a slash of red to mark its jaws. You rise from that dark, a cutthroat trout, ascending blood.

The fish roved in the river currents the way her life did in her skull.

He wondered how long she had waited before her husband came home. Was she playing with the knife or did she just sit there in a terrible solitude? What was it she wanted from him that she should wait until he came home from wherever he'd been? Out with Ernie maybe, somewhere, or alone. McAllister had worked the day shift so he could have been anywhere in the night. What might she have done next with the knife but for Jim finally coming in and finding her?

Once begun, there was no end to such play. Wang Po told him once there was no end to a painting, no end to a poem. Art had seen lonely games in the war, men trading cigarettes butt for butt, taking turns stubbing them out on the tender inner skin of their arms, a bullet in a foot or hand, a wrist opened up with the tip of a bayonet, a man staring at his tendons and muscles, another gazing curiously at the strange repetitive pulse of an artery, blood spraying the air to a tune played by the heart. There were men who took themselves apart like that. And there were men too who tried to put themselves back together. The soldier he saw in a bomb crater near Bruges who kept trying to push his intestines back into his body. The simplicity in the soldier's eyes, the concentration as he asked for help with his own offal. Art wondered if he'd been like that when they found him after the explosion at Moerbrugge. Was he knocked out or was he sitting by the fieldstone wall trying to put his mind back together, picking up a memory here and there and putting them back in his head? When they found him did he ask them the question the corporal a half mile south of Lange Munte had asked?

Give me a hand, would ya?

The soldier only said it the once and then stopped a moment as if tired of trying to understand why he couldn't gather it all up, the tubes of his body slipping through his hands like wet hawsers as he died.

The muscles in Art's shoulders and chest bound him tight. He barely breathed.

He lifted his hand to the dried-out heads of the daisies beside him, the stems and wilted flowers brushing his palms.

McAllister.

As far as he could tell, Jim hadn't touched her but for taking the knife away. He told Art he'd had to unwind her fingers from the buckhorn handle of his hunting knife. He'd held the blade out to Art when they got to the trailer, but Art refused the knife she'd used. McAllister said it was the one he'd skinned moose and deer with. And as Jim described the undoing of his wife's fingers, he asked Art: "Why not one of her own? Tell me that. Why would she go digging around in my stuff to find my hunting knife? There were others in the kitchen just as good."

How was Art to answer such a question? How speak to such a man?

McAllister had left her sitting in her blood when he came down to the cabin to get him, Art Kenning, the one person McAllister thought would be able to deal with what was, beyond his frustration and rage, a complex puzzle he could not for the life of him solve. He could have woken Oroville Cranmer and got Oroville's wife, Gladys, to stay with Irene while he went for help. They lived in the cabin just down the path. But it was not in McAllister to ask Oroville or anyone for help for fear of being beholden. No, he went off into the night to get the first-aid man, the only one he knew who could not only staunch the blood and sew up the wounds but keep what his wife had done a secret.

What had she wondered as McAllister went out the door and left her there bleeding?

Or was there wonder left in her?

Jim must have told her where he was going.

Or not, because Art didn't know what Jim might have said to her, sitting as his wife was on the edge of their bed stuck down in her own blood.

"I'm sorry," Art said to the river which, for all the many times he'd talked to it, said nothing back, the rapids and currents swirling his words away in obdurate refusal to speak its one mind.

When he'd finished suturing the injuries on her left thigh Art had sharpened the needle again on the stone, disinfected the blade, and begun work on the one deeper cut on the right leg, another small shot from the remnant morphine keeping Irene still as the stitches went in, the tug of the diamond needle, the thin itch he knew she felt as the thread pulled through her flesh, and beyond that nothing but the beating of her heart.

He lay against the river boulder, hands wrung and dry, and lifted the whisky bottle he'd yanked from McAllister's hand when he left the trailer. He took a deep drink and then a last one, holding the bottle to his mouth until the faint drops touched his tongue. He rested the empty bottle between his thighs, the liquor burning in his belly.

He would go to Wang Po's. But first he needed to pull himself together.

He laced his fingers around the bottle's neck.

What had it been like for her to go to such a place?

He knew the wounding wasn't a cry for help. In that she was like the man who owned her. And she hadn't given up her life entirely or else she'd have made a better job of it. What she'd done, Art thought, was to make of her body an offering to McAllister, a display of her despair, the blood she shed a kind of message, a missive sent, any kind of written note a lie. Her wounds were like the belongings of a hanged woman's life arranged neatly around her, everything in order, the floors scrubbed clean, food covered with a cloth to keep off the flies, the plate on the table a cold dish for her man to eat when he came home at last from work, clean underpants and brassiere, clean slip and dress. It was no different than a swept floor, a fire banked, the clothes left folded neatly on a toilet seat by a woman who had drowned herself in a bathtub having taken every pill she could find to keep from waking up in the same wrong world.

Or Helga Fyksen last year who walked the CNR rail line all the way to the great outfall of the river at Little Hell's Gate, the double-back eddy below the gorge where the drift trees caught, the river slowly and steadily beating them to splinters against the huge rocks blasted from the cliffs a century ago to make room above the canyon for the railway. She was a woman not much different than Irene. Helga had worn the pants and shirt and overcoat of her husband. Olaf's clothes, not her own. Helga hadn't taken his clothes off when she clambered down to the river and it wasn't that clothes mattered at all, but that clothes with pockets were needed for the job at hand. When they found her body downriver her myriad pockets were full of small stones the river hadn't beaten out of her.

Art had been called to look at her as if saying she was dead confirmed her death to those who'd dragged her lifeless from a sandbar. He had thought of Helga many times since they took him to her. When Art picked through the little stones he found in her pockets he imagined her choosing each one from among the many along the river. One perfect stone, and then another and another, a nimbus around one, a halo, polished ones with white moons, and the coloured pebbles too, the blue and red and green, jasper, carnelian, quartz, iron-flecked, green jade, pyrites, each and all, they were the kind of rocks he knew a woman could lick with her tongue to see if by their shine they were right for her. For Helga, a hundred stones, until she knew she was weighed down with enough beauty to keep from rising up.

A woman like that.

A woman like Irene.

The cuts Irene McAllister made she displayed so her husband might know her and she might therefore become in her suffering what she thought she was to him, his one true and only wife, his pure and terrible dilemma, his hellish Irene.

"See me," she might have said to him. "Look at me in my blood."

"I can't go crazy," Art said softly, but there was nothing and no one to answer him.

The railway tracks behind his head gleamed like silver threads dragged by the sickle moon from his skull.

A little brown bat flittered along the river's edge in search of an errant moth. It cut sideways toward him as if it had an answer to what he hadn't asked. He felt its skin cross his eyes, the spider bones inside the leather wings startling against the moon.

Art had cut his arm with a razor blade once. He had watched his blood well up in tiny blurts, and then cut himself once more just to make sure it was true.

Perhaps it was simply to know he was alive in there, some proof needed in the end.

"Don't," he said, "remember."

Art put his face in his hands. He and Claude were on leave in Paris. The war was over. Late 1945. It was one of the nights just before Claude went home. As for himself, Art knew he'd be staying to work on the graves. The word had come down the line that no Canadian soldiers could be buried in Germany. The bodies had to be brought back from that cursed ground. Claude had arranged for Art to search out the dead and bring them to Groesbeek in Holland. There was nothing for Art back home, nothing to take him there.

Claude had been drunk on black-market Scotch at his table at the back of the Café L'Oiseau Rouge. Hélène was sitting beside him. Hélène, Claude's *petite putain*, the one who had been with him when Claude introduced Art to Marie. She was the girl Claude kept hurting, his disdain for the little prostitute balanced only by his pleasure in using her over and over again for his amusement.

It was the night Claude sold her to a sergeant from the Black Watch.

Pourquoi, Claude, pourquoi?

Claude had ignored her.

"Because it amuses me," is what he said when Art asked him why.

Art saw Hélène only once more. It was on one of his leaves a few months after searching for bodies and graves around Oldenburg. Marie had gone to Marseilles to get drugs, heroin and morphine from the boat in Marseilles that she sold in Paris, the stuff she brought back for him and for her. When he saw her Hélène was standing a little way past the Café Olympique a few blocks from Place Pigalle. Two soldiers were talking to her. He watched them as they led her into an alley, Hélène's skirt partly torn and streaked with oil.

Petite Hélène.

And never again.

Paris.

Sometimes it wouldn't go away.

Hélène was drunk. But she was always, always drunk, wasn't she?

At the end she would sit with Marie in the café waiting for Claude, sipping her wine. Every few minutes she'd lean over the table, her hair in clots falling across her eyes. She'd grab Marie's wrist or the sleeve of her blouse, and say: "*Es-tu heureuse, Marie?*"

Hélène was serious the way drunks are serious, asking and asking the same questions. For Hélène it was wanting to know if Marie was happy. "Are you happy?"

Marie always told her not to be sad. "Don't be sad, Hélène. Don't be sad."

"Are you happy, Marie?"

And Marie would ask why she stayed with a man who beat her, a man who sold her so he could watch.

And Hélène would say, "Because I love."

And it would go on like that. On and on.

And long before that, the leave in Paris when Art first met Marie. Was it after Bruges?

Was Marie happy?

They were happy then.

He couldn't remember if they were ever happy.

Was laughter happy?

Was silence?

But it was Claude's last leave, Hélène going off with the sergeant from the Black Watch. She turned at the door leading out to the alley and asked Claude, again, why.

Pourquoi?

Sometimes it seemed that word was her one song.

Everyone has a song. Art tried to think of one for himself, but he couldn't.

"Maybe I don't have a song," he said.

Art rolled onto his side and saw the cat leaning across her front paws as she lapped a drink from the pool. Sated, the cat pushed herself up and then rolled over onto a patch of moss and offered him her belly to caress. Art knew enough not to be tempted. Touching her belly was to be attacked by tooth and claw, her game, her play. He leaned over and listened to her purr.

"You have a song, don't you, cat?"

The cat slowly got up and stretched. She did not look back at him as she disappeared into the long grass.

Hélène had a song.

Pourquoi, pourquoi?

She sang and sang the same refrain and then she was gone, her wrist in the fist of the sergeant from the Black Watch.

Her hair had banged against the sergeant's elbow, the yellow clots clappers without bells.

A carton of cigarettes and a bottle of Scotch.

Claude said the Luckies and the liquor didn't matter. He'd have let her go for nothing just so he could watch her walk away.

It was after the Breskens Pocket, after the Scheldt, after the Ardennes, the Rhine, after almost everything.

And Paris.

"*Rien ne change*," the words coming unbidden to his tongue. "Nothing changes," he said to the moss where the cat had laid herself down. "Nothing changes, but us wanting it."

"Nothing."

Another bat fluttered toward him as if to touch Art's voice, a strange sound to hear by the river in the night, and so distracted, the white moth veering. The bat missed his kill, the wings of the moth fluttering small and low over the seething water away.

Art rolled his head on his shoulders. Marie, Hélène, the war. There was reason to be crazy. There was McAllister, his wife Irene, and all the rest, the years that had brought him to this village, these mountains, this huge river.

An empty bottle wasn't going to get him through the night. He held it up and imagined it full for a moment, the click of the cap when he cracked it open, the first whiff of whisky. Art looked through the glass darkly and then set it down on the moss.

Things were quiet in the village up the hill. Everyone had gone to sleep. He knew Joel would be perched on his upended log back of the store stealing a look at the Indian girl in her lean-to shack, but he'd be the only one around. The rest of the men were long returned from their Friday night in Clearwater or Blue River. Reiner and whoever else had gone there with him would be passed out in their truck somewhere or laid out on their bunks like discarded bodies. Most of the drunks and the gamblers, the loners and losers, were lost in sleep in the bunkhouses. What had or hadn't happened to them was already dim, almost forgotten except for the groans in their sleep.

Art closed his eyes and saw behind them Wang Po standing on his short stool at the cookhouse, his thin body leaning over the counter as he punched down the dough, those small, hard hands of his disappearing into the body of the bread.

The first loaves would be out of the oven now, Wang Po almost ready to hunch over his pipe as he waited for the bread to cool, the work done, the last of night to dream.

The sea water in the fields, the polders blown by the Germans, and the pig, the pig. The little sow screamed like a child when Tommy cut her throat, blood in dribbling ribbons hanging from his arm.

Art pulled his fingers through his hair.

"Stop," he said, scratching at his skull.

"Just stop."

He needed not to think of Irene McAllister either, because thinking wasn't going to make anything better, only worse. He needed to chase the dragon with Wang Po. The cramps in his belly whispered. He'd go down to the cookhouse.

A few months after he'd come to work at the mill he'd passed by the cookhouse late one night and smelled opium outside the narrow window of Wang Po's basement room. He had talked to Wang Po and they had shared his opium and Art's whisky. When Art told him one night that he could use penicillin to help people Wang Po said there was a way to get some.

All the law allowed him as a first-aid man was Aspirin and

what good was that for a man with his legs broken, a child with a fever he couldn't put out, a woman with influenza, infections, one who'd cut the tops of her legs open?

He wanted Irene McAllister out of his head, even as he knew he'd have to go back up to the trailer in a few more hours to check on her bandages and make sure the stitches were okay, that she hadn't done something crazy and pulled them out to start the cuts bleeding again.

There were hours to go before light.

Irene should've gone out to the hospital in Kamloops after he stitched her up. McAllister had the money for it, and the truck, but Jim had said no to taking her. And Art knew asking Claude to try and make Jim do it would have ended up with McAllister quitting. There was nowhere for her to go and no way to get there short of walking and she couldn't do that. The next passenger train was at noon and it was going north. The Jasper hospital was two nurses and a wish, and Edmonton? Alberta didn't take people from away. The southbound passenger wasn't till Sunday.

Jim had said no to that too.

Art could hear Major Claude Harper of the Fourth Canadian Armoured Division asking him where he was supposed to get another sawyer as good as Jim McAllister.

"Not, for damn sure," Claude would say, "am I going to get a replacement sawyer out of some gondola car on a CNR southbound night freight where I got that winter-frozen, love-besotted Joel kid you made me feel sorry for, an act I regret each time I see the boy at the store mooning over that damned Indian girl that Piet bought for fifty dollars, or for that matter anyone else that from time to time I've needed out of desperation because some other miserable wretch has hit the road with the dream that somewhere out there's a better job in a bigger town with more women in it, a place where if you run out of booze there's a liquor store nearby where you can buy a case of beer or a bottle and so he's caught a truck going south or north or jumped one of the freights like the kid arrived on, the trains that are, at times, my only source of labour: bums and fools, backward children from families who didn't want them or wanted them too much, escapees from fundamentalist fathers or loose mothers, the old men, cripples, cranks, and idiots, the drunks and junkies, and in those I include you, Art, knowing full well you're here only because I couldn't find anyone else to take on the first-aid job so far from a hospital and because too you were with me in the war and I haven't forgotten that even as I've tried to forget it, and the halfwits, ragheads, and retards too, anyone who can walk while he pushes a broom and a wheelbarrow under a gang saw or trim saw or can hold a twelve-foot pole and push a log on the pond toward the chains that will carry it up into the maw of my mill where the steam dogs wait to set the logs on the carriage and the head saws whine in the hands of the sawyer who will, if I'm lucky and all goes well on Monday, send a clean, half-assed fir log into the blades, carving it into the cants that in their turn will be turned into spaghetti lumber by the gang saws and edgers for the half-naked blacks to sort in Louisiana or the Carolinas, Texas or Arkansas."

Art would sit there across the desk from Claude and wait for him to be done.

"No," Claude would say, "McAllister can do what he wants short of murder and even that's got a question attached to it depending on who got murdered and why. If McAllister's wife is crazy enough to carve herself up, then it's McAllister's problem, not mine and not yours beyond you sewing her up so she can go back to being his wife. He's my best sawyer. What he does in his spare time up in that forty-foot tin-can trailer is for him to know and no one else. There's no one in this shithole village I can trust to do a job of things. Not one man . . ."

And he'd look hard at Art, the man he'd known for twenty-five years, in England in '42 and then through the landings on D-Day and on to France and Belgium to the salt marshes and flooded fields of Holland, to the leave in Paris where Marie introduced Claude to Hélène and on to a maybe happenstance, casual, or deliberate meeting with Art in a dead-end bar in what little was left of Vancouver's Japtown four years ago in 1956.

". . . save you."

Is what he'd say.

To which Art would have nothing to reply.

NINE

JOEL STOOD QUIET BESIDE AN OLD FIR TREE and stared across the bulldozed ground at the back of Rotmensens' store. McAllister's trailer was hidden in the trees high above the road, the light from its two lamps a far-off glimmer in the forest behind him. Joel stared at the doorless lean-to built onto the back of the store. The roof was nailed on badly with wide-spaced two-by-fours and hand-split shakes, the low-grade, rejected cedar shards curled and knotted. He knew the spaces between the shakes would be homes for wasps and spiders, mice and rats, and he wondered if Alice was afraid of what might live in the dark above her.

Joel had been in the store drinking a Coke the first time he'd heard of the Indian girl coming to the village. It was at the counter in the back where the Rotmensens sold Export and Player's cigarettes, soft drinks and beans and chicory coffee, baloney and processed cheese sandwiches made with Bimbo bread two, three days, sometimes a week old depending on the last shipment, stale potato chips, penny candy, jawbreakers, candy hearts, chocolate bars, licorice pipes, dried-out Halloween caramels and licorice allsorts left over from a year or more ago, the sugar layers hard as rock, the licorice stiff and grey, Oh Henry! and Sweet Marie bars, their chocolate marbled from months on the shelf. He'd listened close as Imma told Claude she and Piet had got a girl to work for them. So far as Joel could find out in the days following her coming to the store, she was from the Cariboo and she was called Alice. He never heard but that.

Alice.

Imma said that the Brother at the residential school thought maybe she was one of the Toosey people. He'd told her some Sisters found Alice when she was left sitting in the shade under a wagon at the Williams Lake Stampede. There was no one around so they figured she didn't belong to anyone. The nuns grabbed her and took her to Kamloops.

"Who knows if any of that stuff is true," Imma said. "Those Brothers will lie quicker than a snake. Indian people don't know how to care for their kids. They grow up ignorant is what we all know. Anyway," Imma had said, "they grabbed her at the Stampede. End of story. She needs to learn our ways," she said. "I'll be teaching her."

Claude had asked Imma why they'd got an Indian if they were so much work and she said such girls as were Indians trained best. "They're not the same as white girls, Claude. Indians don't run off 'cause there's nowhere they remember to run to and they don't talk back 'cause talking at best is not what they can do much of or seem to want to." Imma dragged her fingers through her bleached hair as Joel watched. Anyway, she said, "This one's young. We've got her for two years. She'll do what she's told or else."

Claude had laughed and asked: "Or else what?"

"Or else she'll find out what," Imma said. "They get lazy easy. They're born to it. Indians need a hard hand. I know, Piet and me, we've did with them before. A good strapping once in a while will keep her in line."

"Isn't she too old for that?"

"She's a child in her head. She needs treating like one."

Joel wondered if the lean-to would be warm enough for Alice once winter came. The walls were rough-sawn planks, the lumber used to build them scavenged from junk piles on the waste ground past the sawmill. Rotmensen never paid for anything he couldn't get for free. The Dutchman had got Mike Obetsky, the cleanup man on the second shift, to haul the oddments of lumber up to the store in a company pickup truck. Joel had ridden in the back. He'd helped Mike load and unload, not knowing then what the room they were building was for.

It was only later he found out they were building a cage to hold her.

The wall boards had been lapped and spiked onto two-by-four studs by Obetsky and Reiner. The high window was crudely cut with a chainsaw and covered over with a pig-wire screen crimped down with fence staples. It sure didn't look like either of them knew the first thing about building an add-on room. But the whole time Reiner kept bragging about how he was the one making the room they'd be keeping the girl in.

"I'm building it and I got the key," he said to Joel as he hammered on the shakes with his claw hammer.

Mike Obetsky had just laughed at that, saying, "The key will be hanging on a chain around Imma's neck."

Joel looked across the deep back lot to where the dirt and gravel sloped by the store. There was only a narrow path beside the wall but it was wide enough for the cedar round he'd placed there, its dusty bark draped with threads of dried bluegrass and blown fir needles. He'd carried the round to the clearing early on after he'd first tried to climb up so he could see through her window and couldn't. Before he got the round he'd had to reach for the sill with his clutched fingers and pull himself up, but when he did she'd heard him struggling there, his boots banging, and cried out for Piet. Desperate, he'd dropped onto the gravel and run across the clearing and hid behind the rusted tractor where the dog was, his hand held tight around its muzzle to keep it from barking. He'd brought it meat he'd saved from the cookhouse to keep it quiet. Two nights later he'd taken the biggest cedar round he could find in Oroville Cranmer's woodpile and carried it to the back of the store. It was tall enough for him to stand on so his eyes could reach the wire.

Behind the lean-to stretched bulldozed gravel with wild grass and shrubs growing. An old Reo truck, its tires gone, the axles resting on boulders, was off in the corner of the lot. Aspen leaves fallen from the thin trees littered the ground beside it, the truck box bent and broken by the heat and cold of the years, the dry winds that swept up the narrow valley from the desert around Kamloops.

The dog lay now under the tractor's curved fender, locked on a twenty-foot chain to the iron steering wheel, the black rubber that had been the grip long ago rotted off and hanging in shreds. The hound lagged its long tongue as it stared across the gravel at him. It didn't bark or howl. Many times these past weeks Joel had filled a Chevy hubcap with water from the tap on the side of the store, or he'd carried leftover pork and steak bones from the cookhouse. The dog knew who he was. It trusted him. Someone else was feeding it too because he'd find chewed bones from moose under the tractor. He didn't know who else was feeding the dog. It didn't matter so long as it didn't starve from Piet's neglect.

Joel had gone to meet the train the Rotmensens brought her in on that early July day. He knew he'd never forget her getting off the train. It was like he'd never really seen a girl before as pretty as her. He stood off to the side just watching, not being able to believe his eyes when he realized she was going to be living in the village.

It seemed like the whole village had watched Piet pull her along, Imma marching behind, all the men talking as she passed by on the crushed gravel and cinders, watching her every step, this girl from nowhere, this girl. Carl Steiner, the station agent, had acted his usual important self, saying this and that when the three of them got off the train, the conductor bowing as Piet took her elbow in his fist.

It was Carl who said he thought the girl was pretty enough for an Indian. "They're pretty if you catch them young," he said. "They don't stay that way long, though. You know—Indians."

Molly Samuels and Carl's wife, Etta, were standing behind him when he said those things. "That's evil thinking," Molly said to him. "They're people too. They're just the same as us." Carl started saying to Molly how she hadn't caught his meaning exactly and that what she'd just said was what he meant exactly.

Etta had stepped in then and told him to shut up about what he thought he knew. "I don't know where I found you," Joel heard her say as she dragged her two kids into the station. When Carl tried to say something more she leaned out the door and said, "Alberta is where, on a road without a correction line. I must've been drunk or blind to pick you out of the poor lot that was there. God only knows why I'm still here. I'd leave if I wasn't trapped by you and the kids." And at that she clapped the door shut.

Carl was still going on about the girl, but Joel didn't care. He couldn't take his eyes off her. He barely heard the end of their talking as he turned and followed Piet and Imma and the girl up to the store. He stayed twenty feet behind, his eyes on her as she stumbled along, her suitcase banging against her leg. Imma kept telling her to hurry and Joel could see she was trying to keep up. He would've done anything to help but all he could do was watch as they stumped up the steps at the store and took her inside.

Joel tried not to think about Imma Rotmensen giving the money to the Brother at the residential school, counting out the ironed bills from that big leather wallet of hers with its polished steel clasps. Or about her saying to Claude that day in the store when Joel was listening, "Come and have a look at her once she gets here. That Brother Whelan said he was sorry to lose her and I can imagine he was." She'd looked close at Claude with those hen-like eyes of hers, the lids coming down on them like half-flushed shutters.

And Claude had said that a good look at a young girl never hurt anybody. Imma didn't say anything to that, just squeezed her eyes down even thinner as if she was adding up something complicated, her mouth tight, her head turned a bit away from Claude like she didn't want him to see how she was thinking.

Joel walked along the trail just below the road. It was the middle of the night and there was no one on the road that led up from the mill and probably no one on the high road north to Little Hell's Gate or south to Mad River. Beyond them was Jasper or Kamloops and after them the world. Joel listened to the night. No one was out prowling, only the grizzly he'd heard banging at a burning drum, and a tick-tormented moose he saw in early rut run across the railway tracks down by the river meadows. The cupped rack of its horns seemed light as curved black feathers under the glow from the last of the moon. He watched until the animal disappeared into a grove of alders.

Wordless, Joel crossed the barren lot, climbed the gravel slope behind the store, and knelt by the round of cedar by the lean-to. He'd counted the rings the first time he'd placed the round there, afraid to climb up so he could see her sleeping, wanting to, but instead of looking, kneeling in the dirt measuring the tree's life, his fingernails stepping ring by ring to the sapling at the heart. He'd counted to himself from the outside ring as a child might in a whisper: thirty-one, thirty-three . . . forty . . . and at forty-four got up off his knees thinking about how the tree the round had been cut from was almost three times as old as he was. Finally he'd placed his right boot on it and laid his hands flat against the lapped cedar wall. He'd balanced himself like a moth on bark, pressed close to the wall, and then he raised his left boot careful up, for a moment rocking there, almost, but not falling over, toes angled out, knees slightly bent, the window at the level of his stetson just above his eyes, the brim pushed back on his head, and then slowly, straining, straightened, his arms outspread on the clapboards as if on a cross, his face risen at last to the pig-wire window.

That night there had been a sickle moon too. It had cast a rim of light on the bed where she lay, he was sure, sleeping. He had not, now he was at last there to see, been able to move. There was the arch of one foot partly out from under the sheet, the toes, all five of them at the sheet's hem looking like impossibly small, naked mice peering out from sun-bleached summer grass, and the curve of her slender ankle disappearing under the tattered cotton. Then her hidden calves, her thighs, and the high curves of her small buttocks covered over, her waist and back, most of her hidden, the sheet fallen from one shoulder, the skin so clean from where it showed from under the pale nightgown she was wearing, and her left arm curled out from the edge of the flat pillow. Her right hand touched her cheek, the fingers curled slightly, lightly. Her face was turned away from him, her black hair undone, splayed across the pillow, the hair loose and long, a flare of darkness that was as much blue as black, glinting as if made from some fragile metal fallen from the moon, and so just to see her breathe, and him, somehow with her, breath for breath, his fingers hooked in the pig-wire, staring down at her sleeping there, Alice.

For how long had he been there, the moon almost gone, the frail light of the false dawn come, the smoke haze from the southern fires that had put the stars out one by one, Venus left behind, a blue diamond gleaming, and Jupiter bright as a drop of wet solder in the east, the planets he knew because his mother had told him once of all things in the heavens their light was sure, unlike the vagrant, blinking stars.

Down the road by the tracks a logging truck started, its engine rumbling, some logger wanting to be the first truck at the log landing up the canyon in hopes of getting three loads if he pushed it hard enough and maybe if he was lucky, the roads dry, the truck not breaking down, maybe, just maybe, four loads maybe for sure, and the power diesels not yet starting up, the lights not coming on in the mill, the millwright, Eddy Draper, sleeping toward the first day of the weekend.

And strange too, another truck so late in the long night, a pickup coming hard out of the dark behind him with its lights off, the glint of metal, black paint barely touched by the sliver of moon behind a cloud, and him only catching a glimpse of it, two men inside, the box piled up with stuff. He couldn't tell who the two men were, the truck gone past in shadowed dust, the wall of the store cutting it off, and then gone up the hill to the high road.

The power diesel's heavy pounding would start in a couple of hours, the cleanup and maintenance men stumbling out of their bunks and heading down to the cookhouse for coffee and breakfast and then to the mill to finish off the work of the week, the shadows of dawn beginning. Monday morning was far off, Saturday already here in the dark. There was a whole day and then the dance at the Hall tonight. And maybe, just maybe, with Imma and Piet gone to Kamloops, Alice would somehow get out of her locked room, if Claude Harper let her out, and go to the dance. And he had to learn how to dance better, today somehow, in case she did come, in case she was there, if he asked her, if he knew how to ask her, because he knew Cliff Waters would be there and for sure he would ask her to dance, Reiner too if Cliff let him, and Cliff knew how to jive and waltz and everything. Joel had seen him dancing with other women before.

"Please, would . . . could you, maybe, like to, want to . . . dance . . . with me, please."

Joel pressed against Rotmensens' lean-to wall, his fingers hooked on the wire, his stetson fallen from his head, and how many times, how few, had he seen her move under the sheet, the moment a week ago when she rolled on her side and he saw, caught, glimpsed, just barely, her naked neck, the wing of a collarbone, and the soft skin below that swallow curve of bone, one small breast swelling, and him balanced there thinking of that breast and not thinking, and slowly turning his head away from her to the mountains across the river, the night still long, and he couldn't remember stepping down off the cedar round, picking up his stetson from the gravel and running wild along the path saying to himself over and over:

"She is what else I want."

—

WANG PO WAS AT PEACE when the mill shut down. The night shift crew had gone, the last cleanup man a shadow on the road, behind him the groan of the great chain as it slowed to a stop in the flume, the last wince of steel licking steel and then the quiet, the kind of silence creatures know when they touch each other at the end of violence, at rest at last. It was at that moment Wang Po emerged from his room and walked alone to the river. The slow susurration of the waters by the big eddy took him back to the Nanjing he knew as a boy by the Qinhuai River, he and his friends sailing lotus lanterns on the river to help the hungry ghosts find their way back to the underworld.

His father had taught him how to make a lantern, the folding and refolding of the paper until it was strong enough to bear a candle and yet light enough to float. There was happiness then around the table, his mother steaming red bean buns, the smells coming from the kitchen. Wang Po was so young then when all was well. They would drink tea and eat and then they would go out to the river and light candles in the lanterns and send them down the river to the Yangtze, him running with the other children along the riverbank in the early night. They followed the lanterns until most of the tiny boats wavered and burned, a few continuing on, their frail lights vanishing in the far waters.

Wang Po sat alone on the smooth white back of a fir tree that had washed high up on the riverbank during some spring flood years ago. This was his eddy in the river, beyond it the beginning of the rapids. It was his night place and though he knew he was not always alone there, his companion did not disturb him. The boy was not always there. Emerson's usual place to watch the river was from a jumble of black rocks high above the shore where the cliffs began. Wang Po looked for him, but he wasn't on the rocks this night and Wang Po missed him. When he turned back to the river the boy had appeared as if from nowhere. Emerson was sitting at the end of the beached tree where the stubbed roots splayed out in search of the place in the earth they had been torn from. It was a comfort to have him there. Wang Po felt they were like any two animals come to rest awhile from the confusions of the day.

Across the river were hidden cabins back in the trees. Art had told Wang Po of them and told him too of the one cabin with glass in its windows, glass that someone had packed in from what would have been Fort Kamloops a century or more ago. Such a short time. Everything was so new in this country where he lived and where he would someday die. He had thought of his death and had at times wondered if he would have his ashes sent back to China, but each time he thought of Nanjing he knew he would never return, alive or dead. Where were his parents' ashes? How could he rest in a place where his parents' spirits wandered without cease?

His would be the first body of his family buried in the New World. If he had children by Chunhua they would outlive him by many years. He had thought at times of having his ashes scattered on the Fraser River where it emptied out into the sea in Vancouver. The North Thompson River at his feet flowed into the Fraser. Each time he came to rest on the tree by the river it pleased him to think that his ashes might someday melt into this northern water.

Wang Po smiled. He had gone far away into his own death and he wondered at his concern for something that was merely the end and the beginning of suffering. His body would die and he would return to go on wandering in *samsara*. He had not lived a peaceful life and even on this day he had indulged in the pipe, his intoxication a continuing betrayal of precepts of the Buddha.

So he would pay for that in his reincarnation, just as he would pay for the Japanese officer he killed in Shanghai who'd murdered what Wang Po had thought was a child.

The starving boy had been down by the docks at the door of a bar in the alley where the soldiers came out to piss. The child had stood in the officer's way when he stepped from the bar and the officer had calmly reached out, turned the child around with his left arm, took out his knife, and cut the boy's throat. He remembered how the officer didn't get any blood on the arm of his uniform. The death had been swift and Wang Po had known instantly that the officer had to have killed many times before for him to so artfully avoid staining himself. It was the casual display of the officer's efficiency that shocked Wang Po, who had seen many terrible crimes in his time in Shanghai. The officer's own death had been as quick.

What he remembered most was not the way the officer had killed the child, and not the officer's own death by Wang Po's hands. It was after, when he looked at the boy lying in the fetid water of a plugged drain. The boy's filthy shift, the only rag he wore, had come open when he fell and Wang Po saw his pubic hair and knew then the boy had been a man. The only thing remaining of what Wang Po would have called the man's body were the bones and the skin that covered them. That and the thin sack of his hanging belly. When he saw the pubic hair he had wished the officer was still alive so he could kill him again except this time more slowly.

The river continued to flow and it took a few moments for Wang Po to come back to the world. He had not thought of the Japanese officer or the man the officer had murdered for a long time. Perhaps his remembering his killing the officer was a way of his killing him again and he would keep on killing him until his own death.

He wondered if knowing he was about to see Art, hear more of the first-aid man's stories, had brought the old memory back to him. Wang Po did not regret its appearance after such a long time. Wang Po thought then of the boy at the other end of the log, but when he turned to look, Emerson was gone. He had vanished as suddenly as he had appeared.

TEN

STUNTED CEDARS ROSE UP OUT OF THE BOG by the gravel lot behind the cookhouse. Joel waited a moment in the shadow of the trees and marked the stink of diesel, a pale smoke stuttering in the air from the power plant. The lights from a logging truck blared past the cookhouse. The truck headed up to the junction and by the sound of it turned north toward the new cutblock above Little Hell's Gate where they were logging.

Was that where the pickup had gone?

Saturday log loads would arrive come dawn, the mill shut down till Monday, a logger hoping to make a few extra bucks working the weekend. Joel gazed at the dark bulk of the sawmill beyond the main-line tracks, the small two-storey station with its grey, weather-burned walls, the light above the short platform by the tracks smouldering with a fitful glow. The freight out of Kamloops would roll through soon and the Express just after dawn. The windows in the station were dark now, the agent and his family asleep.

Somewhere up on the mountainside a machine started high above the road past the shacks where the Sikhs lived. It sounded like the little D4 Cat the company parked by the dump. A crazy night. Who the hell would be up there pushing garbage around? Kids maybe from one of the farms fooling around.

Joel knew Art went to Wang Po's room most weekend nights and always after he'd worked on someone who'd been injured. McAllister's wife had sounded like she was hurt bad. Art would be looking to puff on that pipe of Wang Po's, the one he called his forgetting smoke. Joel asked him once why he called it forgetting and Art said it was because he didn't want to remember what he'd forgotten and the opium took him to a place where nothing was.

Walking out of the shadows he crossed over the rough, bladed ground to the back of the cookhouse. He went in, closing the screen door quietly behind him. Thirty loaves of bread cooled along the counter in the kitchen. The bread hadn't been long from the ovens and Joel breathed deep, the rich smell turning his belly over. He listened at the stairs leading down to the basement where Wang Po lived. Art was down there. Joel could hear their words moving in the dark.

Joel took a loaf from the rack and tore it lengthways with his hands, the white bread breaking open with a fluff of steam. With a butcher knife from the block, he smeared each side with real butter and not the margarine that Wang Po put out on the tables for the crew. He took both chunks to the basement doorway, sat down on the top step, and began to eat, the bread pulp wet and thick, the butter sweet in his mouth and nose.

As he ate, he listened as a word rose like a single soft link of chain from the square of yellow light in the doorway at the bottom of the stairs: "Godelieve."

The name was one Art had said before on other nights in Wang Po's room with its one light hanging from a twisted wire, the yellow glow barely reaching into the corners of the room. Joel slid down to the bottom steps so he could hear better. He could see Wang Po now. The cook smiled at him, but Joel couldn't see Art. He was hidden behind the swung-open door. Joel breathed the smell of opium as it melted in the air around him, listening as Art talked, his voice slow and sometimes stumbling over the spaces between words.

"Tommy was the one went searching in the dark," Art said. "The girl he found was crying. The mother kept saying: Canada? Canada? She spoke our country like it was a question. Dank u. Dank u."

"Same old story," Wang Po said, looking straight at the doorway. He knew Joel was listening.

Turning to the first-aid man, he said, "Listen, Art Kenning, an old poem:

The moon over the northern deserts
means nothing to the soldiers
as they listen to the thunder of the chariots.

Joel leaned forward to listen better, the bread a soft stone in his belly.

"Art, our wars," said the cook quietly. "When are we going to let them go? Everyone is dead back there."

But if Art heard Wang Po he didn't show it. He wasn't in the cookhouse basement room anymore. The whisky and opium had led him back to the flooded fields of the Scheldt peninsula.

"There was no rain in Holland. Not that night. Tommy was cutting gobbets from the pig, someone else's hand reaching for the wet meat barely cooked."

And a voice came out of the night and Art spoke it as she had spoken: "Dank u, Canada, dank u, dank u."

Joel had heard him speak those same words before on other nights at Wang Po's. Art's worst stories always seemed to come after something bad happened. He wondered if what happened to Irene McAllister and Art having to look after it, that maybe that was what started him remembering the Holland story. The woman was Dutch and she was just saying thank you. He listened closely just like he always did. Art was in a place far from him, another world, the stories all his own.

And then Art began:

"There was no moon, only mud, the water deeper, and then the house and barn rising from nowhere. The buildings were on an island, the polders flooded by the Germans when they broke the dikes, what road there'd been had slumped into the sea. We were worn out by the skirmishes, the foraging, crazy wandering trying to find the enemy. Don't you see? The fields were water, the road ahead gone. The fence around the house was crushed before ever we got to the farm, the posts and palings broken, the ground torn up by a tank that'd been there probably only a few hours before, the tread marks German, a Panzer IV."

Joel took his hat off and moved forward so he could see better as Art's hand lowered a whisky bottle to the floor by his boot. The bottle sat there like a small obedient animal. To him it seemed like Art's cat begging, the small beast Art kept alive to talk to in his cabin by the river. Joel lifted the last chunk of bread and chewed on the crust at the end, the butter melted deep in the dough.

Some nights all Art seemed to have was a story. Joel loved him talking about the war and wondered if he'd ever have the chance to go and fight in one, maybe not the Germans or Japs, but maybe the Russians, and not in Holland but somewhere, maybe even here.

Art began to speak again, his voice low and monotonous, the old story from other nights, but not like it was being told tonight. As he listened, Joel felt he was inside the world Art spoke of, his Holland, his war. It was like he was trying to explain something to himself.

"The wall was blown away, part of the roof gone, the kitchen open to the night. A stump of candle burned on a small table in the middle of what was somehow still a room, plates and knives and forks arranged on the table. There were two places set, one plate was pushed back, the knife and fork crooked. And a salt shaker tipped over, the brass top gone, the white crystals strewn on the cloth, shining like crushed silver. The woman was sitting there under the clouds, her hands cupped around the candle. The spilled salt below her hands seemed eroded from her bones. Cran and Elsted were just outside the light. I don't know where we picked them up. They were two Calgaries who'd followed us in. They'd been looking to get away from the war awhile and when they saw our tank they picked us to follow and find a hole to hide in. It's like they knew who we were, who we were going to become. I stepped past the two of them into what was left of the kitchen. There were chunks of wall on the floor."

Joel stepped into the light, ducking his head under the low doorway. Wang Po lay on his cot, his pipe beside him, a thread of smoke rising from the bowl. It smelled like Indian paintbrush burning on the wood stove at home, the smell of the alpine in the flowers he'd picked for his mother, her scattering them on the hot stove because she liked the scent of their smoke when they burned.

"You sit down," Wang Po said to Joel. He pointed at the wooden chair across from Art. "You want a drink? Art Kenning has whisky in his bottle."

"Yes."

Wang Po smiled. "Maybe he will give you some?"

Joel nodded yes again.

"Art Kenning," Wang Po said, his hand out, a thin bird fluttering. "Maybe the boy can have a drink, yes?"

When Art didn't say anything, Wang looked at Joel. "Art Kenning is drunk and he smokes the poppy. Doesn't hear me, doesn't hear you. Hey, Art Kenning. Listen," he said, and began to sing, so soft Joel had to lean to hear him:

I was a boy when I left home.
I come back an old man.

Art turned his head slightly and looked at the cook.

Wang Po's laugh was kind, so soft as he sang it again, this time in Chinese, his language full of the familiar strange sounds. "You like my words?" Wang Po said. "I made them in English for you."

Art didn't seem to hear him. He went on with his story.

"The woman got up from the table. She peered at us out there in the dark and said for the first time our country. Canada, she said. Dank u, dank u. Her hands hung down at her sides, tiny salt crystals falling from her fingers. Her hands didn't seem alive. Tommy came to the lip of the broken wall and stood by Cran and Elsted. He nudged Cran and they both grinned at her. Tommy was rubbing his stomach. He pointed at the empty plates and asked her if there was something to eat. The woman took six steps to where the wall used to be and took two to the side. It was like she wanted to walk through where the kitchen door used to be. Her arms were still hanging. She turned as if in wonder that the door was gone. It wasn't there and then . . . and then she just walked off into the night. We didn't try to stop her. It wasn't like there was very far she could go. There was the barn, a bit of road, part of a field, and a cluster of trees back behind the house, what looked like part of an orchard stretching away, a kind of tumbled-looking shed out there in what was maybe a pasture. The part of it you could see was higher ground. The rest was water, an island that wasn't there before. We'd come in past that field. What looked like a bit of vegetable garden was out there. We all watched her walk away. I remember hoping she wouldn't return. But she had to come back unless she wanted to drown. Tommy followed her along the side of the house. He wasn't going to let her get away anywhere even though he knew she couldn't unless she decided to swim. Easy, Tommy, Alvin said, but Tommy didn't turn around. He didn't want to hear anything from Alvin."

Wang Po spoke into the brief silence. "What happened tonight, Joel?"

"It was the sawyer. Jim McAllister," said Joel. "His wife got cut."

"Cut?"

Wang Po closed his eyes.

Wang Po took the pipe over to Art. He placed the stem in Art's mouth and the first-aid man breathed the pale smoke, shaking his head slowly. He pulled on the stem as if it was a fish hook and Wang Po was trying to pull something out of his skull.

Wang Po followed Art's head with the pipe, Art's mouth chewing on the stem and then his teeth loosening, his lips slack as he let it go. As Wang Po swept the pipe away it drifted past Joel's face, Joel breathing the remnant smoke.

"Alvin should've done something," said Art. "He was the corporal."

Wang Po laid the pipe on the table and picked up the whisky bottle. He poured a little into a glass.

"Here. You drink this," he said, handing the glass to Joel. And then turning, said to Art: "Yes, my friend, he is the corporal in your story."

There was silence and Wang Po said, "Listen. The story is beginning again."

Wang Po settled himself on the cot. He said, "Art Kenning is having a talk with one of the ghosts. They are inside him, the ones he won't let go."

To Joel the cook looked like he was melting. It's the smoke, Joel thought. I'm breathing that dragon smoke.

"Alvin shrugged when Tommy followed the Dutch woman. He told Cran and Elsted to get a big fire going. They started ripping palings from the fence. It was cold in Holland. You could smell the winter coming in on the wind from the North Sea. I watched the men tear up the fence. The candle on the table was flickering. I held my palm over the flame. The fire was a thing in my hand. I held it for a while. I didn't mind it burning me. Cran started breaking boards over his knee and piling them like he knew how to build a fire, Elsted going back for more wood. Alvin told them to put the fire farther away from the house. That's when Tommy came back, the woman trailing after him. He was dragging a burlap sack of potatoes, a smaller one over his shoulder clinking. The woman's muddy skirts were hiked up her calves. Tommy was laughing. Look what I got, he said, and I knew he meant more than just potatoes. Those were bottles clinking in that small sack."

"You want some bread?" Wang Po asked.

"Bread?"

"New bread upstairs," said Wang Po.

Joel told him he'd already ate some.

"Listen, Art Kenning. Song from the old times. No one wrote it down. I learned it a long time ago."

Snow in the mountains. A bitter cold.
Everywhere I look you are not there.
The wind fills the holes in the snow.
The tracks I follow are my own.

Wang Po's song quieted Art. Joel didn't know if Art heard the words or if it was just the sound of the cook's voice that had calmed him. The sounds he made were high and fleeting as if the words themselves were running away.

Art reached down and picked up his glass, but it was empty. He looked at it for a moment, bewildered, and Wang Po stepped over and filled it from the bottle. The whisky in the glass danced and Art, unable to lift it without spilling, leaned his face down to it until his mouth met the rim and then lifted the glass and his head at the same time, the whisky slipping between his lips.

"It was wet in Nanjing, Art. Everyone was dead."

"Nanjing?" Joel asked.

"Nanjing." Wang Po smiled as he looked at Joel. "There are many wars, boy."

"Nanjing?"

"It was the wharf beside the Qinhuai River, everyone falling into the water. My new friend in my arms."

"Where?"

"Nanjing."

"Where's Nanjing?"

"China," said Wang Po. "Nanjing was a city in a war. Not Art's war. There were many people dead in Nanjing. A city of the dead."

"Do you come from there?"

"From Nanjing. A long time ago."

"Who killed them?"

"Cipango."

"Who?"

"The same people you call Japan."

"We're the ones killed the Japs," said Joel. "We killed Germans too."

"You are a boy," said Wang. "You don't know women with bayonets pushed up inside them, hands cut off, breasts cut off. You don't know babies burning. Tanks crushing bodies for pleasure. Men with their heads in their arms, necks talking to the clouds. A cut neck farts blood. You drink whisky, okay? Happy, happy. You like, you like?" And he laughed as he turned in a circle. "Me? I'm just a crazy old Chinaman-chink. I don't know nothing."

"Stop," said Joel. "That isn't funny. You aren't that." He got up and poured a little more whisky into his glass. "I never knew about Nanjing before, that's all," he said.

"It sounds like a bell, that word," Art said.

"Sometimes when a bell is poured it is left alone for many years before it is struck," Wang Po said.

Joel was getting lost. What did a bell have to do with anything?

"It must first learn the sounds of the wind before it is played," Wang Po added.

"I don't understand," Joel said, the whisky and smoke clouding his head.

"It was a war. But listen now," he said as Art began to speak again.

"Alvin saw it first. The little pig was grubbing in the mud at the edge of the berm behind the barn. It had survived the Germans on their pullback to Walcheren island. They were living off the land, the Germans, foraging just like the pigs were. But the Germans had missed the shoat. It was Alvin caught it. Cran and Elsted drove it into deep water and Alvin waded out almost up to his chest and hauled it by the hind legs back to land. Alvin said the shoat was swimming for England. We killed ourselves laughing at that. It was Tommy did it. Alvin was on his ass holding the pig in his arms and laughing while it kicked. Pigs scream like children, like women do when they're held wrong and can't be let go. As Alvin laughed Tommy reached down and pushed the pig's snout up under Alvin's chin and cut its throat. The blood sprayed out across Alvin's arms. For a moment I thought it was Alvin's throat Tommy cut, but then Alvin let the pig go. The shoat grabbed hold of the ground with its feet, but it just stood there on legs that wouldn't do what they were supposed to do. Not anymore.

"Alvin stood up and him and Tommy watched it die into its own blood. Men die like that. Germans mostly, but our own too. The Calgary Highlanders. The shoat. Tommy wiped off his face with his shirt. He was half naked when he gutted it. The offal piled around his feet. The blood in the water looked like sheet copper forgotten in the rain. And then the guns began again off to the west. The ships were shelling Walcheren. I knew we'd be leaving the farm at daybreak, water or no water, roads or no roads."

Art stopped as Wang Po held the pipe stem to his mouth. He closed his eyes again and Wang Po sang.

Coming home in the dark through the broken fields
My cane tangles in the weeds and scattered stones.
Walls in the temple, black from forgotten fires.
I ask an old man to tell me where my mother lives now.
He points to a faint star adrift among the clouds.

"You sing different than us," Joel said.

Wang Po's laugh was the sound of grass scraping on rocks.

"Listen. Listen to Art's war."

"Johnny speared the carcass on an iron bar he found in the barn. He tied the pig around it with brass wire from a roll he had in the tank. The coils bit into the skin. Cran made a handle with a pair of long-handled locking pliers from the tank and Elsted started turning the shoat over the fire. The hairs in the pig's ears turned to flame, the ears beginning to burn. No one cared. Somebody, Cran, I think, pushed potatoes into the hot coals at the edge. We drank the brandy and watched. The woman? I don't know where she was when we were drinking. She wasn't mine to worry about. We were leaving in the morning. It didn't take long before we were tearing off bits of crackling. We couldn't wait anymore. We hadn't had fresh meat in a week. Forage was scant in the Scheldt. Fat kept dripping onto the coals. Little bright fires splurting. Tommy was hunched over the blackened pig. He cut off chunks of meat and tossed us gobs of half-cooked pork. Tommy was nineteen. Only that and the worse for it. Another East End kid from Vancouver. He kept that knife of his razor sharp. Some nights it got so I thought I'd go nuts listening to his steel slide across the Washita stone in the firelight, Tommy spitting, and then, *slick-slick, slick-slick*. The steel sounded like skin slipping on a wet mirror."

"Here's another song for you, Art Kenning."

In the desert the soldiers wake among bones.
They break camp as vultures circle the heavens.

"What does it mean?" Joel asked after a silence.

Wang Po breathed smoke, wisps in his black hair. "From the old time," he said. "A bad-dream song about war."

"Alvin kept raking potatoes out of the coals. The husks were charred, the insides steaming. Tommy sheathed his knife in its scabbard. It hung from a braided leather belt he took off a German officer we found in a ditch. It was after Caen. Tommy was squatted down by the fire and chewing on a shard of crackling. There was grease all down his chin. It dripped on the Iron Cross swinging from his throat. The medal he stole was on a string around his sparrow neck. All the time he was chewing Tommy never took his eyes off the woman, a knot of pig gristle stuck in the corner of his mouth. He had no right to steal what wasn't his."

Joel sat and listened. His head was strange inside. His eyes closed.

"The woman. The candle was cupped in her hands. Her ring was almost worn away. It was like the moon just before it isn't anymore. That last slice thin as a fuse burning ten miles away. I look at paintings in my head. Everything bleeds in the dark. The shadows were so hungry they ate themselves. The candle flame was impossible. It flicked at her skin, at her hair. Blonde clots lay on her shoulders. Up inside her frayed collar were her wing bones white beneath her throat. I can see the flowers on her dress. Blotched poppies. They were the colour of the shoat's blood in the gobbets the men had ate. Watery blood and brandy to thin it. I looked at her slack breasts and looked away. I was so ashamed. Tommy wasn't. Tommy Bilkowski. He stared at her across the fire. He was whispering to the Calgaries.

Cran had that stupid grin on his face. Elsted kept giggling. The ring on her finger told me she had a man. Of course, there had to be one. We were on a farm, for Christ's sake. There was a barn. There were animals or at least there used to be animals. That pig had to have been hers. She was all alone. But I didn't want to know what she was feeling."

"Long time ago, Art Kenning."

"He never told it like this before," said Joel.

"Art's war."

"The story is different than the times before."

"Each day we get older the story gets older. It changes with our lives. That is the way of stories."

Joel hunched down as he waited for Art to begin again.

"She was alone in the candlelight. I wanted to say something, thank her for the potatoes, maybe, thank her for the brandy, the pig. I knew what the men were thinking. When I stood by her, the light from the candle crept into her hair. Can you imagine light hiding? I said I was sorry. I was hopeless as that. I looked at the men and knew the only sure thing was not to feel anything. She lifted her hands from the candle. She stood up and took my sleeve and walked me into the house. It was after we ate at the shoat. There was still some left hanging from the wire. I turned once and saw Elsted twist a leg off the pig. He was rotten drunk. There were bones and bits of meat and scorched potato husks scattered on the dirt. I followed her down a narrow hall into a room at the back of the house. When I got there she took a picture out of a drawer and held it to her chest. Her bed was in that room. I cringed to see it so neat. I remember thinking how she must have believed pulling up the covers over two pillows and smoothing a quilt out somehow made the war not there. As if a careful bed could be a safe place. The window was blown in. The quilt was a sunflower.

Crumbs of brick and dust and splinters were sprayed across it. I wish I never saw that bed.

"I took the photograph from her hand. Godelieve, she said. At first I'd thought it was her name, but it wasn't. No one asked her what her name even was. Not once. Not me. I didn't. Even when I tried to help her she never had her name. The photograph had her in it. She was younger when it was taken. I knew the look on her face in the picture was one she'd never have again. A man was with her, the farmer, the husband, the father, and between them was a young girl. The girl was the girl named Godelieve."

It was the name Joel had heard on the stairs. Half in dreaming, the smoke soft in his head, Joel said, "What?"

"She had on a dress, something that was trying to be special, tiny buttons sewed in a circle just above what were her first breasts. The girl wasn't looking at the camera. She was holding her father's hand and she was lost in his blunt fingers. I don't know. She had on her face what you'd call a fleeting smile. It was a smile that got caught by the camera just as it tried to run away, a smile there only for a moment and going just as the shutter closed. The kitchen wall that was gone was in the picture behind them. There were flowers in a pot by the door. I'd seen bits and pieces of that pot in the rubble outside. The spilled flowers were ruined geraniums, the blossoms like clenched blood. The girl in the picture looked maybe nine or ten. Eighteen years and I still see it, her smile flying away like a bat into the dark. The woman reached out and took the picture away from me. She braced the wood frame against the worn poppies on her belly and looked up at me with the kind of helplessness women get when they think they've lost everything and suddenly know it's not over, not yet. There's never an end to losing, there's always something more."

"*You are a river gull lost in the canyons,*" Wang Po said into the quiet.

Joel listened, a thin silk of smoke shivering above his head.

"The woman was younger in the picture. It's who she was back in '33 or '34. When we were at the farm she was older. There were ghosts in her eyes made of rain. The man in the picture was holding the daughter's hand, the husband, the farmer, the father. Who else? The woman sat on the edge of the bed saying, *Boche*, *Boche*, *Boche*. She whispered the words like some strange prayer. I led her back to the ruined kitchen with her still saying it. The picture was pressed into her belly. When she got there Tommy untangled her fingers from the frame like he was undoing a knot. I didn't stop him. I don't know why. He took the woman by the wrist after he looked at the photograph. I knew even then, I knew. That bubble of pig gristle was still stuck in his grin. I said no, but he walked away with her. The woman didn't struggle. Not even at all. She walked like she was already dead. He looked back at me only once. Tommy, I called. He grinned at me and I knew saying Tommy's name wouldn't be enough. When he came out of the dark he had the girl. The woman, the mother, was behind them. She kept putting her hand on Tommy's back as if by touching him she could make him let the girl go. The woman must have hidden her daughter as soon as she heard us coming along the dike road. The girl was what the woman had left. Her Godelieve."

Wang Po was curled up on his bed, his eyes closed, singing.

The night guards have returned, their eyes closed.
Only the owl remembers the stars.
Its long sorrow is the song of a war without end.
The guns are silent, the far fires turned to ash.
The morning has broken with the screams of gulls.
Another night passed in the dreams of horses and men.

"Tommy knew when first he saw the woman she wasn't alone. He'd seen the two places set at the table: two plates, two knives, two forks. And she was the one brought the picture out to where Tommy was. I don't know why she did that. I don't even know why she showed it to me. There was the smell of the burned meat, the stink of the men, the mist, and the rot lifting from where the tank treads had torn the ground. There were a hundred wars in that dirt. You could dig anywhere and come up with a sword or spear or a Lee–Enfield or Browning. There was grease and oil, shit, sweat, jism, and blood in that dirt. It was worn into our uniforms, our hands. There was water all around us. We were on an island in drowned fields that stretched all the way to the sea. Out in the west were the guns of Walcheren. Ours and theirs. Oh hell, Johnny was the first to follow Tommy when he took the girl into the barn. Cran and Elsted were close behind. Alvin stayed outside with me. He was the corporal, but he didn't say anything to them or to me. He just started breaking more fence palings and throwing the pieces into the fire. What was left of the shoat was burning by then. I looked around for the mother, but she was gone. When I finally saw her she was out in the sea too far to find. Her dress was floating around her like a broken flower. There are nights I can't close my eyes. I remember Tommy's blade cutting the meat, his knife a slow scythe."

I fish for minnows in the lake.
Just born, they have no fear of man.
And those who have learned,
Never come back to warn them.

"Su Tung Po's death song," said Wang Po. "At the end of his life he sang this song."

———

THE SMOKE IN THE AIR had left Joel in a world where a pig burned on a fire and a woman and a girl danced in a picture frame filled with water. He lifted his head and looked at Wang Po. The cook's hands were moving above Art's head and he was singing in his strange tongue. His voice was soft and slow. Joel's mother would have called his song a keening, but Joel didn't think men keened. Only women made sounds like that.

And old Chinamen, Wang Po might say.

Joel tried but couldn't get up off the floor. He tried to lift his empty glass but fumbled it and the glass rolled away. It was the best he could do. He felt like throwing up.

It didn't seem like the first-aid man had moved since he first sat down. Joel watched as Wang Po took the pipe from Art's hand and tapped it on the lip of the porcelain cup, a grey nugget and dust.

"All gone," the cook said, "all over," and he patted Art's head as if talking to a child.

He nudged Joel's leg with his red slipper. "Get up, boy," he said.

"What?"

"Take Art Kenning home."

"Did he finish his story?"

"All ashes, that story," said Wang Po. "He won't let the dead sleep."

"I don't understand."

"He keeps them in a room in his head," he said. "It is where they live now." Wang Po kicked lightly at Joel's foot with his worn slipper. "You take Art Kenning home."

Art's head lolled to one side, his mouth open, a grey pearl in the corner of his eye.

"Why's he like that?" asked Joel as he pulled his hat down

on his head. It seemed too tight for him and he wondered if his head had grown while he was breathing that smoke.

"Art Kenning is a good man," said Wang Po. "Bad things happen in war to men like him."

"You were in Nanjing," Joel said. "That was a war too."

"I am not so good a man," said Wang Po. "I crossed the river when others couldn't. I didn't turn back. The last thing I saw was a mouse swimming in the river. I saved it from drowning." He placed the pipe on the low table. "Never mind Nanjing. That place is lost among the willows across the river."

Wang Po leaned into Art and whispered. All Joel could hear was the faint rasp of Wang Po's breathing, the words faint and far away. As the cook spoke, Art lifted slowly, his body leaning to the side. Joel got up off the floor and stepped behind Art before he fell over. The chair tumbled to the side and Art began to shuffle, taking Joel with him. It felt to Joel like they were dancing to a song he couldn't hear, Art sliding inside Joel's hands, his feet flopping like he had broken ankles, uneasy knees. Joel put his arms all the way around Art's chest.

Art stopped and mumbled, "Okay. I'm okay." He tried to shrug him off, Joel lifting him and him almost falling back.

Joel let him slowly go.

Art swayed but held his ground. His eyes were slit as if the lids had been cut with a razor.

Wang Po said, "Go home. The gulls will start screaming soon."

And they were outside the cookhouse, a high wind crying across the trees.

Art pushed Joel away. "Leave me alone."

Joel watched him stumble across the gravel reach by the cookhouse where the road headed into the village.

Maybe Art would go home.

The village was quiet, the night shift over. The dim light in the drying yard glowed, the stacks of lumber sprawled around it like heavy animals dead on their knees. Joel glanced at the cookhouse and caught the dark of Wang Po's room, the light in the narrow window at the foot of the wall going suddenly out. He wondered for a moment what Wang Po did when he was down there alone in his cave, if he ever missed his home in China. Nanjing, where the war had been.

Joel had only ever felt lonely in the village since Alice came. His sudden wanting never to be alone again was the beginning of loneliness. It was a new kind of fear. It had entered him like a cage enters an animal.

It seemed like the only person Wang Po ever talked to was Art and even then he never said much. When he did, Joel had trouble understanding him. Joel thought Wang Po talked the way a river talks, in swirls and eddies.

Wang Po never went into the village and never went across the tracks to the mill. Joel had seen him on his night walks down by the river where the big eddy turned and turned in its circle. The only other times Joel saw him leave the cookhouse were to take the kitchen garbage out to the oil barrel drums and that time in the spring when he'd caught the train south to Vancouver. He left in the middle of breakup during the high snows last melting, the bush roads impassable. He was gone a week.

The creeks had overflowed their banks and the roads in the bush had become ruts of mud and gravel, some of them washed away by slides. The few trucks that tried for a load remained in the backcountry sunk to their axles in mudholes and gravel slides. Claude had shut the mill down, the workers living on what they'd saved. It could be three weeks or three months before the mill started up again, everyone said. Art told Joel breakup or no breakup, Claude would've shut the mill down anyway. Lumber prices were at rock bottom in the States. And in late spring when the prices rose the sawmill started up again, Claude scrambling to find a crew. When he found Jim McAllister he was happy. A good sawyer was hard to find. Camp cooks too.

Wang Po had only the cot he slept on, two wooden chairs, and a table with a few books on it, the curling pages held down by what Art called his chrysanthemum stones, quartz splayed across the rock like fractured flowers. The books had soft white paper for covers with string stitching and Chinese writing down the side. The writing looked like grouse tracks in snow and Joel always wondered how anyone could make sense of them. Joel had opened a book once when Wang Po and Art were smoking and the book had the same strange writing on the pages inside. They were stick pictures, complicated drawings of things. Wang Po had tried to explain them to him and it made a kind of sense.

Behind the books were three black cardboard folders held together with faded red strings. There were two pottery jars, one with pens in it and the other with thin brushes. Art had told him some of the brushes were made of wolf and deer and others made of scraped feathers. There were even some that were nothing more than sticks frayed at the end as if they'd been chewed. Beside them was a dish with a damp pool of black ink covered by a chamois, and there were a water glass and other, smaller jars, but what was in them Joel didn't know. Art had told him that Wang Po made drawings in the folders with the pens and brushes. One of the pictures had been pinned crooked to the wall above the table. The drawing was of a girl. She didn't look grown-up enough to be a woman.

Art had told him the drawing was Wang Po's new wife in Shanghai.

"Wang Po is saving his money so he can bring her here," Art said. "The drawings are who he imagines. They've never met."

Joel asked how Wang Po could have a wife as young as the one in the drawing and Art told him the marriage was arranged. "He sends money to the family. When he's paid the bride price in full he'll give them the passage money and they'll send her here."

To Joel the cook was old, a man with a wispy beard, shapeless clothes and slippers, and black, black eyes. Those eyes of Wang Po's had lights dancing in them, tiny flashes, winter water.

The woman was only a few lines of ink. It didn't show her feet, just a dress hanging down, her hands inside long sleeves. In the picture she was standing sideways and looking back over her shoulder. Art told him the drawing was beautiful. Joel didn't know how Art saw things. To Joel the picture was sad, the woman lost, someone Wang Po had made up, not someone real.

But maybe that's what beautiful was to the first-aid man and maybe to Wang Po too. Maybe to be beautiful you had to be lost. Joel wished it was a photograph, a real picture where you could see what she was instead of lines of ink on paper. Everything in the drawing was black and grey and white except for a thin red line running down a seam on the side of her dress where an edge of cloth was folded over. Wang Po told him the woman in the picture was as young as wind that rises to melt snow in the wrong season. Joel didn't know what he meant. The only wind he knew that did that was the chinook, a warm wind that blew over the mountains from the ocean and melted the winter snow out on the plains.

Remembering the picture Wang Po drew made Joel think of Alice again and how she'd be awake now, the light streaming across the top of the sky above the mountains. Joel had stared through the pig-wire window a lot of mornings and each time she started to open her eyes he'd duck his head and listen to her feet on the creaking one-by-six boards as she went to the bucket in the corner to pee. It near drove him crazy to hear her pissing.

Thinking of it he felt like the little hunchback kid who used to live behind the post office in Nakusp with his crazy mother. The boy's father had died in the war. He was a funny-looking kid with crooked, bony hands and a humped back. His tiny knuckles were sharp as blades. He loved punching fists. No matter if there was blood running down his wrists and his skin cut to ribbons, he never stopped. Joel felt like him some nights, his head hunched into his narrow shoulders, his fists clenched tight, but why he felt like that he didn't know.

What Joel remembered most from the times he'd seen Alice wake was her smell. It was warm like when a young animal in a barn rises from the straw at dawn. The first time he smelled her he'd had to press himself hard against the wall to keep from falling. He'd wanted so bad to look at her and maybe see her take off her nightshirt, the thin cotton slipping up over her head.

Her smell drove him as crazy as Myrna's did.

But he couldn't go there again now that it was almost light. Someone would see him for sure. Other trucks were starting to move, lamps going on inside some of the cabins. The sky above the mountains was a faded bruise.

There was a world he wanted to hold on to but he didn't know how to hold on to anything.

Joel picked up the first-aid kit Wang Po had handed him at the cookhouse door. Art was ahead of him, staggering as he walked the road across from the bunkhouses. He turned up onto the trail Joel had taken earlier in the night and not the worn path that led down to his river cabin. Joel knew Art was going back to check on Irene McAllister.

A frog creaked small and lonely from the bog behind the bunkhouses. Joel clicked his tongue and the frog stopped croaking and everything got quieter. He stepped through the broken grass in the ditch and moved into the trees. Art wouldn't want him tagging along up to McAllister's so he moved with each tree, each rock and stump, keeping just far enough behind so Art wouldn't see him.

A lamp came on in a shack they passed, a pale face staring between two ragged curtains at the night. There was a muffled groan in a cabin, then silence, a child crying quietly in another, then nothing. It was the fading dark of Saturday morning and most people were buried in their beds, sleeping off going to the bar in Blue River, or lying in the dark thinking about getting up, their sullen, watchful kids wanting breakfast, mothers and wives angry over what happened the night before, men gulping down air with their heavy snores, dreamless and still as snakes in a drought. The Friday liquor train had given most people reason enough to slumber or to seethe.

Joel came around a stump and saw Art kneeling by the creek. The first-aid man was cupping water and thin gravel from a pool and rubbing it into his face. As Joel set down the first-aid kit it fell over and Art reached out and pulled the kit toward him, the corner of it wet.

"I know where you're going," Joel said.

Art ignored him as he lifted another handful of rough sand and water into his face and scoured his skin.

"Wang Po told me to make sure you went to your cabin."

Art fell back on his heels.

Joel said, "Why do you have to go back there?"

Art stood slowly and pulled his shirt out of his pants, drying his face on the tails. His eyes looked like something dead had been dragged through them.

"Go to the bunkhouse and get some sleep, Joel."

"Wang Po said."

"Wang Po's got nothing to do with this."

"You're going up there to see that Irene McAllister."

Art rolled his head to the side and looked at him.

"I was outside before when you fixed her up," said Joel. "I was walking the trail is all. I heard what happened, what she said in there. I know she cut herself."

"Jim'll send you broken down the line if he finds out you know about that," said Art. "What were you doing listening at Jim's trailer?"

"Nothing."

"Don't lie," said Art, taking a deep breath and letting it out slowly. His hands hung between his legs like broken leaves. He seemed to struggle for a moment and then he rolled his shoulders and took another heavy breath. "You spend too damned much time looking in windows and listening outside doors. It's going to get you in trouble some night," he said, rubbing his eyes against his sleeve.

"What about Ernie Reiner?" Joel said. "Sometimes he's up at McAllister's trailer too."

"Ernie goes up there?"

"I've seen him go in there. Jim knows him."

"Jesus," said Art. "I knew they hang around together, but up at the trailer? Reiner?"

"Yup," said Joel and then, because Art looked so stricken, asked, "Are you okay?"

Art leaned out from the tree's shadow and almost fell. For a moment he looked bewildered, staring at Joel as if seeing him for the first time.

"What're you doing here anyway?"

"Wang Po told me to take you home," said Joel.

"No," said Art, staring off into the trees. "I should've done something."

Art was looking far away again. It was like he was there and wasn't. "But you did," Joel said.

"The only thing I did was nothing."

"I don't understand."

The branch Art had been holding swung away. He picked up the kit and walked slowly across the narrow bridge, the planks bowing a little under him.

"Go home, kid." Saying that, Art looked around as if trying to understand where he was.

Joel stared at Art's confusion. He'd seen it before, but this time it was worse than ever. Again, Art said to Joel, this time quieter, "Go home, please."

Joel stood by the pool and watched Art go up the path. Each step the first-aid man took seemed to take a long time. Joel waited until Art disappeared into the dark.

ELEVEN

ART LOOKED UP THROUGH THE TREES rising around him. The stars had faded, Venus low in the south, a single faint light steady above the nameless mountains. The sky had touched upon a pale blue the day would never know again. Only the last of night could touch it. Art felt sometimes he could drink such light, could empty the sky of its colour.

He stepped around a boulder, stumbled over a root, and fell to his knees, his kit skittering down the trail. He knelt there, his hands bracing him against the dirt, and then slowly got up and brushed away the fir needles, grit, and dust on his legs. Small, terrible creatures crawled in his belly, more terrible ones in his head. They wouldn't stop eating him. He wiped at the sweat on his face, his sleeve coming away wet as he carefully got up, picked up the kit, and began to walk again.

He could hear Joel's feet on the path behind him. He swore again, but who or what he cursed he didn't know. The kid should be tired out from the long hours he spent balanced on the cedar round at the lean-to back of Rotmensens' store, let alone the hours in Wang Po's room listening to God knows what. Did the kid never sleep? And what was his plan for Myrna Turfoot? If she wasn't in trouble now, she would be. The girl wasn't slow, she was different. One thing, she was alive in ways another girl might take years to figure out. If it was his own daughter he'd kick Joel's ass all the way to Mad River Junction and then drown him.

And Art was surprised Reiner and his cronies hadn't caught Joel watching the Indian girl. They had to be stupid not to know. Where did they imagine Joel went when he crawled out of bed in the night? Yet Joel was pretty smart about what he did around Reiner and the others. Art knew that. Joel would make sure no one was awake or around before heading up to the lean-to. Art didn't like to think about what they'd do if they found out about Joel peering in at Alice. Especially Reiner. He tormented the kid enough as it was. He'd have a field day if he found out the kid looked in her window. The boy's life was misery enough.

A wisp of woodsmoke slipped past his nose, some morning fire in a shack back in the bush, early coffee burbling. The opium from Wang Po's had drifted away. He was no good without it. He needed a drink, a pipe even, and though he'd sworn to give it up, morphine, a needle. That or, God knows, sleep, but he wasn't sure of sleep. He wasn't sure he knew what sleep was anymore. There were the nightly ravings, the noise as he thrashed on the bed, the cat staring as he woke himself up with his shouting.

He'd dreamed the war again when he was down at the cookhouse and now he wondered if he'd talked too much while he was smoking that black rice and guessed maybe he had. He hoped he hadn't talked too much about those days.

Hell, he didn't even know the kid was there until he was leaving. God knows what he heard him say. The bloody war.

He tried to imagine a loneliness so great it would make a woman pick up a man's hunting knife and cut herself with it. Whoever Irene McAllister was, she thought she'd lost it all. But Art thought again there was no end to losing. He hoped what he'd done for her was enough, the stitches, the penicillin. That drug had saved a lot of men.

Booze. Morphine. Opium. They were the drugs that saved his own life back in the war.

Were they saving him now? He didn't know.

What was his life that he should save it?

The knife she'd used had probably been dirty. Jim had skinned and gutted moose and bear with it. Short of boiling the blade for an hour there was no way it could have been clean.

But Art wouldn't let her get sick.

There in that narrow trailer all by herself day after night after day. What kind of fear did she have in her to keep herself hidden away? No matter the rare moments when she was seen at the store. It was as if Jim tied her up or something. He wouldn't put it past McAllister doing that, but he figured Jim didn't need to. She was just too frightened, Art figured. Or was her hiding in there all she knew how to do?

By God, the first sign of something going wrong Art would have her out of that trailer and down to the hospital in Kamloops. And fuck Jim McAllister if he tried to stop him. Fuck Claude too.

"No one's going to die," he said. And then, as if to the river, the valley, and the mountains surrounding him, he cried, "This village, this mill, these people."

He stopped and turned in a circle, shocked by the sound he'd made. He was sure it was an animal that'd cried out, not him.

But it wasn't an animal. It was him. He had made the noise.

He bit his lip and tasted wet iron, slick on his tongue. He kicked at a loose rock and it caromed off a boulder, clicked against a tree, and vanished into the tangle of saskatoon brush. He turned past a clump of stunted alders and stopped dead at the sudden, musty scent of bear. The rank smell reached into him like a knife pushed deep in meat. He choked, took a step back, and stopped at a hump of root pushed out from a stump.

The bear was close.

He stood and waited till he could breathe. His mind was still tangled by the hours at the cookhouse. He cupped his hands to his cheeks and tried to hold himself steady. He couldn't tell where the bear was, higher up the slope in the trees or off in the scrub. The stench hung over him in a pall. His boot pressed on the root, the other tense in the dirt, ready to stand his ground or cut down through the trees and brush, but he knew if it came to him running the bear would catch him before he took ten steps. He touched a spruce branch, the needles prickling his fingers. His skin was alive.

And the kid behind him?

What about Joel?

He licked at what wasn't a breeze, his own breath, in and out, a slick whisper sliding across his dry teeth as he stared into the dark.

There was what seemed a great fir stump off the trail between two alders.

It hadn't been there before.

The tree closest to the hulk trembled, leaves ashiver.

There wasn't, was, nothing, something, there.

The bear.

Aahhhhh, huh huh huff, broke the quiet.

And silence moved.

Art stared at the great shadow among shadows, the huge heavy shoulders, the wet glint of a single tiny eye.

Grizzly.

The bear moved its great head slow and looked long at him as if to weigh him somehow and then, done, it turned away knowing what it needed to know of him, turned away not in disdain, but as if to have acknowledged his presence.

As if.

An impossible quiet going among the trees, its bulk weightless upon broken needles, dry leaves, and cones.

And gone.

Art listened to his heart.

———

JOEL CAME AROUND THE BEND behind the trailer and crouched down in the flattened bear stink by the choke-cherry, the same bush he'd hidden behind before. He'd seen the grizzly. Art coming along the path must've made the bear move off. The huge animal had looked at him as it passed below him in the trees. For a moment it was like the bear breathed him in. He heard the suck of air as the bear sniffed him. He'd seen griz-zlies before down on the Lake, but never one here and in the village too.

Joel crouched low, ahead of him the trailer in cedar shade, no light in the window back here. But the kerosene lamp was glowing in the front.

Art was standing by the bottom step, the kit hanging from the end of his arm. For a moment Joel thought the first-aid man had passed out standing up, but then Art lifted his free arm and banged on the aluminum siding the way a tired child would who wanted shelter. Not loud, but loud enough so anyone inside would hear. For sure, someone had to be in there. Joel knew Jim McAllister wouldn't have left the lamp on if he'd gone out, no matter Irene's troubles. There was no sound from inside the trailer and Art rapped at the siding again.

Joel looked down the path along the trailer to the other shed Jim had built to keep his pickup truck out of the weather. The truck was a '54 Ford F-100 with an eight-foot box, the wax polish burnished by a tender scour with a soft cloth. It had to be Jim's pride, the truck. He'd kept it clean for what use he had of it like any other man who had a truck that new. But it wasn't in the shed now, it was parked skewed in the narrow driveway. What had he seen when he was standing on the round behind the store? Two men in a truck. It had passed by the front of the store, the headlights off, heading up the hill to the high road. But he'd only glimpsed it. It could've been McAllister's truck, but his wasn't the only black truck. The planer-man had one and he knew of a couple of others in and around the village.

Joel heard a single, sudden noise inside the trailer, and then a quieter one followed by boots rattling on a plywood floor. The footsteps came down the trailer, hollow, pounding, and then Jim McAllister opened the door and appeared in the joy-shack doorway.

Art took three steps back as Jim leaned out.

"What do you want, Art?" Jim's voice slow and quiet.

"I've come to see to Irene."

Jim just stood there.

It seemed to take all he had in him to say, "I got to see if she's okay."

"There's no need," said Jim.

"There is, though, Jim. I got to check out those dressings and make sure they're all okay."

"She isn't here no more."

"What?"

"You heard."

"Then where? Where is she?"

"She left," said Jim. "She's gone."

McAllister stood there with his hands gripping the sides of the door frame. It looked to Joel like the man was trying to force them apart, or worse, pull them closed.

"What?"

"There's just me now," said Jim.

"I don't understand," Art said. He picked up his kit, a torn frond of cedar caught in the strap. "I think maybe you should let me in so I can check on her." There was no response and Art asked again, "Will you let me?"

"No," said Jim. "There's no need you coming in, 'cause she isn't here." He pulled his body back into the half shadows of the joy-shack so all that showed clear were his hands on the wooden frame. It was as if he were holding himself from falling into the dark behind him, his arms a pale white, the skin left long out of the sun, his face back in the muted dark.

"She said to tell you thanks for what you done," said Jim, the voice hollow from the shack it came from.

Art shook his head. "But how'd she go anywhere? She couldn't walk. Not the way she was. And besides, where was she to go? Was there a place you took her?"

Jim thrust himself forward, his arms pulling him half out the door. He craned his head into the last of the night and sniffed at the air like a dog, his nostrils flared.

For a moment Joel thought Jim might scent him and he made himself small behind the bush. As he listened he wondered why Art wasn't telling Jim what he had to do. Why was he just asking?

"C'mon, Jim. Let me come in."

McAllister smiled over his horned teeth and took a deep breath as if making himself relax. "You look a little worse for wear, Art. Why don't you head on home. Have another drink, smoke some of that chink stuff the cook's got. Maybe you should catch some sleep. You look like you've been up all night. And let me know how much I owe you for Irene. I've never been in debt to no man. You hear?"

"She's hurt bad, Jim."

"Look at you. I know you've been down in Wang Po's room under the cookhouse. Your eyes are like two pissholes in a snowbank. Go on home."

When Art just looked at him, the sawyer dropped his head to his chest, took his hands off the frame, stepped back, and pushed the joy-shack door shut in Art's face, a chain on the inside rattling as it was snubbed on what Joel knew, hearing it, was most likely a spike driven into a stud in the wall. Art stood where he was for a long time and then turned away and headed along the trailer and down the rocky drive McAllister had cut out of the forest.

As Joel followed he ran his hand over the hood of Jim's truck. When he caught up to Art he told him the truck was still a little warm. "It was him driving it," Joel said. "And he had someone with him. I'll bet it was Ernie. I just bet."

The narrow track McAllister had cut out of the bush was rough, cedars and firs pushed over every which way and stones and branches piled up in gravel drifts along the side. Joel tripped over a stub of rock as he caught up to Art. "I saw that black pickup on the road," he said. "I was down by the store when it drove by. It was him."

Art gave no sign he heard.

At the bottom of McAllister's gravel rift the first-aid man stumbled over the ditch by the sawmill road and kept on until he turned down onto the trail that led to his cabin by the river.

Joel followed him to the ditch and waited there until Art faded away. He took off his hat and ran his fingers through his chopped hair. The Express would be coming through and he needed to pick up Art's package. There wasn't much time. After that he needed to fall into his bunk and never wake up until the dance.

When he got to the station he could hear the Express calling out of the swamp, the echoes of its horn bouncing off the walls of the canyon. He stood in the weak light under the canopy of the station and waited until the train pulled in. The few people that were there milled about in the shadows as they collected whatever they'd sent down to Vancouver for, Joel waiting quietly until most had retreated up the road or down to the mill. When the last of them had stepped away from the Express car Joel went over and asked for the package from Li Wei for Art Kenning. The man in the car opened a clasped Express box, took out the small package, and tossed it to Joel. "Every month, eh," he said. "Like clockwork."

"It's for the first-aid man. It's medicines mostly," said Joel.

"Yup," the man said. "Art used to always get it for himself but lately it's been you. How come?"

"He gets pretty tired," said Joel. "I'm just helping him is all."

"Good for you. And you're right. The last few times I saw him he looked pretty beat-up."

"He tries," said Joel. "It's just he's kind of worn out."

"Yeah, so you said."

The horn sounded and the man grinned. "Next stop Avola, then Blue River," he cried as he pulled the Express car door shut with a loud clang. The engineer leaned out his window and waved his arm as the train jerked forward, the twenty-odd cars banging against the strain. The engine sounded its horn and Joel began walking beside it along the grade as it pulled away. It was only a little ways down to Art's cabin. The first-aid man would already be asleep or passed out and Joel would leave the package on his table. It would be the first thing Art would see when he woke up.

The cabin was quiet as Joel placed the package beside the empty whisky bottle, the cat watching him warily. Art was lying on his bunk, his legs pulled up against his chest. He was still in his clothes. Whether he was asleep or not, Joel didn't know. "Art," he whispered but there was no response beyond his body twitching. Joel lighted the stove, the fire going enough to keep Art warm for a few hours.

The last he saw was the cat resting on the windowsill. He waved at it and the cat flicked her black tail in disdain. He took the trail up past the store and the Hall. The only people he saw were a few stragglers from the station turning up to the high road, farmers mostly. A couple of them waved, but Joel kept on trudging, the bunkhouses in sight.

The morning sun was still an hour from crossing the eastern range. Its light would careen over the crest of the mountain behind him. There was new smoke coming from the chimneys of a couple of shacks along the road. Coffee pots were perking on the stove, mugs waiting. In one or another cabin a woman was feeding a baby while she pushed kindling sticks into the firebox. Crackle, snap, cedar flaring, the heat up in the cookstove. A pot of mush bubbled on the back of a stove, two-day-old bread slices lay on hot iron, wisps of smoke rising. A man stared hungover from a chair or bed at the wall where a wolf spider waited for the prey that lived in the cracks and crannies. Kids ran or crawled across the floor. Other women stared from bedroom doorways, cups of coffee in their hands, hair uncombed and silent in the way women were when all they saw was less than what they dreamed.

Joel knew who was in most every place, knew what went on. He'd looked through the windows. He'd seen them all and sworn he'd never be what they were. He'd never hurt Myrna, not in a million years. Or Alice either. Especially her. She had that look he'd seen in Indians before, a kind of shadow behind her eyes as if something was crying inside.

As he passed by a cabin he glanced at a boy standing naked on the bottom porch step pissing absently into the dust and grit at his feet. The child's fist was stuffed into his mouth, drool on his fingers dripping. He waved absently with his free hand as Joel passed. Joel paid no heed, just went on by, crossing the road and walking down the side of the bunkhouse to the back. Everything was quiet. He sat on the stub of fir on the porch and loosened the laces that bound his ankles, pulled his boots off, setting them down quietly. There was no one awake yet in the bunkhouse and he wanted it to stay that way.

He gazed at the green wall across the river, closed his eyes, and saw in his head the Monashee range far off to the south, the long blue line of the Arrow Lakes. For a moment he was back home.

Where was he now?

Those old mountains of his were far away and gone. It was strange thinking about what he'd left behind, how he didn't miss it, yet he yearned somewhere for some kind of home. But could anyone really make a home in a place like this? And then he thought of the people who did, the hill people, farmers like the Turfoots and such who had made their lives in the valley. Others too. And Joel liked living up the river. And there was Myrna. She'd be here forever and there was Alice too, but thinking of her made him feel a little lost. Somehow he knew she wouldn't be here any longer than she had to be and he wondered if she'd always be a little homeless, a little lost too, no matter where she was.

The valley where he sat lay in shadow. The light wouldn't reach down into the river until ten o'clock. He got weary to his feet, his boots hanging from his hands as he carefully elbowed the door open. He let it come to rest without a sound.

He thought of Reiner up at the dump some night soon with Jim McAllister, the two of them pit-lamping the grizzly he'd met on the path. The bear was special. Seeing Joel it had lifted its black snout and drawn him inside its great body, the huge intake of air rushing into its lungs and turning him into the blood that swam in the bear's heart. He could feel himself and then felt the bear in him and at that moment wanted to go up the line of bunks and slice open Reiner's throat. Joel could feel him under his hand, Ernie's body thrashing there, blood like Irene McAllister's pooling through his fingers.

Pushing his boots against the wall by his bunk, Joel stripped off his knife and scabbard and pushed it under his pillow. Belt unloosed, he shrugged out of his shirt, hung his hat on its nail in the wall above his head, and fell onto the sheet, lapping the grey blanket over him. He was dead asleep when his head hit the pillow.

TWELVE

YOU'RE MY BABY GIRL, AREN'T YOU?
　　Hearing Sister Mary say those words Alice woke in the dark, thrashing, her blanket tangled and her yanking at it tightened around her legs. She didn't know where she was and then she did. The night was everywhere. Jesus wasn't on the wall staring down at her. Sister Mary had put him under the bed and she was holding Alice.

Alice pressed her hands against her eyes as she tried to close her mind, shut tight the door that let the words in, Sister Mary saying, *Lie still, Alice. You lie still.*

Sister Mary always held her finger against her lips when she came to get Alice from the dorm. Sister woke her up, but she didn't really because Alice was always awake. She knew the nights Sister Mary came. The Sister would take her from her bed, hold her hand, and lead her down the long hall to Sister Mary's room where Jesus slept. He slept there because Sister Mary put him there. When Alice came she'd take the cross with Jesus on it and lay him down under the bed so he could rest. She said Jesus lived everywhere all the time, but when he got very tired he liked to sleep there.

You have to be quiet. You don't want to wake up Jesus.

Alice would climb into the bed and lie facing the wall. When Sister Mary got into bed she would turn her over and hold her tight. Alice would lie very still because she knew if she didn't then Sister Mary would get mad and she didn't want the Sister to get mad. If Alice did then Sister Mary would hurt her. She would tell Alice she was a bad baby. She would say, *You're a bad baby.*

Alice would try to lie very, very still when that happened but it didn't matter how still she was. In the end Sister Mary would tell her she wasn't a baby anymore, she was a bad girl, and Sister would say, *You're a bad girl*, in the quietest of quiet voices, in a whisper so small only Alice could hear it, and she could hear it because Sister Mary's mouth was pressed against her ear, whispering.

You know what Jesus does to bad girls, don't you, Alice? Don't you?

And Alice held herself in the tangle of the blanket in the room that Piet and Imma built to hold her. She wrapped her arms around herself and she didn't move. Not for a long time. When she squinted her eyes open at last she looked up at the window high on the wall with its thin pig-wire bars. Through it she could see the faint stars. It was the false dawn and she knew what that was because Cliff had told her about the earliest dawn, the time before the light became the light. She remembered what he said. He said, "It's the light from the sun before the sun gets broken."

She could ask Cliff anything. He knew everything there was to know.

He was beautiful.

Alice stared up at the window but the boy, Joel, wasn't there. Most nights he came to see her. Not every one, but when he did she could always hear him outside on the gravel behind the wall. Each step he took clicked on the rocks like faraway beetles talking and when he climbed onto the round of wood and clambered up to the window she could hear that too, the little bumps and scrapes he made against the boards. He tried to be quiet, but sometimes after he had been watching for a while she would hear him breathing, his breaths heavy and thick. Alice knew Joel didn't want to wake her up, but she was awake almost every night unless it was the morning. It didn't matter anyway. Alice always pretended she was asleep when she heard Joel come. She knew he wasn't there to talk. He hardly said anything, not even in the café when he asked for his bottle of Coke. He'd just look at her.

He liked to watch Alice and it didn't matter. It made her feel safe to know he was there. It was like he was protecting her. When Joel was at the window she could go a little deeper into sleep and the bad dreams didn't come. Sister Mary and Jesus stayed away when Joel was there. The other dreams too, the beatings, the nights without anything to eat, the wooden box she was put into out by the sheds, the sun beating down. And Alice suddenly remembered Christmas and how Sister Mary never let her eat her cornflakes. It was special, cornflakes on Christmas morning. Once a year. A treat, the Sisters said. For weeks the kids used to talk about the cornflakes they were going to get, but Alice never got to eat them. Only once when her friend Margaret sneaked out a little handful from her bowl. Alice loved how the golden flakes crunched in her mouth, how she tried not to swallow them, the crackle of the tiny bits like magic melting in her mouth. Margaret was her friend, but

Margaret was sick a lot. She coughed at night and if she coughed too much then the Sister would come in and take her away to another room where she had to stay by herself. When the coughing was bad she spit up blood.

Somehow it seemed Alice always got into trouble at the school. She tried to be good, but Sister Mary and Sister Grace always said she was bad and punished her. The worst was when they strapped her legs. She had bruises all up and down her legs from Brother Whelan whipping her. She hated what he did, but it was worse for other kids.

She had been at the school three years when Margaret died. She was a year younger than Alice. One night Brother Whelan came and took Margaret away like he always did and that night when she was brought back to the dorm Margaret was sick in her bottom and where she peed and by the time it was breakfast she couldn't come to eat and when they were in the schoolroom learning how to say English words Sister Grace came and said Margaret was dead. They took her to the pine trees that night. That's where the little kids got buried. Brother Whelan wrapped her in a piece of torn-off canvas and carried her to the pine trees. He stood there with Margaret at his feet and watched while Brother Andrew dug the hole. He had to dig two holes because one of the Sisters said he found bones in the first hole he dug.

But not Alice. She wasn't going to die no matter what they did to her.

She lay there staring out the pig-wire window and then she cast the Sisters and Brothers from her mind. "Cast them away," she said in a whisper, and then because she couldn't hear Mister Harper coming she said it again, louder. "I cast you all away," she cried. "I cast you away."

It was enough for now, no matter her dreams when Sister came to get her in the night.

Alice got out of bed and went over to the bucket in the corner, took the lid off, and sat down to pee. The rim was cold on her bum and she hated that, but she had to sit right on the bucket because once she slipped balancing there and the bucket got knocked over and Imma got mad. She wouldn't let Alice clean it up all day, telling her that if she wanted a smelly room then she could have one. Alice didn't want Imma to get mad again.

Finished, she cleaned herself and dressed and waited for Mister Harper to come and unlock the door. It would be the first time he'd be the one to let her out to work. The day she arrived from Kamloops on the train, Imma had brought Mister Harper to the room. He'd looked at her in the way Piet sometimes did, only Mister Harper's look was worse. It was like she wasn't even alive. Like a piece of meat, that's how she felt. Something you could hang in a cooler.

It was her being locked up that made them look at her that way. That's what Cliff told her. "You're their prisoner, just like at the school in Kamloops," he had told her. "They think they can do what they want with you."

Alice always made sure to get up and get dressed before anyone came, Imma or Piet, but especially today now it was Mister Harper. She didn't want to be alone with him watching her put her clothes on.

Sometimes she had to wait a long time before she was let out of the room, but that was better than being caught in bed. The one time that happened it was Imma who unlocked the door. Imma didn't say anything to her. She just stood and watched as Alice peed and got dressed. Imma was just like the Sisters at the residential school. They watched too. That night when she went to bed Joel didn't come and there was no one to protect her from the night.

But Sister Mary came.

It was like she knew Alice was alone. Sister came in the dark and it was bad.

Alice knew Mister Harper would be coming soon.

She combed her hair slowly and tied it back with a piece of red twine she had taken from a potato-sack tie in the storeroom. The colour was pretty against her black hair. There wasn't a mirror in her room and none in the store. Sometimes she could see her reflection in a window if the light was just right, but it was never clear enough. Cliff had told her she was pretty. No one had ever said she was pretty and Alice wondered if she was.

One day Brother Whelan told her she'd be going to work up the river in a village. He said the people who owned the store where she was going to work were coming to get her in the afternoon and she was to be ready.

Mister Harper still didn't come. The sun was still far away behind the mountains, but there was a fresh light outside the locked room and Alice knew it was almost time to open the store. Alice stared at the blank door that didn't have a handle or a knob and as she did she wondered how the other kids were doing back at the residential school. There was one little girl she'd been worried about ever since she left. Her name was Catherine. Exactly where her mother and father were Alice didn't know and Catherine wasn't sure either. When Alice asked her she just said they lived by a river. That was all she knew.

Catherine was only five years old, a year older than Alice had been when she'd come. Alice found out a while later from one of the girls that Sister Mary was taking Catherine to the room where Jesus slept under the bed. Alice knew what Sister Mary would be doing to Catherine. It would be the same as she'd done to her.

When the Brother said Alice was leaving to go north, she told him about Sister Mary and what Sister was doing when she took Catherine at night. Alice told him what Sister Mary had done to her. That's when Brother struck her on the side of the head with his fist and knocked her down. It was weeks later that it stopped hurting inside Alice's ear. The Brother said Sister Mary was only trying to civilize the girl just like she had with her. *All Sister has ever wanted is to make you good and useful*, he said. He stood there and Alice thought he was going to kick her. She could see his shoes under his soutane. They were scuffed and dirty. *What are we going to do with you Indians?* he asked, but there were only Alice and Sister Grace there to answer and Alice was on the floor and didn't know how to move and Sister said nothing.

Nothing at all.

Sister stood quietly by the door and waited until Alice could get up. It took her two tries before she could get off her knees. When she finally stood Sister Grace took her by the arm and led her out to the front of the school where the truck was waiting in the desert sun to take her to the train station.

Alice heard the front door of the store open and close and then boots walking on the floor. They were the heavy steps of Mister Harper. She stood by her mattress and waited until he stopped at her door and then the snap of the padlock as the key turned, the click of the hasp, and the door opening to him in his canvas jacket, his leather belt. When Alice met his eyes, she closed hers. When she opened them again she was looking down at the floor and she was a little girl at the residential school and the Sister was standing in the dust in front of the huge red-brick building, behind her the desert hills with their cactus and stunted pines.

"Well, you're all ready, aren't you?" Mister Harper said. He stood there in the doorway, looking at her in the way most of the men from the mill looked at her, with the wrong grin, the wrong eyes, the wrong way of standing, their bodies leaned in the way dogs do when they are trying to decide whether to attack or run. Alice almost expected him to come over and smell her. She raised her head and looked up at the sawmill boss and, yes, his body rested in the same kind of slouch. It was his head, the way it was raised slightly and leaning toward his left shoulder as if he was judging, not her, but himself. It was as if he was deciding what he was going to do and whether or not he was going to do it.

"Thanks, Mister Harper," Alice said, her legs moving carefully as she took four steps to reach the doorway, turning slightly so her body could get by him without touching. As she passed she felt her hair move. It was the lightest of touches, a weaving made by his fingers. She felt her stomach tense, her throat thicken. She kept walking, head down as she passed through the door. She stepped around the spot on the floor just past the freezer. It was the damp wood where rusty water leaked, the pool she dry-mopped every day so Imma and Piet wouldn't slip when they stepped from the store to get to the back. There wasn't a sound and then there was, Mister Harper behind her, moving slowly just as she was. It was as if the walk they were taking happened like this every morning, Mister Harper behind her instead of Imma or Piet, the padlock and the hasp, the door opening and closing, and each day his huge hand touching her hair.

As she passed along the aisle of tinned food, she imagined herself continuing through the store and out the front door, but when she stepped down from the deck she didn't know where she was or where she was going. She only knew she wasn't in the store anymore and she wasn't owned by Piet and Imma. Mister Harper was standing now at the open front door of the store watching her walk away. He was waiting to see where she was going. It was a terrible kind of dream she was having because Mister Harper was waiting for her to turn around just past the Hall where the dance was going to be, turn and come back to the store, and she did turn, she did return, and his hand touched her hair as she walked through the door back into the store, his fingers knotted above the red twine bow she had tied there.

The dream vanished as she stepped around the front table where Imma charged the customers for what they bought. Mister Harper walked past her as if she wasn't there, as if whatever had passed between them hadn't happened. There were sandwiches to make, food to prepare, the vegetable bins needed filling, the floors swept, the cash to be counted again and again to make sure it was right, all the things that had to be right before people came. If anything was wrong there would be someone who would tell Imma and Piet and if someone did she would be in trouble.

She went to the cupboard by her room, took out the broom, and began a slow sweeping of the hall that led past the storage room where the canned goods were stored. Halfway down she stopped and leaned the broom against the wall. She put her hand on the side of her head and touched the place where Brother Whelan had struck her. She could still feel the blow, the sudden shock of his fist. She didn't remember falling down. All she knew was that she was lying on the floor and the Brother was standing over her. She had put her hand to the side of her head and felt the numbness in her ear. It felt wet and when she'd looked at her fingers there was blood on them. *Get her up*, was what Brother Whelan said. He was talking to Sister Grace. *Get her up and get her out of here.* And when the Sister helped her up, Brother Whelan said what he said about Indians. She knew then and she knew now that she would never forget what he said about her, what he said about all the children who lived at the school.

She pushed back her hair and felt her ear and it all came back to her, the years at the school, Sister Mary hurting her and Brother Whelan too. She remembered the truck they packed all the kids in when they were taking them away. She remembered the little ones crying when they looked through the wooden slats and she remembered when she was little and she had cried too and how they beat them when they cried. And the wooden box Sister Mary put her in the time she caught her trying to take an apple from the bowl in Sister's room. The Sister had left her in the box all night and when the Sister opened it to take her out her dress was wet from peeing herself and the Sister had beat her and beat her with the stick she kept in the corner by the bed. *You dirty girl. You dirty girl*, she had said as she struck her.

Alice put her hand to her face and it felt wet. When she took it away and looked there wasn't any blood on it. It was clean and it was only then she knew she had been crying. She told herself not to cry.

She was afraid of Mister Harper. She had hated him touching her hair. She didn't want him or anyone else to touch her hair ever again and then she thought of Cliff and how gentle he was with her, but it didn't matter if he was gentle or not. She didn't want him to touch her either, not anywhere, but part of her did want him to touch her, but not in that way and not now. She wanted him to hold her gentle, hold her the same way he talked to her, the way he protected her. He wasn't like Brother Whelan and Sister Mary and Mister Harper and she put her hands up to her face and held them there. She didn't want to see anything. The terrible thing was that when she did that she could only see in and what she saw inside was Sister Mary undressing her when she was still a little girl. Sister Mary's long white fingers were on her skin. They were touching her and she was afraid to cry.

THIRTEEN

ART'S FIRST-AID KIT was hooked over his shoulder, the strap wrapped around his knuckles as he left the cabin and took the river trail along the railroad grade past the bog. The swamp reached out beside him, green pools seething in the sun. Mourning cloaks and fritillaries licked the muddy banks by the tracks with their slender tongues. The blades of their wings willowed in the heat as the butterflies rose into the breeze along the river. They lifted from the mud as the scissored shadow of his trembling legs passed by.

The morning was half gone.

Bone-dry trunks of aspen snags stood crooked in the muck, among them the flayed bodies of red cedars and hemlocks, their needles fallen, their bark stripped away by woodpeckers and flickers in search of grubs and beetles. Dragonflies quartered the air feasting on flies and mosquitoes. Below the skimmers and meadowhawks were the festering pools of their birth. He looked into an eddy by the grade and saw water tigers and diving beetles course the deep as they hunted for prey. Mosquito larvae jigged in the fetid water, their bodies dancing.

The surface of the long pool where the creek met the swamp was dimpled with small trout rising in search of grubs and insects. There was hunger everywhere, an infinite variety of hunter and prey.

The bit of opium he'd smoked when he woke up had settled his body down. He thought his head would clear in a little while even though his body was exhausted. The nightmares had gone back to an uneasy rest after raging through his head. As he walked he caught a glimpse of someone at the edge of a cedar copse on the dry island in the bog behind the bunkhouses, but when he turned to take a better look whoever it was vanished into the dense brush. He thought it might've been the Turfoot boy, Emerson—trust him to be roaming around again already—but he wasn't sure. It wouldn't have been Joel. He'd be sleeping the sleep of the young after his long night's wandering. But that island was where Joel kept his stuff. Art had seen him hiding things there. The kid had better be careful, he thought. He wasn't the only one who noticed things.

Joel. He had to thank him for picking up the package. He remembered then that Joel had been at McAllister's trailer, both times.

Art drew the back of his wrist across his forehead, his shirt cuff coming away wet. What breeze there was cooled his arm, salt lines growing on the cloth. Jim had gone somewhere in the night when they'd been down at the cookhouse. It couldn't have been Irene with him in the truck. Even McAllister wouldn't have taken his wife out of the trailer. She'd have started bleeding as soon as he tried to lift her. And she couldn't walk. She had to still be in the back bedroom where he'd stitched her up.

He swung the kit over to his other shoulder. The whisky he'd drunk at the cabin simmered in his belly. The liquor rode the tremors that attacked him everywhere. He had to keep on walking, the cramps from constipation grinding his gut. He needed to shit, but he knew if he tried all he'd do was crap black chunks hard as blasting rock. The opium had eased the pain a little, but he felt like he was walking in the wrong kind of feathers, goose down made of stone. When he tried to stop moving, his legs betrayed him and he wobbled on loose ankles. He had to cut back on the liquor, the opium too. He didn't know which was worse, the drug or the drink. All he knew was the one seemed to help the other.

The Express had gone through while he was passed out. Joel had dropped off the package and Li Wei had his money. He could see the wrapped package of drugs falling into Joel's hands as the man in the Express car tossed it from the open door. The penicillin, the opium.

Heat came off the swamp in a thin mist. He sat down on the tracks and placed the first-aid kit between his legs. He could barely breathe, his shirt soaked with sweat. He pressed his hands down upon the hot steel of the tracks and felt it burn into his palms. The heat quieted him.

He looked to the river and said to the brown flood: "Hey, deep river, I got to go see if Irene McAllister's okay." He rubbed his hands together as if trying to wipe something off. "Jim just doesn't want me seeing to her now she's stitched up. He says she's gone, but there's no way she could have gone anywhere."

His share of the opium was back in the cabin in a purple Seagram's bag on the shelf above his bunk. He was going to hold off taking that again for a while. The drinking too. He was going to slow down. He could do it. The way he was he was no good to anyone.

"I'm going to clean up a little," he said. He looked out over the river again, but if the river heard him it gave no sign. Its long whispers promised him nothing. The only thing the river offered was the gift Helga Fyksen had accepted. Sitting there he took no comfort from the river, but for listening to it flow. There were times he felt it was a ravenous tongue eating the valley.

A black dragonfly landed on his knee. He leaned down and stared as it rested there, its gleaming scales reflecting the clouds. He moved closer to its double-eyed, bullet head and saw his face in the mirrors there. He hung distorted in the curves of the myriad eyes looking back at him. He shuddered and the dragon-fly, its wings clashing like shaken rice paper, lifted from its perch and circled his head before flying out over the swamp.

He wasn't sure if he'd been blessed or damned. He got up and started walking again thinking of the messages the world sent to him that he never paid attention to, never had time for. He crossed over the swamp by the mill and the cookhouse, passed the bunk-houses, and turned up the raw cut of McAllister's driveway.

Jim's pickup was in the shed.

Art stood a long time before pushing tentatively at the joy-shack door. As he did he heard the loose chain rattle against the two-by-four frame. It wasn't hooked on the spike. He banged on the aluminum wall, but all he got back was quiet from inside the trailer.

He opened the inner door slowly.

"Hello, this place," he called.

The only answer was from a Steller's jay mocking him from a branch of fir outside. He turned and the bird shook its blue wings at him, lowered its black head, and shrieked with a ter-rible rage. At the bird's scream Art's skin came alive, the last of the drugs in him exploding. Electrified chiggers crawled under his skin. He threw his arms out and spun around, the first-aid kit tight in his fist banging against the door jamb as he stumbled from the stoop to the dirt. He knelt there shaking, the bird staring down at him, silent, waiting to see if he dared rise up again.

"Fuck off," he said, as much to himself as to the bird. He got to his feet, exhausted, the bird giving one last scream as he climbed back up the steps to the open door.

The joy-shack's room stretched long and narrow into the shadows. McAllister hadn't cut windows in the thin plywood walls, but sharp cracks of light cut across the spaces from where the wooden sheets had been nailed on badly, three bluebottle flies soaring in and out of the slats of brightness with steady, exhausting drones. The door open, they didn't flee, but kept on in their endless jagged triangles and squares.

The room had been cleaned up since the night before. Jim's chainsaws were still there along with his swede saw and handsaws. The steel tool box that likely held most of his wrenches and screwdrivers, hammers and other small tools was in the corner by the workbench. There were a couple of cartons neatly stacked against the wall, but the odds and ends of things that were there the night before were gone. He remembered vaguely the mess the joy-shack had been. Everything now was neat and tidy. The washing machine that'd been there had vanished. Like most everything else that was gone it was as if it had never been. He remembered seeing the frayed cord hanging from the machine's back, a copper fox tail hanging down, but even if the plug had still been attached the machine wouldn't have worked without electricity. He'd wondered why McAllister would have cut the plug off and thought maybe the sawyer had got a deal on the machine, buying it from someone downriver, someone who had no more use for it than the sawyer had now. Maybe Jim was going to fix the cord if they moved on to another mill town where they'd have power. There'd been a box freezer but it was gone too. Just something else that had been useless up the river.

Jim and Irene storing stuff for another day wasn't any different than everyone else in the village. Most people had packed away junk they couldn't use, washing machines, televisions that didn't work because there was no signal they could get, vacuum cleaners, anything that needed electricity. It was like people were just waiting for the day when they got away from the valley.

All junk, he thought. And then, Irene.

There were only two windows on this side of the trailer, the one down by the bedroom and the other inside the joy-shack by the trailer door. The curtains were pulled close in both. He peered through the thin slit in the curtains by the door but all he could see was a stub of nail pounded partway into a scratched plywood wall.

He rapped his knuckles against the window glass and then louder on the door, but there was no answer. If McAllister wasn't there then he had to be down at the mill or at the store. There was nowhere else he would have gone on foot. Maybe he'd taken off with Ernie somewhere. Either way, Art was glad he was gone. He didn't feel ready to start fighting him about seeing Irene.

The jay gave one last scream as he tried the trailer door, the handle turning with a wince, the metal door scraping against the white rust on the worn aluminum sill.

The knob felt cool in his palm as he pulled the door wider, a last thin squeak crying light. He sniffed and the sharp burn of vinegar and ammonia seared his nose and throat. It brought back the smell of wounds and outcries, field hospitals, wet rubber sheets in ragged tents, the chemical stink of war, the bodies and the graves. He leaned his head into the room and looked long down the narrow hall past the kitchen . . . no one.

Silence.

And then he asked the oldest question in the world. "Is anybody home?"

He let his breath go and took another.

No one.

He told himself that if Jim came back from wherever he was Art would say Irene had called out to him for help. Thinking that, he stepped in and pulled the door shut behind him. The couch against the front wall was a worn brown, the pebbled cloth rubbed smooth, a sheen of grease on the arm closer to the door. A plywood coffee table sat in front of it, a black leopard ashtray in the centre, one of the cat's ruby eyes gone as if fallen or pried out and lost. The plywood tabletop was stained a deep red. It looked like Jim had taken a can of oxblood shoe polish and worked the thick greasy stain into the whorls of wood after he bought it. The ashtray was clean and so was the floor.

The floor, the walls, the table and counter, all clean.

He couldn't exactly remember, but he was pretty sure they weren't like this before.

He reached out and touched the nail in the wall he'd seen through the window. A picture had hung there last night, he was sure now. He remembered it was of a lake, a sunset, flowers, and mountains, the old dream of a wilderness where harmony and peace reigned. Now there was only a rectangle of pale white below the nail, the spot where it had been cleaner than the wall surrounding it.

He looked around, feeling like he'd never been here before. "Hello?"

The kitchen was part of the living room. In the corner by a small wood stove balanced on bricks was a spider-legged kitchen table with two unmatched metal chairs pushed under it, their brittle plastic cushions, one swirled green, the other ruby red, criss-crossed with duct tape to hold the stuffing in. The table was bare, no cloth or bowls, no knives or forks, no remnant breakfast plates or cups. A sink was sunk in the counter, the worn steel scoured clean, no dishtowel, no washcloth. The cupboards above were closed. He opened the one above the sink. There were four plain white plates, five saucers and three cups, some glasses of different shapes and sizes. The cupboard beside it was empty except for two steel forks and a single table knife, the three of them pushed to the back. He opened the drawer by the sink and found a plastic tray with knives and forks and spoons in it. He hesitated a moment and then for some reason he took the ones out of the cupboard and put them in the tray with the others. It made no sense that they should be in a different place.

He tried to remember the night before. McAllister had raged in this room while Art sewed Irene up in the back bedroom. He'd heard a bottle break out here last night. There should have been broken glass somewhere on the floor, but everything had been swept up. For sure it wasn't Irene who had cleaned the place. She was helpless.

He remembered taking an almost-full bottle of whisky away from Jim when he left. It was the bottle he'd been drinking from down by the river, the one he'd woken up to. Just before he did that he'd looked around and he was sure the front end here had been a mess.

He looked down the long hall, everything narrowing to the end, a sliding door blocking off the bathroom.

"Missus McAllister?"

Nothing.

"Irene?"

Maybe she was sleeping.

She had to be sleeping.

He held the first-aid kit out in front of him and went along the narrow passage toward the back. Beside him on either side was a row of cupboards and two narrow closets. He opened one with his free hand. Hanging from the wooden rod were McAllister's work shirts, beside the last one a worn jacket and a hunting vest draped from nails, a row of seven shotgun shells sticking out of the loops of the vest, and a heavy knife, sheathed and hanging from a loop of leather. It wasn't the knife she'd cut herself with. This one had a broader blade. Behind the shirts and leaning into the corner was a .12-gauge Brittany shotgun, the barrels polished to a heavy blue, two boxes of shells on the floor beside it, one box open and three shells gone. Beside it was Jim's .308 Browning.

Art turned around and pulled out a wall-cupboard drawer stuffed with work socks, the one below holding a tangle of worn underwear. The drawer below it was deep, work pants folded in a pile in the bottom of it. He opened a cupboard door on the other side. Hanging from the wooden rod was a white shirt, its collar yellowed, and a red striped tie hanging from it. Beside it was a black suit, an old one, the cuffs worn, the lapels wide. On the floor as if forgotten was a pair of white panties. He touched the panties' frilled edge and remembered the ones she'd been wearing the night before, the blood soaking them. There was a rod in the next closet with nothing hanging from it, just a row of finishing nails below it punched into the wall. Other than the ones with Jim's stuff, the drawers he looked into were empty.

He tried to remember and the image of Marie's room above the café in Paris came back to him. He clenched his elbows against his sides and closed his eyes. For a moment he tried not to be in Paris and then he was. He was in the room with the little couch by the window where she always sat looking out at the street. Marie had a closet but he realized he'd never really looked at what was in it. His own stuff was kept in the duffle beside the door, his extra shirt and pants, socks and underwear, his spare things. But Marie's stuff? He had no idea what she had except that she wore dresses sometimes, other times skirts and blouses. He had no idea where she kept her stockings and underwear.

There was the shotgun and the knife.

Jim hadn't left town, his truck was in the shed, his tools were in the joy-shack.

But there'd have to be things of Irene's in the bedroom. He was sure. He remembered seeing a closet there and a tiny bureau pushed into the corner where her bed was. That'd be where she kept her woman stuff.

Art rolled the sliding door into its slot and entered the tiny bathroom. He took three steps and stopped at the last door, the one that opened into the room at the end, the one where Irene had been, the one where she was.

"Irene?" he said, but there was no answer. He hoped she was sleeping and not scared, good if she was asleep, good if she wasn't afraid.

He didn't slide open the door. Maybe it was best if he left her sleeping.

She was sure to be in there.

But he had to see if her wounds were okay.

He'd look.

He'd look in a moment.

The bathroom was clean, the smell of vinegar and ammonia stronger there than it had been up in the front of the trailer. He looked again in the sink, saw it as it was the night before with its wet pink cloths soaking, the streaks of dirt smeared on the floor where his boots or Jim's had slipped in the water Art had spilled from the basin. Crumpled towels and washcloths and torn strips of a pillowcase he hadn't needed or wanted that had been thrown into the short, four-foot bathtub, everything blotted with her blood, the soaked blanket that was the bedcover where she'd sat and the sheets too. He remembered the stains. They'd been violent red-black lichens on strewn stones, the blood caked at the edges.

He had stood at the sink washing his hands and arms before going in to stitch her up. What else had he done before he went in to see her last night? He knew he didn't want to remember just as he knew he had to. He'd stood there and he'd seen a cobweb in the corner above the bathroom mirror, but the cobweb was gone now, the wall washed clean.

Art placed his palm gently on the thin sliding door that opened to the bedroom and then took his hand away. He wished it wasn't him who was here, that he wasn't the man Claude Harper had found in the hotel bar in Japtown two years ago, that he hadn't come upriver to work and to maybe find some kind of life far from the city where he'd been lost off and on for years. He set his kit on the floor, slipped the mickey of whisky from his jacket pocket, and took a drink. His stomach recoiled and he swallowed a bit more, his belly muscles tight as he capped the bottle and put it back in his pocket. It was still almost full.

He thought he'd call out, only this time maybe a little louder. He didn't want to suddenly wake her, to frighten her.

He said her name again. "Irene?"

Even as he did he knew there'd be no answer.

He tried to understand and didn't quite, the hope, however confused in him, that she'd be in her bed at rest, the hope for her to be better or at least not worse. For her to have passed the first crisis was what he had wanted, to have survived the shock, the primary one, the kind that killed. He'd seen survivors in the war, had seen men wear terrible wounds and live, seen blood displayed on their bodies like wet medals, an arm holding on by a shred of skin, a piece of skull sheared away by shrapnel, the quiet brain seemingly still thinking in the rivulets of blood, the injured man talking to his mother as if she was there in the mud beside him, the man who told his wife that he was sorry.

There was that soldier just before Caen. The man was lying on his back by the side of a ditch when Art saw him. When Art knelt down the soldier opened his eyes and told Art a mortar blast had knocked him out. For a moment Art thought the soldier had lost his legs, but they were only part-buried under dirt-clotted grass and stones. The soldier wore at his throat a blue bandana with white flowers on it and Art remembered thinking he must have brought the bit of rag from home, maybe from the Cypress Hills down by the Montana border or in the desert country in the South Okanagan, somewhere west for sure. A good-luck charm his girlfriend back home had given him, maybe, or sent him in an envelope from home. The twisted bit of cloth made the soldier too human. There was the front of his ruined uniform, his pale face. Art had asked him if he was injured and the soldier lying there on his back said he was hurt only a little. Mostly just knocked out for a bit, he'd said. Art had been going to give him a shot of morphine, but the soldier told him he was all right. He said there'd be someone up ahead who'd likely need it more, and when he'd said that he turned his head away from Art. The man's Lee–Enfield .303 was lying beside him, the barrel nestled in a shattered willow crook.

Art had tightened the straps of his first-aid kit, someone shouting *medic, medic* from a cluster of trees on the other side of the field past the ditch. He had backed down the slight slope and was bent over shrugging into his pack when he saw the soldier just above him turn a little, the curve of his back resting against a rock. The man began to shoot with what seemed to Art intimate care and precision at what Art knew were the distant moving wraiths that were the soldier's enemy.

Two hours later he'd come again to the road, the Germans pushed back to some nameless village crossroad up ahead. He wasn't looking for the injured soldier when he stepped down into the ditch to piss.

The man was where Art had left him. The soldier lay as if at rest, the rifle barrel still propped in the willow crook, his one hand cupped around the trigger guard and the other as if he'd been trying to pull his coat under him to keep away the chill. The soldier must have thought the cold had been coming from the earth beneath him but it was only his own dying.

He had wondered at the wholeness of a body, how it could so easily be taken apart.

The dirt had been dark with the soldier's blood, the hole in his back big enough for Art to put his fist into.

He put his hand on the door and pushed it sideways. It slid open, a single shaft of light from the window stretching supine on the empty bed. There was no blanket or cover, only a sheet stretched tight. For a moment he wanted to reach out and lift the edge of the sheet so he could look at the bloodstain that had to be on the mattress, the outline of her buttocks there, her thighs where the blood had run down and soaked in. He wanted to and then he didn't. Nothing happened for a long time and then he saw his hand resting on the wood and he slid the door back, nudging it into its slot by the sink with a quiet thud. He looked at the door and then turned and went back down the hall to the front of the trailer.

Art sat down on the chair with the swirled green plastic, leaned over Irene McAllister's rickety table, and looked out the window through a shaft of sun. Midges small as bits of dust danced there, their wings touching the edges of shadows and recoiling. In the corner of the window was a slender spider waiting with the immense patience that all still-hunters had for one or another of the insects to blunder into its web.

He remembered a priest in Belgium sliding beads through his fingers as Art talked to him about forgiveness. They were in a windowless shed outside some village. The two Germans at their feet were dead, one of them with his arm blown off, one half of his head in a helmet by the wall. The other soldier lay perfect in his death, his uniform clean, no wound to see. *Wij zijn vergeven*, the priest had said.

Art had wanted to kill the priest when he said that, *we are all forgiven*, and told him so. The little man with his steel spectacles propped on his nose clicked his beads and smiled at the wild idea of his own death by the man who had liberated him. An hour later the priest vanished in a battle, his tidy shed obliterated by a mortar, the little man in the soutane gone as if he never was.

Forgiveness?

Forgive who, forgive what?

All he had was what he remembered and all he'd wanted for these many years was to forget. The soldier lying in a ditch in France with a hole in his back. What was it in the man that he could not, would not tell Art he was wounded? What made him lie there with his rifle, waiting to kill again? What kind of man was that?

The German word for courage was *mut*. What did a word like that have to do with a man's will?

He ran the palms of his hands over the wine-dark tabletop. He knew why he'd come back to the trailer. He'd needed to check her stitches, make sure they were secure. She might have panicked and at worst torn some of them. And her dressings needed to be replaced, her wounds checked for inflammation, infection. He had the penicillin from the package Joel picked up. She needed to take some of the pills.

But she wasn't in bed where she was supposed to be. She wasn't anywhere.

And McAllister had stood at the door of the joy-shack and denied him? Had she been gone even then? Surely there was some decency in Jim? And Art could have been with her, could have told the sawyer he was going to stay from the very first. She'd still be in her bed then, wouldn't she, if he'd just sat beside her through the night? Or would McAllister have thrown him out? Of course Jim would have told him to go. She was Jim's wife. She belonged to him. Jim would have kicked him out if Art had insisted on staying.

Art had wanted him to.

Every thought he had was a betrayal. Had he always lied to himself? The truth was he'd wanted to get out of the trailer and away from the madness in the room, the two of them feeding off each other's misery and hate, the anger, the fear, and the suffering too. They were eating each other alive.

He'd go down and share his whisky with Wang Po and the cook would share his opium with him. It was part of their ritual. The little bit of opium he kept for himself back at the cabin was his to use when he needed something more than whisky to help get him through the night. But right now Art needed the black tar's smoke. He needed it bad. And as he thought of the opium he felt the softness spreading through his body, and nothing for him to think, nothing to feel, only the smoke floating him away. He'd be in that safe place. The opium and the whisky took him far away from the world. The past was just a story then, a long dream that couldn't hurt him anymore. He needed that.

"Fuck," he said. "Fuck."

FOURTEEN

SQUATTED DOWN ON HIS HAMS AND HEELS on the worn boards beside the iron bunk, his whole body pulled into the darkened corner around behind the door where no one coming in from the swamp would ever see him, was a boy. He was hidden in plain sight much as a willow grouse is who hides in a barren field from those who are hunting. He was hiding so perfectly he was as a fallen rock or a clump of winter-burned weeds, something unalive to anyone not knowing how to look, to see. Behind him was the door, the swamp behind the bunkhouse, the sun just coming on, fringes of heat lifting from the windowsill above the bunk.

The boy's face and hands were draped with thin scars he'd endured from passing through the bush on one of his many wanders, the smaller ones from twigs and branches scratching him. The larger scars he'd given himself deliberately with the tip and edge of his knife. He had done that to himself because he'd seen pictures in a magazine picked up from a chair in front of a bunkhouse a year ago. The pictures were of black men in Africa who decorated themselves with scars, their beauty such he wished the same for himself. He would not have called them beautiful for he thought the word wrong for anything about himself, beauty being something girls and women spoke of, not men.

And the new scar still forming on the side of his face he'd given to himself by falling from the osprey tree into the river, the river alive in him still. The fall was now what Joseph and Art had told him, a moment of flight when he became an osprey, the river his hunting water, the great trout and salmon living there his prey. His mother had changed his bandage that morning, careful not to disturb the thin crust that had formed around the stitches. She had gently placed a salve made from lavender leaves, wild foxglove honey, and crushed garlic over the wound to keep it clear of infection. He had watched her mix the salve in silence. Only his mother could make him sit still long. As she bound the wound again with strips of clean cotton, she had spoken to the wound, asking it to complete its journey from the broken to the whole. Then she sang her healing song, the one she learned from her own mother when she was a girl.

Emerson listened and didn't listen, his body wanting to leave the house he had slept in the past night. His mother had made him sleep on a straw mattress she laid at the side of her bed. When he had risen in the night to piss she had followed him out under the moon and waited until he was finished. He knew why she was there and did not go to the barn where his real bed was. She stood behind him, her face turned away from his pissing. He was old enough now for her not to look at his pecker. She had followed him not so much because she did not trust him to stay, but because her love for him was boundless. "I have a boundless love for you," she had told him while she was changing his dressing. "The chains of love were taken away when you slipped from my belly," she said.

To that, Emerson had said not a word. He could feel the scar growing, becoming a thin white ridge that he would wear all his life. He'd been happy as he returned to lie on the mattress beside his mother's bed. Sleep did not elude him. Emerson had learned to sleep standing up. It was a kind of resting that nurtured him. The sleeps he needed were taken in the forest under certain trees, his favourite a cedar whose healing boughs protected him. His mother had taught him the languages of trees and shrubs, the cedar and fir, the chokecherry and the Oregon grape. He had rested the remainder of the night. He knew he had to leave before dawn.

His feet were in dusty boots, his shirt torn at the neck. The thin blue jeans were held up with a twist of what looked like a tanned strip of deer or moose hide. His body was oddly shrunk as if he'd never quite got enough food in him in his early years or more likely, given the love his mother had for him, because he was simply born to be small of stature like his father. He was squatted low on the floor as if nailed there, his arms crossed over his torn pants, his head lolled forward across his wrists. The bones in the back of his neck above the collar were ridged out tight against skin that was both white and darkly red, the demarcation between them showing where the sun had both touched and untouched him. He didn't look like he was breathing, more like something carved and left there.

Emerson had been silent for an hour or more as he'd waited for Joel to wake up. Once a man had walked down the aisle of bunks and passed on through the doorway into the last of dark to piss, but the boy had been so avoidably still he hadn't been seen to be there.

He knew Joel was awake now though and watching.

—

BY THE LIGHT IN THE WINDOW above his head Joel knew he'd only slept a few hours, no more. His eyes were bare slits through which he stared at the Turfoot boy's head, the raked green-blond hair hanging down the sides of his face neither combed nor brushed, but rather turmoiled by the wind and weather and further, likely shaped by him clawing his fingers through it. A bandage was wound around Emerson's head. It showed through his tangled hair. Joel wondered where the boy had got such an injury that it would need such careful binding, but figured he'd find out one way or another.

Joel had been looking at him for a while, thinking upon the boy's purpose. The boy hadn't moved even though Joel had stirred once or twice. The boy's head was bent a little sideways, his eyes part open in what seemed like a half sleep and wasn't. He was carefully awake. Joel knew he was staring directly at him. Between the two of them was a wordless agreement that until Joel made some move to recognize the boy being there, neither of them would stir.

He had to be three shy of the oldest of Turfoot's five sons, unless there were medium-sized or bigger ones hidden away up at the farm. Joel doubted that, given his own regular trips up the mountain. He'd seen this boy at the station the times Arnold Turfoot brought his family down to the train. There was a littlest one, then came this one, and after them the next-in-line three brothers, the bigger kids who did most of the loading up on the wagon when the shipment came in from the Woodward's store in Vancouver. And Myrna, of course, the sister of them all, and the oldest.

Joel couldn't think of a reason for the boy to be in the bunkhouse other than to deliver some message to him from Myrna, though why he needed to hear it given he was going to be seeing her anyway later on was a mystery to him. It had to be important for the boy to be there at all. Farm people had little truck with mill people. The only places the village and farm met were at the train, the store, or the church, the last only on the rare occasion there was a service and that didn't happen often. There was the Hall when there were dances. Everyone showed up for those.

Like the dance being held that night just ten or twelve hours away depending on what time it actually was right then, the sun up, light coming in through the window and door. Come eight o'clock tonight the first record would be spun by Wally Yaztremski, maybe one of those twist songs or the one about the teeny weeny yellow polka dot bikini. Joel had tried doing the twist and figured he was good at it as most people. What he was hoping Wally would play was one of the new ones by Elvis like "It's Now or Never," a song that made Joel crazy for the Indian girl. It made him crazy for Myrna too. Her brother squatting there beside him made him think of Myrna with her dress up and her panties wrapped like an undone shackle around one of her ankles.

A bluebottle fly slipped in through a tear in the wire screen above the boy on the floor. The winged bead moved upon the air like a feral trout in a stream, some human stench drawing it from the bog, a man's heavy sweat or some torn skin or muscle unhealed and smelling close enough to dead to make it worth the looking. Joel heard the fly before he saw it, the weighted drone, its purple belly, and its wings like a bumblebee's seemingly too small and fragile to hold such a body up.

The fly passed over Joel's shoulder and he caught for a moment the sun-bitten glint of blue on the fly-belly's carapace, the wings a faint blur above. It passed over him and lifted above the boy's bent neck, almost touching the line of sharp bones that rose beneath the skin, the bandage with its wound, frays of shaggy blond hair adrift. The boy did not move, though Joel saw the muscles flicker in the boy's hand, another muscle in the wrist tensing so slightly it was less than a whisper. His head hung sideways above the knees and crossed arms, the eyes still seemingly on Joel, though there was a tightening of the lids around them, and now there was a space between the wrist and knee. The fly continued to move as if without purpose, aimless, drifting in narrow circles, descending out of its careen beside the boy then turning a sharp quick angle and grazing the hair on the boy's forearm. As it did, the boy's hand turned and rose in what Joel could only imagine was a rattlesnake's strike it was that fast, vertical and impossible, the boy's hand like a brown and bitten mouth closing upon the desperate carom of the fly.

Joel heard its frantic whir inside the encasement of the brown fist held out over the boy's knee. The boy raised his head, the eyes quick with a blue dark as autumn clouds. Joel blinked once and the boy smiled at him, raised his arm, and dashed the fly onto the floor between his feet, the fly's body cracking there, its dying the sound a bubble of spit makes exploding on hot iron.

Up at the front of the bunkhouse Joel heard wood crackling in the stove, and the hiss of water in a pot, a faint draft of coffee slipping through the still air. Saturday was a morning to sleep in. But someone was up, likely Vern Lupich, the man who most days got the coffee cooking in the pot.

There was the cough of someone waking, but the boy didn't stir. He stared instead back at Joel, his blue eyes opaque. Emerson returned his arm to the other arm, the two resting across his knees again, hands hanging down. When he spoke, his mouth barely moved.

"She told me to get you," he said. "I wouldn't have come for other."

It was Myrna wanted him, who else?

"Get me for what?"

Joel watched the boy ponder the question as if wondering whether there even was an answer and if he might opine it, his instructions from her simple enough, but not in any way he cared to know, just doing what his big sister asked of him. Joel figured his question created a complication the boy couldn't answer to, not knowing what it was she might want Joel for other than in Joel's mind, the boy's mind too, he figured, to rut.

"She never said for what or why." The voice was quick and angry, defensive, as he added, scowling: "You know for what!" and then almost not speaking aloud, in a sharp whisper said: "To get you is what she told me . . . and that's what I'm here to do." And when Joel didn't respond, the boy burst out, spittle a flicker across his wrists, his whisper thin and hard: "You think I'd come for anything else?"

There seemed to be a complex, maddening confusion in him trying to explain any of it. If it was the same for Emerson as what Joel had known back home on the farm in Nakusp then Joel knew that in the Turfoot family the boy was expected to do certain things, not asked to do them and not told to either. He was to split and pile winter stove wood, feed chickens, sheep, the horse and cow, clean stalls, the barn, the workshop, help put in a crop, harvest it, and, or, dig, climb, cut, wield, walk, run, fish, hunt, shoot, cut, pray, or sing, and above all watch the weather and know who to talk to and who not, the latter being all and everyone outside of family except for the exceptions. The boy was expected to do whatever he did, simply, and to ask why made a ponderless dilemma out of the question, one without any logical meaning.

Joel had been impressed by him killing the fly. He'd not seen it done that way before.

"You got fast hands," he said.

Emerson looked at him steady as if he was without thought following upon his outburst.

"I saw you catch that fly right in the middle of the air," Joel said. "That's quite a trick."

"Hell, anyone can do that," the boy said, coming sullen up out of his reverie. He twisted his shoulders and stretched his thin brown arms out in front of him, his small hands pulled into fists, the skinny pyramids of the sharp knuckles shining. He stared hard across them at the walls beyond, seeming already to regret he'd talked at all.

"No, I don't think so," said Joel. "I bet no one else can catch and kill a fly as good as you just did."

The boy's eyes looked quick at Joel, a sudden glint sparkling out of the deep he had inside him, the brightness there as if strangely erupted by chance and circumstance, his being there with Joel at all and, to boot, being told by someone outside of his family, especially someone older, that he was good at doing things. There was a brief moment, a fierce pride Joel could see in him, and then it was hidden away, the eyes opaque again.

"There's lots I can do you don't know about," the boy said, an eye tooth glittering a split second and gone behind his narrow lips. When Joel didn't say anything to that, the boy sulled up again and part angry, part humiliated said: "You think you're smart, I bet. You think you got secrets. Well, I seen you with Myrna. I watched what you two do up there in the rocks above the high field. Don't think I don't know what you've been at. I seen you rut in her lots of times."

Joel stared into the eyes across from him. Other than that moment of pride, they revealed nothing. The boy had translucent eyelids like the haws of a cat, a third lid seeming to roll out beneath the other two, keeping what the boy was seeing a mystery for anyone who tried to read his thoughts.

So the boy had spied on him when he'd been with Myrna. Oddly him seeing them didn't matter to Joel. Emerson was as much animal to him as likely Joel was to the boy, as his sister was to either of them. He wondered if he'd been the same way when he was that age and thought he might, given the way he was still peering through windows at night. Talking to the boy made him suddenly feel older than he'd been a moment before.

He didn't want to think of Myrna. He had kept her mostly out of his mind since he got wrapped up with Art Kenning and McAllister, and the sawyer's wife too, cutting herself like she did. Them and Alice, the way her smell tasted in the back of his mouth.

The boy squatted there stolid, his body, so slight and quick, now seeming thickened. He turned his head away and spoke into the door laid up beside him, saying: "You can call me Emerson," telling Joel what he'd already remembered. And then, belligerent again, quick to tease out an insult, added, "And don't you go calling me anything but that neither."

"I guess I won't do that then," said Joel quietly, adding, "Emerson."

They were speaking in whispers, the boy with his close-set lips hardly making a sound. Joel didn't have to strain no matter he was listening to him with only the one ear up, the boy's voice insinuating in the same way water does when it wicks into a clot or sponge. Other sounds came up through his pillow, reverberations accentuated by the army cot he lay on with its iron frame resonant on the wooden floorboards, the metal struts and wires he was laid on vibrating. Farther off he could hear Joseph from out the front door of the bunkhouse, his scored and scratched guitar, those sharp fingernails cutting notes from the strings, each pick and pluck separate one from another, cruel too in the chords' sweet loneliness. It was no tune Joel had heard before, but a salvaging of what at this moment the gang sawyer's heart had to tell his hands of what it knew, Joel hearing some of the songs, bits of "Blue Canadian Rockies" among the far-off wince of "Cry Me a River." And beyond that too a simplicity so complex in its yearning that he could only feel it, no understanding of such loss and loneliness possible in his short life.

The smell of coffee was rousing other sleepers. Sounds came from elsewhere in the bunkhouse, not far off a foot pushing itself into a stiff boot and then another foot into another boot, a coarse hand slapping at an unshaven cheek or itching an arm to kill some errant mosquito or deer fly, and undercutting these a noise between the guitar and the boots and the slap, the mumble of men up at the front of the bunkhouse by the stove where there was a rickety table with five chairs, the men appearing half dressed from their bunks and all of a sudden starting to play their Saturday morning game of hearts, a penny a point, the odd number rounded up to a nickel when it was time to pay, the game with friendly stakes, nobody drunk, not yet, and nobody foolish enough to change to five-card stud or draw poker, those being games played only late at night after the drinking and carouse, the laughter and loneliness. He heard the shuffle of cards, the flitter as the tired pasteboards melded together, a grunt or two, a soft *the hell you say*, spoken by someone, and another voice responding *is what she said*, any and all other words and comments left to slip adrift in the farther dark of the long room, but over the game he heard boots come banging down past the rank of cots and stop behind him.

Joel breathed in deep through his nose and expelled the stink of Reiner who'd come up to the foot of Joel's bunk. Ernie was staring at the boy by the door, but Emerson didn't move. His arms hung over his knees. The fists he'd made a moment before had turned back into hands, both of them hanging loosely from his narrow wrists, the left one swinging slightly side to side as a single leaf does on a cottonwood when there's no breeze felt.

Joel could feel the boy, the small body compressed and tense in a strange and intimate immensity.

A crow called, guttural, insistent, the men at their cards quiet, no answer anywhere other than the far-off picking of Joseph's guitar as it sought some other relic tune for relief of time along the river.

"Who the hell's this here?" Reiner said from behind Joel, his boot kicking at the iron bed leg, the clunk shifting the bed an inch or two.

Joel kept still and tried to ride it out, this Reiner, this piece of misery.

"None of you hillbillies are supposed to be in here," Reiner said, talking to Joel and staring down at the boy. "Cliff and Joseph and the rest wouldn't put up with it and I won't neither."

Joel sat suddenly, his shoulders and chest bare, his belt loose in his pants. He swung his legs out from under his blanket and stood up, Reiner looming.

"Joseph wouldn't care and Cliff and them aren't here and even if they were, this boy's none of your business," said Joel. "He's a friend of mine is all."

Reiner took a step around Joel and reached down to grab the boy by the arm, Joel moving too late to try and stop him, but there was no need, for Reiner stopped himself, the boy's one hand behind him, reappearing with a knife in his grip, the five-inch blade bare, sharp as a kitten's tooth and shivering. The knife cut within an inch of Reiner's outstretched finger-tips and began to weave slow figure eights, light catching at the steel making it a bright wing.

Reiner stared at the blade and his hand moved a hair's breadth closer in the air between them.

"Don't," the boy said, and quietly too.

"What the hell?"

The knife continued its slow arabesques as Reiner pulled his hand back slow, garbling a few words, and finally spitting out: "You little fucker."

The boy rose slowly up and then slipped around the door and out to the porch where he turned and faced back into the bunkhouse. Looking part bobcat, part wolverine, Emerson squatted on the porch lip in the same position he'd had beside the bunk, the knife gone, vanished behind him where Joel figured the scabbard had to be, a leather sleeve hooked to the boy's belt under the tail of his shirt. It had been something to see the boy catch a fly and kill it, but his bringing out the blade had been faster, a silver trout sporting a riffle.

Reiner took a step out, the boy not moving. "You get the hell on out of here," Reiner said, confused and flustered. "What kinda kid are you?" When the boy didn't respond, he said: "I could break you in half if I'd a mind to."

Joel could see the boy's eyes locked on Reiner's sternum. He struggled into his shirt and ducked around Reiner, his boots with the socks tucked in them hanging from his one hand, the other hand trying to notch his belt where his scabbard hung.

"Leave him alone," said Joel as he turned by the cedar round, half afraid and not.

"Fuck off the both of you," said Reiner.

Joel sat down on the planks above the step, his back to Reiner, Emerson beside him as Joel pulled on a sock and then a boot, tying it tight to his ankles with the leather laces. He started with the other sock as he heard, "Fucking little redneck pricks," Reiner's loose boots horse-heeled in iron, diminishing in blunt echoes along the bunkhouse aisle as he walked back into the shadows.

Emerson stared down the corridor between the bunks at the back of the man who'd tried to grab him, a watchful stillness in him, half tame, a wilding you touched carefully if at all.

"He ain't so much," said Joel.

The boy said nothing, Joel waiting, and then Emerson said, "He's got bear skulls in there that he don't deserve to own. I seen him shoot two bears up at the dump a couple of months ago. He did it just for fun." Emerson breathed hard through his nose as if trying to expel something deep inside him. "He's a coward, is what."

"He is," said Joel. He looked out at the mountain beyond the river. Back at the farm on the Arrow Lakes, Joel's family had toms like Myrna's brother, barn cats that were never fed and never tamed though sometimes when he was small Joel tried, the scars on his hands evidence of their desperation and fury, a kitten, stray, and not yet grown, but just waiting till it was.

And the boy turned to him, still sitting there, his head turned slight, but his eyes holding aslant to the bunks where Reiner had gone, the man's body a bulk fading.

"She told me to tell you to come, so you gotta come."

"You go on," said Joel. "Tell her I'll meet her in the field. She knows where. First I got to go to the café."

"Nope," said the boy turning full around and sitting a careful three feet away. "She told me you'd say that about going to the café and she said not to. And she ain't up in the field and she ain't up in the rocks neither. She told me to get you and that's what I got to do."

"I guess so," said Joel, Myrna suddenly in his head, her belly and breasts, and him not wanting her right then to be there, her white rump, the half moons of her butt raised up, the thatch of hair between her legs wet with his jism, and her hollering, fists holding on to rocks so tight he wasn't sure if she held the earth or the earth held her.

Letting go his fingers locked together, he stretched his hands out backward, palms to the bunkhouse doorway. He had to move or soil himself with his own seed, the boy staring sideways at him.

"Rise up and I'll follow you," and saying that, Joel watched the boy named Emerson come up out of his squat, his body a slip of muscle moving without effort on slender, threadbare bones. Joel barely had his last boot wrapped and tied when he saw the boy slide away along the faint trail forty feet in from the margin of the bog, a trail Joel thought only he knew was there. He got up and went quickly after this Emerson who'd watched him rut with his sister and probably stroked his own little cock while he was doing it. When he caught up to Emerson he was leaning on a boulder. The boy didn't seem frustrated. He was just waiting.

And they went on, a bit more slowly. The railway was far off to the left of them. They were fading steady away from the tracks and river. Joel figured as he ran that if Emerson kept on they'd end up on the low flank of the mountain and there begin a climb to where the farm was.

This was Emerson's swamp, bog, and creek, his hollows, valley, mountains, and river, the earth of this place bred into his bones, just as the Arrow Lakes country was Joel's, the slow reaches of the Monashee Joel's, the mountains' soft peaks that rarely rose to rock, and the high walls of the far Purcells to the south, their peaks snow-bound and rising steep out of Kootenay Lake. The draws and gullies, hidden meadows and creeks, the valleys where he had run, ridden, walked, clambered, crawled, and climbed had been his and, sudden, irrevocable, he almost faltered, knowing the land he'd left behind was lost to him except his remembering it. Joel at his run said to himself the word *was*, and said too *that's when I was younger, young*, his outcry such the boy ahead of him stopped and turned, looked back at him, and called out: "What's wrong?"

And, "Nothing," Joel cried back, his running slowed to a steady pace. "Nothing," he said, and looking up saw Emerson stopped.

Joel stood now on the other side of the swamp copse and glanced down at a red-shafted flicker lying on its back between two chunks of cedar, its belly torn open, the viscera gone. The bird had flung its wings apart when it fell from the sky, the salmonberry feathers cupped as if in supplication, the beak stretched open, a fly perched watchful on its long tongue. There were no maggots and he thought perhaps they'd eaten the viscera entire and fled leaving the meat. Willow leaves had gathered in the lee of one wing, a light breeze stirring them, the wing as if alive, still moving.

Myrna's brother was thirty feet away squatted in the lee shadow of a boulder the size of a dump truck. Joel watched as the boy reached out and pulled two hips off a mountain rose, the brief cardinal swell of the fruit disappearing one at a time between his lips, his narrow jaws clenching down, the seed fuzz slipping from between his lips as he chewed them away.

Joel knew where he was now. In the mouth of a meadow at the mountain's foot was an old, deserted one-room shack of a church. He'd never got to it by going through the swamp, only by following the overgrown track that led down from the high road. It'd been months since he'd been anywhere near. It didn't look any better than the last time he'd passed it by, the roof shakes withered, the glass in a pointed window by the door gone but for a few shards sticking up out of the old putty like knives pointed heavenward.

Joel took off his hat and wiped his face. His breaths were ragged from the long journey from the bunkhouse. He walked out into the open, reached down for a rock, quartz freckles across its face aglitter. He licked it once to see the sparkle and then threw it sidearm at the boulder face above the boy. The rock struck where he'd been aiming it, a foot or so above the boy's head, the rock clicking as it caromed off in a whisper faint as a sparrow's cry. Emerson didn't turn, but raised his hand to him palm out.

He was unsure of whether to join the boy at the boulder or stay where he was. The church looked deserted as always. The grasses in the dry bog at his feet had tilted their stalks south, their heads twisting, last seeds flashing into the dusty air as Joel brushed them with his boot. A high wind moved across the mountain's face across the river, a thin band of cloud against the peaks, white feathers frayed and tattered like troubled wings across the sheer rock and gone, and the wind too fleeing along the mountain face and flanks, firs and hemlocks suddenly astir, needles seething with the sound of cracked grain thrown violently across sheets of tin. Jays and crows lifted from branches in the forest marge and flew out to join the rise of the wind, the murderous bands black and blue shards stark against the grey wall of rain that appeared as if conjured from nothing, pouring down the valley from the north.

It would be upon them in no time, a few minutes, no more. Joel glanced at Emerson but the boy did not move, only stared across the last of the bog at the shack everyone in the hills and village called the Someday Church, laughing when they said it, the boy looking out over the swamp to the river and the eastern range, the church standing in a raised meadow where the trees and rocks started their climb up the mountains.

Joel pulled on his hat and stepped over a fallen aspen trunk, thinking to find shelter, the sudden cold from the storm rolling down the valley wrapping itself in coils around him. As he went around a thick hummock, the door of the church creaked open and he looked up as Myrna stepped out onto the worn porch, her pale hand holding the door ajar. She gazed at him, her eyes even at a distance wide in her pink face. Joel glanced over to see if Emerson was still there, but as he did the boy gave him only a bare and fleeting glance as he slipped around the great boulder and was gone back into the swamp.

The blunt clouds were over Joel now and a cold rain began to pelt down in heavy drops, dust spurting up from the dust at his feet. He held his arm up to shelter his eyes and heard his name in the sudden thrash of wind and water, Myrna crying: "Joel, Joel," her voice high and wild in the swirl. He stood for a moment, thinking almost everything, Art, Irene McAllister who'd cut herself, Joseph and Cliff and Reiner, the smell of the dream smoke in Wang Po's basement, all that had happened in a part day and night away, and then Alice, how he'd watched her at the end of the night. He turned his head away thinking to run back into the swamp but something, he did not know what, made him look again at the church and he saw Myrna's wild and frantic waving, her one arm sweeping like a tree limb in the wind. She called his name as if it were some kind of crazed fragment from a song stuck in a record's scratched groove, some kind of Joel *tick* Joel *tick* Joel, and as he heard his name he took a step and, clothes soaked from the violence of the rain, ran toward the church, all the time thinking, *No*, and again, *No*, and knowing it was the word *Yes* he was saying, and cursing himself for saying it.

Myrna slipped inside when he neared and he followed her, leaping up onto the porch and through the open door and into the room where he stopped, breathless, water running down his face, his hair plastered to his neck. What he saw were two crippled chairs, the back of the worse one wired on to the seat, a scarred three-legged table propped under a back window, a stack of old cedar shakes taking the place of the missing fourth leg, the whole thing teetering, and in one corner a stained mattress on the floor, the cotton worn, torn in places and the tears taped down, the mattress threadbare and plagued with bits of straw and dust. At the mattress's foot lay folded what were sheets and a spare blanket sticking out of a single pillowcase.

All that he recognized of what had been the church was the board altar against the back wall with dead candle stubs burned into dry puddles, their wicks twisted and dry. Along the altar dishes and pots were arranged, a few pieces of cutlery, two knives, some spoons of various sizes, and a single fork, two tines missing. Under the altar was a stool with a wash basin and a galvanized pail dented and scraped from long use, streaks of tar gone hard in drips down the sides. In the far corner was a dented Queen heater vented out the back wall and likely to burn the whole place down if it was ever lighted, wood piled beside it, bits and pieces of sticks and limbs she must have gathered from the forest. A broom leaned against the wall in the corner, the floor swept clean. There were two cardboard boxes with what looked like clothes and other things, rags and towels, and part of a plastic clock sticking out from under what might be a sleeve, the ticking loud in the room.

And Myrna by the altar shelf, the window arched above her with a few cracked panes of old rolled glass still left, the holes for the missing panes covered with oiled butcher paper tacked to the frames.

There was the mattress and the thin quilt folded at its foot and her standing by the altar holding her belly with spread hands. He stood quiet in his boots, the wind blowing the door shut behind him with a dithering crack. What he wanted was to return to the storm, wondering why he was there, what he had come for, the nakedness of what she'd be when he wanted her to be, knowing it, and then his being in her and rutting as always, and yet there were her hands on her belly, the fingers splayed. And suddenly wanting her as he always wanted her from the very first time he saw her, there on the wagon back when she sat there looking at him down at the station, her riding away on the buckboard staring back at him, and then up by the caves at the top of the field where the trail led to the high country and the cold, clean mountain spring where all the water in the world began.

He stood in the ramshackle church unsure in his sureness, at last, at least, there. The boy, Emerson, had taken Joel exactly where Joel was supposed to be, just as Joel had known all along where he was going, and, yes, he didn't turn back, no matter his wanting to, knowing Myrna was at the end of where he was going.

She said: "Joel, Joel, look."

And he thought he was and did again.

And seeing him seeing her at last, she said, plaintive, proud in her joy, "I got your baby inside me, Joel. I got your baby."

FIFTEEN

CLAUDE LISTENED TO HIS MILL, the Saturday morning cleanup crew almost done, the fire in the burner starting to gut out as the shards and shattered bits of wood and bark, the endless dust, fell into the desultory flames. He was discontent. He missed the workweek, the saws, the screams and chatter of the machines, the belts whining, and the rattle of the chains and cables, power diesels pulling down hard when a big log slammed into the head saw, the great slab carved off and falling away to be carried up the conveyor to the burner.

And he missed the whistles, the story of the mill. Familiar as breathing, they spoke through the shifts: one whistle to start up or shut down, two whistles for the millwright, three for the foreman, four for Claude himself, and five for the first-aid man. The whistles called their needs through the days and nights of the week, their shrieks coiling up and down the valley, the wailing echoes sounding along the river and mountains, moose, lynx, cougar, and bear no longer lifting their heads into the terrible outcries they endured, the beast they heard crying out in pain, the animal that never died.

Claude longed for the convulsive fury when the mill was working full throttle, the way it consumed everything leaving nothing behind but loaded boxcars, smoke, and ash. It wasn't just the logs and the saws that tore them into lumber. It was the men on the mill floor. He loved the waste of his men's bodies, their exhaustion when they walked off the floor. When the shift was over they passed below his window in clumps and clusters, no one talking, their lunch buckets hanging from their hands. Every shift the men tried for bonus, a few extra dollars twice a month, the difference between lard and butter, hamburger or chops, powdered milk or cream. The crew lived off the sawyer's sweat. The sawyer set the pace in the mill and Claude's best sawyer was Jim McAllister.

The only decoration in the room was last year's calendar, a naked blonde wearing a Santa Claus hat sprawled on a red sheet, big tits, a great ass, and a crotch barely hidden by a wisp of satin pulled taut between her thighs. It didn't matter what man came in, they always looked at the calendar. The months below her had long ago been stripped away. The dead days of 1959, last year's December staring out the same window as the girl did, as he did. He had his desk, his chair, and a single old kitchen chair for whoever was asked to sit and that meant mostly no one except for right now, Art Kenning, who was sitting beside a four-drawer tin-can cabinet and an ancient hand-crank telephone in a wooden box screwed to the wall behind his shoulder. It was one of the three phones in the village—this one, one at the train station, and the last at Rotmensens' store. Every time Claude cranked the phone to raise some operator in Kamloops he felt like he'd fallen back into the century before the Boer War. They all lived in this sawmill town beyond any civilized world, no television, radio static, newspapers always a day late, and on and on.

Saturday morning, ten o'clock, the sun high enough to reach over the lip of the mountain into the valley bottom, light struggling to get through the last of the rain clouds that were passing over. Even on a clear day the light mostly failed in here, the wet clot of sun barely seeping through the opaque patina of dust and charred smoke and oil on the window. Claude long ago figured it would require a chisel in the hands of a patient man to clean the years away.

He looked at his first-aid man, who hadn't said a word since he sat down.

"What do you want, Art?" Claude said.

When Art didn't move or speak, Claude spoke a little louder, his voice almost tired: "Gawdammit, Kenning, get off your ass and get a cuppa coffee. Get one for me while you're at it. You know where the pot is."

Art shook his head as he dragged himself to his feet and went out the office door to where the young company clerk sat doing unpaid extra hours adding log scale on a manual machine as he kept the minimal accounts the mill required, head office far away in Vancouver. The clerk looked demented as he pulled the crank for the ten-thousandth time that morning, adding up the numbers on the columns of figures that seemed to go on forever. The coffee pot was on a hot plate behind the clerk's desk, the pot sitting on a coiled wire burner, the coffee cooked black by the hours.

Claude looked out the window and watched one of his Saturday cleanup crew cross the yard and disappear through a door's maw into the mill, the wheelbarrow he was pushing full of bits and pieces of broken wood. The turban on the man's head was black with soot from working around the burner, flecks of sawdust fretting his beard. Claude didn't know what Sikh it was. To him they were all the same except for the one called Jaswant Singh. Claude didn't know why they all had the same name Singh. This Jaswant was the leader of the green chain crew. The Sikh told him once he'd been a teacher back in India, but Claude figured he was lying. If he'd been a teacher then why was he working in the north on a green chain in a dead-end, spaghetti mill?

Art came back from the other room and set a cup of brackish coffee on Claude's desk. The first-aid man sat down again on the chair, his one hand turned up on a knee, the other holding a second cup.

Claude ignored him as he watched his mill yard.

The door the Sikh had gone through hung from one hinge, the bottom boards frayed from scraping the dirt, the sill rotted away. Everything in the mill needed fixing, the buildings falling apart, the nails holding the tin-can corrugated iron on the rafters rust-rotted, the iron panels skewed. What parts of the roof he'd had fixed were those above machines, rain and snow coming through most everywhere else. Scoops had been carved in the boards by the hobnail boots of workers. They reminded Claude of the stairways in old monasteries and castles he'd seen in France. The mill was on its last legs and he was under orders to run what was left of it into the ground, squeezing every nickel and dime out of it before it got sold to one of the big American outfits who wanted the timber quota. Whoever owned the quota owned the watershed. Claude had been high-grading Douglas fir and hemlock out of a big cutblock east of the river for two months. He'd told the fallers to take down the cedar and leave it to rot. The loggers dropped the cedars and crushed what there was with Cats, cutting or pushing over the trees, calling them widow-makers and blowdowns, there being no market in the States for the softwood. His fallers had been under orders since spring breakup to cream off the fir and trash the rest.

The guys from the Government Forest Service down in Kamloops had taken their money and turned their backs on what he was doing. The cash he'd passed out had been worth every cent. Money talks and bullshit walks. He'd learned that in the war.

When he was done with the cutblock there'd be nothing left but a few scattered pecker poles hanging over the carnage of stumps and limbs and crushed trees, the salmon creeks jammed with rocks and mud, the steep ground sliding toward the river, the bush roads waiting to wash out in the first runoff in the spring. It was as bad as the war. You slaughtered, slashed, and burned, and then you walked away, leaving what was left for the locals to deal with.

He could see his battered boxcars at a loading dock outside Baton Rouge, men leaning into their work, the lumber piling up on some bayou siding, redneck drivers in flat-deck trucks with bald tires and worn brakes lined up to haul it away to construction sites for floors, walls, and roofs. Shotgun shacks and mansions, they were all the same. The sweat would be running down those black backs. He could smell them. His own men stank the same, the sun hot on their bare arms and necks, their skulls cooking inside hard hats and turbans on the loading docks and chains, blackflies and horseflies swarming on their skin, salt sweat running down their chests and bellies as they filled his boxcars.

They were lucky they had work at all.

Another year, maybe two, and he'd be gone. Once the big outfit down at the coast sold the government log quota they'd fire everybody, auction off the equipment, and torch the buildings for insurance. In five years the Americans would own everything from Kamloops to Jasper. The last few independent mills along the river would die. The towns and villages would shrink back to farms and horse ranches and the mill workers and loggers would walk away from their trailers, shacks, and houses and head south to the city to look for work, most of them ending up on labour gangs or construction crews, collecting welfare, pogey, or down on skid row smashed on booze and drugs when they weren't hanging around the union hiring halls for a chance to work the fishing boats or catch a few weeks logging off some float camp up the coast. Some would head out to the prairie but there was only summer work there. In the winter everything on the plains died in the cold.

He looked at Art Kenning sitting in his chair with a mug of bad coffee. Art was telling him again what had happened at Jim McAllister's trailer last night, the wife his sawyer had.

Claude shuffled the papers on his desk. "It sounds like she left town," he said. "Women do that, you know. They just up and leave."

"But how? She couldn't walk or anything."

"That doesn't matter," said Claude. "You said she was small. Easy enough to carry her out to his truck if he needed to. Anyway, Art, she's his business and you keep out of it. If he says she's gone, then she's gone."

"She's disappeared," Art said. "Vanished, just like that. There isn't a trace of her anywhere in that trailer."

He waited but Art said nothing more. Claude knew Art had spent most of the night drinking and smoking down in Wang Po's hole under the cookhouse. Art didn't look completely wrecked, but he wasn't totally there either. Claude didn't care.

What Art did with his nights was okay with him so long as he was close enough to hear the whistles. Art was on call twenty-four hours a day. His job was looking after the men at the mill when it was running and when it wasn't. That was number one. On top of that he could look out for the local farmers and hill people, their wives and kids and sometimes even their animals, so long as he didn't forget who he was working for, who was paying him his wages.

But this morning he looked beat.

"You get too involved, Art," Claude finally said, tired of the man sitting there. "You always have, in the war, back when I first met you. Your problem is you think you can fix things. You can't, you know. Most all a man can do is keep a foot or two ahead of whatever's dragging at his heels."

Art looked up from his coffee. "Marie told me my lifeline was broken."

"Who?"

"Marie. You remember her. Marie in Paris."

"Christ, Art, what the hell are you thinking about that old stuff for?"

Art tried to smile. He tried to show Claude he was okay. "But what are you going to do about Irene?"

Claude shrugged. "Nothing changes, Art."

The mug in Art's hands slowed to a stop, his finger tracing a crooked line along the handle. When Claude didn't say anything more Art began turning it again.

"Why not?" Art asked.

Claude took a breath and let it out slow. What kind of a question was that? He'd long ago given up trying to figure Kenning out. What Art didn't seem to understand was that people like McAllister were the same as they'd always been, in the war or up here on the river.

"I don't know where I am today, Claude," Art said. "Sometimes, like now, I don't even know who I am. Every time I look I find someone different."

"Who? You mean other people?"

The hot coffee in Art's mug slopped over onto the knee of his pant leg, but he didn't seem to notice. He rubbed at it absently with his free hand. "Why do you keep asking me? I told you already."

"Jesus, Art, you're a mess."

Claude picked up the stack of waybills the station agent from across the tracks had delivered an hour before and shuffled them into a loose pile. Seven boxcars loaded for Baton Rouge. They'd go out on the Sunday night freight to Vancouver, then to the States.

"Look, Art, Jim was in to see me an hour ago," Claude said.

Art's hand started shaking. He put his mug on the floor by his boot. "What did he say?"

Claude ignored the question. "You know how important Jim is to this outfit, don't you?"

"Claude," said Art. He began to speak slowly, carefully. "Jim's woman cut herself up with his hunting knife. I was there last night at the trailer stitching her up and now McAllister says she's gone. What I want to know is where'd she go? It's not like she walked away or caught a train. The only train last night was the through freight to Edmonton."

When Claude said nothing, Art leaned forward, his hands on his thighs. "Christ, Claude, she couldn't even crawl successfully. Joel, he was there listening at the back of the trailer. He knows what happened."

"What the hell was Joel doing up there with you?"

"It doesn't matter," said Art. "He's not important, Claude. He was just there. You know how he wanders the village half the night. I'm sorry I even brought him up. This's about Jim having his wife cut herself. What I want to know is what did he do with her?"

"Dammit, Art, wake up. I swear the shit you're smoking at Wang Po's has addled your brain."

Art placed his face in his cupped hands as if trying to stop it from sliding off his skull. "I'm going crazy," he said. He dropped his hands and attached them to his knees again, his fingers gripping the worn cotton of his soiled jeans. "You're still the same gawdam major you were in the war."

Art waited and then spoke into the silence. "Claude, she'd have bled to death if I hadn't gone up to that trailer. It was McAllister who came and got me at my cabin. He's the one asked me to help her. Didn't he tell you that?"

"He never mentioned you or Joel. We talked about the work that needs doing on the draw cables for the carriage on the head rig. They're going to need replacing. Look, Art, you and me were in the war together. We saw all kinds of things. Sometimes I look back and wonder if half of what I remember even happened. The parts I do remember, I work hard to forget. Listen to me. You were down at the cookhouse drinking whisky and smoking with the chink all night. How the hell do you know anything? Remember, I gave you this job as much because of the war as because you were hard up. I found you in Japtown down in Vancouver and I can send you back. You can sit in the same bar on Water Street and go into the same gallery and die with a pipe in your mouth and a bottle in your arms, the rest of you wrapped around a toilet that won't flush. Don't try to make me pick between you and McAllister. I can get another first-aid man up here Monday on the passenger train from Kamloops, maybe not as good as you, but what does that matter so long as he knows what a bandage or a sling is.

McAllister's the best I've got for cutting second-rate, crap timber into usable spaghetti two-by-fours and sixes. I'll never find another sawyer good as him to come up the river."

"She cut herself the way you'd cut meat," Art said, his eyes closed, his body beginning to rock backwards and forwards.

Claude waited and when Art didn't continue, he went on: "Why don't you go get some sleep. There's the dance tonight up at the hall. You should rest awhile and then go and take a few turns with somebody's horny wife, some half-assed farmer's daughter. If you're lucky you could take one out back of the hall into the bush. Old Turfoot's got that girl of his, what's-her-name, Myrna? You could have her if you want. God knows your friend Joel does her every chance he gets. And there's always the Indian girl at the café. It's me who locks and unlocks her this weekend and she's going to be at the dance. You could take a run at her. She's prime stuff."

"She's just a kid, Claude. Jesus Christ."

"There's never enough women there for the men to dance with. The men deserve some fun. Her too. She's been in that lean-to every night for months."

"You haven't changed."

"What's that supposed to mean?"

"You were the same in Paris."

"What the hell's Paris got to do with anything?"

"Remember Hélène?"

"Who're you talking about?"

"That night at the Olympique, remember?"

Claude just looked at him.

"Hélène? Remember her?"

"*La petite pute?*"

"She wasn't a whore," Art said. "She was just a girl in the war. You never understood that, did you?"

"That was a long time ago, Art."

Claude said what he said cold. He said it like he was somewhere else, alone.

"What about Irene McAllister?" As Art spoke he knocked over his coffee mug, the coffee spilling. The mug rolled under his chair and he left it there.

Claude sat quiet a moment as if he were pulling wayward parts of himself back into line. "Art?" he said quietly. "Leave it alone."

"I'm not crazy, Claude. You had to see that trailer today. He cleaned up every sign of what happened last night and he took her stuff away. Even the joy-shack's cleaned up. There's nothing in there but Jim's tools and a few boxes."

Claude slapped at a mosquito on his arm and missed, the tiny insect circling up around his head. He leaned back and clapped his hands together, the mosquito lifting in the fluff of air above his fingertips and crooning across the room. "I don't know anything about his gawdam joy-shack," he said.

"Don't, Claude."

Claude watched as Art bent down and fumbled for his coffee mug. He caught at the handle and set the mug upright beside the chair leg. There were times Claude wished he'd never found Art down in Vancouver. Art was a good first-aid man, but he didn't know how to leave the drugs alone, the booze. There was never enough for him. What was he supposed to do when Art was like this? The opium twisted Art into knots after he came down from it, yet he'd go back and do it again and again. And the war? Hell, Claude didn't know how many times he'd heard about that Dutch farm woman. He should've had Art shipped back home when he got wounded. They'd been fighting a war, for Christ's sake, too busy to worry about a couple of women. And by the time Art came to him about it they'd moved on toward Amsterdam. By then the Scheldt and Island were yesterday's news. The Dutch could look after their own.

Art had told Claude he had to talk to the corporal who'd been there, but the corporal, Alvin something or other, had got himself wounded right after it happened and was back in England on the way to being shipped home. Claude never did try to run him down. Hell, he should've had Art shipped back home when he got wounded at Moerbrugge. Anyway, it was years ago, for fuck's sake. And he'd heard the Tommy kid was killed on leave in Paris later. Beaten to death in an alley, knifed, or shot, he couldn't remember. What was his last name, Bidowski or Bidumski, some bohunk name. He was a shifty prick. And Paris? Christ, Art couldn't leave that alone either.

"Jesus, Art," Claude said. "Let it go."

Art sat back, his hands coming apart like wood does when it's split.

"What?" Claude cried. "What do you want from me?"

Art stared into his hands.

"Go home, Art. Go back to your cabin. Come Monday morning when the start-up whistle blows I want to see my sawyer sitting in the saw box. When that first log rolls onto the head rig I want McAllister breaking it down into slabs and cants." He took a deep breath and went on: "Listen. I count on you to do what needs to be done, and what needs to be done here is for you to leave all this alone. You understand?"

Art got himself up slowly.

"And leave the pipe alone. Stay away from that stuff."

Claude watched him shamble out of the office. Art looked beat-up and broken down, but it seemed to Claude that whatever the beating was it took place a long time before Irene McAllister. The war didn't do Art Kenning any good, Claude thought, and then, a little belligerent, he spoke into the quiet of his office: "Well, it screwed up a lot of people, didn't it?"

Loose papers were scattered across his desk. Between his hands in a messy stack were the week's production figures and invoices he had to sign off on so the clerk could authorize payment. There was the guy down in Kamloops asking for another donation to the Social Credit Party war chest, an election coming up in a few more months. There were the Forestry guys to pay off and the highways minister too. That asshole. It never ended.

A vague image of Hélène, one of the little whores he'd had whenever he was on leave in Paris. *La petite pute*. He always called her that. She never seemed to mind. She knew Marie, the woman Art always saw. He couldn't remember if Marie was a whore too. Why did Art always bring those days up? Whatever was the matter with him might go away if he quit the booze and the drugs. His first-aid man. Christ!

"Fuck 'em all," he said as he pushed the papers away. He glanced at his watch. Eleven o'clock. He'd unlocked the Indian girl at seven that morning. She'd be making sandwiches for the men now, pouring coffee, men leaning over the counter trying to catch a look at her tits, her legs and ass. Pretty little thing. He'd have to lock her back up when the store closed. But he'd be talking to her later one way or another anyway, the dance and all. Maybe he'd take her over to the house for a drink before taking her to the Hall. Get her going a little.

Maybe.

What the hell.

Another year, maybe two and he'd be gone just like the mill would be gone. Once he was finished here he'd move the wife and kids out of that house in Kamloops and take them down to Vancouver or over on the Island. Things were starting to boom again down there.

Art would be at Wang Po's again come night. Claude knew it like he knew the sun goes down. They were the two men in the village he didn't have to worry about. They had nowhere to go. All Art needed was to get his mind off Jim McAllister and his wife. If Kenning did go to the dance later, he'd go wrecked on booze and whatever else he had. What happened up at McAllister's? Hell, Art would have trouble remembering any of it tomorrow.

Claude went over to the window and looked down on the mill yard. Art appeared below him walking almost steady in his boots. One of the Sikhs waved as Art passed by, but the first-aid man didn't wave back. Head down, hands in pockets, Art crossed the main-line tracks and out of sight.

Claude sat back down, picked up the waybills, and shook them together again, tapping them into a pile on the desk.

"McAllister," he said. "If it's not one goddam thing it's another."

SIXTEEN

THE OPEN BOX OF REDBIRD MATCHES and beside the box a delicate pile of charred matchsticks, little withered twigs, crinkled and black from burning. Art held a burning match between his finger and thumb and watched the flame creep down the pine splinter and sear the blackened blister on his skin as the flame consumed itself.

Gentle, almost tender, he placed the fragile stem on the stack with the others. It was important that the carbon sticks not break. If one did then somehow it would be a failing, the burning of his finger and thumb wasted.

He tried to feel the pain, but it was far away, and happening to someone else, not him. His stomach was a knot inside him, the bleeding from ulcers that wouldn't heal. His morning shit had been as usual studded with black blood.

The cat jumped up onto the table and brushed against his arm, a white-footed mouse squeaking in her jaws. The pale, translucent ears of the rodent flared as if hearing something huge and unimaginable, its tiny eyes staring wild from its frail skull.

Black and screaming.

Art didn't waver as he pushed the cat gently to the floor. He watched her crouch and kill what she had offered him, the tiny bones crackling wet in her teeth. Finished, the cat sat in the patch of light coming from the window. One ear was tilted forward listening to the room, the other turned to the door and the end of the early morning rain. The quick shadow of some small bird, a siskin or nuthatch, flittered across the streaked glass. Something alive out there in the world. The cat stretched, then settled onto her paws, closed her yellow eyes, and purred.

Art let his breath go, slowly, surely.

"God . . . damn . . . Claude," he said, each word slow and separate.

A pale light in the window glowed, a few last drops of rain falling in a slow mist as the sky began to clear. Clouds stumbled over the mountains across the river. Swamp grass moved barely by the marsh. He looked to the last of the alders across the field by the raised grade of the railroad. Their leaves shivered like small animals shaking water from their backs. Beyond the berm of the railway lay the river unchanged by the rain, constant in its flow.

He imagined it, deep and brown, flowing and flown.

An empty bottle stood on the raised plank shelf by the door. He'd taken two long drinks before going to see Claude at the mill. He'd needed something to clear his head after the long night, what little sleep he'd had passed out and dreaming. He'd finished what was left of the bottle when he got back, his belly still raging, but quieter by the hour. Beside the empty was another, sentinel, the whisky swirl three inches below the lid.

"No," he said quietly, absently, the hand on his leg unclenching, the one that wasn't burned. He laid it flat on the table alongside the blistered one and pushed himself up, the chair rocking back as he swung himself away.

"Fuck you," he said to the Seagram's bag and the opium that was inside it. "Just fuck you."

He took down the bottle from the shelf and took a jolt, the harsh liquor searing his throat. He took another and put the bottle back, the drinks at last settling his gut.

"Hey, cat."

Lifting a paw, the cat ignored him from her perch by the window, taking one claw at a time in her jaws and cleaning it. The *tic . . . tic . . . tic* as the cat pulled a claw through each interstice was a sound Art loved. He loved the cat, even now, ruined as he was. He glanced at the floor by the door and saw the head, paws, and tail of another mouse, a streak of blood like a comma under the mouse's tiny jaws.

It didn't matter what McAllister had said or not said to Claude earlier that morning. That Irene was hurt or she'd gone away or disappeared were what Claude didn't want to know. Hurt or not hurt, here or not here, what Claude didn't need was trouble for his sawyer. Trouble for Jim meant trouble for Claude.

For the boss things were simple. The work went on.

Nothing changed.

Art sat back down and lit another match. He watched it burn down to his finger and thumb. Just before the pain flashed he saw Major Claude Harper on Pender Street back before the war, young again, a drink in his hand, laughing at something, at nothing.

He dropped the match before it burned him.

The cat stared at him, perfect and alone.

Art reached out and ran his palm over the notches in the cat's scarred ears.

The cat shook him away and then swatted at him when he wouldn't stop. He lowered his forehead to the edge of the table, resting it there. His sweat pooled on the dark wood.

He thought and thought, anything to get his mind off the opium in the bag. He needed to keep his mind clear for Irene. And then he thought of Jaswant and the baby of the woman who'd wandered into the village. What was her name, Gerda something? Dinkle or Dunkle.

He talked to the floor, his eyes following a seam in a fir plank, dirt ground into it. "That baby," he said, "I'll help that baby," and he raised his head slowly up.

He'd take the penicillin up there and see if it worked. He'd promised he would and he'd forgotten. From what Jaswant had said, the baby was sick and getting sicker. But Jaswant hadn't been back this morning to remind him so it was probably all right. Or it wasn't.

One thing he knew, Irene wasn't far away. Jim wouldn't have dropped her off up in Blue River or down in Little Fort. Who would he know to trust her with? Who'd take her in and with such injuries? And there was no one Jim knew in the village who could care for her. The sawyer was a stranger in the river country, just as Art was.

Shadows of cloud drifted over the forests and high cliffs on the far side of the river. Light broke through in the west. There were small birds flying in the blusters of the wind, and leaves too in the alders shining.

He pushed his fingers up his face and into his hair to stop them from shaking.

Something had to be done.

The cat slipped through his legs and was gone, her black tail brushing against the sill log at the corner of the cabin.

"Hey, cat," he said. "Where you going?"

He waited a moment, but he got the answer he always got from the cat. The grass and the trees the same. They never asked and never answered. They just kept on living. The cat walked by herself just like the cat he'd read about when he was a kid.

Standing there staring at everything and nothing he put the baby back into his head. The last time he'd seen the baby it seemed to be wasting away. When was that, a week ago? The baby was probably okay now in spite of what Jaswant had said, and even if it wasn't what could be done? He'd tried Aspirin, steam under a towel, told him to keep it warm, make sure it got enough to eat. Maybe penicillin might help. He had some now.

He should go there right away.

He'd go in a little while.

He turned back into the confine of the cabin, leaving the window open enough for the cat to come back in. He straightened the covers on the bunk, picked up *From Here to Eternity*, folded the corner of the page he'd been reading, and put the book on the shelf. Page ninety-one, the same page it was yesterday and the day before.

James Jones knew what it was all about, no matter his war was a different one.

He knew, but Jones didn't tell it all.

The light from the east shone across the back of the table as he reached for the Seagram's bag and undid its golden strings. He took out the small ball of opium he'd taken from the drugs that'd come up from Vancouver, peeled back the silver foil, and pinched off a tiny bit from what he'd kept for himself. He held it on his palm, the opium rolling gently along his lifeline, his heart line, and he remembered Marie reading his palm in her room above the Café Olympique. She'd told him how he was going on a long journey, and how there was going to be a struggle. He'd always thought the struggle was the war, but she said it wasn't. She spoke of the things that they always do, teacup readers, palm readers—his life, his spirit, his heart. One night just before he went back to his unit she'd turned his teacup upside down and spun it slowly three times with the handle ending up pointing at him. She asked him to turn it over and when he did she looked into the cup for what had seemed a long time, and then picked it up and washed it in the tiny sink she had by the bureau. When he asked her what the cup's story was she said it was nothing. *C'est stupide*, she told him. But when he asked again she wouldn't say. She never read his cup again.

But his palm?

He remembered the last time she read it.

Ta ligne de vie est brisée—ici, ici, she'd said, scrolling her fingernail in the groove of his hand as she pointed out the breaks. *Pauvre garçon*, she said, and she had laughed as he stared at his hand, thinking obscurely of what it meant to have a broken life.

And then he knew. He'd seen people broken. He'd seen them break into so many pieces you didn't know it was a man anymore, a woman, a child.

He knew what kinds of death there were.

Being with Marie was enough.

It was, wasn't it?

And he rolled the foil back onto the ball and placed the opium in the Seagram's bag and put the bag back on the shelf. He looked at the tiny bit of opium on his palm. "It's only a little," he said. He looked around for the cat but the cat was gone.

He hesitated for a brief moment, for just a pinprick of time, and then careful, very careful, he put the ball on the mesh of his pipe and held the lighted match over it, the opium softening and then the smoke and he pulled hard on the pipe, his lungs filling, knowing at that moment there was enough of everything now and then he didn't know anything at all.

———

THEY WERE LYING PARTLY ON THE QUILT, a frayed corner covering Myrna's bare legs. It was a patchwork quilt, a crazy quilt is what his mother would've called it, the bits and pieces of cloth all different shapes and colours sewed together any which way. He looked down at Myrna's pink arm as she pulled the corner of the quilt farther up over the patch of blond hair she had down there, the swell of her belly curving around the damp fray. Joel knew he had to say something after what they'd just done, again, seeing how it was what caused what was in her belly, the baby she said she was having and was. He wasn't sure he could even make sense of it. How could he? And why would she lie if she wasn't?

If it wasn't?

And if it was, then what about Alice? And he felt himself thinking of her and knew he shouldn't. He had just done it with Myrna. For a second he tried to think of Alice, but Myrna's scent filled up the room, the sweat, the smell of her wet from his leavings.

Closing his eyes, he could just see Alice lying on her bed.

He wouldn't think of her, not now, but as he thought of Alice waking in the shack she was in his head and he squeezed his eyes shut at the thought of her lying there.

"Get away," he said, trying to drive her away.

"What? Why do you want me to go?"

"Not you."

"But who then? Who?"

"No one," said Joel. "It's no one I was talking to."

This Myrna Turfoot, he said to himself, his hand on her breast, quiet, her hands nesting her belly, a mist slipping down the valley.

The trouble was Myrna didn't know how to lie, he thought. It was like she was born to be honest no matter how it confused things.

Angry in a way he hadn't been before, Joel said: "We can't live here," and then wondered why he'd said we. And frustrated, yes, not angry, he wasn't angry, not that, he said, "I mean, I can't live here either. You," he added, in case she wasn't getting it. "Neither can you. What if the baby came and you were living down here alone? What then?"

"I wouldn't be alone, don't you see? I'd have you, I'd have the baby."

When she didn't say anything more, he said, "Look, this's no place to live," knowing she was what . . . different? Some people called her slow and, maybe, yes, slower than some in ways, but not all, and not stupid, just Myrna Turfoot from the hill farm who for whatever reason, crazy or not, loved every-thing, loved even him? And why?

He sat up, the quilt awry his thin legs. "There isn't any running water for one thing," he said, "and swamp water's no good for you to drink either. What do you think's going to hap-pen? You think you can haul water here from your father's farm? Or from the village? Do you think I'll haul it here? Through the swamp or around by the road and then back down here? I don't have a truck or nothing. Is it 'cause you're having a baby, this baby you say is mine? Is that what you think?"

She laughed and said, "It's you gave me this baby, Joel. Now it's ours."

She said it somehow with her whole body, rolling toward him and gripping his waist with her arms and speaking into his chest. "Joel. Joel. There's a spring a ways back behind these trees. It's real close. Emerson found it. He says it's been there for a long time. He says you could run a plastic hose down from the spring where it pools back in the trees up high. There'd be lots of water then. Emerson likes to think he's real smart. He is, but sometimes he's not. He's a wild one, that Emerson. That's what Father says about him. But he's not wild. He's special. Joel, look in the jug on the table. It's clean water from the pool. You look, why don't you?"

"Yeah, well, still," said Joel, hesitant now, because if there was water, well then, then what?

"It isn't just water that you'll be needing," he said after thinking for a moment. He tried to get out of her arms, but she only held him tighter.

"We'll be all right, Joel."

"And what about your brother, Emerson?" Joel said. "What about him?"

"What about him? He's my brother. He looks out for me just like I look out for him. It's what my father told us to do. Look out for each other. He's to look out for you too, Joel. I told him so. And he will. He's good that way. If you're true to Emerson, he'll be true to you."

"He told me he watched us," he said. "He saw us doing it."

She started to laugh.

"Oh, Jesus," he said. "Stop laughing, why don't you. Listen, this here's no place. I know you and Emerson tried fixing this old shack up and all, but there's a lot more needs to be done. And it's a church. You can't live in a church."

"No one's been using it since forever. It's just empty all the time."

"And if they did? What if there was a preacher come? What then?"

"He could do his preaching at the other church near the Hall. Or he could preach right out front here in the grass, Joel. Sure, why not out there? There's room for plenty of people. I know they'd be happy standing there singing. They could bring blankets for sitting on, and food too. People can give a lot when they want to. Preachers can preach outside. One came to the farm one time. A Baptist, my father said he was. I don't know what that is, Baptist, but I never forgot the word for him. My father said the word came from the Lord baptizing people back by the River Jordan in the olden days. The preacher preached out in our pasture. Sheep and all. Even the horse came and the preacher blessed him too. That horse has lived a long time since the preacher blew into his nose. It's how horses know each other. They blow into each other's noses. The preacher said he'd blown into the noses of a lot of horses, but our horse was something special. My mother blows into mares' noses and they blow back and after that they are like sisters to each other. She whispers horses. And people came from all around to see the preacher. Some came down from Blue River and from Clearwater too. He put people right into the horse trough and turned them to God. He tried to do it to me, but Mother stopped him. She said it wasn't her way with a daughter. She said I was different than the boys. But Stan and Tom did it. Even Eldred. They said they couldn't even breathe and my mother was crying, but Emerson ran away when the preacher tried it with him, so he's not a Baptist or anything. He's like Mother, is Emerson. Stan and Tom said they didn't feel any different afterward anyway. Father said it was worth trying the once, but there wasn't any talking between my mother and him for near two months. Mother says there's a spirit in trees and in everything, trout and bears and hawks. Even in rocks. And it's in us too. She said we didn't need to get near-drowned in a horse trough to find the spirit. She said a beetle has just as much spirit as we do. I remember that. I wouldn't kill or eat a critter without first asking it to forgive me."

Her arms loosened as she pushed her head up into Joel's neck, her long blond hair splayed across his arm. "We're going to be here, Joel, and if it starts raining again, why we'll be okay, won't we. When our baby comes it'll be born here in the house where a god used to live."

"That doesn't even make any sense."

"Our baby's going to be beautiful. Just like you."

"Stop it," Joel cried.

"You be quiet now," Myrna said, as if talking to a child. She took his hand from the quilt and placed it on her belly, her own hand circling his wrist, and quiet, her voice a whisper in the room, said, "Feel me. In there's the baby where you put it. It's yours and it's ours too."

Joel tried to pull his hand away from her grip, but she held on to his wrist and his hand pressed against her white skin. Her skin felt warm and different than when they were doing it. He'd looked at her belly when she'd taken her dress off. He couldn't help it. He wanted to see if it was true she was having one. And he'd looked at it too when she was laid back on the mattress and he was over her, looked down past where her breasts were fallen to the side like they did and down to where he was stiff and hard, the blond hair of her damp and waiting there, and saw her belly. He'd looked at her when she was first undressed naked and he'd asked if it would hurt the baby, doing it, though somewhere he knew even if it did he didn't care, but was only asking, and wondering too if he'd have done it if she'd said it would. Hurt. But she didn't. She'd pulled him into her and all.

Her belly wasn't huge yet like what other women's bellies looked like. The bellies he'd seen before were way different when other women were going to have a baby. But it was early on. Still, Myrna's stomach wasn't exactly the same as what it was a month ago. Her belly was pushed out now in a way it wasn't before. He lifted his hand and then let it rest back on her skin and wondered if he held it there awhile and pushed down a bit, would he be able to feel it, the baby what was in there? His mother had told him once you could feel a baby kicking after a while. But maybe it was too early for that. He was going to ask her if she could feel it move, but her hand relaxed on his wrist. Gentle now, he slid his hand out from under her loose grip.

What would he do about Alice now? What would Alice think if she knew Myrna was having a baby, his baby? She wouldn't want to have anything to do with him then. So he wouldn't tell her, but she'd find out anyway because there were no secrets around women. Girls talked and so did grown-up women. They all did, his mother and her friends, almost like their lives were a party line. And Myrna was almost like a grown-up now, some-how, because she had the baby in her. And Alice didn't love him, not really at all, but maybe she would if he asked her to. Maybe at the dance tonight. Before someone told her about Myrna. Maybe he could explain it. Maybe she'd understand it wasn't his fault.

But what to do with Myrna? She said she was going to the dance too.

He felt like he was going clear out of his head. For a moment he felt like almost killing Myrna and then he wondered how anyone could kill someone who loved them that much. Loved him, like she said she did, and did too, love him, else why would she have gone to all this trouble?

"This here mattress is going to be a home for rats and mice quicker than you can blink," he said. "You can't sleep on a floor like this."

Myrna smiled. "You can build us a bed with some boards. My father will let you borrow his hammer. He has lots of nails in tobacco cans."

Joel reared up. He couldn't stand it that she thought this old, wrecked church was a house. He swung his arm out at the room. "More of it is falling apart than is holding it together."

"Hush," she said, and then she started giggling. "Why're you so crazy?"

"I'm not crazy," Joel said. "You have to have a real bed to sleep on if you're sleeping here," and when she kept on giggling, he told her to stop, adding, "If you're going to stay here, which you can't. This here is like a play house. It's not real."

"Our baby's real. And if the baby's real, so are we."

Joel felt like she had punched him, his gut sucked in. He could hear the wheezing in his chest. He couldn't almost breathe.

"There isn't even any proper glass in these windows mostly," he stammered, gulping at the air. "That over there is oiled paper, not glass. And the door. Look at the door. You could slide a one-by-four under it without touching either the door or the sill. How are you figuring to keep critters out? Tell me that. Let alone the winter snow blowing in under there. No matter if you even had a stove that worked right, there'd be no difference what with the cold and all."

"The baby's three months," she said. "This here baby is three whole months alive."

"Hell," said Joel, letting out a huge breath and falling back onto the mattress. "It isn't alive until it's born."

"Yes, it is."

"How do you know that?" Joel said, starting to shake.

"Why are you talking so crazy? It's just a baby."

"How do you know it's alive?"

"I can feel it in there," Myrna told him. "You just have to push down a little and you can feel it." She held out her hand to him, pleading. "Joel, I sing songs to this baby." She placed her head on his shoulder. "You want to hear one of the songs?"

"No. I don't want to hear you singing."

Bye, baby Bunting,
Daddy's gone a-hunting,
Gone to get a rabbit skin,
To wrap the baby Bunting in.

He was afraid of the singing she always did, and there she went and sang anyway, even after he told her not to.

"That's a lullaby, my mother says. She says she sang it to me when I was inside her. We were all inside our mothers one time. Like this baby inside me. Isn't it? Isn't it?"

"Stop," he said. "Just stop."

"Will you get this here baby a rabbit skin like the song says?"

As she said it he looked to her eyes and there were tears there.

Quieter, the strength going out of him, a different kind of strength pouring into him suddenly, feeling it like a muscle he didn't know he had, he said: "You sing pretty. You do. So please, please, don't start crying. You don't need to cry what with the baby hearing it, I mean feeling it. But tell me, please, what are you going to say to them up at the farm? You think you can just move down here to this old church and they won't notice you're gone?"

"Mother knows."

"Where you are?"

"She knows."

Joel lifted himself all the way up off the mattress, pushed to his feet, and kicked at the quilt tangled in his feet. Myrna pulled it over, covering herself. He stood naked by the shelf where the preacher must've stood as he wondered what to say next. It was like whatever was outside in the world wasn't there right then. He tried to think of what else he was.

She said, "You're so beautiful."

But he didn't hear what she said. He was thinking about Missus Turfoot knowing Myrna was having a baby. That meant Mister Turfoot knew it too or was going to know it soon enough.

And what then?

He spoke as if to himself. "You mean you told her when you never told me?"

Myrna said, "She knew it was a baby when I stopped bleeding."

"But you never said anything about that before. If it's three months ago, then how come you never said anything to me about her knowing? How come you never said anything to me?"

"'Cause Mother told me you can't be sure the baby's going to be okay in here," she said, placing her hands on her belly again. "The baby's got to take hold is what Mother said. It's got to grab on and hold tight. It can't let go. When you know that then it's okay to tell, is what she says."

"And your father? What about him? What'll he say?" He grabbed his pants and started pulling them on, but his foot got stuck sideways in the one pant leg and he stood there rocking on one foot trying to stay balanced. For a moment he thought of the round of cedar behind Alice's shack at the back of the store. It was like he was standing on it looking down at her and then he almost fell over and started hopping around the room.

"Stop," Myrna said, giggling again. "Father knows too."

"He does?"

"It's okay," she said. "And you'll come back later and help with this house of ours."

Joel managed to get his one leg into his pants and was starting on the other leg. "What?" he said.

"Here," Myrna said. "You'll come here."

SEVENTEEN

CLIFF CAME IN THE BACK DOOR of the bunk-house after taking one of the log-boom boats out. He had crossed over to the other side of the river just above the rapids and tied up where the trail started, the one that led to the old log cabin in the meadow hidden behind a stand of old fir trees. The cabin was mostly empty except for a rusted-out tin heater and what remained of a handmade pole bed with shreds of canvas hanging from it that must have once been a mattress stuffed with cedar-tip fronds. When he first discovered the cabin what kept him coming back was the old sewing machine sitting beside the window. It was a Singer and he had looked and found a date on the base. The numbers were 1885.

When Cliff had told Art Kenning about it the first-aid man said that was only a few years after the Barkerville gold rush back in the 1860s. That's an old-timer's cabin, Art had said. Art went on to tell Cliff about the prospectors, old Sinjun and the others like him, how they trailed down into the Interior to look for colour when their luck ran out up in the Yukon. Art marvelled at a woman living up the river that far back in those days. He said a sewing machine had to have been packed in from Kamloops on a horse or carried on a miner's back. Either way, he told Cliff, that cabin's on the east side of the river. Rough country over there.

Cliff had gone back to the cabin that morning and sat in the chair in front of the rusted old machine with its cracked foot treadle. It's what he did every time he crossed over the river, only this day he had thought of an older Alice sitting there sewing something, a dress or maybe curtains for the window. He knew she was only fourteen now, but he imagined her there anyway, them living together in a cabin somewhere. She'd be a year or two older, of course, maybe sixteen. He thought of himself bringing fresh trout up from fishing in the river and Alice watching him from the window where she was sewing.

He wondered what her real home had been like before the Sisters grabbed her from the back of the wagon at the stampede in Williams Lake. He knew she hadn't been a lost or forgotten child. She hadn't been deserted or left behind by anyone. Her mother and father might have left her alone for only an hour or two while they were talking to friends. They might not have been gone more than a few minutes. And they might have left someone else looking after her too, maybe an older sister or brother, and they'd gone off to see the bull-riding or the chuckwagon races. He could see kids wanting to do that, telling the little sister to stay on the wagon until they came back. He tried to think of what the parents must have felt when they found their daughter was gone. Stolen.

He shut the bunkhouse door behind him and walked up the line of bunks. When he saw Joseph sitting by the card table where the men played cards, he stopped and stared at the brightness of the light shining through the front door into the shadows.

"You okay?" Joseph asked.

"I know what I gotta do," Cliff said.

"I think you do," said Joseph. "You got the look of someone who knows something he didn't know before."

"What I got to do right now is figure out exactly how to do it."

"What I'll do is play you a song while you're figuring it," Joseph said.

Cliff nodded and went out onto the porch and sat on a chair in the shade.

Alice, he thought.

The first time he saw her he was coming out of the Rotmensens' store. They were walking up from the train and taking her into the lean-to. She'd come from the residential school in Kamloops. Imma and Piet had bought her from the Brother there for fifty dollars. Art had told him that. Cliff remembered the wonder he felt when he realized you could buy a human girl for fifty dollars.

Cliff leaned back against the wall in the rickety chair listening to Joseph's music come through the open door. It was a tune he didn't recognize. He asked what it was called and Joseph told him it was a country tune from a long time ago.

"Has it got a name?"

"It's called the 'Lonesome Road Blues,'" Joseph said, and he sang Cliff a line, *lonesome road comfort me.*

Cliff leaned out, glancing back through the doorway and seeing Joseph smile that quiet smile he sometimes had when he was in what he called his Joseph place. Once, Cliff had asked him what that place was, but Joseph just said he only had that one name for it. "It just is," he'd said, "and when I'm in it that's where I'm at. This tune I'm playing gets close to where I am. Make sense?" he'd said as he put down his guitar. Cliff said he thought it did, but Joseph didn't sing anymore that day and Cliff didn't ask why.

What Cliff wanted to do on this afternoon was sleep, the music from Joseph's guitar lulling him. And he almost did sleep and in that half-dream place he saw Alice walking behind Imma Rotmensen along the gravel road from the train station. He couldn't take his eyes off her and it wasn't just because she was a pretty girl or that there were other men watching her pass by. No, whatever she was she caused in him a kind of sadness he didn't know he had. It just happened to him, that was all. No matter she walked with her head down, her long black hair trailing down over her back, her poor clothes, and it wasn't the cheap cardboard suitcase hanging from her hand either. It was the moment she looked sideways at him that made him feel so alone. Her look at him was there and then it wasn't and why she chose him to see it he didn't know, but whatever was in those eyes of hers burned right into him. That was the only way he could think to describe what he felt when she saw him, really saw him. She burned a look into him and bonded his heart. The moment she did his life was changed. He hadn't known what his life had changed into or what was going to happen now it had, he only knew that day he wasn't the guy he'd been before she went walking by on the heels of Imma Rotmensen.

He couldn't stop looking at her as she went on. He watched her walk up the road until she turned at the corner by the store. When she was gone was when he knew what the lean-to was for that Piet had built onto the back of the store. He knew the room with the high pig-wire window was where the Rotmensens were going to keep her locked up.

It was a week after that first day when she arrived in the village that she began going down to the station with the wagon to pick things up for the store. Piet had made it clear that no one was to help her pull the wagon when it was loaded up. He said he didn't want people bothering her. Cliff didn't care what Piet said. He helped her twice before Claude pulled him aside in the mill and told him if he wanted to keep his job he'd better leave her alone. He told Cliff to keep his eyes and his hands off her. He called her *that Indian girl*. Claude told him she belonged to Piet and Imma until she was sixteen years old.

"Crowchild."

That's what he had said that first day when she passed from sight behind the store.

It was a word he hadn't said in five years. They had risen from deep inside him and because they had he said them again out loud.

"Crowchild."

It wasn't something new he'd been changed into that day. It was something old.

Saying those words now stopped him remembering that first day he saw Alice. It wasn't yesterday he needed to think about, it was what he did today that mattered. He got up from the chair and stepped back into the bunkhouse.

"What was it you said just now?" Joseph asked.

"Crowchild."

"What's that supposed to mean?"

"Nothing," said Cliff. "It's just an old name I know."

"You okay?"

"I think so," Cliff said. "I think I am."

Joseph nodded as he turned to his guitar.

Cliff only half listened to the chords as he walked down the line of bunks. When he got to his he sat on the edge of the mattress. He sat very still, the shadows on the floor changing as he stared at them, and then slowly, with what seemed great effort, he reached between his legs and pulled his duffle bag out from under the bunk. Taking it by the strap he stood and heaved it up onto the rumpled grey blanket where he'd been sitting. Before he opened the duffle he looked up and down the row in case someone had come in when he wasn't looking, but there was only Joseph sitting by the summer stove playing his guitar, another tune he didn't know the name of.

There was no one around that might take an interest in what he was doing. He didn't know where Reiner was, maybe out hunting along the river meadows. Cliff hadn't seen him when he docked the boat, but that didn't mean anything. Reiner could be anywhere. There were a few men at the next bunk-house sitting out front on their porch next door, but they were mostly older guys waiting out the afternoon before going down to dinner at the cookhouse. Cards or checkers and they weren't about to come into his bunkhouse anyway. Not without asking. And the kid, Joel, was gone too, probably up in the hills to the farm where he was playing around with the Turfoot girl.

Piet and Imma had gone to Kamloops. They wouldn't be back until late tomorrow afternoon. Alice would be at the store right now selling whatever people might be needing from the crap they had for sale there. The junk in the store didn't mean anything to him, but Alice did. She mattered a lot.

Claude would lock her up at six.

Alice.

He remembered how one morning when the store was quiet and no one was around he'd asked her if she knew where she came from before the Catholics stole her. She told him the only real memory she had was the residential school in Kamloops. All she knew of the time before that she'd heard from the

Sisters talking when they thought Alice was too young to understand or remember.

Cliff hadn't forgotten what Alice told him that day.

Sister Grace told the other nuns how Sister Mary saw Alice sitting under the back of a buckboard wagon at the stampede, no more than four years old. It was in Williams Lake back in 1950, the Sister said—that's how Alice knew she was fourteen. It was Sister Mary who saved her, Sister Grace said.

When Alice asked Brother Whelan about her mother he said her mother was dead. When she asked him about her father he told her she never had a real father like other children. Brother Whelan said her father was God.

Alice said she cried when he told her that.

She told Cliff she was little when the Brother told her God was her father. She said it scared her bad. She didn't want her father to be God. She wanted her real father. The one she had before they took her away.

What she said had stayed in Cliff's mind like it was tattooed there, Alice saying she remembered her father holding her. What she said was she remembered his hands. And then Alice's eyes got bright and she turned away.

Her coming up the river to the village had changed everything for Cliff. Talking to her that afternoon had brought a lot of his own stuff back, stuff he'd worked hard to forget.

And he was finished with Reiner and some of the others too. Sure, he'd gone drinking with the guys up in Blue River a few times, but he was done with them now. All the bragging and the bullshit in the bar added up to nothing but a wild ride down the canyon home and a hangover the next day.

Those men didn't know Alice like he did. They didn't know anything about him either except what he'd told them and most of that wasn't true. Being around Alice brought things back he'd hidden away inside. His own secrets, his own life.

He dug down into his duffle and found the old work sock he'd hidden in the bottom. Undoing the knot he'd tied a long time ago, he shook the sock out over his bunk, the stuff he'd tucked away tumbling out. He didn't remember the last time he'd looked at any of it. He pushed his hand up into the sock's toe and pulled out the papers stuck in there. The elastic band holding them in a roll had dry-rotted and it flaked off in his hands as he plucked at it, the papers unfolding. There were a few letters, some from his mother that she wrote after his father got killed in a fight in Cache Creek. She told him he'd been working on a paving crew there. Some kind of trouble anyway. There was always some kind of trouble. There were a couple of other letters, ones from his sister. She'd got married and had a kid. Lived down in Wenatchee in the States the last letter he'd got. When was that, three years ago, four?

And there was his birth certificate.

Cliff picked it up and unfolded it, the paper heavy and brittle.

"August 23, 1936, Williams Lake, British Columbia, Canada. Cliff Crowchild Waters."

That's who he was.

That was his name.

His mother had given him the Indian one. She told him when he was born a crow came to the Jack pine outside the window of the shack they lived in back then. It was the first thing she saw after he came out of her. She told him the bird's spirit talked to her and so she gave him the name, Crowchild. The bird was a sign and she made his father put the name on the birth certificate when they registered him. Cliff's mother had told him what the name was in their language, but the lady at the courthouse wouldn't even try to write the Indian name down. She said she didn't know how to even speak it let alone spell it. She said Crowchild wasn't a real name either, but his father made her do it. Cliff couldn't remember the old name now. All he had was the English.

Cliff remembered when he was a boy they lived in Riske Creek before moving onto the Gang Ranch. His father worked there part-time as a cowboy and part-time at whatever they told him needed doing. He'd been thirteen when his father took them back to Williams Lake, a year younger than Alice was now. His old man had been drinking heavy again, and there were fights, yelling and screaming, his sister hiding, strangers drinking, the house parties, shame. There was little money and sometimes no food. They barely kept going. Things had been bad in that house they had. His father was white and his mother was Indian. She was one of the Toosey people. He didn't know what his father was. English, he guessed. He missed his mother after he left home, but not enough to go back.

He tensed up, his hands turning into fists when he started thinking about his mother. When they moved back to Williams Lake they lived in a cabin up Soda Creek Road in a broken-down trailer. People in town said he must live in a ditch tent on a road allowance he looked so poor. One thing Cliff decided when he turned fifteen was that he'd never be a Métis. Not ever. The one good thing his father left him was skin that didn't look Indian. He was almost white. When he left Williams Lake he swore no one was going to ever call him a half-breed again.

He wasn't a Métis.

He was Cliff Waters.

And he had told himself he wasn't from anywhere.

He stood quiet, staring at the bunk next to him and the skulls on the shelf above it. Reiner's bunk. The darkness behind the holes in the curved white skulls of the bears stared back at him, their eyes full of shadows.

"Crowchild."

He said his name just like he'd said it to Alice up at the café.

And she'd said his name back to him.

It had sounded strange to hear the word coming from her mouth. When she spoke his name it sounded beautiful.

And he said it out loud looking down at the piece of paper that told him of his birth.

"Crowchild," he said.

His hands were steady as he folded up the birth certificate. He pushed it back inside the sock along with the letters from his mother and sister and then shoved the sock deep in his duffle.

He looked at the other stuff on his shelf, his shaving things, soap, a couple of magazines, stuff and junk. Most of it he didn't need, didn't want. He pushed what clothes he had lying around into the duffle bag. There wasn't much else.

Crowchild.

His name had sounded wonderful coming from her.

There was one thing for sure, she wasn't going to any dance.

———

ALICE HAD CLEANED and cleared everything up after Mister Harper had left the store. When he had walked out the door in the early morning she hadn't dared move in case he returned, but he hadn't. She could still feel the slam of the front door and his boots going down the front steps. After what seemed a long time and was only a few minutes Alice had started to work. Imma had spent two hours with her the night before making sure Alice knew how to handle the front store,

the lists she had to make of everything people bought, and especially the cash box in the drawer, exactly how much money there
was when she started, and how the money at the end of the day
had to match exactly what she had sold.

Missus Steiner and Missus Short left with their bags of
groceries. They were talking a mile a minute and they kept on
talking as they went out the door. Alice stood behind the
wooden counter, tired from running back and forth to the café
and the cash at the front. It was late now in the morning. Each
time she looked at the front door it brought back the daydream
she had of Mister Harper waiting for her, the sharp tug in her
hair as he pulled her back into her room, the door closing
behind him, the lock clicking shut.

She pinched the skin under her wrist, the quick pain
bringing her back to the goods Natalka Danko had laid out
on the counter: two loaves of the last three-day-old white
bread, the wax paper wrapping torn on one of them, the bread
at one end dried out and curled, canned peas and beans, their
labels stained, a single roll of toilet paper, a package of what
looked like soft hamburger taken from the narrow walk-in
freezer at the back of the store, wet rust leaking from the freezer's hinges. As Alice wrote down the numbers of the goods,
Natalka scuffed her shoes on the floor, the cheap linoleum
cracking and lifting. In front of the cans was a cabbage, the
skin scarred and wilted. The outer leaves were loose, the edges
wrinkled and dry. Alice sat on the stool figuring it all out,
writing down what things cost. She tried not to look up as
Natalka began complaining.

Natalka was a small woman, but that didn't stop her arguing. What she wanted to talk about was the cabbage. "You got
that cabbage wrong," she said to Alice, reaching out and stab-
bing with her forefinger at a pencilled number on the bill Alice

had made. "That there should be ten cents. Once a cabbage goes brown like this one is, Imma drops the price."

A little nervous because of Missus Danko's insistence, Alice said, "Imma wrote in the book that cabbages are twenty cents."

"Don't think I don't know that. I can read numbers upside down, you know. But there's a different number for cabbages that're going bad. Imma must've forgotten to write down what the discount was."

Alice turned the scribbler around and pointed at a column and the word *Cabbage* halfway down, beside it the price written there, *twenty cents*, and beside the sum in brackets, *for one*.

"Imma said I have to follow what's on here or else."

"I don't care what it says in a book. It's ten cents when it's old like this one here. You change what you wrote down."

"But I can't," said Alice. "She'll be mad if I let you have it for that."

"Imma will be madder if she thinks you're out to cheat me over a cabbage that's almost not even worth eating. I wouldn't be buying it at all if Martyn didn't tell me he had to have haloopse for dinner. Look at that old cabbage." She reached across the counter and prodded it with the same finger she'd poked the scribbler with. "It's not even worth five cents, let alone twenty. Anywhere else they'd throw it away."

"I don't know what to do, Missus Danko. Missus Rotmensen, she's going to look at everything I write down." She held up the scribbler. "She'll add up the money when she gets back. She'll count the cabbages. She'll know."

"Never mind that. I'll talk to her come Monday," said Natalka. She rapped her knuckles on the edge of the counter. "Just do it."

Alice didn't know what to say. She was almost crying. If she changed the price Imma would find out. Or worse, Missus

Danko would tell her and either way Alice would be in trouble. Tears startled in her eyes and she hated them for being there. Each time she cried in front of people she swore she'd never cry again and now they were there again. It was like the early tears at the school when she was little. She'd been so afraid back then. But why was she crying now?

"I can't, I can't," Alice said. "She'll find out and then I'll get it from Mister Rotmensen."

As she wiped the tears away with the back of her hand the bell over the door clanged and Ernie Reiner came in. When he heard them arguing he came over and stood behind Natalka Danko.

Alice tried not to look at him as he swung his head from side to side as if looking for someone or something. "Where's the girl who makes me my grilled cheese sandwich, eh? I don't see her nowhere," he said. "Where is she?"

"It's me," Alice said, on her guard, knowing Reiner was going to make something from what Natalka was arguing about. "I'm here," she said. "You're looking right at me."

Ernie swung his head around again, pretending he couldn't see her. "Where's that Indian girl?"

She looked first at Natalka and then at Ernie. Alice wasn't confused. She knew what Ernie was doing and like always she didn't like it. His teasing caused trouble, mostly because he never knew when to stop. And too, it was the way Ernie looked at her. It was just like Mister Harper had that morning when he unlocked her. There were other men too who did that, but Ernie was the worst. There was always something dirty behind what he said. But she couldn't walk away. She had to deal with Missus Danko and then maybe she could go to the back and get whatever Ernie wanted to eat or drink. She hoped the coffee wasn't too burned from sitting on the stove.

"You know I'm right here, Mister Reiner," she said as she tried to get him to stop. "You can see me, can't you? I got to do this here before I can make you a sandwich. I got to look after this stuff up front here and back at the counter too while they're away. You go sit down and I'll be right there."

Ernie ignored her and reached out and tugged at the bib of Natalka's purple babushka lying on her back, her head wobbling. "How come you got that girl crying?"

"I'm not crying," said Alice.

"You were," Ernie said. "I can always tell when a woman's been crying. You just look at their eyes."

"You never mind, you," Natalka said, bridling as she twisted her head to get him to let go of her babushka. "It's none of your business if she cries or not. She's a stupid Indian is all."

Natalka glared sideways at Ernie as she reached out and pulled the cabbage toward her. It rolled off the edge of the counter into the open canvas bag she had ready, the bag and the cabbage in it thumping onto the floor, her shoulder jerking at the pull of the handles. "I'm taking this here cabbage," she said. "No charge. And I'll be talking to Imma, you can count on that. Now you add up the rest."

"But that's stealing," Alice said.

"That's for sure," said Ernie. "Anyway, you can't hardly carry it, you're so little."

"I got me a buggy out the door. I don't need to carry it."

"Aren't you a little old to be pushing a baby buggy?" he said.

"Please stop," said Alice.

"You be quiet," Natalka told her. She turned to Ernie. "I told you this's none of your business. This Indian here's trying to cheat me."

"No, I'm not," said Alice. She held the scribbler up to Reiner.

"Look," she said. "It says cabbages, twenty cents for one. It says so right here."

Natalka Danko pushed the scribbler aside. "Just forget that book of yours. How much is all this other stuff?" she said, pointing at the goods on the counter.

"If you're not paying for that cabbage, then I think you better put it back where you took it from," said Ernie.

Indignant, flaring like a defiant hummingbird, Natalka said: "This's between me and this Indian girl here. You keep out of it."

Ernie bent down and with one hand took the cabbage out of her bag, Natalka jerking at the rope handle, telling him to leave her cabbage alone. He lifted it high above his shoulder, a grey ball in the cup of his hand. "You're either buying this or you're not," he said. When she didn't reply, he lowered the cabbage to the counter and rolled it into some piled-up cans, knocking them over. Alice jumped back.

"Well," said Natalka Danko, her breath coming hard. "I'll just see what my Martyn says about this. He's not going to like not getting his cabbage rolls. He asked for haloopse tonight."

Ernie looked on solemn as Natalka told Alice to charge her for the cabbage.

"You put the full amount down and you draw a circle around the twenty cents you're writing there," she said. "You can bet I'll be talking about this to Imma first thing Monday morning."

Alice stared at her pencil stub, the scribbler back on the counter. Her hand shook as she wrote, her pencil scribbling on air.

The front door opened and Cliff walked in. He'd been standing in the porch and heard the last exchange between

Ernie and Natalka. He stopped and looked at Alice. "Are you all right?" he said.

"I'm okay, Mister Waters. Really," Alice said as Cliff turned to Ernie. She could see the anger in his eyes.

"Tell her what she owes," said Cliff, his shoulder bumping Ernie to the side.

"Watch it," Ernie said to Cliff, and then he laughed and stepped back from the counter. He raised his open hands. "No trouble, no problem," he said.

Cliff ignored him as he smiled at Alice. "After you're done with Missus Danko you can make me that grilled cheese sandwich like you always do, Alice." Cliff could see her name felt good to her when he said it. "And maybe this time you can fry up a little crispy bacon and put it in there."

"Me too," said Ernie.

"You boys," said Natalka, almost spitting it out. "I'll be telling Martyn about you."

"We'll be right here if he needs us," said Cliff, stepping around her. He walked down the aisle, Ernie behind him stumbling on a curled-up bit of worn linoleum as he tried to match him step for step. When they got to the back of the store Ernie sat down on the stool at the end of the counter by the wall. As he did, Cliff stepped around the lunch counter, pulled a Coke, and popped the cap on the edge of the cooler.

"Hey," said Ernie, "how about getting me one."

Cliff just looked at him as he took a drink from his bottle.

"I bet you wouldn't mind having a slice of her to go with that Coke," Ernie said. "Maybe tonight at the dance you can try some. I hear Claude's letting her go."

Cliff took three long steps, reached over, and grabbed Reiner's shirt, pulling him halfway across the counter. "Shut your fucking mouth, Ernie."

Ernie stood up and grabbed Cliff's wrist, twisting away from him. "Leave off," he said. "I got enough trouble without you grabbing me."

"What do you mean?"

"Never mind."

"Anyway," said Cliff. "You can just shut up about her."

"Jesus Christ," said Ernie. "What's your problem? She's just an Indian."

"She ain't just that," Cliff said. "She's a nice girl."

"I was only talking."

"Yeah, I know," Cliff said. "It's what you do."

"Jesus, you'd think you liked her or something," Ernie said as he sat back down.

"Yeah, well," said Cliff, turning away.

"What?"

"She's not just an Indian, you know. She's one of the Toosey people," Cliff said as he saw Alice coming from the front. When he saw her he came around the counter and took a seat near the middle where Alice made the lunch sandwiches.

"What do you mean, Toosey? What's that?"

"People who live up the Chilcotin nearby Williams Lake. It's where I come from too."

"You come from up there?"

"What'd I just say," said Cliff.

"I never heard of those people," said Ernie.

"Yeah, well, you've heard one of them now. And you can leave off talking about her like you do."

"Toosey, eh? That's a funny thing to call someone."

"Just shut it, Ernie," Cliff said as Alice came down the counter.

Alice stopped at the sink and washed her hands, wringing them out on her apron.

"You take off," Cliff said to Reiner.

"What?"

"I got things to talk to Alice about."

"Yeah, sure, whatever," said Ernie. "Hey," he said to Alice.

"Do you want something, Mister Reiner?"

"Bugger off," said Cliff.

When Reiner was gone Cliff leaned forward, his hands wrapped around the coffee she placed in front of him. "Crowchild," he said.

Alice pressed back against the sandwich counter, her hands clasped together.

"We're from the same place, you and me," Cliff said. "They stole you from the Stampede at Williams Lake when you were just a little kid. We've talked about that. What I want to tell you is I'm taking you back there."

"Where?" Alice said. Her hands rose to her throat.

"To the Cariboo, the Chilcotin country," Cliff said. "That's where you come from. You're not going to live in a locked-up wooden cage no more." He put his hand out, cupped palm up at the edge of the counter. Alice put out her hand as if to touch him and then didn't, her hand in the air between them.

"Never mind them," Cliff said.

"I'm afraid."

"I'm the same as you," said Cliff. "Say my name."

She took a step and placed her hand on his. "Cliff," she whispered.

"No," he said, his voice soft. "Say my name."

There was nothing in the air between them. Not a sound anywhere. Alice felt the silence all over her body.

"Crowchild," she said.

EIGHTEEN

JASWANT'S TIDY CABIN WAS STUCK back up against the wall of fir and hemlock, one old cedar leaning almost against it, long low branches sweeping across the roof, moss growing on the shakes under its pans of needles. A glacial stone the size of a truck box, huge and grey, was lying in the grass, the wall mottled with red and yellow lichens. Along the front of the cabin was a covered porch running the length of it, a purple couch pushed back beside the screen door, the worn cushions sunk on broken springs where mice had found homes. There was a cracked window by the door and beneath its sill a long box with dry pansies in it, yellow leaves reaching on thin stalks into the still air. A rocking chair, its curved runners bound by rounds of black wire and electrician's tape to hold them together, sat by the couch in an angled blade of the sun.

In the chair was Jaswant's woman, slowly rocking. On the purple couch close by was Gerda Dunkle, in her arms the baby, her naked legs protruding from a twist of worn yellow cotton. The baby's legs hung bent from the mother's arm, the feet looking like tiny corn kernels that had been left in the sun too long and withered away. Gerda Dunkle was singing what seemed to Art a lullaby, her voice so small it seemed hardly to exist at all. As she sang she rocked the child gently in the cup of her shawl. As he listened she began to repeat one of the lines of the lullaby over and over as if somehow she had become stuck in the song.

Art Kenning stood at the edge of the road, his first-aid kit hanging from his fist, his eyes closed, his body turned toward them. He strained toward the woman's song as it began again to weave itself through its endless repetitions. He had been there on the verge of the narrow road for what he realized was a long time because he had begun to murmur along with her the iterant harmony, together their voices an impossible duet, the woman's singing a kind of prayer and his whispered harmony a kind of wish he accepted without thought.

The opium he had used back in his cabin had begun its first quiet leaving, soft tendrils slipping away along the blood vessels in his arms and legs, thin velvet ropes undoing in him, letting him go. He could feel the vanishing and knew soon the world would come back in all its terrible clarities, its cramps and sweat, but not yet. Now there was only the song of the woman as she cradled her baby. Art knew he was there because he had the penicillin. If what the baby had was some kind of bowel or blood infection then it might help.

He didn't know what to do for the mother. Hers seemed a long grief, a sorrow that spanned centuries, a woe as long as life, the present one. What the woman had told him when he'd first looked at the baby was that she barely fed from her mother's breasts. The baby shit thin gruel, vomited, fed, and vomited again, her body wasting away. He knew little to nothing about babies. He'd seen them in the war, sick and starving like their mothers. Their fathers were dead in battle, wounded and recuperating in some Allied encampment, or had drifted off and were lost. The mothers had been unlocked from concentration camps or were simply refugees from bombed-out towns and cities, all of them wanderers in the forests or along the roadsides. There were the German women and children in the camps after the war, the bad food the French gave them, the spare bits of bread, the rotten vegetables, potatoes weeping, soft onions covered in blue rust, the rapes, the murders. There were the girls with shaved heads beaten by women and men who hated them having consorted with German soldiers. There was hate and revenge, shame and desperation everywhere. And there was Marie's baby, the one she would never explain, never say where it was except to say it was or had been a girl. Seeing Jaswant's wife had brought Marie back once again. Art shook her away, the mystery of Marie's baby girl more than he could bear. He waited there on the roadside until her presence faded away.

The one thing Art knew of women was they would do anything to keep their child alive. He'd seen mothers trade their bodies for a half cup of powdered milk, a can of Spam, a chunk of mouldy bread, a bit of chocolate. Soldiers—Canadian, American, Poles, Brits, whoever—used them while their child watched in stillness, a little one in a box or crib in the corner, not weeping, silent, having learned that crying placed everyone in danger.

Art pushed them all out of his head, the German prisoners in the camps at Rennes and Rivesaltes reaching through the wire, the ones the French slowly starved, and he couldn't stand thinking of them all and drove the camps and cemeteries away. He drove Walcheren away too, drove away the guns, and the Dutch woman, her *Canada, dank u, dank u*, words slipping through his ears like the cry of a rat surrounded by a murder of crows in broken corn. She became the German mother on the road toward Rennes offering her ten-year-old child to anyone who would take her, anyone who might want her, all of them and none. He wanted them all gone from him, away. He didn't want to be on the road listening to the mother's song, didn't want to be in a room in Paris with a woman bleeding milk, without words, without anything, her baby disappeared, given away, sent away, lost. He didn't want to think of the war and what he'd seen, what he'd done.

He had come to see Gerda Dunkle's baby with some kind of hope. There was a chance the penicillin would do some good. The real help was with the doctors down south in Kamloops, but this woman had no money to pay for doctors. If there had been any money then it was likely with the man who left her, the father of the baby, the one who promised he would return. And what good was such a vow? Men made such promises believing they would come back, but how frequent were their returns?

The child was sick and would die or not, no matter the medicine, no matter Art's ministrations.

And then what?

A grave, where? Outside the fence at the deserted village church whose very earth was limbo? Limbo was everywhere. The altar was a limbo, the sacred cup and chalice limbos, the vestments and robes the stuff of limbo. There was no sanctuary, no place safe from harm.

He turned and looked up the road to where the track climbed to the dump. He thought slowly through the dwindling fog of opium and whisky that he would go to the dump after he gave the baby the medicine.

Joel had said he'd seen a truck leaving the village in the night.

Where would a truck go but to the dump? It was either that or up the canyon road to Avola or Blue River or south to Clearwater or Little Fort and who would have been going there near dawn, night fleeting? He went over it again, his mind soft, the complexities eluding him. Maybe it was McAllister's truck, but why would he have gone to the dump unless it had something to do with Irene? And Joel said there were two of them, so one might have been Irene—or if not, then who? The only person Jim ever talked to was Ernie. Could it have been him in the truck?

The questions flew around inside his head liked crazed sparrows. Art placed his kit in the yellowed stalks of broken grass by the side of the road and rubbed his face with his hands. He felt for a moment that if he could just take his eyes out he could wash them clean in the sweat of his hands. If he could do that then he might be able to see things clearly and so make sense out of the day and the night before, the night to come, the days and nights going on till they didn't anymore.

He wanted to understand what had happened to Irene McAllister, where she had gone, and how she had gone, her with the legs so badly injured. It had been Jim who had taken her, who else? But where and why? To what end?

And he started walking again, the road ahead climbing beyond him past a rutted curve into the trees and then another quarter mile to the dump. As he stared at its vanishing he felt something brush at his shoulder and he turned to the touch thinking it a bird or animal, some wild thing wanting him to leave, and saw a woman staring up at him. She carried a baby in her arms. It was wrapped in a yellow cloth, the child's legs sticking out like two small twigs, and, "Yes?" he asked, bewildered, for a moment not understanding where he was that a woman should have touched him, and, "Who? Who are you?"

"Raaka Kaur," she said. "You know me. Jaswant's wife."

"Ah," he said, suddenly knowing where he was. He was at the shack where the Sikhs lived. The woman held the baby enclosed in the scoop of cloth, the child who would not get better.

He looked up from the baby. "And you?" he asked, confused again. "What's your name?"

"Raaka," she repeated. "You know me." And softly again, when he still looked bewildered, "I am Raaka, Jaswant's wife."

As he hesitated, she said, "Come."

She picked up the first-aid kit and placed it in his hand, took his arm, and helped him down into the ditch and up the other side to the path that led to their cabin. "Be careful," she said as he scrambled in the loose fall of gravel.

He followed her to the little porch where she sat him down on the sprung couch, his body sinking into the collapsed cushion, his knees at his chin as he stared at Gerda Dunkle.

The woman named Raaka slipped around his long legs to the screen door and went into the shack after placing the baby and the shawl in the other woman's arms.

The baby was going to die. It can't look like what it does and not, he thought. Maybe it was dead now and she was holding a lifeless child and thinking that made him want to flee. He struggled to get up, but when the woman smiled at him he sank back relieved, not quite knowing why.

Jaswant's wife returned a moment later carrying a small black tray with a cup of yellow tea on it, bits of leaves and twigs swirling in a circle. She was about to offer it to Art when the mother got up from the couch and took the teacup from Raaka and gave it to Art.

"Thank you," he said, awkward, the cup hot, burning the blisters on his fingertips. He set the cup beside him on a round of cedar at the corner of the couch and blew on his fingers. He couldn't remember how they'd gotten burned, one of the blisters weeping pink blood.

The baby had swung out from her when she had leaned forward with her offering of the tea and then had swung gently back, her arm cradling it to her chest. The little legs had settled back into the cup of cloth. The woman saw him looking at the slight swelling where her child lay and said, "Her name is Beate. My baby. You remember. Beate is her name."

When he looked into her eyes, she said, "It means blessed. It is a holy name."

Not knowing what to say to that, he said, "Holy, yes. Babies, this one, your baby girl."

"Please, can you help her?"

It was the same as when he'd seen her that first time. He lowered his head to the question, unable to fully comprehend its meaning.

After a moment he turned to Raaka and quietly asked where Jaswant was.

"He is working at the mill," said Raaka. "A special shift."

He closed his eyes and saw the lean brown man working in the sawmill, shovelling sawdust and wood chips into a wheelbarrow and hand trucking it all to the flume that led up to the burner mouth.

He knew Jaswant was a hard worker and he was also a man who had taken onto himself the burden of a stranger, a woman with a sick child. Jaswant's woman was named Raaka. They had taken Gerda and the baby into their home and now Raaka was asking him for help. He looked down at the floor and picked up the teacup, his one hand holding it and the other hanging from the end of his knee as if no longer a part of his body.

Jaswant's wife touched his arm and Art raised himself up, a few drops of the tea spilling across his burned fingers. He tried to feel the pain and he did. "Yes?" he said.

"Medicine?" asked Gerda. Her eyes were pleading. "You have medicine for her?"

"Yes," he said, remembering why he had come. "I have medicine. It might help. I don't know."

Gerda lifted her hands. "It will make her better, please?"

Art leaned down and placed his teacup on the round of cedar. He asked her to give him the baby.

She leaned toward him, her body trembling under the band of yellow cloth as if under the fabric small animals were moving across her shoulders and down her thin arms.

"Beate will be better?" And then as if to herself, "She will, she will."

"Give me the baby," he said, and she did, unfolding the sack of cloth, the baby appearing feet first and then the whole child. He looked at the tiny girl, his mind clearing a little, and thought she was smaller than the last time he'd seen her. When had that been? A few days ago, a week?

As the mother placed Beate in his hands, the baby pulled her legs into her belly, almost disappearing between Art's upraised knees. The tiny wrinkled face appeared between them, supplicant, a human thing.

He held the baby, thinking she couldn't weigh more than four or five pounds. She settled in the crotch of his belly and thighs as he undid the buttons on her tiny shirt, one thin leg straightening, the baby's mouth making a mewing sound, and then the leg returning to bend tight against her belly again. The baby's ribs were narrow ripples on slow water. Her thin chest rose and fell, the great brown eyes staring through him, seeing something beyond him he knew was out there, something he didn't understand. A thin whisper came from her mouth, a sound Art understood to be the kind of song a baby learns in its mother's belly. It had a kind of meaning to it that he had lost, the child without the strength to make an outcry, only sing. She was as nothing in his huge hands as he took her up and held her close to his face.

"Beate," he said, amazed at something so small and yet so human. "Your name is Beate."

"You will heal her," Gerda said, the tips of her fingers nesting against each other as she squatted down before him, a tent of prayer nestled against her lips. There was something in her voice, a terrible desire. She pushed her palms together, her hands blades of bone and skin.

"Hold her," he said, giving the baby back, Gerda settling the baby into the yellow pouch. Art lifted himself out of the hole in the couch, teetering for a moment on the worn boards of the porch before opening his kit and taking out the envelope of penicillin and a tiny bottle of Aspirin.

He dripped a few drops of water from a glass Raaka held out and mixed into it the tiniest tip of penicillin with a few grains of Aspirin. They might help, he thought, it might be enough to give the mother hope, because he knew hope was what the mother had. It was him who was without it.

He pulled the pouch out from Gerda's body, nestled the tip of the spoon to the baby's lips, and gently pushed it into the hollow of her mouth. He gently massaged her sparrow throat, her huge eyes watching him. As she swallowed, Gerda brought her close again and pressed the baby to her chest.

He sat back down, perched on the edge of the couch, and gave Gerda the tip of a teaspoon of penicillin in a fold of paper and a few Aspirin. "You saw how much," he said. "Don't give her more than I did. It would kill her. Give what I showed you twice a day."

"Yes," she said, tears starting in her eyes as she gripped the paper and the pills.

"The medicine might not help her," he said, "but it is all I know how to do. You need a real doctor, not me."

"Thank you," she said. "Thank you."

He startled in fear at her terrible words, the same ones the woman in Holland had said to him. It took everything he had not to cry out. He felt the tears in his eyes and he closed them and turned away, his mouth twisted with a sob.

"It is all right," Raaka said, her hand touching his shoulder.

He told himself he was in the north, at the western edge of the Cascade Mountains where a great river washed its silt south to the sea, and he stared down the road to the valley where the thin smoke from the burner wafted into the wind come down the canyon. He was not staring out at the sea on the Scheldt peninsula, he was not in Paris with a woman who would not tell him what had happened to her baby, who she was, what she'd done, and he was not lying on a mattress on the floor in the rooms that looked out on the alley behind Pender Street in Vancouver. He was not being ministered to by Li Wei. He was not.

He gathered himself together and thought of Molly Samuels and how she might know some way to help this woman and her child. He'd talk to Molly. She would know what else might be done.

"Thank you, thank you," Gerda said.

Art nodded desperately.

Jaswant's wife spoke into the quiet between them and said, "I thought at first it was you driving up here last night. I thought you were coming here."

"Me?"

Art thought for a moment of his sometimes coming up to

the Sikh shacks with a bottle of whisky to drink with the men in their shacks higher up the road, but he never drove, he didn't own a truck. And sometimes too he came to minister to the wounds of the men when they had drunk too much and fought. He asked Jaswant once what they fought about and he said they fought over the memory of their women or just over the thought of a woman, isolated as they were in their wretched shacks outside the village, lonely as they were.

"Last night?"

"Yes."

"Who was it?"

"The sawyer," she said. "My husband saw his truck. He said it was the sawyer. Mister Reiner was with him."

Then not Irene, he thought.

—

PIECES OF ABANDONED MACHINERY lay half buried in gravel and yellow mud, struts of iron rearing out of the wreckage, the pitted rust the bars wore like diseased emblems of decay, shafts, arches, and housings, worn tractor treads and engine blocks, bald tires, patches peeling from their innards, truck boxes, hoods of cars, a twisted flume, a wringer washing machine, a steering wheel bent into curled wings, a child's buggy without wheels perched on top of a Ford engine that was balanced atop a blasted cedar stump, the engine like an otherworldly space machine, below it the canopy of a front-end loader, a crushed hard hat hanging from a twisted strut. A blue blanket like a tattered flag hung tangled with a sheet of rotted canvas. Bush cable was wrapped around two twisted car axles with the wheels attached, the hubcaps long gone. Around the blue flag and mixed in with the detritus were discarded oil-soaked rags, ripped and patched clothing of all kinds, torn bits of sacking, rubber belts and pistons, shafts and transmissions, wheel hubs, engine blocks, cracked sinks and worn-out galvanized tubs and pails, tobacco cans, liquor bottles, and among it all cracked and broken sacks and boxes with scraped shoulder and leg joints sticking out, bits of des-iccated sinew hanging from the scored skulls of dead beeves and horses, moose, deer, and bear, their many spines curved and twisted into fragile arabesques, their bodies torn apart by bears, random bones of all kinds, ribs, legs, and tails, rot-ted vegetables and bits of pebbled fat and marrow seething under a hovering film of flies, wasps, and hornets, the insects searching among the effluvium of village, farm, and mill for anything they could eat or suckle on, the flies to lay eggs in discarded skull pans creating bundled nests of maggots feed-ing on soft brains, and rib cages half filled with earth where tunnels had been dug for the grey hexagonal nursery cells to hold the eggs of yellow jackets, the baskets of paper hanging from under the scapulas of moose where hornets sang their grubs to sleep, the crows and ravens above them in murder-ous dozens screaming along with the gulls their stories of feasts and famines.

All had been dumped in a rocky gulch between the moun-tain's side and a long curved hillock of gravel left behind by a retreated glacier, a cut of open earth and stone, a catchment to hold whatever it was humans had no use for, a place for feral children to forage in for unimaginable treasures, a hole where men could discard what they had worn out and wasted, ruined machinery and tools, cracked sinks and crockery, an icebox without a door, a cupboard with one, a washing machine, a Western Flyer wagon without wheels, dented oil drums, cracked and broken things that could not be mended or fixed, a place of refusal, a depression to hold what could not be reclaimed, every kind of home for rats, mice, moles, snakes, shrews, beetles, and ants.

Art sat on the grey back of a cracked stone staring at a white dress caught on a timber whose flare bore blots of dark and crusted red, a dress that might have been worn for a wedding or a birth, a dress both fragile and rare and now the everyday ordinary uselessness of a thing gone past use with no meaning now to anyone, the blood upon it ineradicable except for the feasting of the flies that coursed in jagged circles around its emblazoned stain. He sat there above the dump and stared at the dress as three black bears worked the drop-off high above where garbage from the cookhouse had been dumped, hemp sacks torn open, their contents bulging, the bears tearing at sacks and ripped meat boxes that held stubs and chunks of tired bread, pork and steak bones, wilted vegetables, cans and bottles, broken crockery, the effluvia of what was left of the week's eating at the cookhouse by the bunkhouse crew.

Deep in the heart of the dump was the grizzly. The great bear lifted with a paw the end of a fractured piece of broken cedar wall, flinging it aside, nails jarred loose and boards flying, beneath it some pocket of gore he had smelled buried in a hole. His long grey snout lifted for a moment, coursing the air, a stunned swarm of flies tearing briefly apart before re-forming across the grizzly's shoulders. Almost blind, it turned its heavy head toward Art and snuffed the air as if trying to catch his scent, but there was no wind, no breeze, only the heavy stillness of the dump, the rummaging of the other bears.

Twenty feet below the timber where the dress hung was a cardboard box. Some tremor from the wall the grizzly had moved made what was left of the fractured lath and plaster fall over and half a side of green moose ribs and spine folded out across a scarred bathtub ten feet away. The side of meat was instantly taken up in the jaws of a black bear sow. As she bolted through the dump toward the safety of the trees, two yearling cubs squealed after her, clambering over junk in pursuit of her find. Behind the three of them a black bear with a missing ear raged as the scent of her find reached him. He heaved his bulk over a mass of broken lumber, trying to catch her as she passed and take from her what she'd found. The sow turned at the edge of the dump, claws tearing at the broken gravel, her cubs scrambling partway up the trunk of a dead fir tree. She turned and straddled her prize, rearing as the boar came at her, swiping with her paw at the boar's shoulder. He ducked her blow and grabbed at the meat. She roared and dropped down, taking a corner of the wet slab in her jaws, the boar biting, pulling back, her huffing wildly as she reared away, the mottled ribs and meat ripping apart and the boar sliding back down the slope into the dump, a piece of the torn moose side hanging from his jaws, the sow above him holding the rest. She retreated with it to a tangle of saskatoon bushes, her cubs crying piteously as they slid down the tree to follow her.

The black boar didn't watch them go. He turned to the meat he had stolen, ripping thick gobbets away, swallowing chunks whole, glutting as fast as he could. Below him the grizzly heaved his heavy body up the slope, the smell of rancid flesh swirling in the grizzly's flared snout. The two bears roared as they met, the black bear falling aside, a chunk of green fat in his jaws, the rest of the side gathered between the grizzly's paws.

Art didn't hear, he didn't see the black boar flee, or hear

the grizzly grunting as it carried in its jaws what was left of the moose side back to the heart of the dump. Art was staring at the dress. He knew whose dress it was.

He had taken the hem of that dress and rolled it in his hands up over the belly of Irene McAllister, her blood squeezing wet between his fingers.

NINETEEN

THE SWAMP AND THE CHURCH clearing below, Joel sat upon a drift stone behind sprayed needles of stunted firs, the afternoon sun glancing off the branches, the beams slipping across his eyes so what he saw was mostly light. Far off in the distance he could hear the last desultory banging of the chains in the empty flumes leading up to the burner, but the mill was far away from him now. He had come back across the swamp and climbed to where he could look down at the busy world of Myrna.

Wisps of white burner smoke drifted down the river and lost themselves in the forest on the other side, but he did not see them pass. He was watching the Someday Church where he had lain with her that morning. After leaving her he had gone back to the bunkhouse where he had collapsed on his bunk and caught two or three hours of sleep. When he came back to the church he heard the ruckus and, instead of walking into what was going on, climbed a little ways up the slope of the mountain to watch and wait from behind a low frieze of brush. He wasn't far away.

Myrna was sitting on the corner of the porch packing dry moss into a pillowcase. Even from where he was he could see the pansies stitched on the cotton, the flowers so alive they might have grown on the yellowed fabric, a kind of work impossible for him to imagine anyone doing, the painstaking weeks it must have taken to draw coloured threads though cloth and make out of them images where there were none before. It was a painting made with thread and he thought it was a wonder. His own mother had pillowcases like that but she hadn't done the stitching herself. The ones she had were done by Joel's grandmother and weren't used, but saved as treasured mementoes from another time.

The church below him had been deserted for years, a house that had once been given over to God. Joel knew part of its story, the disuse and neglect that had left it a shell of what it once had been, no hymns now ringing from the windows, no sermons chastising those who had gone astray. The mock steeple tacked onto the front of it looked to him as if it might fall if a heavy wind were to touch it. It'd be a real danger if Myrna was going to try and live there. If he was going to live there.

If.

Joel wondered for a moment why boys from the nearby farms or the village hadn't burned the old church down by accident or even on purpose. It's something he might have done had he grown up on a farm around here, a deserted building like this an invitation for him and some of his friends to at least vandalize it. Knowing what he'd seen of it inside and out it looked like some of the vandalizing had already been done.

He had been sitting quietly for half an hour watching Myrna and her father, Arnold Turfoot, his sons, her brothers, all of them at their tasks. Beside the church was their wagon stacked with oddments of lumber in various dimensions and a dozen bound bundles of cedar shakes. The old horse had been unhitched and gaunt as ever was grazing upon sparse hummocks of grass at the edge of the encroaching forest. Its ribs stuck out, its hide stretched over them. As he watched, one of the Turfoot boys, the smallest, carried to the horse a wash basin, the water in it scooped from a pool nearby where the creek came down from the mountain. Some of the others were cleaning up around the church, picking up shingles and shakes fallen from the roof and then carrying them over to the clearing where they were splitting them into kindling with small hatchets.

Joel listened as Mister Turfoot spoke to the son as the horse drank from the basin.

"You're a good one, Stan," his father said, his hoarse voice rising up in a scraped whisper to where Joel was sitting.

"That horse loves him the same as he loves Emerson," echoed Myrna, tufts of soft moss in her fingers as she felt through it for twigs and cones. "I think Stan may grow up to be as wild as Emerson."

"Stan needs caring for," said Mister Turfoot. "To tell the truth, the three of them need to be," and he gave half a grin as Myrna cried aloud, her round face pink with laughter.

Wanting to hear more closely, Joel slipped off his log and, crouching, made his way down a little through the trees to a rock at the edge of the clearing that he could hide behind. He needed to hear more clearly what they were saying. Maybe they'd be talking soon about Myrna being pregnant and about her thinking he was going to live in the abandoned church with her in the same way as if they were married.

He figured though that he knew what they were thinking, what with the work they were putting in on the church.

The two oldest boys were clambering over the old roof tearing off tattered cedar shakes. The biggest one was Tom, the other one Eldred. They were replacing the old shakes with clear ones from the bundle they'd carried up the ladder to the roof from the wagon back. The broken-open bundle was tipped precarious against the steeple, the shakes slipping easily to hand. The *tic* and *toc* of their hammers tapping nails fretted the air, the roof turning into a crazy quilt of cedar feathers lapping. Why the Turfoots thought such a patch-work would keep the rain and snow out of the building was beyond Joel.

Myrna was talking to her father.

"Joel will be here real soon," she said. And when Mister Turfoot didn't say anything she said, "Oh, I know for sure he's coming. You might pretend he isn't, but you know he's coming just like I do."

"We'll see," her father said.

"Don't you tease me," she said. "You don't know him really well yet. He'll be here soon as anything. I know it."

Mister Turfoot dropped the two-by-fours he had dragged from the wagon. They clattered on the pile he'd made by the porch. "Well," he said, "I figure he isn't very far away. What was his name again? I forget."

"You know his name, Father. I've said it enough times and Emerson has told you over and over. It's Joel. His name is Joel." She looked up from pushing a last clutch of moss into the pil-lowcase, suddenly excited. "If he's so close," she cried, "where do you think he is?"

"Close by, I think. So's Emerson. I'm pretty sure the two of them are pretty near."

Myrna tied off the pillowcase, knotting the ends tight. As he spoke she dropped it beside her, her face pink with blush.

"Where is he?" she asked.

"If it was me had got a girl with child, then I'd be more than sitting up a mountainside watching people work," Mister Turfoot said in a loud voice. "I'd be down here helping with the fixing up of this old church that's turning into a house for him and you right in front of his eyes."

Saying that, he hitched at his pants, loosened his belt, and hooked it higher on his waist, his thick fingers grappling with the tongue, the brass buckle tight across his belly. Brushing his hands, palm to palm as if breaking a walnut, he clapped them suddenly together, the crack a sharp cry in the quiet. He looked up into the trees where Joel was sitting behind the fir, and said in his hoarse voice: "You, Joel, come down here."

And then as if an afterthought, added quieter, "Emerson, you too. You've done enough tracking of this fellow for one day."

There was a silence in the dry glade, the shatter of a dragonfly's wings at the edge of the bog the only sound to break it.

The quiet stayed quiet for what seemed to them all as forever.

"Come on now," Mister Turfoot said, "there's work to be done here on your new home. And Emerson," he said, louder as if speaking to one who was by nature recalcitrant, "you put that knife of yours back in the scabbard where a knife belongs. You play with it too much, you hear?"

Joel turned at the sound of dry gravel sliding slow behind him, Emerson passing him by. Joel waited a moment, thinking he might run, and then followed Emerson down to the clearing where Myrna was waiting.

—

ART PICKED HIS WAY ALONG the crumbling lip of gravel where strands of yellow grass and bracken trailed along the broken edge of the dump. As he gazed into the pit, he saw the wreckage of a blasted street in Moerbrugge, a ditch full of broken walls and stones. He saw again a child in the rubble, a girl whose face had been burned, her hair melted, and her mouth a dark O that made no sound, a silence that stared at him just as it did when he dreamed himself staggering through the ruins trying to find her, the twisted streets leading him nowhere. He had picked her up from the cracked stones and charred timbers of a blasted house and carried her in his arms to the medics working on a soldier in a side street near the bridge. The older medic looked first at him and then at what he carried and told Art she was dead.

Art thanked him as he carried her over to a torched truck whose tires had melted in the battle and sat on the cracked bumper. He held her in his arms for a long time, her small mouth open, her lips burned black away. He didn't know how to put her down.

A broken street in Moerbrugge after the battle, but was it Moerbrugge? Maybe it was Eecloo or Oostkamp, or was it in Belgium at all?

France? Maybe Caen, yes, in Caen.

Holland was Godelieve. *Dank u, dank u*, Godelieve's mother, *thank you, thank you*.

He pulled his arms across his chest and held himself to stop from crying out.

And he did, his cry inward, a sound he swallowed.

The trembling vestige of the drug was burning in him like a wick in the last of a candle. He started to shake, but he held himself tighter, no matter the sweat, no matter his hands.

He wasn't in France or Belgium and he wasn't in Holland.

He was at the dump where Irene's dress was hanging.

His arms took themselves apart, unwrapping themselves from his chest. It took what seemed a long time until he could start walking again and when he did he tried to ignore the cramps in his belly, the sweat running down his back. His eyes were almost clear as he went step by step along the precipice, the steep bank falling away into the hole. As he moved he kept watch of the bears on the other side of the dump.

The black sow had made her way back from the forest where she'd been hiding. She was on the opposite bank now, her cubs crowding behind her, their grunts and whines all fear and hunger. The smell of rotting meat hung wet in the air. The dump hung in the air. All the odours of days going on days under the sun rose up in a miasma redolent of every unimaginable thing thrown away, discarded, relegated to oblivion, all of it rotting, flies seething.

France.

He wasn't there, not anymore. The burned girl he'd carried and held in Caen was a trick his mind had done when he looked at the garbage in the dump. She wasn't Godelieve. The girl in Caen had no name, no lips to speak a sound, no voice. For a fleeting moment Marie's face slipped through his mind, her dark hair brushing against his cheek. Her hand was over her eyes and, startled, he glimpsed her standing down in the dump by the rusted door of a truck that had been pushed into the oblivion, and then she was gone too, melted away.

The sow on the other bank was holding her head low. She was licking at the dirt where the slab of meat had been, swinging her head side to side, snuffling every few moments at what breeze there was riding up from the river valley. The black boar that had attacked her had retreated high up the side of the dump near the mountain's rise, leaving behind what was left of the chunk of moose meat he had tried to swallow before the grizzly could get to him.

The grizzly was below Art, the bear hunched down between the rusted hull of a Dodge coupe and the undercarriage of a Reo truck. It was tearing at the slab of meat. Every few minutes it lifted its huge head, its nose coursing the air. Up the slope from the grizzly was the dress. It hung from a broken timber, swaying slowly as though there was still a body in it, something thin and alive, moving.

Art's head was weary now, the opium and alcohol in his body elusive, almost gone. He was drenched in a sweat from the drug heat, from the withdrawal. He had used too much back at the cabin. Everything inside him was thin and sour. It came out through his pores smelling of viscera.

The weariness was a part of him now. He stood as still as he could, looking down at the bear. The grizzly knew he was there. The bear had tracked every step he had taken, measuring with its ears and nose how near, how far away he was. He could feel the bear smelling him.

Art felt as if the grizzly had chosen him.

Every living thing in and around the dump, every wasp and fly, mouse and rat, crow, raven, dog, or wolf was known to the grizzly. The bear was afraid of none of them. It knew every creature on the dump needed to live and each was willing to risk much to survive, even if it meant another's life. Hunger drove the maggot and the fledgling, the mothers of both willing to die or kill to save their own. Of all the creatures on the dump, the grizzly had respect for only two, the black sow because of her yearling cubs, and Art because he was a man.

What Art wanted was hanging from a timber halfway down the slope, thirty feet above where the grizzly ate.

Irene's dress.

Art closed his eyes and heard the knock at his cabin door again. It was Jim McAllister. He had come to Art's cabin and got him to go up to the trailer and help his wife, his Irene. And he had. He had done what he could. But none of that made any difference now. What mattered was something terrible had happened since then.

If he had the dress he could show it to Claude. Claude would know then he'd been telling the truth. He'd have to admit that McAllister's wife had disappeared. With the bloody dress in front of him Claude would have to do something.

Art had to have the dress.

Jim couldn't get away with driving his wife to such an end as to mutilate herself and then, what, vanish? Or did Jim drive her to cutting herself? Or was it something she did to herself because she wanted to? He remembered the spiderweb of scars on her arms. He had seen such lines before, women cutting themselves. But for her to just disappear? Where? To the dump? Here?

Was she still alive or was she dead now?

He squatted on his haunches on the rim of the dump and stared down at the bear as it stared back at him. He felt the grizzly knew him. He remembered the bear had been close to him on the way to McAllister's trailer last night. The grizzly had known who he was. He felt it in his bones.

Now the grizzly was waiting again. What was it the bear wanted him to know?

And as he asked himself what that was he felt a sudden heave in his belly and a blow of nausea struck him. He rocked forward onto his knees and tried to puke, but there was nothing in his belly. There was only the last fumes of the whisky he'd drunk. He dry-heaved, choked a moment on his own spittle, and spat out a clot of phlegm streaked black with blood.

He coughed and spat again, holding himself until the tremors in his stomach passed.

He reached inside his jacket pocket then and took out the whisky. The bottle was a little more than half full. He held it up and stared at it in wonder. He thought he'd finished it. How crazy he was, he thought. He always saved some, didn't he?

He unscrewed the cap and raised the bottle to his mouth, took a mouthful, and let it go down slowly in dribbles, the liquor sliding to his belly where it flowed into a pool of sharp, exquisite pain. He felt like throwing it up, but held the whisky down and took another drink. He drowned his teeth and pushed the liquor down a bit at a time. Each time he swallowed the pain was less and then it was gone.

Done, he pushed the bottle into his pocket. He rolled his head back and rested on his heels for a few minutes before taking a deep breath and getting up. The whisky fumes were in his head now, a dizziness that eased his body until it too vanished. He stayed like that until his eyes cleared.

"Okay, okay bear," he said.

At the sound of his voice the bear stopped eating. Art's eyes were closed. He was standing perfectly still. When he opened his eyes the grizzly had raised itself up on its hind legs and began to turn in the narrow space between the rusted vehicles. It look to Art like the grizzly was dancing, the meat between its legs, its belly protecting the torn slab.

Art stepped down off the dump's rim and picked his way to a pile of broken boards. When he stopped there the bear dropped on all fours and then lifted up again. Art knew if the grizzly decided to charge it would have to make its way over the clutter and detritus of the dump. Yet it would take only a minute or two to reach him. By the time the grizzly got to where he was standing Art knew he'd still be in the dump trying to make it back to the rim. He wouldn't have a chance. And the farther he ventured into the dump the closer he'd be to the grizzly and by the time he got to the dress there would be no way he'd escape a charge. He remembered how fast the grizzly had been when it chased after the black bear.

Art moved to the edge of the pile of boards, took three steps, and dropped off onto a swirl of loose gravel beside the box of what looked like the back half of a rusted-out Chevy pickup truck. He stood on the loose rocks, faced the bear, raised his arms, and turned in a circle.

He turned again and then waited a moment, trembling, but the bear didn't charge. Instead the grizzly spread its great front legs, its paws turning in on themselves the same way his hands had. They faced each other and danced.

Art dropped to his knees when the bear dropped down. The grizzly snuffled the air, picked up the last of the moose meat in its jaws, and made its way up the slope on the other side, disappearing into the trees. He knew the bear hadn't gone far.

Art stood up then and made his way to where the dress was hanging. He balanced carefully on a crushed barrel beside the timber and was about to reach up and take the dress down when a breeze caught at the stained satin. The cloth moved desultory, the clean white folds gliding among the bloody ones.

Images from Caen and Moerbrugge fluttered in and out of his mind like elusive moths in a field of shifting grass, their tank rearing out of a ditch, three chickens roosting in a tree without leaves, the chickens dazed, the corporal, Alvin, picking the birds off the branches like plump apples, a small boy smiling when Art gave him half a chocolate bar, a blonde woman standing in the mouth of an alley beckoning him, two little girls behind her hiding behind a broken door.

He stopped, his hand inches away from the dress, and looked down at his feet. A horde of wasps and flies had risen from below the barrel and swarmed around his legs. Stretching as high as he could he took hold of the collar and lifted the dress off the spear of wood. The dress hung weightless in his hand as he lowered it down upon his arm, making sure the satin didn't touch the crumpled metal below his feet. He didn't want the dress to get dirty. When it was safely in his hands he began to roll it up, the fabric turning in on itself, a small flake of dried blood flittering away, a single wasp following it down to the crushed metal below.

The flies and wasps tried to slip into the folds, the wasps whining and the flies intersecting the air in precise geometries. The insects didn't matter to him, their needs their own. When the dress was rolled up tight, the insects lifted from it and wreathed his head and shoulders. They circled until he could no longer see clearly, the dress a thing his hands cared for by themselves as they pushed the rolled satin inside his jacket against his chest.

As he pulled up the zipper a wasp crawled across the back of his hand. It stopped to rest upon the knuckle of his thumb. Art stood very still and waited until it had cleaned its eyes and lifted away from him. He leaned then against the timber and looked out over the dump. His eyes went from rim to rim, wall to wall, hole to hole. Everything was quiet except for the endless buzz and hum of the flying creatures as they fed and searched among the cracks and crannies everywhere around him. The grizzly was gone.

He took the mickey from his pocket and raised it to his lips. The shakes quieted as he drained all but an ounce. He placed the palm of his hand against his jacket, felt the small bundle as he stared at the wreckage around him.

There was something still out there that made him uneasy. There was something that wasn't quite right, but what it was he didn't know. He looked at the chaos and confusion, the glut and turmoil of the waste, but nothing caught his eye, nothing explained his feeling.

Irene, Irene, Irene.

Was she out there too?

She had to be. Where else was he going to put her but here.

He picked his way back to the rim of the dump and the clearing where the D4 tractor with its blade was parked under the trees. The marks of its tracks were scored into the earth as they led to the dump's rim and then down the narrow cut that led into the wreckage. Where Jim must have driven it.

Art thought and thought, his head a mess, the dump, the tractor, the stuff McAllister had taken from the trailer, the dress. And then he remembered. He had to show Claude the dress. That was what he had to do.

TWENTY

THE SOUND OF THE HAMMERS ceased and the dragonflies hovered, the silence gathering the world to itself. The first sound breaking was the river's weight soughing at its banks like a prisoner at his walls. And then came birdsong, the sparrows quarrelling in the berry bushes, the wings of a grouse breaking the air as it lifted from the dense grass by the swamp's edge, and too, the leaf and needle sound, a rush as of rough hands moving on an axe handle, a handsaw's brush on bark, the whisper of a woman praising the day, Myrna lifting her arms, her broom held high in her two hands, her cry of "Yes."

"Come," Mister Turfoot called to the others, "rest awhile."

Joel rose up on his knees, his hammer hanging from his hand, the board he had set in the corner not yet nailed down. He placed the hammer on the floor by the tobacco can part full of two-and-a-half-inch nails. It was the last board and he had thought to finish the job when the youngest son, Stan, raised his head to the window hole where the old sash had been removed and told Joel to come outside. The boy was shy with him, only his eyes showing from under his tousled blond hair. "Father says to come, Joel," his voice quiet against the wall he pressed against. Joel looked up at him and saw the boy's head pulled down out of sight as suddenly as he had showed it. It reminded him of himself at Alice's window and for a moment he felt that peering in windows was a thing that children do, not men.

Joel poked at a board with the hammer and watched out the window as the Turfoot family put down their tools and set themselves in the shade to drink cool water from a pail. He tried to understand why Mister Turfoot hadn't taken him into the swamp and shot him. Instead, Myrna's father had talked to him like he was grown, a man, not a boy, asking him to start work on the floor and he had, picking up a hammer and a can of nails and going into the church. When he did, Myrna had run in from where she'd been hiding and taken him whole into her arms, his hammer and nails falling on the floor. "Joel," she said, "you're here."

Joel had held her for a brief moment, then disentangling himself he'd gone back to ripping up the old boards under the altar where they were worn and by the stove where they were charred and partly rotted. Myrna stayed beside him. It felt good to have her there. It felt good to be doing work on the church, wanting to help Myrna, the baby too, inside her growing.

And Mister Turfoot?

Joel hadn't said a word to Mister Turfoot. He wasn't ready for that yet.

As the boards came up he'd piled them to the side where Myrna squatted with a small hammer, pulling each one to herself and tacking out the old nails, straightening them on a loose board and dropping them in a jam jar. Beside her was a small bag with the candle stubs from the altar. She told Joel all the while that some of the boards could be saved while others would make kindling for the fire, the candle stubs good for starting wet wood to burn. "You never know when you'll need a spare nail or wax shavings," she said. "And we'll need wood for cooking and even more when it's winter. We won't be wanting our baby to be cold."

He wondered again at her joy in everything around her. He didn't say anything for a while and Myrna said into the quiet, "Will we, Joel." And then again, "Will we?"

Here he was, almost married, and he was going to be a father too. And a baby and how do you look after one?

It would have to be looked after.

What was happening?

What was he doing?

"We'll get wood in," he said, tired of trying to figure everything out, Myrna's excitement catching hold of him in the way it did up on the mountain with her, him feeling now like he did after they were naked and breathing under what seemed the whole sun, the heat beating down on their bodies. "There's lots of deadfall along the edge of the swamp," he said. "But I'll need a chainsaw and I don't have a chainsaw. I don't even have an axe or anything."

It was quiet and Myrna said into the silence, "Don't worry, Joel. Father's got extra of almost everything. He's got a chainsaw too. And my brothers will help us haul the wood. Emerson will know where to find it. He knows every tree everywhere, just like Mother does. He even has names for them."

When Joel didn't say anything she got up and reached down a hand, a great smile on her face. "Let's go outside and sit with the others," she said, the breeze off the river blowing in her hair.

Joel sat back and hunched over his knees as she left, saying, "I'll be along. I just need a minute."

In the first moments with her gone a hundred things lurched into his skull. The first one was Alice. He could see her sleeping in her bed, her bare arm showing, and Irene too who'd cut herself and disappeared. She was there too, her legs bleeding. And there was Art and his war, Wang Po and Nanjing, Myrna, the baby, the smoke in Wang Po's room which Joel could smell just thinking of it, the Someday Church he was working on so Myrna could have a home for the baby, the baby, the baby, and all and everything, and Alice too.

If I don't move I'll stay here forever, he thought, his muscles so tense he was sure if one more thing happened he'd explode.

And.

"You better go out there," the words coming close to his ear, Joel's body a green stick bent and ready to spring. He didn't move to see, knew it was Emerson. He hunched tighter, not knowing where the boy's knife might be.

"I know what you're thinking," Emerson said, "and you can stop thinking about her right now."

Joel turned his head slow.

Emerson was behind him hunkered on his heels, close enough for Joel to touch, but far enough away not to.

"What?"

"I know you look at that girl behind the store. And don't tell me you don't. I seen you staring at her nights, perched on that chunk of cedar by her window. Well, you can stop that. You're with my sister Myrna, her and the baby she's having." He took a breath and added, "Yours."

"You don't know what I'm thinking," said Joel, his arms crossed tight across his knees. He took off his hat and laid it down on the floor. Wiping his forehead, he glanced at the hammer just within reach and saw Emerson's foot push it aside, the boy's body balanced on one bent leg as he did it and then drawing the other foot back under him once the hammer was far enough away.

And then there were steps on the porch, feet shuffling on the new boards as if someone were struggling to move on sore feet. Joel looked to where the door used to be, the opening filled with Myrna's mother, Isabel, her long cotton dress draped white with faded flowers on it hanging to her swollen ankles, her feet stuffed into bead-dibbled moccasins sewn in bird-wing arabesques.

"You go now, Emerson," she said. When neither of them shifted an inch, she looked at Emerson until he looked back, her head cocked to one side, her long hair with streaks of early grey swinging. "You," she said to him, not unkind, but direct.

Joel didn't move, but Emerson did. He slipped to his feet like he was made of water falling upwards, so fluid the gesture of his body. Isabel raised her hand as he ran by her, his rough yellow hair passing like parted wheat between her spread fingers, his thin body a stream weaving through the narrow space between her hip and the door frame. "There aren't a thing that boy won't do, but that I love him for it anyway," she said. "He brought me two white-streaked feathers from a young eagle this morning. He said they fell from the sky." She hummed for a second or two a tune Joel didn't know, a lightness as of feathers falling. She looked long at him as if judging who he was and who he was to be.

"Myrna will feel the same about who she's carrying. She'll have the same love when she has her a son," she said in words that were music. It was as if she was singing what she said. He wasn't sure if she was even talking to him.

"I figure it's a boy she's carrying. The baby's high up. Could be she'll have a boy like my Emerson, but that isn't likely, there never being any like him before. Still," she said, "no one's cast the reeds so there's no knowing. My sister Thelma has a way with casting truths, but she's out in Saskatoon visiting her husband's folks, they're close to dying. But there's young ones on the way—there's no end to babies. We're a family that knows how to make a child, you can give us that."

She hummed again the same tune, looking down at him.

When Joel blinked, she said, "As for you, you get up off the thoughts you're having. They're just confusions caused by doubt and doubt is the preoccupation of weak men. I brought food down from the house. Father and the rest are sitting out there in the shade. That creek water is good for drinking. It'll be fine for cooking with too. It's just back in the trees a ways. Arnold will be running a hose line and soon enough you'll have water here. The lot of them are probably eating about now. A rest has turned into a meal. Well, we don't have time for that right now, do we?" She looked out the window a moment and Joel figured it was to see if Emerson had gone.

"Emerson's not far off," said Joel.

"Don't you mind Emerson," she said. "I think we need to have a talk. Don't you?" She held out her hand, small and soft to the touch as he took it and wondered how it could be soft knowing the work she'd done and did. She gestured to him and he rose to her bidding and followed her outside into the sun.

There was no one in the clearing as she walked across the ruts of the road to where the horse slept, one hoof toed down and the rest of its body balanced on the other three legs, snoring, Isabel saying, "Yes, yes," to the horse as they passed, her affection agreeing with the momentary peace the animal had found. Joel walked a step behind and to the side thinking how of all the people he might have talked to about Myrna and the baby, Isabel was the last one he'd have chosen.

But then he thought, who else but her mother?

When they got to the edge of the clearing she parted two cloudberry bushes and stepped through onto a narrow animal path, one the deer and moose had made over the years as they followed the marge of the bog, here and there a cleft print pressed and marked in mud from the rain. He ducked through the gap and fell in behind her, Isabel's bulk filling the available space in front of him, barring any chance he might have had of seeing where they might be going other than knowing they were moving south along the edge of the swamp. As she walked Myrna's mother started singing.

The words *sweet dreams of you* rose up only to fall quieter when she touched the sad words in the refrain. Joel hadn't heard the song since he was back on the Lake. It made him think of Alice and how he was going to have to forget her and start anew like the song said.

Her voice slipped away, Isabel stretching out the last notes in whispers. It was quiet for a time along the trail until they passed through a barrow of logs jammed up against a gravel bank left behind by some long ago spring flood. Isabel hummed a bit more of the song and said, "I do love Miss Patsy Cline and her sweet dreams."

Climbing up the side of a swale, gravel running under their feet, they came over a slight rise to an opening in the forest where an ancient cedar stood, its river-side bark charred from a long ago lightning strike. The wound had healed, but the tree bore the scar, a black ribbon running like a snake's tongue twenty feet up the trunk. The few living limbs hung high up, their green fans swaying sultry in the heat. Below them in a broken chorus hung a torrent of branches from far-off years, the trunk festooned with their broken stubs, some of them ten feet long, a frayed startle like a worn wire brush, the trunk climbing among them into the sky. Beside the tree was a massive stone, a great one maybe left behind by the glaciers. Around it were strewn small rocks and pebbles, each different one from the other as if struck from different mountains.

Joel hung back as Isabel stopped by the stone and took from the side pocket of her dress a pebble with a stripe of green curling in a band around its intense red. It was no bigger than Joel's thumb. She rolled it across her palm and, turning toward the tree, threw the pebble high in the air. Joel followed its flight, the green band flashing in the sun as the pebble fell back into her hand as a bird might to the nest it had left.

Still facing the old cedar, she spoke again in the way people do who have spent time talking alone to themselves.

"Nothing's easy, not love, not nothing, but we can make it better by letting what was go. We have to turn yesterday into what used to be, yes, we do. What we have is today. What we have is now. You taught me there are no choices, there's only doing and doing what's right and what's good. I listen, for how else know a sparrow's wings in first flight, the songs of the beetles as they burrow in the moss. Here I am with this young man who's going to be the father of my grandchild and I am filled up with love for my Myrna and for him."

She stood a moment, then turned toward him.

"What is this place?" Joel asked.

"This is a learning place," Isabel said. "Soon enough you'll find your own elder tree and you'll begin to know. I come here to worry away the world when it starts aching me. I was taught by my grandmother when I was a young girl to leave a stone at the foot of an elder. This tree is two hundred years old. It knows more of this world than we ever will of storms and floods, of fury and travail. Leaving a stone is a sign of willingness and respect that was taught me by my grandmother who learned it from her grandmother and the mothers before her. I taught this to Myrna when my own mother died in her time. Myrna has an elder of her own. Here's where my joys and troubles get taken. Here's where I lay my burdens down."

"Why've you brought me here?"

"It's not a question you need to ask. You think you know why, but you don't." When he didn't reply, she said, "Listening is the hardest thing to learn, Joel."

She quieted for what seemed hours and was only minutes. She said, "This world doesn't change even though you might wish it would. You think things changed when Myrna got with child, but everything's the way it's supposed to be. You look in a pool of water and there you are. Swirl that water up and when it calms there you are again. Things happen as they must. I was walking this morning in the high pasture when this pebble spoke to me from a dust devil the wind blew up by the fence where you and Myrna always meet. A few feet past is where the trail goes up the mountain to the spring where sometimes you sit and worry your days."

How does she know that? he wondered.

"The pebble had a red in it I never saw before in these mountains. The green band around was shining bright like it'd been licked by a snake. I've walked by that spot a hundred, hundred times and I swear that pebble was never there before. Who knows where it might've come from. It spoke and that's when I knew what had to be done. I tucked it in my pocket here to keep it warm," and she patted the side of her dress. "I knew right then I'd be coming here to talk to the elder tree. The other thing I knew is that I'd be coming here with you."

"How'd you know I'd be here?"

Isabel went on as if he hadn't spoken. "Joel, there's a spirit in everything around us just as there's a spirit in this pebble. I know the name of what I hold. My grandmother would have called this stone Chalsey Doney. I love the name of it. It sounds like a horse dancing. That was its name far back where my people come from."

"Where was that?" asked Joel.

"An old, old country. My grandmother carried such a pebble all her life. When she died I placed it under her tongue so she'd be safe on the other side. She told me a Chalsey Doney drives away the dark and protects the one who holds it."

She held out her hand, the green band brilliant in her palm. It held the sun alive inside it, the green surround like a cloud in a forest swirling. "This's for you," she said, "but only for a little while. When you're done with it bring it to this place and give it to this here elder. You're borrowing it is all. You'll find your own stone soon enough."

He took it from her, the stone still warm from her touch. "What do I do with it?"

"It's not a matter of doing. It's knowing. Now it's time for you to go back to the village and do whatever it is you have to do."

"But I thought we were going to talk about things?"

"And what might they be?"

"You know, Myrna and all. The baby."

"Oh, we did that," Isabel said. "Weren't you listening?"

TWENTY-ONE

ART WALKED SLOWLY down the road from the dump, dusty weeds sprawled along the ditches, fir cones lying among scattered stones like ornaments the trees had lost. As he walked he told himself again he'd stay away from the pipe and the bottle. He spoke out loud, angry, saying, "That's it. You're cutting back. You have to." But even as he spoke he knew he wouldn't. He had made those promises before.

He pressed his hand against the roll of cotton resting against his chest. "I will," he said. "I will."

When he came to Jaswant's shack he stopped and stared at Gerda Dunkle sitting on Raaka's porch. She was holding the baby, the familiar bundle cradled against her breast, the baby breathing or not, healing or not, still loved. It tore Art to see her. Gerda gave him a small, tentative wave when she saw him. It was not an invitation and not a dismissal. All she is trying to tell me is that she's here with her baby waiting for Beate to live or to die, he said to himself. He wanted to say something to her, but he didn't know how. All Art knew was that the little hope she had was for her baby, for Beate. There was little to nothing left over for her to share.

He tried to smile, but his lips didn't work right, so he waved with his free hand and moved on, the road descending the mountain in tight curves and switchbacks. He crossed the high road and walked down the hill to the village. At the cemetery he turned instead of going on and stepped over the fallen palings of what had once been the churchyard fence. He wasn't ready yet to go into the village or go to the mill. He held his hand inside his jacket touching the dress as he made his way among the wooden crosses, the few that were standing. Most of them had fallen over or were propped up by rocks, the old names carved or painted, most of them unintelligible, worn away by the sun, the rains, the winter storms. Seeing one turned white by the years, it took him back to the graveyards in France, his work there after the war, the narrow building where the crosses were made, quiet men putting them together, others painting them white, and then the names, the insignia, and too, the crosses without names, the unknown soldiers they buried, small bags in wooden boxes, bones in canvas sacks.

He stopped at the back of the church and pressed his face against the wall, his hand gripping the dress. He stood there for a long time with his body leaning into the weathered wood.

The sun was moving past noon as he passed out of the church's shadow, runnels of tears in the dust on his cheeks. He wiped at his face as he stepped through the unhinged gap where the gate stood propped against a crooked post and started to walk down to the road again. He could see the women carrying things into the Hall in preparation for the dance. It made him almost feel safe to know the rest of the world was going on without him and he wondered if there would ever be a time when he could be like that. He was going to turn at the corner and go to the mill to see Claude, show him the dress, and ask him to do something about McAllister, but Art wasn't ready to do that yet. He wasn't ready to give up the dress. Claude would take the dress away from him and he didn't want Claude to have it. Not yet. Instead he went on to the store.

In the arms of the women passing him were cardboard boxes full of decorations, coloured streamers left over from the last dance and the one before that, the paper bedraggled and torn from being taken up and pulled down too many times. Seeing the women brought him back from his confusions. "I'm going to be all right," he said, his voice sounding normal to him as he took his hand from inside his jacket. He thought of the Christmas lights that Joseph would always try to make work at the Hall dances. Some of the bulbs were always burned out and Joseph would try to solve the mystery of finding out which bulb was dead so the string of lights would work. Art smiled as he thought of Joseph laughing and then accepting that the lights would never work no matter them being brought to the dance yet again. In boxes and baskets some of the women were carrying there would be plates and cups and glasses, forks and spoons, hard-boiled eggs, shaved moose and deer cold cuts, sausages, Jell-O and bean salads and cabbage salads, platters for sandwiches, baloney and cheese slices, wilted lettuce, oddments of eatables, potato salads, cabbage rolls, all kinds of crockery people could risk getting broken, stolen, or lost. Tables would be set up at the back of the Hall and wooden chairs of all kinds and shapes lined up along the walls.

Art knew Wally Yaztremski would have his speakers hanging from spikes on the wall with his record player on a table in the corner where it was least likely to get bumped by some dancer thinking a woman was meant to be thrown around in imitation of some foxtrot, waltz, or jive he'd watched being done somewhere else. Back of the Hall in the field a few trucks and cars were parked. Most of the drinking would be done out there. Liquor wasn't allowed in the Hall, but it got in disguised in paper cups of pop and lemonade and tea, beer in coffee mugs. In the shanty leaning from the side of the Hall was where coats, hats, boots, shoes, and children were left, the parents picking up clothes and kids sometime after midnight, most of the children asleep, the rest weeping, fighting, or simply playing in the beds they'd made for themselves there, the little ones burrowed under the coats for safety or just to find a little quiet, muffled as they were in wool or cotton or fur, empty pop bottles and candy wrappers scattered about, the music loud, their parents talking, laughing, or fighting in the Hall, among the trucks, or in the bush, depending on the hour, the wrong partner, the right one, no partner, too many partners, the wrong tune or corner, brush or back seat, the girls who were supposed to be babysitting the little ones long ago having deserted their posts in the shanty in favour of taking off into the shadows with some boy they knew come down from the hills or better some boy arrived from Blue River or Clearwater, a stranger, exotic and wild, the touching, the being touched.

It was all so ordinary, so perfect. None of them knew that he was carrying the blotched dress of a woman who was probably dead. He was almost at the store when he remembered he had to find Molly. That was what he was supposed to do. Still he wasn't ready yet to give the dress to Claude. He didn't want to think of Claude holding it in his beefy hands, what he would say, what he would do with it. No, he'd find Molly and tell her about the baby and then after that he might go down to the cabin and have a drink. Just a small one, just enough to put an end to the clutch in his belly, the sweat under his arms, between his legs. But no more opium. He'd had enough of that. Opium made him lose his mind and he needed his mind now. He touched the bottle in his pocket, but knew if he drank what was left there'd be nothing more until he could get to the cabin and he couldn't go there yet. He wiped at his forehead and his hand came away wet.

Molly.

She had to be somewhere close by now that the women were decorating the Hall. He'd go and see Claude after he talked to her, after he went to the cabin. If he went to the cabin. He looked around but none of the women filing in and out with their boxes was Molly Samuels.

Parked angle-wise to the side of the store was Eddy Gibson's green pickup truck, his wife, Ethel, taking a carton from the back.

"You seen Molly?" he called across the road.

Ethel smiled. Art had helped her son the year before, talking him out of running away. The boy was at school in Kamloops now. "I saw her a few minutes ago," she called back. "Hey," she said, "you're looking a little the worse for wear."

"I'm okay," he said as he tried to smile. "A bad night is all. I haven't been sleeping."

She tilted the carton against the truck fender and leaned against it to hold it up. "How come you're looking for Molly?"

"No reason. Just need to talk."

"Yuh," she grunted as she took the weight of the box in her arms, settling her feet in the gravel.

"You need a hand with that, Ethel?"

"Nope," she said. "I been carrying stuff like this for years. It wouldn't do to break the pattern by having some man help out."

"Yeah, well," said Art, "there's always a first time."

"First time? Hell, that was back when the little toy dog was new," she said, and laughed. "Keep looking," she said. "Molly's around here somewhere."

He watched her carry the carton to the Hall, relieved he'd been able to talk to her as if it was just a regular day, as if he hadn't just been at the dump dancing with a grizzly bear and getting a dress covered with blood.

The long porch in front of the store was shielded from the sun, dust floating in the air above the step planks. Ernie Reiner was sitting in the shade on a bench against the wall, a bottle of Orange Crush pop gripped in his hand. Beside him was a guy Art knew from the mill. The man had been brought in a few weeks ago to replace someone Claude had fired off the boxcar-loading crew. A cigarette was hanging from the corner of the guy's lips, smoke running up the side of his face. Ernie said something to him that Art couldn't quite hear and they both laughed.

The two of them were watching the women coming down the road from their cabins and shacks with boxes and bags, others parading back and forth from truck to Hall. And then Art remembered who the new man was. His name was Dave. Art stepped back off the road into the shadow at the side of the Hall. He wasn't up to dealing with Reiner and his new friend.

Ernie sat there grinning. "I wouldn't mind having a bit of that," Reiner said as Natalka Danko's daughter Kateryna came up the road with two huge pies balanced in her arms. "There's nothing like getting them when they're young."

Reiner said it loud enough for the girl to hear, Kateryna lowering her head and crossing over to where the women were gathered in the shade of the big fir tree by the Hall.

"Betcha her pie'd be awful tasty," the guy called Dave said and they laughed.

Joseph was sitting at the other end of the porch, putting a new string on his guitar. When he heard that last from Dave he got up off the porch and as he took a step toward them, Art called to him.

"Joseph," Art said.

Joseph turned, hesitated a second, and swung his guitar behind his back, nodding as he jumped off the porch into the weeds. "Those two aren't worth looking at," Joseph said as he came alongside Art.

"Fuck you," Reiner said, stretching his legs, his body lazy on the bench.

The screen door screeched open and slapped shut as Molly Samuels came out onto the porch, a canvas bag of groceries hanging from her hand. The wilted stems of carrots hung from the bag rim like tired flags. "What's going on?" she asked. When no one answered her, she said to Ernie, "You don't need to talk like that. There's kids around here."

Myrtle Gambier hurried over from the fir tree on the other side of the road and pointed at Ernie. "That man," she said. "He was saying bad things to Natalka's girl."

"You," Molly said. She switched the bag of groceries to her other hand.

"I didn't do nothing," Reiner said with half a grin.

"I know you, Ernie Reiner. That's just a girl over there," she said, pointing at Kateryna who was hiding behind the other women. "She's just twelve." Molly took a step toward him, the bag swinging from her hand. "What's the matter with you?"

"I was just kidding around."

"Men like you are why women leave men. You're a sore on the face of the earth, you are."

"C'mon, Ernie," Dave said, grabbing Reiner's arm. "Let's go down to the cookhouse and see if we can get a cup of coffee."

"Fuck her," Reiner said, giving Art a sideways, nervous look as he saw the first-aid man crossing the road.

"You seen McAllister today?" Art called out.

"Who?"

"You heard me," said Art as he came up to the porch.

"He's locked up inside his trailer," said Ernie, his voice nervous as he looked around. "That's where he was this morning when I tried talking to him. It doesn't matter anyway where he is," he said. "I don't want nothing to do with him anymore." He started to walk down the porch but stopped when Art spoke.

"What happened, Ernie?"

"I don't know," said Ernie. He jumped down into the dry grass, turned and looked for Dave, but Dave had gone into the store.

"Last night," said Art as he followed him. "When you were with Jim. You two drove up to the dump."

"Nothing," he said. "Nothing happened."

Art stood there waiting.

"I don't know what you want," said Ernie. "It was Jim. He wanted to get rid of a bunch of stuff."

"In the middle of the night?"

"He came down and got me from the bunkhouse. He said it needed to be done right then so we did it. What's the problem?"

"What stuff?"

"We cleaned out his joy-shack and he had other things too from inside the trailer, clothes and other stuff in boxes," said Ernie.

"What about Irene, his wife?"

"What do you mean?" asked Ernie. "I never seen her. She was in the back room, Jim said. I never went down there."

"And that was it?"

"What do you mean, Art? We took everything up there like

what I said and then Jim started up the D4 and pushed it into the rest of the crap up there. There's nothing wrong with that. It's the dump for Christ's sake. That's what the Cat's for. Besides, who're you to be giving me a hard time about it. You wanna know what's going on about that stuff, go ask Jim."

Art stood there very still, waiting for what else Ernie had to say.

"Anyway, fuck it. I gotta go," Ernie said as he went around the corner of the store.

"What was that all about?" Molly asked as she came down off the porch.

"Oh, Molly," he said, as if he hadn't known she was anywhere near. The bottle of whisky sitting on the table back at the cabin was what was in his head. He'd forgotten her.

"You wanted to talk to me?"

"Oh yeah, I remember. There's someone who's got troubles," he said. "I think you can help her."

"Is it Jim McAllister's wife? Is she okay?" Molly asked.

"No," he said, for a moment confused. "No, not her."

"Who are you talking about then?" she asked.

"Up at Jaswant Singh's place. There's a woman there needs help with her sick baby."

TWENTY-TWO

CLIFF PUT THE EMPTY COFFEE CUPS in the sink behind the counter with the spoons and plates, Alice just behind him cleaning the countertop of crumbs and spills. A bluebottle fly swung in a slow curve above Alice's head, following her as she moved down the narrow aisle past him. As she did she pressed her body as close to the counter as she could get, but her hips still touched his as they brushed against him. She felt his body tense as breath by breath she passed him by, her hand scouring the cheap Arborite, digging with her fingers into the scratches and scuffs, cleaning out the initials scored into it by bored men. Their knives had created hearts and pistols, breasts and buttocks, names and initials, all and everything their weariness asked of them in the hours they sat alone nursing cup after cup of brackish coffee as they waited out the morning or afternoon before going down to the mill for their shift.

Everyone had left the store now, the afternoon worn down to after five o'clock. The Closed sign dangled from its hook over the front door, the dance starting in three more hours, eight o'clock, the men who had sat out pieces of the afternoon talking to or teasing Cliff at the counter having left, gone down to the cookhouse for dinner or to the bunkhouse for a few drinks before the dance began.

"What do you want me to do with all these dishes?" Cliff asked. It was the first time in his life he had ever looked into a kitchen sink except to wash his hands and that had been at home a long time ago.

"It's okay, Mister Waters," Alice still hesitant, saying, "I mean, Cliff. I don't need any more help."

"You know what I told you," Cliff said. "You can call me Crowchild."

"I know," she said. "I'm sorry."

"And stop saying you're sorry. It's them who lock you up should be sorry."

Alice came back down the counter and Cliff moved around to the customer side and stared at Alice's back as she leaned into the soapy water and washed dishes, putting them out to stand and drain in wire drying racks. "You can go now," she said into the steam. "I've got to wait for Mister Harper. He has to make sure everything is all right before he puts me in my room."

"But I'm coming back for you."

"I know," said Alice, turning around and brushing back her hair from her cheek with her wrist. A few drops spattered the front of her dress. "But he isn't here yet, so I don't know what he's going to do."

Cliff watched the drops fall, small, delicate spots appearing on her blouse. "Remember what we talked about?"

"I don't know," she said. "I'm scared."

"Say my name," said Cliff.

She faced away from him, her hands gripping the sink. In a whisper she said, "Cliff."

"No. My real name."

"Crowchild," she said in a small voice. "Your name is Crowchild."

"Louder," he said. "Say it louder."

"Say what louder?"

They turned as Claude Harper came down the aisle, his girth filling the space between the shelves. He slung a bag lightly up onto the counter, the bag settling there as if there were something soft inside.

"What's she supposed to say, Cliff? You want to let me in on the secret?"

"Nothing," Cliff said. "We're just talking."

"You're not supposed to be in here after closing. You know that, don't you?"

"I was helping," he said. "She was all alone here and I figured—"

Claude interrupted him. "You figured what?" When Cliff didn't answer, Claude said, "She's a girl and she's alone in here, you know."

Cliff looked at Claude and slowly, carefully, impossibly, he wanted to hurt the man who could do what he liked with Alice. He wanted to hit Claude so hard in the face the man would go blind.

"I'm sorry, Mister Harper," said Alice. "It's my fault. I asked him to stay and help."

"You did?"

Alice closed her eyes, her wrists crossed on her chest as if with her hands she could fly into herself and disappear. "I'm sorry, I'm sorry," she said, tears startling from her eyes.

Cliff tried to unclench his fists, arms rigid at his sides.

"You sorry too?" Claude asked, a thin smile cut into his face.

"I gotta go, I gotta go," said Cliff, desperate not to leave Alice alone with Claude, but not knowing what else to do. He didn't look at her, saying, "You'll be all right, Alice. Don't worry."

"Go on, get out of here," said Claude.

Claude stood with his back to Alice, Cliff stumbling down the aisle and out onto the porch, the door banging shut behind him. The glass in the front window shivered from the blow.

"Young men like that," Claude said. "I saw his kind in the war. They never lasted long. They got so angry they went crazy and died. I think maybe he's one of them."

Alice barely breathed, her hands still pressed against her chest.

"You go to the back room now. I need to lock you up."

When she didn't move, Claude turned, took a step, leaned on the counter, and said slowly, "Go to the lean-to."

Alice stared at him, stricken, afraid.

"Do as you're told," he said, and pointed down the narrow hall. He stepped around the counter and took her arm. She didn't resist as he pulled her behind him to the lean-to and opened the door, pushing her inside. She was crying as she sat down on the mattress. He went back and brought the bag he'd thrown on the counter when he'd first come in.

"There's some stuff in this here bag for you to get dressed up with. I found it in a cupboard over at the house. The last guy who ran this outfit had a daughter your size more or less. He's running a mill down in Merritt now. Another year and I'll be out of here too. You put on something pretty and I'll be back later to let you out."

Alice stared at the floor.

"You be ready," he said. He raised his chin and sniffed at the air twice, smiling as he closed the door and locked it, the padlock snapping sharp against the hasp.

—

JOEL DIDN'T GO BACK to the Someday Church after Isabel talked to him. He told her he had things to do back in the village. She just nodded and waved him away. He left her then, cutting through the swamp, turning every few minutes to memorize the new path he was taking so he could find his way back. He'd run through the same swamp when he followed Emerson, but there was no way he'd find his way if he tried to retake the boy's wandering path. When he got to the railway tracks he climbed up onto the grade, marking a leafless tree standing sentinel in the bog so he'd know where to turn next time, and headed back toward the village. Far ahead the mill shone in the sun, its corrugated iron siding shimmering. The late afternoon light slipped along its walls to the beehive burner, the rusted red the roan of dusty horses. Wisps of pale smoke seeped from the mesh cone, three gulls wheeling, their shrieks faint in the still air.

The river flowed past, its brown back raked by drifting trees ripped from their moorings on the banks upstream of the canyon. They rolled in water thrust up from hidden rocks, their trunks scoured, bare roots flailing the river before sinking again into the current as they made their way to Mad River.

He stopped a few feet past a railroad culvert, creek water flowing out and falling onto tumbled rocks. The sound of the river moving seemed bottomless to Joel, a breathing deep and heavy, the water dense with dirt scoured from the mountains the river passed through, every canyon wall, every poplar and aspen flat adding to the burden of soil it carried to the sea. Joel had sat and listened to it every night of every month he'd spent in the valley. Art said the river through the mountains was a long wound. It needed to heal each summer, its song as lonely as the land itself.

Joel had thought about all the things that Art said many times, but his hour with Myrna's mother had given him a glimpse of another kind of thinking, a way to understand things, especially her asking him at the last if he'd been listening. He realized for the first time he should keep his mouth shut not just so he wouldn't look foolish but so he could hear what people said behind their words. She'd passed something on to him, but what it was he couldn't explain except to know she'd given it to him in the shape of a pebble, a Chalsey Doney stone as old as forever almost. He was supposed to do something with it or it was supposed to do something to him. One or the other or both. She told him he'd know when the time came.

But it wasn't just Isabel who'd given him another way to know things. He realized Wang Po had given him something too. And Art, his stories about the war and what happened in Holland at the farm and to Marie in France. Out of the many bits and pieces of Art's story Joel had created an impossible place called Paris, a city made from words and make-believe pictures, strange streets, people in cafés, beautiful women who laughed and cried, and men, hard men who had fought a war only to find at the end something broken. Wang Po gave him his war with Nanjing and the slaughtering of his people by the Japanese. Maybe everyone had something they couldn't make better. His mother did, his sister too, her going through the field to the shed behind his father, and the crippled Elsie Crapsey with eighty acres and no one to share her life with, Irene McAllister with her knife, Art with his dreams, what he called his torments, and Alice, and Reiner and Cliff, Emerson, Isabel, all of them with stories that explained nothing and yet explained everything if you really listened to what they said.

Wang Po's story was Nanjing and Shanghai. Art's was Belgium and Holland, France and Paris.

Somehow their stories were the same. They just didn't know how to finish them. Their lives were in a mill wheel going round and round without end as it ground them to dust. Especially Art.

Joel gripped the Chalsey Doney stone in his pocket. It burned into his palm like something alive. He stopped and sat down on the steel rail of a railway bed almost a hundred years old. Before that there wasn't even a wagon road, just a trail busted out of the forest and the swamps. A tatter of wild daisies grew out of the gravel bed by the tracks. He leaned on his knees before their tough frailty, his hands cupping his chin. The river flowed. It was always changing, it was always the same.

He reached into his pocket, took out the Chalsey Doney stone, and rubbed it with his thumb. The sun caught at it and the band flared, a green fire burning inside.

He knew there wasn't a name for what he felt. It was a kind of sadness. The only person he knew who didn't have it was Myrna. If she had a sadness it was a happy one. There was joy in her life all the time. And that was the difference. That's what made Emerson and Isabel, her father too, the three of them to protect her, the three of them to love her. And him too. When he was with her he wasn't afraid.

A hawk slashed the air beside him, its sudden passing a blow to the right of his shoulder. Its sound was a pale scream, the hawk streaming into the grass by the river's edge and stopping with a jolt, the wings outspread, the broad red tail feathers flaring for a moment before the hawk lifted, a wood rat hanging below its clenched talons, the rat's tail curled beneath it like a question mark. Joel watched the hawk lift and glide out over the river before curving back to the forest's edge by the mountain. He waited until it vanished into the arms of a big fir tree and for a moment wondered where the red-tail's mate might be. He remembered seeing the smaller male that spring in a courting flight. The male had come down upon the female's back in the air and then her turning her body upside down and grasping the male's talons, rolling over and over with him in free fall, only letting go of each other a few feet from the treetops. The female screamed when they let go, the male rising until he gained enough height to tumble over her as she passed beneath him. And he thought of him and Myrna up on the mountain. Like the hawks whose cries had stilled the day.

Joel placed his hand on his shoulder as if to touch the air the bird had breached as it flew by. There was a coolness there. The day had moved on. Isabel would be talking to her elder tree by the great rock fallen from the ancient glaciers. She'd be listening to the world, each grass blade twisting, a nuthatch searching the bark of her elder tree for a grub or beetle. While she did, the rest of the Turfoots would be turning the church into a house for Myrna and the baby and while they did he was sitting watching the river, a warm pebble in his hand, and now a hike to the mill and then on up to the cookhouse and a meal.

But before he went back to see Myrna he had to go into the bog behind the bunkhouse and get his tobacco can from its hiding place. He needed to get his money out so he could take it back to her. They were going to need it to buy things for the church that was going to be their house now and they needed to get things for when the baby came. He didn't know what exactly, but Myrna and Isabel would know. Maybe Myrna and him could go down to Kamloops and buy some things. It'd be exciting to take her there, just the two of them. They could get a room in a hotel or a motel. He'd never done that before. It sounded exciting.

Suddenly he was starving. He looked back the way he'd come, taking it in once more, memorizing each tree and bush so he could find his way back if he had to. There would still be a bit of a moon later on. He'd be able to see okay.

There was an ache in his belly. He needed to eat something.

He thought of Wang Po. There was a moon in one of the poems the cook was always singing out loud. In the spring he had made Joel memorize the English he had made it into, the Chinese sounds impossible for Joel to make. Wang Po told him the man who wrote it was from a place called Sian. Joel tried to say the poem:

A full moon over the river.
All of heaven burning.
A night without sleep.
I blow out the candle,
See your face in the dark.

It didn't seem quite right the way he said it. He thought maybe he'd mixed up the words. Some of it didn't make sense except for the people far apart. Maybe the two people are looking at the same moon far apart. He thought how strange his life was now, how only a night ago he was looking down on Alice from his perch on the cedar round. Now he was going to be living in an old church with Myrna. And he knew a poem by heart. Who ever thought that would happen?

And he was going to be a father.

A shiver went down his arms and he turned again to the swamp, thinking the hawk might have returned for a second kill, and saw something in a clump of dying cedars fifty feet back in the swamp.

Emerson.

The boy was trailing him again.

It didn't matter now to Joel if the boy was there or not, if he followed him or didn't follow him.

What Joel needed was to find Art. He hadn't seen him since Art had talked to Jim McAllister up at the trailer and Jim telling him Irene was gone. There'd been too much going on since he dropped off the package in the morning. Art had still been passed out then, but Joel knew he'd be somewhere else by now, trying to figure out where Irene McAllister was. And Joel knew what was in the package from Vancouver. Art might have used some of the drugs but Joel hoped he hadn't.

He got to his feet and stretched his arms over his head. His body felt alive as he stepped onto the railway ties. He looked far down the tracks to where they came together and became one steel line and he began to run, his feet touching the ties, three and then four, then three, the railroad passing under him. Far behind him the cry of the afternoon freight train sounded coming up the grade from Mad River crossing. The train was miles away, the horn in the distance a wolf's faint howl. He would be at the station before the freight came around the bend below the swamp. As he ran he didn't turn around. He knew Emerson would be pacing him, the boy's thin body running the rails with him.

The sun had passed over the mountain above the village, its shadow crossing the river. In a few more minutes it would begin the slow climb up the green slopes to the east. The mountain the shadow climbed had no name and neither did the one to the west. Maybe the Indians had names for them but there were none around to ask except for Alice and he didn't think she'd know.

The Brother down in Kamloops who sold her to the Rotmensens wouldn't have taught her anything about Indians or their names. All she'd know was what the school taught her. Her story was that she'd lost her story. Joel figured she'd have forgotten most everything from when she was a little girl up in the Cariboo. Her last memory would be of a wagon back and white hands lifting her up and taking her away.

His feet drummed on the railway ties, bits of gravel skittering from under his boots.

The dance would start in a few hours.

They'd be playing the Everly Brothers and Buddy Holly records, maybe "Peggy Sue" or a slow one like "My Special Angel."

He thought about dancing to "Bye Bye Love" with her, but then he couldn't decide who he meant. It didn't matter. He knew one thing for sure, he'd be dancing.

Alice or Myrna, he couldn't wait.

—

THE ROAD WAS DUST and there were women with black wings. Their hands were white birds and they were pecking her. And the dust. Alice remembered the dust. She went away sometimes and dreamed the day they took her. The dream was full of sounds, words she didn't understand, faces she didn't know, all but one, Sister Mary holding her, and in the dream she was crying. And there was dust in her nose and mouth, and it was hard to breathe, and in the dream sometimes there was a blanket around her head, and she kept trying to breathe through it, and there was Sister Mary's voice, and she kept getting it wrong and she didn't know if it was Sister Mary's voice that first day or if it was her voice on all the days, all the nights, and her crying was only on that first day because she remembered lying in the bed in Sister Mary's room and Sister Mary telling her she couldn't cry and when she did Sister Mary hurt her so bad she never cried again. Not once and, no, she had cried when her friend died, and she had cried when they wouldn't tell her where they buried her, Brother Whelan and the Sisters, because she had begged them to tell her and that night Sister Mary took her, Sister Mary took her, and she couldn't, she wouldn't remember that, because the blanket was tight around her head, she was dying and there was no way she would ever find her way back if she brought that night into her dream, and, Oh, the road was dust, and it was dust, and she couldn't breathe.

But she had cried since she came here. Yes. She knew that. Mister Harper had made her cry and so had Imma. They had both made the tears come into her eyes, but she wouldn't let them hurt her like they did at the school. She remembered the children leaving to go back home in the summer. But not all the children went home. She didn't and there were others like her. They were the orphans. How she hated that word *orphan*. It sounded so pretty and it was so ugly, that word. And sometimes they said the word *foundling* and they told her that's what she was, a girl who was found, but she knew she was stolen. The Sisters and Brothers were the ones who used those words. They said she was an orphan, a foundling, so that's what she was, words, and they meant she didn't have a father or a mother, but Cliff said she did have a mother and father and he would help her find them up in the Cariboo among the Toosey people. Maybe she was one of them, she prayed she was one of somewhere, one of someone.

Cliff, Crowchild, and how she was afraid to say that other name because none of the children were ever allowed to say their real names, and she had never had a real name like Cliff, like Crowchild did. She didn't have any kind of real name. Alice wasn't her name and whatever it was, whatever it had been before the black wings and the white hands took her, before the dust, had been lost. It was the day they stole her. And the fear and the hurt came back, and she was covered in the blanket in the dust, in the dust.

Alice couldn't remember how long she had been sitting on the mattress, just that it was where she was and that she must have been dreaming the dream again. It was why she was so tired. And she reached out and pulled the bag toward her, the one Mister Harper had left. She placed it on her lap and she undid the knot Mister Harper had tied in the top of the bag and she pulled the bag open and began to take out the things he had put in there, the pretty things, the white dress and the skirt, the two sweaters, and the other clothes, the underwear that was coloured pink, and then she couldn't look at any of the things anymore. She couldn't look at them and she picked them up and she pushed them back in the bag, she pushed them back in the bag, the sweaters and the skirt and the dress and everything, the pink underwear, the panties, the red shoes, and she pushed them in hard and she tied the string in a knot and she made another knot and then another one until the two strings were one string, a long string of knots she had made, and she didn't cry, she didn't cry, not once she didn't cry.

TWENTY-THREE

JOEL SAT IN THE EMPTY ROOM at the end of the
second table in the cookhouse, a thick slice of sirloin
steak, its fat charred at the edges, taking up half his plate,
a mound of rough-mashed potatoes beside it, the spuds drenched
in gravy left over from Wednesday's roast beef. The pallor of
canned peas shone a pale green, smeared with melted margarine.
He picked up the salt shaker and shook it over the food, following it with pepper and an extra lump of margarine on top of the
gravy, the fat in oily pools trembling. Taking up his knife
he took another scoop of margarine and covered a thick piece of
Wang Po's bread with it, dredging the end of the slice into the
gravy and pushing it whole into his mouth. As he chewed he cut
a wedge of meat from the steak and forked it into the potatoes,
gravy dripping from the tines.

He felt like he hadn't eaten in a week, no breakfast, no
lunch, Emerson calling him away to the swamp and the church

before he'd had more than an hour or two of sleep. Then working at the church again in the late morning, him fixing the floor, stacking odds and sods of lumber, building shelves under the altar. And Myrna's mother taking him on that walk to the old tree and then giving him the little rock. Myrna's rock was different than his, but the rock he'd got from her was just as important even if he couldn't figure out why.

Myrna's brother flickered in his mind and he wondered if Emerson was still hanging around. He didn't think it likely the boy had any more to eat that day than he did, so busy he had been watching Joel whenever he could as he helped his brothers fix the roof, punching raw clay mixed with cement between the stones so the foundation might hold a few more years. Joel forked another piece of meat into his mouth and when he was done chewing and swallowing he picked up his plate and carried it around the empty tables to the kitchen where Wang Po had begun the cleaning up. Joel walked in and put it down by the cutting block.

The wood of the block was cupped from the years of cooks, Wang Po adding to the shape over the three years of his butchering, the sides of pork and beef reduced to steaks, roasts, chops, hamburger, and stew meat by Wang Po's artful knife, the bones boiled for stock. Joel had watched him many times, the blades and sharpening steel, the whisper of the knife as it entered the meat never nicking a bone, the knife edge slipping along a rib like a feather caressing a breast.

"You hard sharpen a good blade only once," he'd said to Joel, "After that you touch the edge to steel, like what you call an eyelash." Wang Po had held up the knife he was using. "This blade is no good," he said. "Needs sharpening all the time." He rolled his shoulders. "Your country can't make a knife," he said. When Joel had asked why he used it, Wang Po said, "I left all my knives in China."

Joel had asked where in China and the cook had tipped his head to the side. "A soldier in Shanghai has my best knife." He smiled. "Cipango. He used it only once."

Wang Po didn't look up from the sink full of dishes. "What do you want, Joel?" he asked, pushing clean plates into the racks for drying. "More? The steaks are in the dish over there," he said, nodding in the direction of the counter by the door. "Three pieces. You take one, leave the others for Art when he comes, okay?"

"It's not for me," said Joel. He hesitated and then said, "There's this kid follows me around. Emerson Turfoot from up the mountain. Anyway, I don't think he's had food today. I'm pretty sure he's outside waiting for me to come out so he can follow me again. Do you think, maybe he could come in and eat something? I could give him part of my steak, if that's all right?"

"I know him," said Wang Po, his arms elbow deep in soapy water.

"How do you know him? I mean . . ."

"He eats here sometimes," said the cook.

"I've never seen him at the cookhouse."

"He talks a lot, that boy," Wang Po said as he stacked dishes in the steel cradle for drying. When Joel looked at the cook in wonder, Wang Po said, "He's out there," and he pointed with a butcher knife at the door, a blanket of flies clinging to the screen.

Joel put his plate down on a stool and went out, the flies scattering in a cloud before returning as the door slapped shut. He looked at the wall of cedars beyond the garbage cans and parking lot. "Hey, Emerson," he called, "you out there?" When there was no answer, he yelled, "Come get some food." As he spoke, the flies ceased their monotonous whine, the gulls alone crying in their wheel.

"Emerson," he called. "It's okay. Wang Po's got lots left over."

Branches shifted in a clutch of sapling aspens and Emerson stepped out and peered into the shadows to see if anyone else was there.

"It's okay," Joel said again. "It's Saturday and there's an extra steak. Potatoes too, and gravy."

Emerson took a last look toward the road and the station and loped over to the cookhouse, his boots slapping on the hard-packed dirt, his body hunched as if not wanting to be seen.

"Quick," said Joel as he opened the screen door a crack, the boy turning sideways and sliding in, Joel right behind him.

"You let the flies in, you better kill them," said Wang Po from the racks.

Behind the cook were the yellowed oak cutting block and two stools. Joel's plate was there and beside it another plate, both piled high with food, knives and forks, and a tall glass of milk for each of them.

"Better here in the kitchen." Wang Po waved a pot in the air. "Quiet. Nobody here but us chickens," he added, laughing into his beard.

Joel took off his hat and set it down in the block, the two of them pulling stools up and, straddling them, set to emptying their plates. Wang Po glanced at them every few minutes making sure they were eating it all, ready to pile on more potatoes and gravy. A separate plate with a steak and potatoes sat on the blackened steel rack in the oven, the door partly open, the last of the fire's heat keeping the food warm in case Art came late to the cookhouse.

As Joel ate he thought of Guwang Wah and his wife Bao back in Edmonton, how they had fed him in the past winter when they found him cold and hungry on the street, Bao leaning down to put more noodles or rice in his bowl at closing time, sometimes a mound of chow mein, and every day at noon chop suey, chopped eggs and strange vegetables mixed up and piled on rice. What they cooked was different than anything he'd ever eaten. Wang Po cooked that kind of food for himself with a pan called a wok when he wasn't busy. Joel loved the smells, remembering Whyte Street, the Elite Café. A great river flowed in Edmonton's valley just like theirs, a soft and muddy one that rose from the mountains he loved. That was only months ago. He was just a kid then, like Emerson. So much had happened since that night when he almost froze to death in the gondola car, Bill Samuels hauling him out and dropping him by the tracks. The first good thing he remembered from that night was Art bringing him here to the cookhouse and Wang Po giving him hot soup and a sandwich of bacon and sausage.

Joel knew he wasn't the same now.

And Emerson beside him attacking the steak and potatoes, crusts of bread propped against his plate soaking up gravy, margarine smeared on the crust. What made the boy want to follow him? He knew it was Myrna and him up the mountain made Emerson start, but why was he still around?

"Hey," he said to Emerson.

Emerson looked up from his bread and gravy.

Joel took a bite of steak and said, "Wang Po says you talk to him."

"You got a good hat," said Emerson as he pushed a chunk of meat into his mouth.

"My hat?"

"Yup."

And then it was silent. Finally, Joel said, "You don't have to follow me everywhere, you know. After I'm done here I'm going to take a shower in the bathhouse. And after that I'm going to the dance. I saw you there at the Hall one time when there was a dance going. You were hiding at the back where the coats were piled."

Emerson kept working on the steak and potatoes as Joel talked. His fork moved like a small backhoe shovel, his mouth either full or being filled. Joel had never seen anyone so small and skinny eat so much, so fast. "Slow down," he said.

Emerson kept going at his food, using the bread scraps to wipe up the gravy slopped over the side onto the board.

"I need to find Art," Joel said. "He needs help. You can come along if you want." When Emerson didn't say anything, Joel said, "If you're with me at least I'll know where you're hiding."

Wang Po was hanging wet cloths and towels on the line above the stove as Joel talked. "If you can't find Art Kenning, he's at the cabin, or down by the pond he made out of the creek where he sits sometimes," Wang Po said. "It's where he is if he isn't anywhere else. If he's not there he's nowhere."

Emerson busied himself with his knife scraping at the last bits of potato and gravy stuck to his plate.

Joel wondered how Wang Po knew about Art's pool. And about him too. It seemed to Joel like everyone knew what he was doing before he knew himself. Art, Isabel, and now Wang Po. Emerson too. He showed up no matter where Joel was. Emerson got to wherever Joel was going before Joel did.

Wang Po left the kitchen and went out into the dining room to clean tables and return the room to order so it would be ready for the eight o'clock Sunday breakfast. The door to the kitchen closed behind him. The last crust eaten, Emerson looked warily around. It seemed to Joel Emerson hadn't kept watch of anything but the food in front of him, but he knew that wasn't true.

Emerson leaned away from Joel and slipped off the stool,

his fist at his pants as he pulled them up his slender waist, undoing his belt and tightening it again.

"You gotta good hat," he said.

"I got it back on the Lake before I came here," said Joel. "I found it on a post down on the Monashee."

"It's a good one," he said.

"You don't have to follow me," Joel said. "I'm not going anywhere secret."

Emerson took a step back from the stool. Joel took it as a sign the knife hadn't appeared from wherever the boy had it hidden. After seeing what he did with Ernie at the bunkhouse Joel needed to be sure Emerson's hands were empty whenever they appeared from anywhere near his scabbard. The kid was staring over Joel's head at the window.

He tried to figure out what Emerson was thinking. Old boots and scruffy pants, the shirt buttoned wrong, the boots with no socks, and the pants looking like they'd been dragged rough. Joel figured nobody was around when the boy left home that morning. If Isabel had been there she'd have arranged his buttons. He wondered what the boy was thinking. Myrna said Emerson liked him. There seemed no sign of it other than he had come out of his hiding place in the aspens when Joel had called him. It was like Joel had a wild shadow near him all the time.

Maybe Isabel and Arnold let Emerson run wild because that's what he was.

Joel had a dog when he was a kid back in Nakusp. He remembered it showed up one winter starving, its flanks so thin you could have played its twenty-six ribs like a bone guitar. In the beginning he fed it what food he could slip from the house knowing his father would shoot the dog if he knew it was hanging around. It showed up to eat and drink and it slept sometimes on an old crib mattress they'd got from the Crapseys. Missus Crapsey said her birthing days were done when Elsie came out bad. In the end Joel's father said the dog could stay. There were no more lamb or chicken kills after it arrived. The dog kept the wolves and cougars away. Even the mink and marten steered clear of the farm.

Joel had just called it Dog. To him that's what it was. "Hey, Dog," he'd say, and the dog would come to him, its tongue lagging, its eyes soft as butter.

Part boxer, part shepherd, and somewhere in there a breed that might have come from Russia where they bred wolfhounds or so a neighbour had told Joel's father. Paul Urbanowski was from the Ukraine. He came over to Canada after the war. He knew about such dogs. He said the Ukrainians hunted the Germans with dogs like Joel's when the Germans were retreating toward Poland. He said they didn't shoot the Germans they captured. They gave them to the dogs to kill.

The dog he called Dog was always around, following close in the bush when he was hunting willow and blue grouse. The animal knew his whistle. Before they headed home Joel always gave it a kill, a squirrel or rabbit, never a bird. The dog didn't run in a pack like the game warden's hunting dogs and it ignored the loose gangs of village dogs when they ran does and fawns in spring. Joel loved Dog, but the animal was its own creature.

Joel thought maybe Emerson was pretty close to being the same as what Dog was. If he was, then there'd be no real knowing of him beyond trust and that was something you didn't ask for, you couldn't buy.

Emerson hooked a thumb into a loose belt loop and rubbed his other hand across his mouth, wiping away the grease from his meal. He looked halfway past Joel and said, "That McAllister man unplugged his trailer and took it off the blocks. Pumped up the tires too."

"What?"

"He hitched his truck."

Joel sat back on his stool.

Emerson stood where he was, waiting.

—

ART HELD THE BOTTLE IN HIS TWO HANDS and carefully poured whisky into his glass. It felt good not spilling any. He could still do that. He held the bottle to the moonlight coming through the window by the door. The amber liquor moved in the bottle like stray silk drawn through oil. He lowered the bottle to the floor beside him, holding its neck to make sure it didn't fall over. The cat lay on his lap, her ears turned back, listening as she always did to Art's meanderings, the soliloquies that had neither beginning nor end.

"It was almost spring and I thought it would always be spring somewhere and wherever it was there would be the sun, but there was no sun in Paris, there was no sun in the Gare Saint-Lazare. It was the last of winter. I wanted spring, but I didn't want it, because I didn't want Tommy to die in the spring. I wanted him to die in winter, in Holland. But it was Paris and Tommy would never go back to Holland again. Tommy had forgotten that place."

"*Mon chat*, my little one," he said, his hand resting against the cat's flank. "Paris was Tommy's city. I knew it the day I saw him walking past Saint-Séverin, the church they built on a hermit's grave. Every time I went by that church I wondered at how a simple life can turn into an empty vault made of stones. Saint-Séverin was only a little way from where Marie lived. Marie. Ah, my cat, how long did she live in that little apartment above the café? How long did she live anywhere? A month, two? Another rooming house, a café room, a hotel, another empty space she occupied. Did she really go back to Marseilles? Ever? I don't know. She said she did. But she didn't trust me, my little friend. She didn't trust anyone. And she never told the truth. Her stories changed every time I was on leave with her in Paris. Little things, a detail, a wrong season, the wrong flowers in the vase in Lille, tulips in November, anemones in March. But that first night with her in Paris. What I remember most was the pale blue milk, her asking me to drink from her breasts. Drunk, she called me her baby, her *petit*. She cradled my head as I suckled her. Sweet, *mon chat*, a woman's milk. And the baby? When I asked where it was she told me it was gone. *It*, not her, not him. Just gone."

His hand moved down the cat's back, the dark fur lying down and then lifting, a shudder running along the cat's spine, a moan quiet as a distant grouse cry falling.

"*Pauvre* Marie. Her cat was a stray that came each day to her window above the café and slept in the empty flower box. There were no geraniums in 1945. *Mon petit chat, ma jolie*, is what she would have called you, and she would give you a scrap of the chicken she stole from La Closerie des Lilas where she worked in the kitchen. Her hands were rough and chapped from the bad soap, the cold water. A black cat like you, but a tom, not a queen."

He heard his voice but it seemed another's. It seemed made up, a storyteller's voice, someone who pretended what he did, what he seemed to do, what he'd done. The cat was all that held him still. He reached out and stroked her ears flat. "Listen, *mon amie sauvage*," he said.

"In the Gare Saint-Lazare the glass roof went on forever.

The sky that morning was dirty and the rain wouldn't wash it away, the heavens smeared with soot and dirt. I looked up and saw the glass ceiling like a blunt knife jutting into the sky, its blade tearing at the clouds as they passed over. The station was almost deserted but for a line of soldiers carrying litters with the bodies of men upon them, all of the bodies alive, all of them broken, their heads, their hands, their hearts. The wounded called to each other. There was the laughter, the jokes, but there was crying too, there were the silent ones. I could almost hear the breathing of the injured, the labour of their lungs. Soldiers were carrying them to the trains, the echoing slaps of their boot soles on the marble, the dull thuds of their heels. And one of those soldiers was Tommy. Yes, he was there. The concourse at Saint Lazare was like an extended hand, cement fingers reaching past the hospital train into the open in the hope the falling rain might clean them. The cars were dead-ended in the station, no engine to be seen. The rails beyond the cars stuttered in the thin mist rising from the sleepers."

Art took a long drink and then tipped the glass and emptied it. He felt nothing, his body numb. The cat on his lap lay very still.

"It's okay, little one, it's okay. There's more," he said. He placed the empty glass on the table, his other hand burrowed in the cat's fur.

"I sat in the little café near the west gate, the one whose window was always smeared with steam from the kettles and the yellow catarrh of the cheap cigarettes the poor smoke as they wait for a chance to make a few aluminum centimes carrying heavy bags to the taxis. A few pennies, a rare franc or two from a soldier on leave, a real dollar from an American soldier showing off to his girl. There was still a war somewhere. The wounded were being carried to the hospital train and then on to Le Havre. I looked out the café window and remembered the church on rue Saint-Séverin, the one with the twisted pillar and the bone garden, the one where if you stood in the Gothic chapel in the apse at dawn you could hear the dry tears fall from the eyes of the two old women who sat every morning at dawn a pew apart to mutter their rosaries, their bodies gently rocking, their heads nodding as if moved by strings held in the hands of angels.

"Marie hated it when I went to the chapel, *mon chat*. But I went there for the quiet, not the god. She hated the Church, she hated what it had done to her, the priest who hurt her when she was a little girl in Marseille. And she hated her mother who did not believe her even as Marie bled in her arms. *Pas le père Boniface*, her mother said. *Pas lui, pas ça*, she said again and again. *Il ne ferait jamais ça.* He would never do that, her mother said. She was so angry. *Pas le père.*"

Not the Father.

"And Marie hated and she hated until she wept in my arms from the exhaustion of her hate, the weariness of her body when it refused to cry for her, the inexhaustible journey of her heart."

The cat looked to the door, but Art didn't notice Joel sitting outside listening. Art reached out for the glass on the stool beside him, but his hand was shaking so badly he couldn't pick it up.

"*Mon petit chat*," Art said, the cat beginning to purr again, the tips of Art's fingers hanging on to the table edge, the other hand stilled in the cat's thick fur. *Écoute, mon chat.* It was a month later on the rue Saint-Séverin, a different leave. I was coming out of the church when I saw Tommy again. He was crossing the street. The woman with him tripped as she stepped from the curb, a broken shoe in her hand, the high heel hanging from the leather heel by a thread. She spoke his name. I'd only seen his face for a moment but when she said *Tommy*, I knew.

"I stood in the shadow of the church door and saw Tommy pull her across the street, the girl stumbling as she tried to keep up. *Mon chat, ma jolie*, she was just another woman from the quarter, someone who had made it through the war only to discover the war wasn't over. I followed them to a little hotel in an alley off the rue du Cherche-Midi. The clerk told me Tommy had been living there for a week. I looked at the register and saw he was with the Royal Canadian Army Medical Corps. Tommy Bukowski, a corporal. *Dank u, Canada, dank u.* Tommy who told me Godelieve died because she choked and couldn't breathe. The girl is always with me, *petit chat*. I remember the fear in her face when Tommy first brought her from her hiding place into the light at the farm. Yes, and I watched her mother drown. I did nothing, *mon amie*. I didn't stop them raping Godelieve. I didn't stop Tommy."

The cat shifted its body on his knees as Art finally got the glass into his hand. He lifted it to his lips, tipped it up, and drank the emptiness.

"I'm sorry," he said, the cat digging its claws into his knees.

Art wept.

"Ah, I don't know," he said, rubbing his eyes. "I didn't report him when we reached Walcheren after the farm and when I finally did, Claude said it was too late. But it wasn't, *mon chat*. Claude was the major. He could have done something even though we were on a short leave in Paris. A telephone call. It would have taken nothing to call someone. When I got back to the unit Tommy had transferred. I could never get anyone to tell me where. Claude told me later he was killed in some alley fight over a girl, but I didn't know if I could believe

Claude. Alvin said he was sure it wasn't true Tommy got a transfer, that Tommy had either died or deserted. One day he was there and the next day he was gone was what Alvin said. But he wasn't dead. There he was, Corporal Tommy Bukowski of the Royal Canadian Medical Corps, walking down the rue Saint-Séverin. *Arrête de me blesser.* Stop hurting me! the girl cried. Poor girl, I thought, to be with him."

Joel's voice was soft. "Art," he said. "Wake up."

Art looked at Joel, but he didn't see him. He turned his head and spoke to the empty doorway where Joel was standing. "Tommy was in the Medical Corps. It didn't take long for me to find out where he was stationed. He worked the hospital trains. I followed him. I knew where he stayed in Paris then. Little Tommy Bukowski, a corporal. I remember wondering how he got the rank. He should have been demoted. He should have been in the stockade. He should have been hanged."

Joel said Art's name again.

Art's hand went still when he finally heard Joel's voice, his palm resting on the cat's back. The purrs went on, a small motor somewhere in the cat's throat. Art nodded his head slowly. "Joel," he said, a voice coming out of a dream. "How long have you been there?"

"It's okay, Art," said Joel. "I came to tell you Jim McAllister took his trailer off the blocks. He's hitched it to his truck."

Art spoke from far away. "Did Claude look after it?"

"Claude?"

"Have you told him?"

"Me?"

The cat stood then on his lap and arched its back as Art ran his hand up its long black tail. She jumped down, glanced at Joel, then slid past like moving smoke, disappearing like a shadow into the tall grass under the window.

"I'm sorry," Art said. "I was thinking of someone else."

Joel shrugged his shoulders.

Art took his feet off the apple box he used as a stool and stood, balancing himself as if on a rocking boat, his back straightening, his shoulders pulling themselves up, knees clicking into place. He reached back and put his hand on the chair and braced himself as he prepared for a first step, wanting to make sure he got it right. His other hand gripped the empty glass, his knuckles white with the strain of not dropping it.

"There's something I'm trying to remember," Art said. "It's driving me crazy, but I don't know what it is. It was up at the dump where the dress was."

"Dress?"

"Irene's dress. Jim threw it away on the dump. Other stuff too."

Joel nodded, suddenly seeming to Art older than he was, older than all of them.

"I think I fixed it," Joel said.

The Express going to Vancouver went by on the tracks. They were quiet as they listened to it pass. When it was gone Joel heard far off the engine on the southbound night freight start up. The freight train had been pulled into the siding waiting on the Express.

"What are you talking about?" asked Art, Joel coming back into focus. "Fixed what?"

"I got Emerson to slash McAllister's truck tires. There's no way he can get them repaired. Not with the men from the shop at the dance. He's not going anywhere tonight."

"Emerson? The Turfoot boy?"

"He's good with a knife," said Joel. "Don't worry. Jim will never know it was him. Emerson's a ghost."

"Why him?"

"He's been following me around." When Art looked at him, Joel said, "It's because of Myrna," he said.

"Is she okay? Myrna, I mean."

"She's going to have a baby." Art stared at him, Joel adding, "My baby."

"Yeah," Art said. "I think maybe Molly told me." Art was half in one world and half in another. "I think maybe she did," he said.

He took his hand from the chair, leaned down, and picked up the whisky bottle, gripping it by the neck. Ignoring Joel, he took a step to the cold wood stove and, trembling, placed his glass on the iron. He slowly poured it half full of whisky, spilling a single drop on the iron. He set the bottle on the stove and looked at the drop for a moment as if unsure whether to leave the drop or lick it up, then cupped the glass in both shaking hands, but didn't lift it. Bending down, he placed his lips to the rim, raised his head and the glass at the same time, the whisky draining into his throat. He stood there, the glass pressed against his teeth, and waited for the clouds in his head to lift.

He was no longer in Paris with Marie. He was no longer looking for Tommy. Saint-Séverin was full of ghosts, the first one a poor hermit living alone near the Seine. Art was sure the last thing the man had wanted was a pile of stones built on top of his home.

I'm in my cabin by the North Thompson River and Joel is standing in the doorway, Art thought. Joel is in the shadows, but I know he's there because I'm talking to him. Art poured another drink, his hands steadier, and drank three more fingers, a fleeting image in his mind of a line of soldiers carrying empty stretchers across a field of snow. One man dressed in a red coat was screaming, another man was pushing his entrails into his body. Art did not know them.

He placed the glass on the stove by the bottle and looked around for the cat, but she was nowhere to be seen. He went to the bunk and sat down. He rested his elbows on his knees and placed his face into his waiting hands. It felt good for his face to be held.

"Joel."

"What?" Joel asked.

"Go away," Art cried. "I can't help you."

Joel closed his eyes.

Art sat on the edge of the bunk and went over the past day and night and day as he tried to figure out what was driving him crazy. The drinking and the drugs didn't help. All they did was make him forget and right now, at this moment, he was tired of forgetting. He concentrated as he tried to force the people in his head to go back to sleep. It was the dump he needed to be thinking about. The grizzly bear kept coming back into his mind. He'd smelled it on the trail, he remembered that. The stink of bear. And the bear smelled him. The stink of man.

Holland, he thought. When he was first at the farm. The two plates and two sets of knives and forks on the table. Tommy had seen them too. But it wasn't until the mother had shown Art the photograph that he knew what the table setting for two people meant. Tommy had figured it out right away. He was the one who went into the night and found the girl in her hiding place.

"Christ," he said into his hands. "I know Godelieve's name, but the mother didn't have one. I never asked." He pressed his hands into his knees and looked through the doorway into the night. "What's wrong with me?" he whispered.

He could hear his voice, the sound he'd listened to ever since the war. He knew just as he'd always known there was nothing he could do about any of it. Tommy just did what the

Tommys of the world always do. And Art had let him take her into the barn. And then the others went in after them. He'd known what they were going to do. How did doing nothing make him the better man?

"What have I done?"

And there was a howl in him, and he knew it would break him if he ever let it out. He opened his mouth and far off he heard the sound of an animal crying and he wanted to help, but he didn't know how.

———

JOEL SAT ON THE TOP STEP outside Art's cabin, scared. Art wasn't supposed to fall apart. He wasn't supposed to break. Not like this. He was a soldier in the tank corps. Soldiers don't cry. What did he mean when he asked what he'd done?

No matter how hard he tried to keep them out, Myrna and Alice refused to go. They swirled behind his eyes like wild blossoms in a wind. The dance would start soon. He couldn't wait for it to begin, couldn't wait until she was there. He could feel Alice's skin in the palm of his hand, his arm around her waist, Alice smiling at him, a thickness in his throat, his cock getting hard. And then Myrna's white body was under him, her groan as he entered her. Myrna dancing with her father, dancing with him, the baby in her belly dancing too.

A cool breeze off the river slipped across his back and he shivered, Buddy Holly singing "Heartbeat," the Hall going crazy. He was dancing with Myrna and the record was playing full blast.

The cat passed by through the grass, a soft meow and then silence. No matter what, Art loved that cat. Joel's mother came into his mind and he remembered her and how no matter the grief in her life she had loved him. He wondered what she would say did she know he was going to be a father. For a moment he didn't know how to understand where he had come from and where he was going. Maybe someday he would take this child of Myrna's and show it to his own mother. But his father? What would his father say, knowing the Crapseys' eighty acres was forever gone? Joel didn't know. The baby that was coming wasn't real to Joel. It was, but what was it? He could hear Art pouring himself another drink and it was quiet inside. He went back in.

Art was sitting on the edge of his bed, but this time with his .30-30 Winchester 94 lying across his lap. When Joel saw the rifle he was scared of what Art might do and asked him if he was going to kill himself.

"What're you doing here?" Art asked. When Joel didn't reply, Art said, "I got no time to kill myself. I got a cat to look after," and he tried to grin, almost making it.

Joel said nothing, only watched when Art took the rifle over to the table and began to strip it down. After a few minutes Joel realized Art had already forgotten him being there. It was as if nothing had happened, nothing had been said, no story had been told. It was always like this, Joel thought, but this time Art didn't look right. Something was different. Joel wasn't sure if it was safe to leave him now. "You sure you're all right?" he asked.

"What do you mean?" Art said.

"Why are you cleaning the rifle?"

"It's something I've been meaning to do all weekend," said Art.

"That's all?"

Art didn't reply as he took up a screwdriver so he could take the tang out of the rifle.

Joel left the cabin again and circled around the side. He watched through the window as Art pulled the tang and then the stock and was unwinding the last screw so he could drop the lever. He looked concentrated on the job at hand. Sure it was going to be okay, Joel slipped away.

He had to go back to the bunkhouse and clean up before the dance. He'd hung his only clean shirt on a wire hanging down from his window. He hoped the wrinkles had fallen out, but he doubted it. His clothes were always wrinkled. It wasn't until Myrna and Alice came along that he'd started to think about how he looked.

One day when Joel knew Myrna was coming down to the train station Joel had changed out of his work clothes into what few clean things he had. Wang Po saw him from the cookhouse door and called him over, asking Joel who the girl was he was dressing up for. Joel told him there wasn't any girl and Wang Po laughed. "Here's a love poem for you, boy," he said. It was one Joel knew he remembered right because he'd asked Wang Po to tell him the words again and he wrote them down on a scrap of the cook's drawing paper.

> *I watched you comb your long hair.*
> *Your hands were small birds in the shadows.*
> *If I had wings tonight I would fly to you,*
> *Nest in your darkness.*
> *But you are far away by the River Chin*
> *And I am in the north on the endless sea.*
> *I touch the spare grasses and I weep.*

Joel had asked him why all his poems were sad and the cook told him love was sad.

"But the pictures you drew of the girl back in China are beautiful."

"Maybe beautiful is only sad in China," Wang Po replied.

"Is the man in the poem a sailor?"

Wang Po told him it wasn't the ocean in the poem. It was the northern desert. He said soldiers were sent there in the old days to guard the frontier. Sometimes they weren't allowed to come back for many years. "In China the desert is called *Hanhai*," he said. "It means 'the endless sea.'"

When Myrna had seen him at the station in his wrinkled shirt she'd smiled.

She wasn't sad like girls were in China. He wondered if Wang Po would make a picture of her for him so he could hang it in their new house and then he thought he couldn't do that because someone like Reiner would come and tear it down or make a joke of it.

As Joel walked along the path the shadows grew deeper. Far off he saw the front of the store, its lights off. The only light on the road was the one from the Hall. The windows there were lit up and he could see women moving around getting the last things ready. The double doors in front were open. A few men stood together in the shadows just beyond the doorway. Their cigarettes danced like fireflies in the dark. Two of them stepped aside when a woman walked by holding a platter of food. One of the men said something and the others laughed.

The dance wouldn't start for another half-hour. There would be drinking out back where the trucks were parked. People would come from Clearwater and Blue River and from the gyppo mills, the ten-acre farms, and the two-cow ranches along the way. The real dance didn't get really going until midnight.

Joel wondered what it would be like to live far away from someone you cared about. He thought then of Alice and wondered if she was in the lean-to at the back of the store. Claude had said he would let her out to go to the dance. Joel was sure she was in there waiting for Claude to unlock the door. He wondered what she'd be wearing. He didn't think she'd have much, just the stuff she'd brought from the residential school. Anyway, it didn't matter what she wore, he thought. She'd be beautiful no matter what. And she wouldn't be sad either like in Wang Po's poem about the man on the endless sea. She'd be happy to be out of that room.

"She'll be dancing with me," he said out loud. And then he felt guilty because of Myrna and the baby, because Myrna would be at the dance too and she'd see him dancing with Alice after he danced with her and maybe she'd know he liked Alice, he liked her a lot. But he liked Myrna too. He really did. She was having his baby and later she'd be at the old church. It's where he was going to be living too. He'd be looking after her now she was having a baby, his baby. And he wondered what they'd call the baby, what kind of name they'd give it. And for a moment it seemed impossible to deal with any of it.

And there was Myrna's mother too. If Isabel saw him dancing with Alice tonight she'd know. She'd know for sure, he thought, because she had some kind of special powers. He kicked a rock into the ditch and watched it carom off into the darkness. He didn't care. He was going to dance with Alice anyway. It'd just be the one time he'd be able to.

He hadn't been able to talk to Art about it because Art was drunk and there was Irene McAllister to find and then Emerson cutting McAllister's truck tires. Joel stepped over the narrow ditch and cut through the cedar trees at the back of the lot behind the store. Just up the road and around the corner was the driveway Jim McAllister had cut into the bush to hide his trailer and his wife. It was driving Art crazy not knowing what happened to her. At least Joel getting Emerson to cut the tires gave Art time to find out where she was. And where was McAllister anyway? For sure he must know his truck tires were flat. He should be raging around, Joel thought, but he's not. And what about Reiner? And he thought again of walking down to his bunk while Reiner was sleeping and cutting his throat. He could do it easily. And no one would know it was him because he'd be down at the church with Myrna, and he could see the blood filling Reiner's throat.

He looked up and down the road from the darkness of the cedar trees behind the cookhouse lot. A couple of cars and a pickup truck came down from the high road, their headlights cutting into the night. The guy in the truck beeped the horn and Joel could hear a woman laughing. There was something beautiful about the laughter and he waited for it to end. When it stopped he stepped out from the trees and went over to where the Rotmensens' dog was tethered. It whined when he squatted beside it. Its water bucket was full, and the pan had a few bones in it Joel didn't recognize. It leaned its shoulder against his leg and whined. He scratched its ears and then took the tether off the dog's collar. He wasn't sure why. Maybe it was the dance made him do it.

There was a pale light shining from the high window in the lean-to. Joel knew it came from Alice's small lamp. She kept it by her mattress plugged into a cord that ran under the door. It meant Alice was in the room. He imagined her lying back on her mattress resting before Claude came and let her out. Maybe reading the Bible they'd let her have. It was her only book.

It was closer to full dark when he crossed the lot, the dog following him. More cars and trucks were arriving, people talking and laughing. Folks were walking along the road as they came from the bunkhouses, the cabins, and small bungalows between the mill and the Hall. Couples were coming from the river shacks by the station. There were kids yelling and carrying on, parents telling them to stop running, the kids ignoring them.

Most of the people coming along the road had flashlights, thin streams of light picking out this family or that, a child fallen into a ditch, a boy and a girl trying to slip away into the bushes, a mother calling her daughter back, a couple arguing, another couple laughing. One old couple from a farm up Aspen Flats carried a coal-oil lamp, its yellow flame fluttering through the smoky glass. Joel recognized Judy and Sam Newly by the light, Sam hobbling along with his cane.

No one was lonely tonight.

Joel climbed the slope behind the store and resettled the cedar block under the window, a line from Wang Po's poem on his lips, *Your hands were small birds*. He could see Alice's hands combing her hair, her fingers like little nuthatches appearing and disappearing in dark river moss.

He was only going to look this one last time. His boot set on the block, he pulled himself up, his belly and chest flat against the wall, his arms outstretched for balance. The block was too close to the wall. He was going to get down and set it back six or eight inches, but he couldn't resist looking. Holding himself as still as possible he placed his fingertips on the ragged wire that closed off the window, and looked down into her room.

She wasn't there.

The door was wide open, the store beyond it dark. Her bed was made like it always was, but there were things missing, the stuff she kept on the little table by her bed, the Bible he thought she'd be reading, her soap and toothbrush, the rags she washed herself with. Her clothes were gone from the box where she kept them and so was her suitcase, the one she'd carried up from the station when she got off the train with Imma. There was a strange bag in the corner, but he didn't know what was in it. He'd never seen it before.

Joel hung there from the wall like a midnight moth, his arms flattened against the bare boards. It had to be Claude, Joel thought. Claude was the one going to let her out.

Alice was going to the dance, but if that's where she was then why were all her things gone? None of it made any sense. Alice was gone, with Claude or without him. But where would she go by herself where she wouldn't be found?

The breeze picked up, a wind coming soft from the south. It touched his bare arms, the back of his neck. He slid down the wall so he could get his feet on the ground. When he did he kicked the cedar block down the slope onto the gravel and looked around, unsure of what to do.

A voice came out of the shadows by the corner of the shack. "They went down to the siding."

"Emerson? That you?"

"Yup."

"Who's at the siding?"

"Cliff and her went there."

"Why the siding?"

Emerson got up and stood against the wall looking out over the empty lot to the road. A woman, already drunk, yelled, "You bastard." The man beside her cursed her back as she staggered in the light from his torch. He held the light away from her so she couldn't see where she was going, laughing as she stumbled.

The dog got up from the dirt beside Joel and went over to Emerson. The boy reached down and scratched behind its ear, his eyes still on the road. "How come you let him loose?" Emerson asked.

"The dog?"

"Yeah."

"I don't know," Joel said. "You been feeding him?"

Emerson squatted down and put his lean arm over the dog's back. It snuffled at his chest, its tongue lagging. "He gets hungry," he said. "Needs water too."

"I know," said Joel. "I feed him too sometimes." And he shook his head. "Jesus, Emerson," he said. "Why did they go to the siding?"

"They got in a boxcar," said Emerson.

"You mean the night freight?"

"Yup."

It was the freight Joel heard leaving earlier.

Emerson sank back into the shadows, his hand on the dog's collar, his breathing stilled. Joel hunkered down on his heels. They both stilled as they heard Claude's voice raging inside Alice's room, the walls shaking. Something, a fist, struck the wall above Joel's head, the boards rattling.

They heard Claude curse and then he said, "Who the fuck let her out?"

Joel thought of Cliff and Alice heading south in the freight and then he heard people laughing from the road. "Mystery Train" began to play at the dance, Junior Parker singing. He wished she was there and hadn't gone with Cliff. If she was he'd be dancing with her, maybe a last dance, but he'd be holding her and all at least once before he started living with Myrna and the baby.

"It's that fucking Cliff," Claude muttered from behind the wall. "He took a bar and pried the lock right off the door. God damn him."

The lean-to door slammed, and Joel could hear Claude stomping back through the store, his boots pounding the floor.

It was quiet for a moment, the song at the Hall over, and then voices got louder again, Wally Yaztremski putting on Little Richard, kicking things off again with "Tutti Frutti," the beat of his piano crazy, the night retreating.

The two of them waited until the song ended.

"I'm glad she's gone," said Emerson.

Joel stood, his thumbs hooked into his belt, his hat pulled down over his eyes. Emerson nudged the dog with his boot and it went over to Joel and licked his hand. Emerson called the dog back. It came back to him and leaned against his knee. "Myrna," he said. "She'll be looking for you."

"I know," said Joel.

"They got the church fixed up good," Emerson said. "There's a couple of windows need doing and other stuff." He took a breath and said, "Myrna's told everyone she's moved in there." When Joel didn't say anything Emerson picked at a sprung knot in the wall.

Joel looked out over the river to the dark shape of the mountains beyond and he put Alice in a place where he knew if he searched he might never find her again. It was a good place for her to be now. The only way she could come back from there was if she decided to, not him. There were other people he'd put there, his father for one. So far none of them had ever come back to haunt him. Just before he left her there in the place he closed his eyes and saw again her sleeping in the lean-to, the curve of her shoulder and the single lock of black hair upon her warm skin. He closed his eyes and breathed the thought of her in. When he opened them Emerson was hunched down, the dog under his arm, both looking at him.

"I don't care."

It was all Joel knew how to say to what he was already working at forgetting. He took off his hat and slapped it against the wall, dust flaring out from the brim.

"Quiet," said Emerson as he pointed across the lot.

Someone was walking through the far cedars with a rifle, the torch in his hand dimmed. What light there was he kept aimed at his feet. Metal clicked on stone, the man's boots moving with care, for no other sound came to them but that one.

"Who's that?"

The man passed behind the wrecked car where Piet leashed the dog. "That's a Winchester he's got," said Emerson.

"I know," said Joel, wondering as he slipped down the slope how the kid knew what the rifle was in the dark. "It's Art."

"Where you going?" Emerson said as Joel moved down the slope and into the dark.

"Where he's going," said Joel. He stopped and looked up at Emerson, the boy waiting for him to decide. "You might as well come," he said. "It helps you can see in the dark."

Emerson grinned.

"What the heck," Joel said. "You're going to follow me anyway." As Emerson took a step, Joel said, "You better put the leash back on the dog if he's coming along."

"He's been with me other nights. Now's no different," said Emerson as he slid down beside Joel. "He's a good dog. Like my mother says, he abides."

"If you come I don't want you talking about Alice or about Cliff either. They don't matter to me anymore. Okay?"

"Yup."

"I mean it."

"Yup."

They watched in silence as Art waited until there was a gap between people going to the dance before crossing the road in the dark. His faint light seemed to pull him down into the ditch and up again into the trees.

"The dump," said Emerson. "He's going to the dump."

TWENTY-FOUR

A LIGHT FLICKERED IN THE SHACK on the dump
road, the glass shade of a coal-oil lamp casting a warm
glow in the room where three women sat at a table drinking tea. Gerda Dunkle faced the window, the scoop of cotton
hanging around her neck and shoulder. The baby was a small
bulge in the cloth's curve. Beate was supported by her arm,
Gerda's fingers splayed against her baby's body, the skin and
bones and breathing of her child.

Beate wasn't dead.

Art breathed a breath and then another as he sat down on
a rock by the side of the road, his rifle resting across his thighs,
his forearms on the stock and barrel. Seeing the four women
gave him an interlude of comfort, a brief respite of hope before
going on to the dump.

Molly and Isabel sat quietly talking as Raaka listened and it
looked to Art that whatever they'd done for the baby had been

good. He was glad Molly got Isabel to come and help. And maybe the penicillin had made a difference after all. He was gladdened by that.

Molly knew kids. It's why he'd asked her to see what she could do. She'd had three of her own and she'd delivered half a dozen others in the past couple of years, women calling on her from village and farm when their time came. The last baby was Anne Steiner's back in April, an easy birth for an unhappy woman according to Molly.

He wondered for a moment if Jaswant had come back from the mill, but knew if he had he wouldn't be around with two strange women visiting no matter their purpose, no matter their helping the child. He'd be in one of the shacks up the road talking with other men or gone to a quiet place where he could be alone to cry or pray or both. Art thought maybe Jaswant was one of those men who could cry. He'd seen men like that in the war. What he didn't know was who or what Sikhs prayed to. Some kind of god, he guessed. Whatever kind it was it had to be a fierce one. Jaswant carried a special kind of knife on him a lot of the time.

"Knives and gods," he whispered.

He saw Molly smile as she looked out the window into the dark, Raaka's hand touching her arm, Isabel pouring tea. Gerda adjusted the baby in the shawl, shifting her across her chest. He imagined the child's tiny breaths and the breathing of the mother too, rocking the baby in her sleep.

Seeing them together made him feel good, but it was a goodness he didn't understand. He barely recognized it for what it was. He had always felt he lived far off from all that happened around him. All he'd ever been was a watcher. Ever since the war he'd lived alone. It was as if goodness was a stranger he'd met along the road, someone he could see but never

know. He knew what evil was, but goodness had escaped him.

Art flicked on his torch, its light lying among the stones at his feet. He got up and looked a last time at the house. He turned his flashlight off as the shack door opened and Molly came out on the porch. The light from the room created a glow around her as she called out to him. "Art," she cried. "Is that you out there?"

He stood up, rifle in hand, but didn't answer, unsure of what to say or do. The gravel road before him led up into the mountain. He had to go. Ahead was the dump and the bear. The grizzly was waiting for him.

He took a step and Molly called to him to wait as she stepped down off the porch and made her way across the grass and stones to the ditch beside the road. "Where are you going?" she asked.

"The dump," he said.

"At this hour?"

He didn't want to talk, to ask, but he did, his hand gripping the rifle to keep from trembling, the drugs and alcohol alive in him still helping him to forget, helping him to remember. He was beginning to feel things even as he wanted to stay numb.

"How's that baby?" he asked, not knowing what else to say.

"She's going to be okay, I think," Molly said. "I wanted to thank you for asking me to come up. Gerda's a good mother in spite of it all. Sometimes when you're alone you don't know what to do. She's had a hard time of it what with her man deserting her and the baby sick. But she's going to be all right now the baby's taken a turn to get better."

"I know," said Art as he turned his head and looked up the road. "I got to go," he said.

"To the dump? That's crazy," she said. "Come in and have a cup of tea. I know Gerda wants to thank you."

"What?"

"You helped her, Art. Don't you know that? And Isabel helped too. She gave the baby something and it perked up a bit. Isabel and me are going to raise some money along the river tomorrow and send her and the baby down on the train to Kamloops on Monday. There's a doctor there who knows about kids."

"The baby's going to be okay then, is she?"

"A bit stronger than she was a while back. She started crying an hour ago and that's good. The baby feels some pain and it's telling her she wants to live. She even took a little milk from Gerda and kept it down."

"What did Isabel give her?"

"She told me it was fennel, goldenseal, and black tea. There was something else in it but she said it was a secret her grandmother told her years ago and she couldn't reveal it."

"The baby kept it down?"

"Yup. A tiny spoonful."

Art looked off into the dark. "She's just skin and bones," he said. "I saw babies like that in the war."

"This isn't the war, Art."

Art smiled quietly at what she'd said. "I have to go."

"Are you okay?"

He shrugged.

"What're you going to do with that rifle?"

"Rifle?"

"The one you're holding."

"It's nothing."

"Okay, Art," said Molly softly. "You take care. And Art?"

"Yeah?"

"Gerda thanks you and so do me and Isabel and Raaka."

Art shifted the rifle to his other hand and watched as Molly

walked back to the house and joined the women at the table. Molly said something and it looked like Gerda was going to get up, but Molly stopped her. She spoke and Gerda sat back down. She raised her hand to the window, a kind of farewell, not a goodbye.

Art wondered at what he felt and then he didn't.

He couldn't hear the boys but he knew they were only a little way behind him where the road took a hairpin turn around a rock bluff. They had Piet's dog with them. He'd heard it whine a hundred feet or so back. The three of them had been with him since he passed behind the store. They'd been standing under the lean-to window. Joel must have been stealing a look at Alice and Emerson had come to stop him. The boy had his sister in mind when it came to Joel. They had looked his way when he was passing and took up behind him on the path and along the road. It didn't matter, he thought. Joel knew what Irene McAllister had done to herself and the Turfoot kid had slashed Jim's truck tires. They were a part of it now.

"A baby," he said, thinking of Arnold Turfoot's Myrna carrying a child and of Gerda Dunkle's baby too. We come into this world weeping, he thought.

The road lay ahead as he walked into the gut of the mountain. Art didn't call the boys to catch up. He let them stay back out of sight as he climbed slowly through the shadows till he came out at the lot overlooking the dump. He went over to the D4 tractor and rested against the worn seat. This's what Jim used, he thought. He'd needed to cover up what he'd done.

As he picked his way down into the wreckage he glanced back and saw the boys come to the rim with the dog. He clambered over the garbage to the timber sticking out of the junk. The stained white dress he'd taken from the timber that afternoon was still inside his jacket. He remembered the blood on his fingers when he'd taken the dress down. He hadn't taken the dress to show Claude or to show Jim either. They'd both acknowledge the dress and the blood, but without Irene it meant nothing. It was just something Jim had gotten rid of. And too, the dress was somehow a comfort to Art, a promise he'd made to Irene. He put his hand inside his jacket and pressed it against her dress. The cotton felt soft and somehow safe where it was, far away from Claude's heavy fingers, from Jim's white hands.

He stood there and looked down at a rotted tarpaulin at his feet, the cotton weave cracked and torn, weeds sticking through its mesh. It lay as if flung down a ridge of gravel into the dump. Art stepped out on a corner of the canvas sprawl. At his feet a cluster of rusted cans floated in a truck fender turned upside down, the rusty water shining with oil. The broken moon rested on its glaze.

Art didn't move as he stared into the pit at the grizzly bear swinging its huge head from side to side. When it located him the bear stopped moving and Art felt it breathe him into its body. There was a stillness then in them both. It was strange and perfect, he thought, the great bear standing at the heart of everything people had refused.

And him too, what he had refused in his heart.

They were quiet for a long time, his breathing and the bear's breathing one thing, and then the bear turned from him and made its way over and around and through the wreckage to a mass of junk fifty feet away on the other side of the dump. On the rim above the bear's head long clusters of yellow grass hung down like a fallen shawl and it was under the cape the bear stopped and turned its head toward Art.

He knew the bear couldn't see him now it was dark, its eyesight poor, but it could smell him still. The great head raised itself up and the bear held Art in its body, breath upon breath. The bear knew where he was and who he was and the bear knew too what he was looking for. The grizzly had known that ever since Art had taken the dress down.

The bear growled deep in its chest. Art lowered his head as the bear's jaws chopped the air. Hearing the sudden jolt dropped him to his knees.

He stared across the dump at the back of the grizzly as it rolled its heavy shoulders and then with its great paws began tearing at the wall of garbage in front of it. As it did, the wall began to collapse, heaps of garbage and junk falling as the bear dug deeper, digging at what remained. When the rest of the pile had fallen away all that remained was the top half of McAllister's small box freezer. Art knew Jim had used the D4 tractor to bury it there where no one would ever find it.

The bear batted the white metal box with a heavy paw and, done, shouldered its way past what it had unearthed and climbed up the steep slope, the grass shawl parting as it pulled itself onto the rim and on into the forest where it disappeared into the arms of the cedars. The limbs closed behind and it was as if the grizzly had never been.

Art stood and remembered when he first smelled the bear. It was when he'd gone back to McAllister's trailer that he smelled the stench of the animal in the dark. Art looked down and saw the moon shine upon oily water in the upturned fender. The bear had been breathing Irene's blood spoor outside the trailer and it had been breathing him too. The bear had known even then.

Across the dump was the box freezer.

It was still half buried in the garbage, beside it a rusted ploughshare from a far-off time. The freezer had sat in the shack at the trailer. The only thing different about it was the long strips of duct tape pulled tight across the lid, binding it to the box below, sealing what was inside.

———

A DOOR BANGED AND THE FOOTSTEPS of the boy crossed the floor above. Wang Po waited quietly, Joel coming down the stairs, his boots barely touching the steps. Wang Po turned as Joel came through the door.

"What's wrong?"

"It's Art," Joel said, his breath moving in wisps. "You have to come."

"You sit and wait a few moments." As he spoke he gestured to the chair by the mattress and told Joel to sit down. The boy was shaking. "Breathe," he said.

Joel gulped air.

Wang Po raised his hand and said, "Slow, slow," his hand hovering like a hummingbird. It was as if he was pressing down on a column of air, forcing it into Joel's lungs.

Joel gasped and swallowed, took a breath, and then another.

"Sit," said Wang Po. He waited as Joel went to the chair and put his body on it, each move careful, his hands on his knees trembling. Wang Po waited, knowing Joel needed to hold all of himself together before he could speak well enough to make sense.

"Three breaths," he said and waited. "Yes, good," Wang Po said, Joel finally still, each breath quieter than the last. "Nothing can't wait. This long, yes?"

The cook composed himself, his eyes at rest, his hands folded together on his lap. "Now say what is wrong about Art."

And Joel did.

He told Wang Po about how he and Emerson had followed

Art and how Art stopped at Jaswant's shack and talked to Molly Samuels and then went up to the dump and the bear looked at Art and Art looked at the bear for a long time and how Joel was sure the bear was going to charge, and he wondered if the Winchester would bring it down if it did charge because the bear was only twenty feet away, no more, and the rifle's caliber wasn't large, a .308 would have been better, but Art didn't raise his rifle at all, and Joel said it was the grizzly bear, the same one that had been on the path behind McAllister's trailer, and after a long time looking at each other they seemed to know the things each of them had to do. The bear left after it tore away everything covering the freezer, and that was when Art went over to what Jim had thrown away. Art took his knife and cut the duct tape around the rim. He lifted the lid and looked into the box for a long time and then he reached in and took something out and put it in his pocket. After that he took the loose tapes he'd cut and stretched them back over the freezer again, the lid sealed down like it was before.

Joel breathed and said how Emerson and him had gone down the road with the dog. Art was with them but the first-aid man wouldn't talk to them. Joel asked Art if it was Irene in the freezer, but Art wouldn't say anything and he wouldn't say what he took out of it either.

"Do you think it was the woman in the freezer?" Wang Po asked.

"What else could it be? It's where McAllister took her."

"Yes," said Wang Po.

"Then he told Emerson and me to go home. He told me Myrna was waiting."

"The girl with the baby, yes?"

"After that he didn't say anything again," said Joel.

"Tell me," said Wang Po.

"He went to McAllister's trailer. There was a lamp burning in the front room," said Joel. "Art went in there. He didn't knock. He just walked in and closed the trailer door behind him."

"Yes."

"Art has his rifle," said Joel. "McAllister's in there with him."

Wang Po nodded.

"Emerson snuck into the shack and looked through the trailer window. He said McAllister was sitting on the couch and Art was sitting on the chair by the sink. He's just looking at Jim."

"Yes."

"We don't know what he's going to do. Art's rifle is pointed right at him."

"How?"

"How what?"

"How does he hold the rifle?"

"Like this," Joel said, and he leaned against the back of his chair, crossed his leg, and pretended to rest a rifle on it so it pointed at the cook.

"Yes," said Wang Po. "His finger on the trigger?"

"I think so."

"Think?"

Emerson had said his finger was inside the trigger guard. "His finger is on the trigger."

"And they are not talking. No?"

"Yes," said Joel. "I mean no, no, they're not talking. Emerson said they're just looking at each other."

"Emerson is at the trailer now?"

"I told him I was coming to get you. I told him I'd be back."

Wang Po held up his hand, thought a moment, and then told Joel what he had to do. "And make Joseph come. Vern Lupich and Oroville Cranmer too. Bring no one who is too drunk. Don't tell Ernie Reiner, he will only make trouble. The foreman Bill Samuels and Claude Harper. At the dance," he said. "They will all be there."

"You know their names," Joel said, surprised.

"I'm the cook," Wang Po said. "I feed them."

He waited, but Joel never moved.

"Wake up," said Wang Po.

Joel blinked his eyes and took the stairs two at a time.

Wang Po listened to the running steps on the floor above and the far-off slam of the cookhouse door.

He turned to the table, took up his wolf-hair brush, cleaned it, and placed it in the case. It was a little longer than the other brushes. He was very careful not to crimp the tip. He put away his ink-stick in a Redbird matchbox with the others and covered the inkstand with a piece of damp chamois so the ink wouldn't dry out. Perhaps there would be time later to work on another drawing.

His tools safely put away, he got up and shrugged into a heavy red shirt, the one given him by Murray, the chokerman who had quit two years ago and went south. They had strange words for things in Canada, he thought. *Chokerman.* Wang Po climbed the stairs, looked at the bread in the kitchen, and thought about putting it into the ovens. The loaves were covered. He slipped on his shoes and went upstairs. He made sure the door to his room was closed behind him. There would be time later for the bread. Right now Art was pointing his rifle at Jim McAllister.

Wang Po stepped out onto the gravel and began walking. The moon was up in the southern sky. Pebbles were strewn across the empty lot. They glistened with evening dew. Their backs looked like thousands of tiny turtles swarming. The pebbles and the deodar branch he'd finished drawing brought back his childhood home and memories of his mother. She had told him long ago his name meant "white soul." The name was about the earth where the feelings are born. His father told him he had to work hard at removing the heart, that he had to drive out the bad demons there, but his father was Confucian, not Buddhist. Wang Po had spent many years with his father's wishes. He had nurtured patience and kindness as best he could after leaving Nanjing, his mother and father dead, buried alive in a trench in the park by the river. The Cipango laughing as they covered his parents' heads so slowly, his mother staring at his father's eyes as he tried to breathe, her eyes and nose covered last. Revenge had left him long ago, just as anger and greed had fled. He remembered, that was enough.

Turtles had swarmed on the banks of the Qinhuai River when he was a boy. One day he'd brought a bucket of young turtles home to his mother. She made him take them back to the river and instructed him to ask their forgiveness when he released them. Po, his white soul, his heart made of earth and darkness. When he died he would return to the earth as *kuei*, a ghost. His mother told him not to be afraid. The earth is your mother too, she told him.

He had never forgotten what she had told him.

I am the ant on the pine cone, he thought. I am the wolf-hair brush at rest.

He had forgotten the mouse in his pocket after they crossed the river. It was only after he'd walked miles into the rice fields that he remembered it. He was lying under a willow tree by a ditch when he felt the tiny animal move. He took it from his pocket and opened his hand in the grass. The mouse sat on his palm and cleaned its paws before walking off his fingers into the world.

There is much to be grateful for, he thought.

He heard the sound of music playing at the Hall down in the village, but didn't recognize their song. All such music was foreign to his ears. He smiled at the word, *foreign*. He said it out loud.

"Foreign."

He knew where the path to McAllister's trailer broke away from the road. He knew the way. He had walked the village paths when he first came to the valley. He needed to know where he was, where others were. As he walked he remembered "The Song of the Cicadas." The wind played music in the air around him. He imagined his woman waiting patiently in Shanghai. He could hear her plucking the *pipa* for him, the delicate sound of the strings in her small hands. "The Cicadas" was one of his faraway songs. Its sadness gave him pleasure whenever he remembered it.

———

"TODAY I WAS DRAWING THE CEDAR BRANCH on the deodar tree, Art. I was sitting at my table in the cookhouse, but I was by the Qinhuai River too. When I was a child the river was my outside mother. The deodar I drew was down the street from where I lived. The third day of the invasion I was hiding in a house far down the street from the deodar tree. In the morning I woke up. I was still in the narrow place above the highest room. Soldiers were shooting into the ceiling. They did not kill me. I do not know what people had lived there. It is strange to lie still and hear soldiers raping a girl. When they stopped is when they started the shooting. It was very quiet after so I knew the soldiers had taken them away to be killed or the people were already dead. I don't know what you call a room like that in your words. It was very tight to lie down and there was a small window with bamboo sticks to let in the air and keep out rats. There were many rats in Nanjing, many rats in the house. I had been there two days and two nights. They burned down that house where I was hiding. I do not remember how I got out. We don't know why we are saved, Art. I think we do not know why things happen. There were rats in the street. They came out when the burning started. Why was I still in Nanjing? Sometimes you fight and sometimes you hide. It is not important. Later I will tell you about the river and the mouse," he said. "You will laugh, I think."

"Jesus, fuck," said McAllister. "You crazy chink. Just take the rifle away from him."

Wang Po turned his head and held up his hand. "It is not a time to talk for you."

"Do something," said Jim. "I have to piss."

"Then piss," Wang Po said.

"What?"

"It is not hard to do, I think," he said. "It is not good to hold water."

Jim was going to speak again and Wang Po reached out and touched the barrel of Art's rifle.

Art didn't move.

"For you, sitting still is good," he said to McAllister. "Quiet is good."

Emerson sat cross-legged inside the dark joy-shack staring through the open door into the trailer where the men were.

Wang Po inclined his head at the boy, his eyes on Art.

"Yes," Emerson said, nodding. "They're coming," he whispered.

"Go get Claude," said McAllister. "He'll put a stop to this."

"It is okay to shoot him, Art," Wang Po said. "If you want. It is okay for me."

McAllister sat very still inside his fear. He looked afraid.

"Ah," Wang Po said. "Quiet is nice."

"Listen, Art. I want to tell you about Chungshan Gate. Cipango made us pile the corpses in the street on the way to Hsiakwan. All day I dragged the dead there. Many had run away to that village in order to die. From Nanjing. Why? There was nowhere to go. Chungshan Gate was one place. The dead were everywhere, soldiers, women, horses and babies, dogs too. We piled them up. When we were done they drove their tanks and trucks over the bodies and ground them to meat and bones. They called that place Shi Jie, what you would call Wet Street."

McAllister sat there, his mouth open, his breathing loud.

"They are stories, Art," Wang Po said softly. "I remember them because I remember. It is a life and I have it."

Art didn't move.

"So, there is another story. We were taken to the riverbank. They lined us up on the wharf in Hsiakwan. There were many hundreds of us. Cipango made us stand all day. Then they brought the machine guns, ten, twenty, and shot everyone. I was in the back of the wharf. When the guns started I fell into the water. Other men fell on me. Dead men, alive men. A corpse was in the water beside me. I pulled him to me and held him in my arms. My head beside his head, my cheek by his cheek. We swam together. The officers stood on the wharf laughing as they shot the water. They tried to kill the dead men with their pistols. The man I held was shot three times. Down the river we floated away, my dead friend in my arms."

Wang Po smiled.

"You're crazy," McAllister said, and in a whisper, as if Art couldn't hear him, pleaded, "Can you help me?"

"I think if you talk more he will shoot you," said Wang Po. "It is best for you to be quiet again."

McAllister crossed his arms on his chest and leaned forward, holding himself. After long minutes looking into Art's eyes, he said, "Please tell him to stop looking at me."

Wang Po settled deeper into himself as the sound of men coming up the gravel road broke into his thoughts. Hearing them, Emerson slipped from the doorway, not a sound from his boots as he vanished.

"They're coming," said McAllister in a whisper. He was speaking to himself. "I can hear them. They're going to help me."

"Stop," said Wang Po. He held up his hand.

McAllister winced as if he'd been struck. "Don't hurt me," he begged. "Please."

"Art," Wang Po said. "What is it in your lap?"

The pad of Art's finger moved slightly on the curved trigger of the Winchester. A single high note rose from McAllister, a wail slipping from his lips. It was like the cry of a child when he is faced with a punishment he can't avoid. "Help me," he pleaded.

"Art?"

The first-aid man reached into his pocket with his free hand and lifted up a necklace, passing it across the rifle to Wang Po. A string of black glass stones clicked against the barrel. Wang Po held it up to the yellow light from the lamp. The silver chain lying across his fingers looked stained with rust. He brought the necklace close to his eye and thin flakes of blood fell from the links into his palm.

McAllister turned his face away, his hands burrowing into each other.

Emerson was in the doorway again, his back to the room. He was looking out into the dark. Joel appeared as if from nowhere and stood beside him, shoulder to shoulder, but Joel facing into the room, his eyes meeting Wang Po's.

"Art?" Joel asked, his name a question.

"It's all right, Joel," said Wang Po. "Be quiet. Everyone be quiet." He turned back to Art and held up the necklace. "What are these?"

"Alaska black diamonds. They were Irene's."

Jim hung his head and stared down at his hands. They wrenched at each other as if they could take each other apart and undo their clasp.

That was when Wang Po reached out and placed his finger-tips lightly upon the barrel of the Winchester and shifted it an inch to the side.

Art smiled as the barrel moved.

"Jesus, Jesus, I'm sorry!" McAllister shouted when he looked up and saw only Art's smile, his hands at last undone. He held them out to the first-aid man. There was a deep quiet for only a moment as he cried, "Can't you hear me?"

Art turned his head and looked at Wang Po as he pressed the trigger.

McAllister fell forward from the couch onto his knees, his body violent in its shaking. His pursed mouth opened and closed like the vent of a dying fish. Helpless, his hands patted at his chest for the blood that wasn't there.

The first words Wang Po heard were Claude Harper shouting at Emerson, men crowding behind him in the joy-shack. He could see Joseph's face and beside him, Bill Samuels. Two or three others were in back trying to see. He recognized Oroville Cranmer, but the others in the shadows he couldn't make out.

"Put the knife down, you little sonufabitch," Claude said through his teeth.

Joel turned around and saw Claude raise his hand as if he were going to strike Emerson.

"Don't you try and touch him," said Joel. He pushed past Emerson and struck Claude's chest with his fist. "He's my friend."

What looked like Joseph's hand reached out and pulled Claude back by his collar just as he was about to throw Joel aside. "He's just a kid, dammit!" Joseph said. He shook Claude, the boss's head jerking up and down as he pulled him close. He spoke quietly into Claude's ear but Wang Po heard the words: "Shut up, you fool."

Claude stopped struggling and looked over Emerson's head at McAllister, who was kneeling on the floor by the couch, his face in his hands.

"What in hell's going on?" Claude asked, but no one paid any attention except Emerson who still blocked the door, his knife weaving in the air above Claude's belt buckle.

"Just don't you try anything," said Emerson. "You're not too big to bleed."

Bill Samuels looked down at Emerson with a half smile on his face. "Jesus," he said. "Where the hell did you come from?"

Wang Po placed his hands on his lap, one on top of the other. "Where is she?" he asked.

"In the box freezer at the dump," Art said.

Everyone in the joy-shack heard him.

Claude hung from Joseph's fist, blinking his eyes.

Emerson slipped his knife into his scabbard and turned to look into the trailer beside Joel.

A few of the men Joel had brought from the dance crowded into the joy-shack, trying to peer past the others. The ones behind Claude and Joseph told the rest what Art had said, the men starting to talk and argue, Bill Samuels telling them to settle down and be quiet. "We'll know soon enough what's happened here," Bill said. "Some of you go find Ernie. He'll be at the dance. Take him down to the mill and keep him there. According to what the kid tells me he's got a part in this."

The boys moved into the room.

Wang Po placed his hand on Art's shoulder and whispered a fragment from a poem he learned as a boy in school.

We wandered far into the mountains in search of bones.
Like the moon we cried out when we were broken.
This path and that path. We did not stop to listen.

Art lifted the rifle to his chest, cradling it in his arms. He leaned his face against the barrel. "I killed Tommy," he said. His voice was the voice of a child.

"I know," said Wang Po, gentle as he took the rifle from Art's hands and laid it on the floor at his feet.

TWENTY-FIVE

THE OLD MAN HAD CRUMPLED NEWSPAPERS and stuffed them inside Joel's coat and pants and helped him into the lee corner of the gondola car. He'd sat Joel in front of him, pushed their legs into a gunny sack, and wrapped them both in thin grey blankets, a stream of snow seething over the metal rim above them, the tiny grains finding their way into the cracks and crevices of what covered them, filling them in, leaving no room for anything but the snow. Joel had sat between the old man's legs, his arms in a cross, his hands pressed into his armpits. The man's arms surrounded him, holding him close to what warmth there was in his body. The wind screamed through the night, the storm covering them with the breathing of mountains. Joel had felt he was a small child as he curled himself into the old man's chest and belly, his head under the curve of the old man's jaw, their two faces looking into the whirlwind as the train careened down the canyons.

In the other lee corner of the car two men lay prostrate under greatcoats, a voice finding its way through the wind's howl as a man sang "The White Cliffs of Dover" repeating and repeating the refrain until it became a crippling whisper in Joel's head. After a long while he no longer knew if the man was singing or if the man had died and the song was all that was left of him in a world made entirely of winter. Beneath Joel was the ceaseless chatter of the wheels on the rails, its endless clatter becoming a part of the man's song, "*just you wait and see.*" A fragment formed inside him, a sonorous cascade made from words hanging in his mind, the "*wait and see, wait and see, wait and see*" going on forever.

And what he saw last of the man who had saved him, a wretched face hanging over the rim of the gondola alongside the visages of the other two men as the old man pleaded to be let down from the car. Bill Samuels told the three of them to stay where they were, Joel shaking as he walked away from the tracks, Art leading him toward the lights shimmering in the cookhouse window. Joel knew he would remember it forever, his not thanking the old man for saving his life in the storm that lasted the hundred miles between Jasper and the village where he lived now.

Joel stared up at the lapped-board ceiling of the church that was going to be his home and thought of the old man in the gondola car last winter holding him in his arms. And he thought of Cliff holding Alice in the boxcar as it threaded its way through the mountains and canyons and into the ranchlands and farms of the river valley where it opened up at Little Fort and beyond. It was in the drylands at the junction across the river from Kamloops where they must have got out and run across the lines of tracks to the bush and at last over the bridge to the town where they could find the bus depot restaurant and bowls of Campbell's tomato soup, and a grilled cheese sandwich maybe, before boarding a bus going to the north that would drop them on the side of the highway at Williams Lake. There they could hitch a ride in a pickup truck to Riske Creek where the Toosey people lived.

Cliff must have held her all that way, them talking, the wind in her black hair, telling each other the stories of their lives, and maybe touching each other too, and then Joel couldn't think anymore about them and what they might have done or not done to each other, with each other, because he wasn't looking at the ceiling anymore in a dream, he was looking at the curve of Myrna's shoulder, a lock of her blond hair lying upon her soft skin, a spray of pale freckles across the top of her shoulder blade looking like the Milky Way in the night sky, the sheet moving ever so slightly as she breathed. For a moment he could see Cliff looking at Alice's shoulder, her skin, and Joel closed his eyes because he didn't know how he could have Alice in his head at the same time Myrna was lying beside him in their bed.

He knew Alice would come and go in him before she left forever. He knew that. He had dreamed her for what seemed to him now forever. He'd thought about Alice for just a moment when he'd come back tonight to the light of the oil lamp in the window. She vanished the moment Myrna took his hand and pressed it against the quickening in her belly. He tried to imagine the baby moving in there and wondered at it aloud. Myrna laughed at him thinking so and he laughed too, and after a long quiet they slept in each other's arms.

As he lay there in the middle of the morning the past night came back to him. He watched again as Joseph and two other men took McAllister away, Claude telling them to tie him up and lock him in the supply shed down at the sawmill. Others were sent to the Hall to find Ernie Reiner and take him to the sawmill too, but when they got there the men at the dance said Ernie had taken off in his pickup. They told them Ernie said he was quitting and headed over to the bunkhouse to get his stuff. A few minutes later they saw Ernie's truck head up to the high road and he was gone, which way, north or south, they didn't know.

What Joel remembered most was the moment when Claude told Art to come down to the mill with him. Art had looked up at Claude and whatever it was passed between them was enough to make Claude turn away without a word and leave the trailer. When everyone was gone Wang Po told Art he was going to the cookhouse to bake the bread for Sunday breakfast. Art nodded. Joel asked Wang Po what Art was going to do and Wang Po smiled and told him he should go home. "You leave Art alone now," he said. "Art is enough."

Joel had left then with Emerson. There was the end of a bright moon when they went down to the bunkhouse. Joel put what little clothing and stuff he had in a kit bag a worker had left behind when he took the train out one day months ago. Joel's hat had been sitting on the foot of his bunk and when he turned to pick it up he saw Emerson holding it. Emerson's thumb ran along the braided leather that scrolled the crown, his thumb touching the faint crusts of grease and salt left there by Joel and the man who'd worn it before leaving it on a fence post down on the Lakes. The three red-tail hawk feathers slid through Emerson's fingers as he stroked the vanes, the barbs catching and the feathers finding the shape of the wind again. The hat turned slowly in his hands. Joel thought of Emerson squatting by the bunkhouse door when Reiner confronted him, Emerson backing Reiner off with that knife of his.

Joel remembered Wang Po telling him Emerson looked up to him like an older brother. Joel knew he wasn't kin to Emerson, no matter his being with Myrna and the baby, but Emerson had chosen him as someone beyond blood. Joel hadn't had that kind of friend before. Emerson was a strange kid with his knife and his secretive ways, but his knowing of the river and the forest was deeper and different than how Joel knew it. What Emerson had were gifts Joel was only beginning to understand.

"Hey, Emerson." When Emerson looked up, Joel said, "Keep that hat, why don't you. It doesn't really fit me right."

Emerson slit his eyes a bit as if thinking about what it meant for Joel to offer it, then nodded, knowing that a gift was a gift and not to be refused. "I don't know if it'll fit because of the bandage," he said. He took it by the brim in his two hands and pulled it down on his head, the hat sliding over the bulge by his ear. "It's too big, anyway," he said, lifting it off.

"Don't worry about that," said Joel. He stepped out the back door of the bunkhouse and tore a strip of moss off the side of a boulder. "Give it here."

Joel tucked moss inside the hatband on one side, testing the fit on Emerson's head until it sat right. He tucked a bit more moss in and put the hat back on Emerson's head. "It's just right now. When you get that bandage off you can put more moss in there, especially 'cause the moss is going to dry out anyway. The hat'll settle in once you grow into it. Hey," he said, "it looks a lot better on you than it ever did on me."

"Thanks," said Emerson, a grin on his face.

The two of them had stood there and listened to the river. There'd still been a couple of hours until dawn, the moon above the mountains to the west. The Milky Way spread across the sky, a great band of light becoming brighter as the moon paled. Orion was tilted in the east, the stars of his body leaning into whatever new struggle was coming through the heavens. Wisps of horsetails brushed the rim of the mountains to the west.

"There's weather coming," Joel had said. "We have a last thing to do before I go to the Someday Church and Myrna. C'mon," he'd said, going back into the bunkhouse, Emerson beside him. The two of them made their way down the row, a single brown moth circling the light from a coal-oil lamp burning on the shelf above Ernie Reiner's empty bunk. There was nothing much left of what he'd had. Joel didn't look at any of it, socks and old boots, empty cartridges. It was the skulls of the bears Reiner had killed Joel was looking at, two on the shelf and the other on the floor under the bunk.

Joel had picked up the fallen one and told Emerson to take the other two. When they got back to Joel's bunk Joel grabbed the kit bag and threw it over his shoulder. They were outside on the back porch of the bunkhouse. He remembered telling Emerson he'd learned a lot of things in the past days. "Wang Po and Art taught me a lot," he'd told him, "but so did Myrna and your mother, Isabel." And then he told Emerson how Emerson had taught him a few things. And it was because of what he'd learned that he was trying to think what he should do with the skulls. He said, "They're all that remains of the bears Reiner killed. It's like you said—he didn't need to kill them. The bears weren't dangerous. And they weren't hunted. He just sat on a rock at the dump and picked them off when they came for food. He didn't respect them at all."

"Yeah," said Emerson.

"I'm just glad he never shot that grizzly up at the dump." Emerson nodded.

"I don't know," Joel said. "Bears mean a lot to Art Kenning and he's a friend of mine and a friend of yours too. I thought at first I'd bury them someplace special because of Art, but that doesn't seem right, so I thought I'd ask you what you think we should do."

Emerson picked up a handful of dirt, smelled it, and put it back where he found it. He lifted his head and coursed the air like a small animal questing. "Can you smell it?" he said. When Joel nodded, Emerson said with a big smile, "It's the river. It wants the bears to come home."

"You show me where's the right place," said Joel in wonder at this boy who'd come into his life. "You lead, I'll follow."

Emerson turned to run and Joel stopped him. "I got something to get before we go," Joel said. "You get those skulls while I'm doing what I gotta do."

Emerson passed Joel like a wraith as he went back into the bunkhouse. When he came back out with the skulls tied up in a shirt that looked like one Reiner must have worn, Joel was sitting on the porch with his tobacco can beside him.

"You went and got that out of the bog," said Emerson. "I thought that's what you were gonna do. It's why I took so long getting the bear skulls."

"You knew about my tobacco can?"

"Yup."

"Hell," said Joel. "There isn't a secret I've got that you don't know about."

"Yup," said Emerson.

"Okay," said Joel as he pushed the can into the bag with the skulls. "Let's go."

A half-hour later they were far south of the mill. They'd passed the church where Myrna waited, a lamp burning in the window. Joel didn't say anything as they went by. He had to finish things. He had to clean things up.

They stopped where the swamp dwindled away, great rock cliffs jutting up from the river where the rapids began.

A small cove curved past their boots, the quieter water gathered to the inside of the river's bend. Joel placed the skulls on the gravel and waited while Emerson searched out the cupped slab of cedar driftwood he needed. When he brought it back Emerson placed the three skulls in the red curve, tying them there with twine he'd had tucked in his pocket. Joel held the skulls down while Emerson knotted them there, the skulls in a line from smallest at the back to the largest in front. The shadows of their eyes stared out at the river between the mountains.

Done, Joel took up the cedar canoe with its cargo of skulls and carried it to the corner of the cove where the current pulled past with the full force of the river. He could hear the faint, far rapids north of the outfall of Mad River.

Joel passed it to Emerson. "It's yours to give to the river," he said. "Your bones were made here just like the bones of the bears."

The two of them had knelt down as Emerson placed it on the water. Emerson held the cargo of skulls a minute, the feelings of each boy his own and belonging to no other.

His hand sure, Emerson had pushed the craft out into the river, a curled wave catching at it and throwing it sideways into the heavy waters beyond. The two of them had knelt there in the last hour of the night and watched until the skulls disappeared in the mist.

When Emerson got up from his knees Joel had stayed where he was, listening to Emerson's boots on the river gravel and then grass brushing against grass, a sound only the wind could make, and then he was alone and there was only the river. Joel shifted and leaned against a driftwood log that was sticking out of the bank, looked up, and saw a meteor streak across the sky. It left a stream of smoke behind it as it passed over the mountains. Joel waited until the burn turned into streams of mist, melting into the cirrus clouds coming out of the west. The colour of the sky, the moon's light shining through the path left by the meteor brought words into his mind and he spoke them aloud:

> There's a girl who remembered me for me.
> It was before I ever came to the deep river.
> She heard me down on the lakes when I was lonely.
> It was her laughter brought me here through the snow.
> Her stone and my stone and the stone growing inside her.
> There is a light in everything I see.
> By the mountain she sings for me a river's song.

Joel had said the words. They came into his head and he said them and then he said them again so he wouldn't forget them. "It's a poem," he said, amazed. He was almost afraid to say the word out loud. *Poem*, he said. He said it and then he said it again. He thought, maybe, if he was brave enough, he'd say the poem to Wang Po some night when he was down there. And then he wondered if he was brave enough to say it to Myrna because she was who the poem was about.

He'd stayed a few minutes more and then followed the river out of the dawn light and passed through the swamp the way he had made himself remember it. The lamp still burned in the church window. It shone through the new glass and as he walked out of the swamp and up the long slope to the church he stopped, a small cedar tree shading him. The church door opened and Myrna came out onto the porch. She hadn't seen him yet but something in her blood had drawn her from the room into the morning. Perhaps it was simply the light, the unseen sun streaming its rays across the tops of the eastern range. Or maybe just the sound of the birds in the dawn chorus crying. She'd stood in shadow, but Joel could imagine her face looking out for his coming and he was, he'd realized, at last coming home.

He'd put his hand in his pocket and felt the pebble Isabel had given him, the Chalsey Doney warm against his thigh. It had been with him throughout the night, sometimes warm and sometimes cold, but it was a deeper warm now than he'd felt before. He took it out of his pocket and held it in his palm. The pebble glowed, the green band shining with something that wasn't light, the pebble burning. The small bit of shining rock was also coming home. Joel closed his hand, held up his fist, and saw the shadows of his bones shining through his skin. He turned then home.

He lay there in the bed with Myrna and he remembered it all. The pebble was on the windowsill and he saw how it caught the light of the morning sun, the green band shining. Myrna's mother had told him to return it to the tree and that was what he would do, but not yet. He turned onto his side and as he did Myrna also turned, the warm animal smell of her filling his arms, and she said, "Joel, you're here."

And he said, "Yes."

———

THE NEEDLE LAY ON THE FLOOR beside Art, his arm bent and hanging over the side of the bed as if broken from his shoulder. A leather strap lay coiled on the floor, the shed skin of a black snake. Late morning light angled through the window above his head. It burned across the wall and carved itself into an ancient newspaper from 1914, glued there by a man who was going to a war he would not return from, by a light he could not reach, a wound made from nothing but a star. On Art's chest lay the cat, her paws folded around the mouse she had brought back from the world as an offering, the cat's lean black body rising and falling with Art's life. The cat's purr melted into the river's breathing as it made its way to the sea.

ACKNOWLEDGEMENTS

—

I WISH TO EXPRESS MY GRATITUDE to McClelland & Stewart, including Anita Chong for her early help with this novel and John Sweet for his fine copyediting. I especially owe a great deal to Melanie Little whose consummate skills and immense patience, kindness, and understanding helped me complete the novel through the months of my recovery from a debilitating illness when at times I was barely able to edit a sentence let alone a paragraph or chapter. As well, thanks to my agent, Dean Cooke, for his support.

I wish also to thank Arthur Waley for his translations of Chinese poetry first published in 1918 and Kenneth Rexroth's translations in *One Hundred Poems from the Chinese* published in 1965. Rexroth's own poetry as well as his essays and translations proved a guide to a young first-aid man in a small northern town more than half a century ago. I owe them both a great deal. Rexroth's translations of Su Tung P'o's poem "Epigram" from the Eleventh Century and Ho Ch'e Ch'ang's poem "Homecoming" appear in this novel.

My wife, the poet Lorna Crozier, cared for me through the last two years when I was very ill. Her fierce love kept me alive through many long days and nights. The Sung Dynasty poet, Hsu Chao, wrote, "You can find shelter in my heart." And in my wife's heart I did, I do.

PATRICK LANE's first novel, *Red Dog, Red Dog*, was a national bestseller, a finalist for the Amazon.ca/*Books in Canada* First Novel Award, the Rogers Writers' Trust Fiction Prize, and the Ethel Wilson Fiction Prize, and was longlisted for the Giller Prize and named a *Globe and Mail* Best Book of the Year. Lane is one of Canada's pre-eminent poets, and his distinguished career spans fifty years and more than twenty-five volumes of poetry. His memoir, *There Is a Season,* won the Lieutenant Governor's Award for Literary Excellence and the inaugural British Columbia Award for Canadian Non-fiction, and was also a finalist for the Charles Taylor Prize for Literary Non-Fiction, the Hubert Evans Non-fiction Prize, the Pearson Writers' Trust Non-Fiction Prize, and the Barnes & Noble Discover Great New Writers Award for Non-fiction. He has been a writer in residence and teacher at Concordia University in Montreal, Quebec, the University of Victoria in British Columbia, and the University of Toronto in Ontario. Patrick Lane lives near Victoria, B.C., with his wife, the poet Lorna Crozier.